The PEN/O. Henry Prize Stories 2012

The PEN/O. Henry Prize Stories 2012

Chosen and with an Introduction by
Laura Furman

With Essays by Jurors
Mary Gaitskill
Daniyal Mueenuddin
Ron Rash
on the Stories They Admire Most

ANCHOR BOOKS
A Division of Random House, Inc.
New York

For Elinore and Michael Standard,
dear friends for so long

AN ANCHOR BOOKS ORIGINAL, APRIL 2012

*Copyright © 2012 by Vintage Anchor Publishing, a division of
Random House, Inc.*
Introduction copyright © 2012 by Laura Furman

Permissions appear at the end of the book.

The Cataloging-in-Publication Data has been applied for.

ISBN 978-0-307-94788-8

Book design by Debbie Glasserman

www.anchorbooks.com

Printed in the United States of America
10 9 8 7 6 5 4 3 2 1

The staff of Anchor Books makes each new PEN/O. Henry a pleasure to work on and to read, and the series editor thanks them for their excellence. PEN America works for writers all over the world and to them the series editor gives thanks also.

Mimi Chubb and Kate Finlinson read, wrote, and thought with intelligence, taste, and grace, and made the job of the series editor even more of a pleasure, for which she thanks them again and again.

Publisher's Note

A BRIEF HISTORY OF THE PEN/O. HENRY PRIZE STORIES

Many readers have come to love the short story through the simple characters, easy narrative voice and humor, and compelling plotting in the work of William Sydney Porter (1862–1910), best known as O. Henry. His surprise endings entertain readers, even those back for a second, third, or fourth look. Even now one can say " 'Gift of the Magi' " in a conversation about a love affair or marriage, and almost any literate person will know what is meant. It's hard to think of many other American writers whose work has been so incorporated into our national shorthand.

O. Henry was a newspaperman, skilled at hiding from his editors at deadline. A prolific writer, he wrote to make a living and to make sense of his life. He spent his childhood in Greensboro, North Carolina, his adolescence and young manhood in Texas, and his mature years in New York City. In between Texas and New York, he served out a prison sentence for bank fraud in Columbus, Ohio. Accounts of the origin of his pen name vary: One story dates from his days in Austin, where he was said to call the wandering family cat "Oh! Henry!"; another states that the name was inspired by the captain of the guard in the Ohio State Penitentiary, Orrin Henry.

Porter had devoted friends, and it's not hard to see why. He was charming and had an attractively gallant attitude. He drank too much and neglected his health, which caused his friends concern. He was often short of money; in a letter to a friend asking for a loan of $15 (his banker was out of town, he wrote), Porter added a postscript: "If it isn't convenient, I'll love you just the same." The banker was unavailable most of Porter's life. His sense of humor was always with him.

Reportedly, Porter's last words were from a popular song: "Turn up the light, for I don't want to go home in the dark."

Eight years after O. Henry's death, in April 1918, the Twilight Club (founded in 1883 and later known as the Society of Arts and Letters) held a dinner in his honor at the Hotel McAlpin in New York City. His friends remembered him so enthusiastically that a group of them met at the Biltmore Hotel in December of that year to establish some kind of memorial to him. They decided to award annual prizes in his name for short-story writers, and formed a Committee of Award to read the short stories published in a year and to pick the winners. In the words of Blanche Colton Williams (1879–1944), the first of the nine series editors, the memorial was intended to "strengthen the art of the short story and to stimulate younger authors."

Doubleday, Page & Company was chosen to publish the first volume, *O. Henry Memorial Award Prize Stories 1919*. In 1927, the society sold all rights to the annual collection to Doubleday, Doran & Company. Doubleday published *The O. Henry Prize Stories*, as it came to be known, in hardcover, and from 1984 to 1996 its subsidiary, Anchor Books, published it simultaneously in paperback. Since 1997 *The O. Henry Prize Stories* has been published as an original Anchor Books paperback, retitled *The PEN/ O. Henry Prize Stories* in 2009.

HOW THE STORIES ARE CHOSEN

As of 2003, the series editor chooses the twenty PEN/O. Henry Prize Stories, and each year three writers distinguished for their fiction are asked to evaluate the entire collection and to write an appreciation of the story they most admire. These three writers receive the twenty prize stories in manuscript form with no identification of author or publication. They make their choices independent of each other and the series editor.

All stories originally written in the English language and published in an American or Canadian periodical are eligible for consideration. Individual stories may not be nominated; magazines must submit the year's issues in their entirety by May 1. Beginning in 2013, editors may submit online fiction for consideration. Such submissions are to be sent to the series editor in hard copy. (Please see pp. 439–40 for details.)

The goal of *The PEN/O. Henry Prize Stories* remains to strengthen the art of the short story.

To Reynolds Price (1933–2011)

In 1990, when I was starting *American Short Fiction,* I sent letters to the writers I admired most, asking for stories. One bold move was to write to Reynolds Price, and I never expected an answer. Price was the author of *A Long and Happy Life,* one of my favorite novels. Everything about it pleased me—its characters, setting, and above all the lyricism and earthiness of the author's voice. To my surprise, Reynolds Price sent in first one story and another later. Both appeared in the new journal.

"The Enormous Door" ran first in the first issue. It told of a young boy whose parents are in the process of moving, staying in a boardinghouse in the new town until their own house is ready. The boy is given a room by himself, with a bathroom in between his and the next room. He looks in the bathroom's keyhole and sees—what he sees is an embodiment of spiritual and physical beauty, a vision that prepares him to grow up whole and healthy. "The Enormous Door" is both a realistic story about a scared little boy whose life is changing beyond his control, and a magical tale about an angel. The story works on every level.

Reynolds Price had great artistic gifts, and also the instinct for generosity to other writers. For this reason among many, *The PEN/O. Henry Prize Stories 2012* is dedicated to his memory.

Contents

Introduction

ONE OF THE most fascinating, and annoying, questions asked of writers is about the origin of a story. We hope that if we could pinpoint the real beginning of a story, it would reveal all that a story holds—certain aspects of the author's personal history; the experience, fact, or image that caught the author's imagination; the path through language from imagination to a coherent work of art. We wish to be able to extrapolate the mysterious process of writing fiction.

Many stories draw upon either the experience of the writer or another's experience as reported to the writer. This is not an assertion that every story is autobiographical (or biographical), only that something of the writer's own life is of necessity part of every story. A number of writers find their stories through research, a method of educating oneself and also of procrastinating. For still other stories, and other writers, the inspiration may be as fleeting as a landscape glimpsed from a passing train.

But the process of writing always remains mysterious. There can be no definitive answer to a question about a story's origin because the best stories are manifold and open to multiple understandings. A single origin doesn't seem enough for the stories we love and reread. Furthermore, a story presents changed meanings over time to a faithful reader, for the story we read in middle age is different from the one we first encountered in adolescence. A single glance from a train doesn't account for a story's beginning—it's too monocular, too limited—and yet that may be the way the story's creator remembers it. A story undergoes many changes as it's written, making it a complicated journey from the starting point.

We do want to know where a story came from, and by that we mean the whole story, not only the tiny flash that began the imaginative process. Implicit in the question is the respect we have for the story, and the answer we suspect: Not even the writer really knows where the story came from. If that were known, why bother to write?

John Berger's "A Brush" epitomizes a kind of silence I associate with the short-story form. In the story, the reader finds a slow, almost offhand perception that presents itself when one is looking the other way, or, as W. H. Auden said in "Musée des Beaux Arts," "While someone else is eating or opening a window or just walking dully along."

We are all self-preoccupied; the narrator of "A Brush" is no exception. In Paris, he makes his way through his routine, giving no evidence that he is either lonely or happy in his solitude. We experience what he wants us to—chance meetings, a slow revelation of character and history by those he notices, and, finally, the shock of understanding, a moment of real attention. In the story's ending, we understand how much the narrator has come to value and gain from his urban friendship. The narrator of "A Brush" is both the reader's informant and a character involved in the story's action. Berger's masterly writing conveys with equal grace the recent history of Cambodia and the patient skill required in making art. At the story's simple and exquisite ending, the narrator summons both fact and feeling.

Salvatore Scibona's "The Woman Who Lived in the House" has an eccentric and delightful ending. The story is about many varieties of togetherness. Ásmundur Gudmundsson has a few easy relationships—with his father-in-law, and with a sister and niece—and several complicated ones—with a dog who's crazy about him, an unsuitable lover, and his disgruntled wife. Scibona throws us right into the story with the announcement from a television set that Ásmundur's latest investment, the one he and his wife put everything into, has failed. In no time at all, the marriage follows suit, in Ásmundur's determination an act of God, who, "after twenty years of giving them the stamina and will that makes young Eros turn into the companionship of married love," ends it in a comical street accident. The whole story is a dance of attachment and separation, connection and alienation, and, finally, of love lost and love renascent. The ending is both a surprise and a joy; the one we didn't know we were waiting for at last is back with us.

Anthony Doerr was included in *The PEN/O. Henry Prize Stories* in 2002, 2003, 2008, and now appears, for a fourth time, with "The Deep," a story that combines the author's preoccupations first with the natural world as it is seen through science and then with the interior, often secret, lives of his characters. In the case of "The Deep," Tom's interior life is dominated by his heart, a defective organ: "Atrial septal defect. Hole in the heart. The doctor says blood sloshes from the left side to the right side. His heart will have to do three times the work. Life span of sixteen. Eighteen if he's lucky. Best if he doesn't get excited."

The voice of science—and Tom's mother—urges extreme caution. Tom's spirit looks at those small numbers—sixteen, eighteen—and wonders how cautious can he be and live. Tom's heart keeps him slow, careful, and quiet. His life is different from that of the other children, particularly other boys. The tension in the story is between the restrictions imposed by his literal organ and the desires of Tom's metaphorical heart.

In Lauren Groff's "Eyewall," a hurricane rages outside and inside the narrator's three-hundred-year-old house, flinging this way and that her chickens, furnishings, books, and her past. For all that is destroyed, something whole and new is created by the rollicking lively narrator. Groff's story is poetical and laced with humor, as the dead drink excellent wine with the living, and the storm rocks on.

Christine Sneed's "The First Wife" narrates a story about inevitability in a doomed relationship, a kind of wry love letter from the cautious, somber narrator to her beautiful, unfaithful, and predictable husband. The story is a consideration of a cliché—the handsome movie star's infidelity. A reader might well ask the star's wife: Why is it that we go on asking questions to which we know the answer, starting things we know will end in failure? The answer is what Jean Rhys called "Hope, the vulture," and because it feels good to bet against the odds.

Often the ending of a short story brings a reversal of fortune, character, or the expectations established at the start. In Sam Ruddick's well-choreographed "Leak," there's a comical reversal. A man believes he's having a straightforward and, for all parties, satisfactory adulterous affair. Before long, it's clear that he's the innocent in the crowd that gathers, like clowns exploding from a car, at his assignation. The story's title is a definition of what happens in every aspect of this lover's duet, trio—no, quartet. Ruddick has a gift for understatement and for moving his characters along in ways that surprise and delight the reader.

It's often said that in marriage one partner is the brakes and the other the gas. In Alice Mattison's "The Vandercook," the narrator is the caboose and his wife the engine. When the narrator, his wife, and children move across the country to the narrator's hometown to aid his aging father and keep the family business going, the marriage's balance of power and love is fatally disturbed. The narrator's calm, rational voice doesn't conceal the pain of a new understanding of his past and consideration of his future. By the end of the story what was whole seems corrupted. The beauty of the story lies in its sense of the continuity of the lives narrated. The characters will go on, but with a telling difference. Mattison's story will be read and reread to trace the narrator's understanding of his wife's character and his own.

Dagoberto Gilb's moving story "Uncle Rock" narrates a similar movement toward understanding, though in the case of Erick, whose difficult, compromised childhood is explored, there's freedom rather than disillusionment in the end. Confronting cruelty, Erick gains a new understanding of his mother, of masculinity, and of his own strength. The boy who doesn't speak in either of his languages ends the story with an evasion that protects both his imperfect mother and her lover. By speaking, Erick steps toward adulthood. He sees what he didn't wish to, understands the unintended consequences of lush, powerless female beauty and male power, and moves into his own complicated life.

In Kevin Wilson's "A Birth in the Woods," the mixture of realism and fantasy pushes the reader into a nightmare. A young boy's parents isolate themselves in the joyful, arrogant belief that they can make a new Eden and raise their child in a utopia. The story's narration of a mother's love, and her manipulation of her weak husband and young son, mixes with the elements of horror. The blood announced at the beginning of the story covers the family by the end. Wilson's story is most brilliant in capturing the innocent ignorance of the child and the ways in which every child is a victim of his parents' choices.

Cath in Keith Ridgway's "Rothko Eggs" lives in London with her mother. Cath's parents are divorced, and she feels like their caretaker, more knowledgeable about them than they are about themselves. She loves art and thinks about it, but just as often thinks about how to think about it. The story's diction is striking; simple sentences, repeated, varied, until there's a pileup, a fender bender of thoughts and words. The narration is a close-up third person, so close that we are nearly in Cath's mind as she puzzles out matters of art and sex, and, oddest of all, her parents' shared history before she was born. Cath is central to them, but, she finds, only part of their relationship and not the whole of it, as she once thought. Ridgway's story plays with articulating inarticulateness. For Cath, an intelligent and sensitive young woman, the impossibility of describing abstract art is nothing next to the impenetrability of other people's motives and emotions, and her own.

As in Kevin Wilson's and Keith Ridgway's stories, Hisham Matar's "Naima" has at its core a child trying to accommodate himself to his parents' choices and secrets. "You need adulthood to appreciate such horror," the narrator tells us. A useful question when reading first-person stories is, *Why is the narrator telling this story?* A general answer is, *To understand what happened.* In the case of "Naima," the narrator is trying to understand his parents' marriage, his mother's death, and the place in his life of Naima, the family's servant. His parents so overshadow Naima that the reader also initially wonders why the story is named for Naima rather than the mother or father. The beauty of Matar's story lies in the narrator's delicacy as he seeks to slice through memory without destroying the past.

Adulthood doesn't much benefit the narrator of Ann Packer's "Things Said or Done," nor does the wry humor with which she copes with her father's egomania and hypochondria. "Other people throw parties; my father throws emergencies. It's been like this forever. When I was a kid I thought the difference between my father and other parents was that my father was more fun. It took me years to see it clearly. My father was a rabble-rouser. He was fun like a cyclone." And then there is the narrator's mother, a model of distanced cool, an escaped prisoner who refuses to risk her freedom to help her daughter. If the father were all monstrous, the story wouldn't be as good as it is, nor would the narrator be as sympathetic a victim of herself and her family. The story's intertwined characters are testimony that there are no easy answers for those trapped by love and loyalty.

For the second year in a row, fiction by Mark Slouka and Jim Shepard is included in *The PEN/O. Henry Prize Stories.*

Last year's story by Mark Slouka was about an estranged father taking a terrible chance with his young son; this year's story is also about a father and son. In "The Hare's Mask," the narrator begins by announcing how much he misses his beloved father, then goes on to tell a complicated tale of himself as a boy trying to imagine himself into his father's past. Something primitive is stirred as the narrator realizes that the world existed before he did. He pieces together a terrible loss his own father suffered at his age. The narrator tells us he had a "precocious ear for loss" and "misheard almost everything." In this brief, layered, beautifully told story, the narrator moves from a child's innocent inability to comprehend the past's sorrows to an adult's wonder that human beings dare to risk such pain again.

The narrator of Jim Shepard's powerful "Boys Town" lacks, among other things, the capacity to weather loss and sorrow. His mother is a foulmouthed bully, and he is incapable of freeing himself from her. "Boys Town" is the story of a person without resources, internal or external, who has neither the education nor the emotional means to grow beyond his limiting circumstances. When he looks outside of himself at a movie seen long ago, he sees a hero who has nothing to offer but empty promises. "Most people don't know what it's like to look down the road and see there's nothing there. You try to tell somebody that, but they just look at you."

The hero/narrator of "East of the West" by Miroslav Penkov is named Nose for his "ugly snoot," the result of his cousin Vera's punch, which crushed "it like a plain biscuit." In other ways, too, Nose is broken into pieces by Vera. "East of the West" centers on the river that divides Nose from his cousin, as it divides Serbia from Bulgaria. The river brings tragedy and heartbreak. The river covers the past, and Nose gathers his courage and swims to a drowned church with his cousin. The question of identity—who's a Serb? who's a Bulgarian?—rides through the story and becomes a larger question: *Who will dare to change?* When you finish reading some stories you feel you've listened to a song. Miroslav Penkov's "East of the West" is such a story.

The main character in "Mickey Mouse" by Karl Taro Greenfeld is a Japanese artist in wartime Tokyo assigned the task of creating a cartoon character to represent his country and displace the globally popular American rodent. The atmosphere of war, survival, and danger is so skillfully created by Greenfeld that it isn't until the end of the story that the reader understands what the artist hasn't about his peculiar and impossible assignment.

Steven Millhauser's "Phantoms" is about the memory of a whole community as it lives with its all-too-present past. The phantoms, or ghosts, appear and reappear, a continuity after death that brings little comfort to the living. The presence of the past creates problems for the parents of the town: to tell or not to tell? What frightens a child more—ignorance or knowledge? Humorous, wise, and smart, the first-person-plural narrative covers the life of the haunted town and its people, making its consciousness of its phantoms and its willful forgetfulness seem more or less like our own relationships with our own ghosts. As ever, the strangeness in Steven Millhauser's fiction pulls us in, intrigues us, entertains us, and makes us reflect on our own odd lives.

Steven Millhauser's work has appeared in *The PEN/O. Henry Prize Stories* before, as have the stories of Wendell Berry, who is also well known as a poet and essayist. "Nothing Living Lives Alone" is about Berry's recurring character Andy Catlett, in several stages of his life. As ever, Berry meditates on the qualities of home and the relationship held by generations to the place they think of as their own, the "home place." In this lovely, slow story, Berry is particularly interested in the entrance of the mechanical into the lives of the animals and people there, and he examines different ideas about labor and freedom, including the freedom some feel to destroy the planet on which they live. The story concerns worlds gone by and their place in our present. Once more

Berry gives us intelligent, vibrant fiction, the product of his own excellent labor.

Each year, three jurors read a blind manuscript of the twenty short stories I've chosen for the collection, and each picks a favorite. This year's jurors are Mary Gaitskill, Daniyal Mueenuddin, and Ron Rash, three wonderful short-story writers who could hardly be more different from one another. The fiction of all three jurors has been celebrated in *The PEN/O. Henry Prize Stories*. Each has written an essay on a chosen story, and I invite you to enjoy them in "Reading *The PEN/O. Henry Prize Stories 2012*," pp. 411–18.

The favorite stories for 2012 are by Yiyun Li and Alice Munro, two writers whose work has been included before in *The PEN/O. Henry Prize Stories*.

"Kindness" by Yiyun Li is the confessional autobiography of a woman who's lived in isolation and recalls those few who noticed her, ambivalent attentions she regards in the end as kindness. The narrator is humble, modest, and calls herself "an indifferent person," which can be taken in two ways, that she is like many others and that she is immune to others. Her isolation stands out in her crowded Beijing neighborhood, in school, and during her time in the Red Army. Her life is circumscribed; the reader recognizes a war between her individuality and the demands of her society and of other people. Both the sourness and loneliness of "Kindness" are more predictable than the narrator's final declarations about the kindness of others, hinted at in the story's beginning when she says, "I have few friends, though as I have never left the neighborhood, I have enough acquaintances, most of them a generation or two older. Being around them is comforting; never is there a day when I feel that I am alone in aging." Her apartment house is derelict, threatened with destruction by Beijing's newly prosperous developers, but the life she lives and has led has filled her with stories, which alone keep her company.

Alice Munro's "Corrie" is also about a woman without husband or family, a rich girl in a small town. Corrie, lame from polio, has a quick mind and self-possession to a remarkable degree. She takes what she wants from the life she's been given, at least in one way, and she looks her losses and gains in the eye. Corrie is not sentimental, which saves her. The ending of her story is its most surprising part, and Corrie's reaction to a revelation seems both exactly what the reader would expect her to feel—and its opposite. Reading the story, I didn't want to be anywhere else, doing anything else—once again receiving a gift from Alice Munro.

—*Laura Furman*
Austin, Texas

The PEN/O. Henry Prize Stories 2012

Dagoberto Gilb

Uncle Rock

IN THE MORNING, at his favorite restaurant, Erick got to order his favorite American food, sausage and eggs and hash-brown *papitas* fried crunchy on top. He'd be sitting there, eating with his mother, not bothering anybody, and life was good, when a man started changing it all. Most of the time it was just a man staring too much—but then one would come over. Friendly, he'd put his thick hands on the table as if he were touching water, and squat low, so that he was at sitting level, as though he were being so polite, and he'd smile, with coffee-and-tobacco-stained teeth. He might wear a bolo tie and speak in a drawl. Or he might have a tan uniform on, a company logo on the back, an oval name patch on the front. Or he'd be in a nothing-special work shirt, white or striped, with a couple of pens clipped onto the left side pocket, tucked into a pair of jeans or chinos that were morning-clean still, with a pair of scuffed work boots that laced up higher than regular shoes. He'd say something about her earrings, or her bracelet, or her hair, or her eyes, and if she had on her white uniform how nice it looked on her. Or he'd come right out with it and tell her how pretty she was, how he couldn't keep himself from walking up, speaking to her directly, and could they talk again? Then he'd wink at Erick. Such a fine-looking boy! How old is he, eight or nine? Erick wasn't even small for an eleven-year-old. He tightened his jaw then, slanted his eyes up from his plate at his mom and not the man, definitely not this man he did not care for. Erick drove a fork into a goopy American egg yolk and bled it into his American potatoes. She wouldn't offer the man Erick's correct age, either, saying only that he was growing too fast.

She almost always gave the man her number if he was wearing a suit. Not a sports coat but a buttoned suit with a starched white shirt and a pinned tie meant something to her. Once in a while, Erick saw one of these men again at the front door of the apartment in Silverlake. The man winked at Erick as if they were buddies. Grabbed his shoulder or arm, squeezed the muscle against the bone. What did Erick want to be when he grew up? A cop, a jet-airplane mechanic, a travel agent, a court reporter? A dog groomer? Erick stood there, because his mom said that he shouldn't be impolite. His mom's date said he wanted to take Erick along with them sometime. The three of them. What kind of places did Erick think were fun? Erick said nothing. He never said anything when the men were around, and not because of his English, even if that was the excuse his mother gave for his silence. He didn't talk to any of the men and he didn't talk much to his mom, either. Finally they took off, and Erick's night was his alone. He raced to the grocery store and bought half a gallon of chocolate ice cream. When he got back, he turned on the TV, scooted up real close, as close as he could, and ate his dinner with a soup spoon. He was away from all the men. Even though a man had given the TV to them. He was a salesman in an appliance store who'd bragged that a rich customer had given it to him and so why shouldn't he give it to Erick's mom, who couldn't afford such a good TV otherwise?

When his mom was working as a restaurant hostess, and was going to marry the owner, Erick ate hot-fudge sundaes and drank chocolate shakes. When she worked at a trucking company, the owner of all the trucks told her he was getting a divorce. Erick climbed into the rigs, with their rooms full of dials and levers in the sky. Then she started working in an engineer's office. There was no food or fun there, but even he could see the money. He was not supposed to touch anything, but what was there to touch—the tubes full of paper? He and his mom were invited to the engineer's house, where he had two horses and a stable, a swimming pool, and two convertible sports cars. The engineer's family was there: his grown children, his gray-haired parents. They all sat down for dinner in a dining room that seemed bigger than Erick's apartment, with three candelabras on the table, and a tablecloth and cloth napkins. Erick's mom took him aside to tell him to be well mannered at the table and polite to everyone. Erick hadn't said anything. He never spoke anyway, so how could he have said anything wrong? She leaned into his ear and said that she wanted them to know that he spoke English. That whole dinner he was silent, chewing quietly, taking the smallest bites, because he didn't want them to think he liked their food.

When she got upset about days like that, she told Erick that she wished they could just go back home. She was tired of worrying. "Back," for Erick, meant mostly the stories he'd heard from her, which never sounded so good to him: She'd had to share a room with her brothers and sisters. They didn't have toilets. They didn't have electricity. Sometimes they didn't have enough food. He saw this Mexico as if it were the backdrop of a movie on afternoon TV, where children walked around barefoot in the dirt or on broken sidewalks and small men wore wide-brimmed straw hats and baggy white shirts and pants. The women went to church all the time and prayed to alcoved saints and, heads down, fearful, counted rosary beads. There were rocks everywhere, and scorpions and tarantulas and rattlesnakes, and vultures and no trees and not much water, and skinny dogs and donkeys, and ugly bad guys with guns and bullet vests who rode laughing into town to drink and shoot off their pistols and rifles, as if it were the Fourth of July, driving their horses all over town like dirt bikes on desert dunes. When they spoke English, they had stupid accents—his mom didn't have an accent like theirs. It didn't make sense to him that Mexico would only be like that, but what if it was close? He lived on paved, lighted city streets, and a bicycle ride away were the Asian drugstore and the Armenian grocery store and the corner where black Cubans drank coffee and talked Dodgers baseball.

When he was in bed, where he sometimes prayed, he thanked God for his mom, who he loved, and he apologized for not talking to her, or to anyone, really, except his friend Albert, and he apologized for her never going to church and for his never taking Holy Communion, as Albert did—though only to God would he admit that he wanted to because Albert did. He prayed for good to come, for his mom and for him, since God was like magic, and happiness might come the way of early morning, in the trees and bushes full of sparrows next to his open window, louder and louder when he listened hard, eyes closed.

The engineer wouldn't have mattered if Erick hadn't told Albert that he was his dad. Albert had just moved into the apartment next door and lived with both his mother and his father, and since Albert's mother already didn't like Erick's mom, Erick told him that his new dad was an engineer. Erick actually believed it, too, and thought that he might even get his own horse. When that didn't happen, and his mom was lying on her bed in the middle of the day, blowing her nose, because she didn't have the job anymore, that was when Roque came around again. Roque was nobody—or he was anybody. He wasn't special, he wasn't not. He tried to speak English to Erick, thinking that was the reason Erick didn't say anything when he was there. And Erick had to tell Albert that Roque was his uncle, because the engineer was supposed to be his new dad any minute. Uncle Rock, Erick said. His mom's brother, he told Albert. Roque worked at night and was around during the day, and one day he offered Erick and Albert a ride. When his mom got in the car, she scooted on the bench seat all the way over to Roque. Who was supposed to be her brother, Erick's Uncle Rock. Albert didn't say anything, but he saw what had happened, and that was it for Erick. Albert had parents, grandparents, and a brother and a sister, and he'd hang out only when one of his cousins wasn't coming by. Erick didn't need a friend like him.

What if she married Roque, his mom asked him one day soon afterward. She told Erick that they would move away from the apartment in Silverlake to a better neighborhood. He did want to move, but he wished that it weren't because of Uncle Rock. It wasn't just because Roque didn't have a swimming pool or horses or a big ranch house. There wasn't much to criticize except that he was always too willing and nice, too considerate, too generous. He wore nothing flashy or expensive, just ordinary clothes that were clean and ironed, and shoes he kept shined. He combed and parted his hair neatly. He didn't have a buzzcut like the men who didn't like kids. He moved slow, he talked slow, as quiet as night. He only ever said yes to Erick's mom. How could she not like him for that? He loved her so much—anybody could see his pride when he was with her. He signed checks and gave her cash. He knocked on their door carrying cans and fruit and meat. He was there when she asked, gone when she asked, back whenever, grateful. He took her out to restaurants on Sunset, to the movies in Hollywood, or on drives to the beach in rich Santa Monica.

Roque knew that Erick loved baseball. Did Roque like baseball? It was doubtful that he cared even a little bit—he didn't listen to games on the radio or TV, and he never looked at a newspaper. He loved boxing, though. He knew the names of all the Mexican fighters as if they lived here, as if they were Dodgers players, like Steve Yeager, Dusty Baker, Kenny Landreaux or Mike Marshall,

Pedro Guerrero. Roque did know about Fernando Valenzuela, as everyone did, even his mom, which is why she agreed to let Roque take them to a game. What Mexican didn't love Fernando? Dodger Stadium was close to their apartment. He'd been there once with Albert and his family—well, outside it, on a nearby hill, to see the fireworks for Fourth of July. His mom decided that all three of them would go on a Saturday afternoon, since Saturday night, Erick thought, she might want to go somewhere else, even with somebody else.

Roque, of course, didn't know who the Phillies were. He knew nothing about the strikeouts by Steve Carlton or the home runs by Mike Schmidt. He'd never heard of Pete Rose. It wasn't that Erick knew very much, either, but there was nothing that Roque could talk to him about, if they were to talk.

If Erick showed his excitement when they drove up to Dodger Stadium and parked, his mom and Roque didn't really notice it. They sat in the bleachers, and for him the green of the field was a magic light; the stadium decks surrounding them seemed as far away as Rome. His body was somewhere it had never been before. The fifth inning? That's how late they were. Or were they right on time, because they weren't even sure they were sitting in the right seats yet when he heard the crack of the ball, saw the crowd around them rising as it came at them. Erick saw the ball. He had to stand and move and stretch his arms and want that ball until it hit his bare hands and stayed there. Everybody saw him catch it with no bobble. He felt all the eyes and voices around him as if they were every set of eyes and every voice in the stadium. His mom was saying something, and Roque, too, and then, finally, it was just him and that ball and his stinging hands. He wasn't even sure if it had been hit by Pete Guerrero. He thought for sure it had been, but he didn't ask. He didn't watch the game then—he couldn't. He didn't care who won. He stared at his official National League ball, reimagining what had happened. He ate a hot dog and drank a soda and he sucked the salted peanuts and the wooden spoon from his chocolate-malt ice cream. He rubbed the bumpy seams of his home-run ball.

Game over, they were the last to leave. People were hanging around, not going straight to their cars. Roque didn't want to leave. He didn't want to end it so quickly, Erick thought, while he still had her with him. Then one of the Phillies came out of the stadium door and people swarmed—boys mostly, but also men and some women and girls—and they got autographs before the player climbed onto the team's bus. Joe Morgan, they said. Then Garry Maddox appeared. Erick clutched the ball but he didn't have a pen. He just watched, his back to the gray bus the Phillies were getting into.

Then a window slid open. *Hey, big man,* a voice said. Erick really wasn't sure. *Gimme the ball, la pelota,* the face in the bus said. *I'll have it signed, comprendes? Échalo, just toss it to me.* Erick obeyed. He tossed it up to the hand that was reaching out. The window closed. The ball was gone a while, so long that his mom came up to him, worried that he'd lost it. The window slid open again and the voice spoke to her. *We got the ball, Mom. It's not lost, just a few more.* When the window opened once more, this time the ball was there. *Catch.* There were all kinds of signatures on it, though none that he could really recognize except for Joe Morgan and Pete Rose.

Then the voice offered more, and the hand threw something at him. *For your mom, okay? Comprendes?* Erick stared at the asphalt lot where the object lay, as if he'd never seen a folded up piece of paper before. *Para tu mamá, bueno?* He picked it up, and he started to walk over to his mom and Roque, who were so busy talking they hadn't noticed anything. Then he stopped. He opened the note himself. No one had said he couldn't read it. It said, *I'd like to get to know you. You are muy linda. Very beautiful and sexy. I don't speak Spanish very good, maybe you speak better English, pero No Importa.*

Would you come by tonite and let me buy you a drink? There was a phone number and a hotel-room number. A name, too. A name that came at him the way that the home run had.

Erick couldn't hear. He could see only his mom ahead of him. She was talking to Roque, Roque was talking to her. Roque was the proudest man, full of joy because he was with her. It wasn't his fault he wasn't an engineer. Now Erick could hear again. Like sparrows hunting seed, boys gathered round the bus, calling out, while the voice in the bus was yelling at him, *Hey, big guy! Give it to her!* Erick had the ball in one hand and the note in the other. By the time he reached his mom and Roque, the note was already somewhere on the asphalt parking lot. *Look,* he said in a full voice. *They all signed the ball.*

Alice Mattison

The Vandercook

W HEN MOLLY AND I had been married for thirteen years—
splendid Molly, difficult Molly—she took over Conte's
Printing, a New Haven business my grandfather had started in the
thirties. My father ran it when I was a child, and I spent much of
my time in the shop. A teenage boy, Gilbert, ran errands for my
father after school and also kept an eye on me. When I was in college I fooled around on the letterpress printer my grandfather had
used, and Gilbert, who still worked there, teased me for caring
about something old-fashioned. He was a shy black kid from New
Haven's Hill neighborhood who had grown into a moody guy
who worked closely with my father all week and played the saxo-
phone at New Haven clubs on weekends. A few years ago, Dad
finally had to retire when he broke his hip carrying a box of newly
xeroxed pages to a customer's car. By then, Gil had been his manager for years.

"We'll have to sell the store," I said, when we heard about my
father's accident, and Molly said, "I want it." We were living in
California, where Molly had done well marketing software, but
money was becoming less plentiful, and she was angry with her

boss. This was shortly before money—and what it may buy, including a sense of adventure and possibility—became less plentiful in other places; the software industry had trouble first. Molly's instant certainty delighted me. I wanted to save the family business without running it myself, but the thought of her running Conte's Printing hadn't occurred to me. I was teaching a history class and assisting a letterpress printer—I'd retained my interest in letterpress without getting good at it—but I could find a teaching job in Connecticut. I missed New Haven and my old widowed dad. Our boys, Julian and Tony, would grow up near their grandfather.

But I was cautious. "Is this because of what happened at work? You'll forgive him."

"I won't forgive him," Molly said, and I knew that might be true. She and her boss had had a bad fight, and I'd told Molly I thought he was right.

Dad was an ascetic-looking man, small and neat (I'm tall and disheveled) with pale, closely shaved cheeks and dark hair that had grown thin but never gray. People thought he looked like a priest. Starting a joke, he'd lower his voice and touch your arm, like someone delivering bad news. Sometimes he irritated me, but I respected him and was glad he respected my wife, a businesswoman who deserved his admiration. Still, I was surprised when Molly reported after a long phone conversation that Dad was ceding her full control of Conte's Printing. Despite what Molly had said, I'd imagined all of us conferring. Then I realized that given Molly's background, any other arrangement would have been insulting.

"And what about Gil?" I said as she turned away.

"The manager? He'll stay on," she said. "I can work with anyone."

Molly was restless—she did not rest. She had messy brown curls I loved touching, muscular arms and legs, and firm convictions. Now and then her hair flopped over her face and she flung it back with a look of surprise, as if this had never happened before. She was blunt, sometimes critical—often outrageous. Once she came to a decision, she was alone with it; even if the decision made everyone unhappy—including her—her determination was unwavering. The two of us mostly shared political beliefs, but it was Molly who went online and made the donation, led me and the kids to the protest march, phoned the senator. Occasionally Molly marched on the wrong side. For a couple of months she had unaccountably believed George Bush about Iraq, and would not hear me. When several events in my life with Molly might have made me take heed, I did not take heed.

A day or two after that long phone call with my father, Molly asked, "Can you work that old printing press?" In the back room, Dad still had the Vandercook that had been the foundation of my grandfather's business, along with a cabinet of type cases, each full of hundreds of pieces of type in different fonts and sizes, though everything was either photocopied or offset by now.

"I guess so," I said. The California press where I'd worked printed literary books in small, well-crafted editions. I couldn't do that, but I could print a little. She wanted the business to offer letterpress printing. I'd have a reason to be in the store, and to work with Gil—who might tease me again, something I'd always enjoyed.

Conte's Printing had thrived during the forties, then gotten less trade as demand for sales brochures and wedding invitations disappeared into the suburbs. When photocopying came in, Dad prospered, but then he had trouble competing with chain copy shops, and struggled further when computers made photocopying less necessary. But more recently, savvy Yale professors had used our dusty little establishment for putting together course packets. Conte's seemed to honor Gutenberg in a way big copy shops didn't. And then Yale and New Haven decided to change people's image of my hometown from a scary place where you might not want to send your kid to the coolest little city in the Northeast. Yale bought derelict buildings in the store's neighborhood and fixed them up. The city chipped in with Dad on a new facade. Upscale businesses wanted good stationery, and people moving into expensive downtown apartments used Conte's Printing for party invitations. There was even a demand for letterpress.

New Haven had become all but trendy in my years away, and the downtown we arrived in with our children seemed not glamorous, but less dingy than it used to be. Molly began learning the printing and copying business, and I got a job at a nearby prep school. I set about refurbishing the Vandercook and learning to use it on weekends, and took pleasure in my father's pleasure, and just in his continuing life and his delight in my boys, who were eight and ten when we arrived. To my surprise, Dad came to the store every day, and sat on a straight chair at one side, greeting old customers.

Gil, who'd been quietly running the store for years, was reserved, but welcomed us. He was in his fifties now, with the world-weary air of an expatriate musician in Paris in the twenties. He had a wife one rarely saw, and one son who had some kind of unspecified problem. Gil's formality contrasted with Molly's brashness. She'd thump her hands on the counter for emphasis, and he'd become that much quieter, until he spoke in whispers and communicated with raised eyebrows. He called her Molly Ann, though that's not her name.

Two years later, I'd completed some modest letterpress jobs when I could find time around my teaching job, and Molly had attracted enough new business that she had to hire several part-time workers. But during the third summer after we moved, I sensed that something was different. It wasn't that Molly spoke to Gil in an angry or even exasperated tone. But she spoke to him quickly, as if he weren't present and she were leaving a message.

He rarely spoke to me, even though I was in the store more often because I had a tricky letterpress job—tricky for me—with a deadline. A foundation had asked me to print a book of poems written by inner-city children in a program it funded; it would be distributed at a fund-raiser. The poems were short, but the work went slowly. The shop in California where I'd worked was run by a quiet woman who had taught me and kept me steady. There, I wasn't trying to accomplish something while Molly talked on the phone in the background, my father made familiar jokes, and customers explained complicated needs. The store had two back rooms, one with the Vandercook, one for storage, but the rooms had no doors and opened onto the area behind the counters where the copying machines were: it was really just one big space.

One cool night late in that summer, Molly and I began joking and touching in bed, and ended up making love. Sex and laughter were closely connected for Molly.

I was easing into sleep at last when Molly said, "There are people I could kill if I had to, and people I couldn't kill, no matter what."

"Where do I fit?" I said. I was used to being startled by what she said, but she still regularly startled me.

"I think I could kill you," she said. "I mean if I had to—say, to save the life of one of the children. I could shoot you or stab you."

"How would killing me save them?" I turned on my side to look at her.

"Oh, I don't know, Zo—I'm not talking about that." My name is Lorenzo but she made up this nickname when we first met.

What Molly had said seemed funny, but it wasn't simply funny. The next morning, working on my big job at the back of the store, I was still thinking about her cool assessment as to whether she could kill me. I knew she wasn't a murderer and wouldn't become one: what interested me—and, okay, scared me—was her freedom of thought. I tried to get myself to imagine killing Molly—I chose a gun—but I couldn't. So I was distracted, and then Doris, the flower lady, arrived. She sold sturdy carnations, a dollar apiece, on the same block as the store. My father and Gil were nice to her. She'd leave her flowers in a bucket of water in our bathroom, then wrap them individually in sheets of spoiled copy paper, so a flower might come in a fragment of someone's dissertation on the Holy Roman Empire. Now Doris began wrapping flowers in the storage room, talking. I liked her, but soon became impatient. I'd already made mistakes setting one of the poems. Spacing words evenly requires mental arithmetic and I kept losing track.

"You hear there's gonna be another movie?" Doris called.

The state offered reduced taxes to filmmakers, and the city administration had been courting them with closed streets and considerable freedom. Harrison Ford (or his double) had ridden a motorcycle through the Yale campus not long ago; Robert De Niro had been spotted emerging from a house in my father's neighborhood. According to Doris, in a movie that was about to be made, an actor she'd heard of would be shot to death in front of our store. Surely Molly was getting irritated with her chatter. Abruptly, I decided to go home—maybe so that if Molly said something I wouldn't hear it. Anyway, I was getting nothing done. When I washed my hands and started toward the door, my father called, "Lorenzo?"

"Should I drive you home?" He tired lately. We walked slowly to my car, my father in a gray cotton hat. Driving through the dusty, late-summer streets of New Haven, where brittle leaves bordered with brown were beginning to accumulate near curbs, we were silent.

"You have to understand," my father said, when we were a few blocks from his house. "Gilbert has problems he may not mention."

"You mean with his son?" I didn't know why we were discussing Gil.

"Well, that. His son is doing better."

I'd never been clear on what was wrong with Gil's son, maybe a learning disability.

Again my father began, this time as we neared his block. "Of course, Molly is a wonderful girl . . ."

I realized he was telling me something—or, maybe, telling me there was something that wouldn't be told. I checked my rearview mirror to make the turn. Next to me, my father seemed the size of one of my boys. He didn't take up the width of his seat, and he slid a little with each turn. He'd always been slight, but I couldn't get used to the way he'd diminished in old age.

"I don't know how much you know about Gilbert's personal life," he said.

"Very little."

"He doesn't say much, even to me," he said. "But of course I know there's a secret. Some people—no secrets. Molly. No secrets. Maybe temporary secrets or minor secrets. You and I have always had some secrets, and I don't just mean you from me, me from you. This is to be expected, between father and son."

"But Gil?"

"I don't pretend to understand his life," my father said.

I couldn't think of a reason to drive around the block again. We reached his house and I went inside with him and stayed for a little, but he didn't say anything more.

That evening, Julian, our twelve-year-old, told me he planned to audition to be an extra in the movie that was being made downtown. Day camp was ending and the filmmakers wanted boys his age. "How did you find out about it?" I said. I was cutting up zucchini with my back to him, but I knew how he'd look as he answered, his thin, long upper lip quivering slightly as he tried to keep from smiling, to seem cooler.

"Internet." He had Molly's unruly hair, but darker. He hadn't had his growth spurt. Maybe they'd think he looked too young for the movie. I wasn't sure about his being in it. Too much standing around, part of an enterprise created by adults for their own benefit.

I turned as Molly came into the room. Tony was behind her—wider than Julian, with a chubby face. She set the table while I began stir-frying our dinner.

"Mom, I want to be in the movie," Julian said, and Molly said, "Fine!" as I had known she would.

"What movie?" Tony said, and for the rest of the evening it was all we talked about. Molly had become interested. People from the film company had come through that afternoon, talking to the merchants. They wanted to replace the CONTE'S PRINTING sign on our facade temporarily. The movie would take place in the thirties, and they planned to hang something like the original sign, which they'd seen in photographs. I remembered its sober lettering.

Two nights later, the phone woke us at two in the morning. Someone had smashed the front window of the store and broken in. Molly insisted on going while I stayed home with the boys, calling her often. Nothing seemed to be missing but the intruder had flung anything that was loose onto the floor, dumped out the paper trays of the copying machines, and smashed holes in the walls, maybe with a baseball bat. In the room where I worked, Molly reported, the Vandercook looked fine, but the vandal had scattered my stacks of completed pages, ruining everything I'd done for weeks, and—heartbreakingly—had spilled type from the big old wooden cases, hundreds of letters, numbers, and punctuation marks for each font.

It was unthinkable that at this terrible moment for the business, Molly had more right than I did to be there. Somehow my father and I had made a mistake. By the time I got to the store the next morning, after the boys had gone to day camp, Molly had been interviewed by police and press, neighbors and customers. The store was closed and the broken glass covered with cardboard. Scattered copy paper had been gathered together, but much of it would be of no use to anyone except the flower lady. My father, who'd come by taxi early in the morning, paced and fretted. I worried about a heart attack. Molly, in shorts and a loose white T-shirt she'd pulled on in the night, was sweeping up glass and plaster, and Gil was on his hands and knees in the room where I worked, trying to save the type. The floor there was still covered with trampled pages. I tried to make sense of my predicament. I didn't know if I could sort out the type, or how much of it had been damaged, but for the time being I put the neat little metal shapes, each with its letter, number, or punctuation mark backward on top, into a carton. We were closed for days, while the insurance company and a contractor did their work.

Checking e-mail in our bedroom a couple of nights later, I heard voices from the next room: Molly and Julian. We already knew he'd been chosen to be in the movie, one of a group of boys playing near our store, but every little while he remembered something more to tell us. It was a relief to have something to talk about besides the break-in. Now Molly came into our bedroom, stepped out of her sandals, and stretched across the bottom of the bed. "They want him to get a haircut," she said.

"He'll never do that."

"He's doing it. He'll be playing jacks. Three or four kids play jacks, and they run away at the sound of the gun." She was lying on her back now, bicycling her bare legs. "I'm so upset."

Of course she meant the break-in. "Me too."

"When your father saw it, he cried." She turned on her side and drew her legs into the fetal position. "I think it was Gil. I think your father thinks it was Gil."

I stood up so fast—as if I was going to hit her or shake her—that my typing chair tipped over. "Molly, that's insane! My father doesn't think that!"

Molly stood up, too, took her hairbrush from the dresser, and began brushing her hair, something she did more often when she was upset.

I righted my chair and sat down, watching her. "You're not serious."

"I'm serious." She laid the brush on the dresser, closed the bedroom door, and began to undress. "I need a shower," she said.

"But what do you mean?"

She paused. "I don't know what I mean." She faced me, in her underwear. "The cops kept asking me about enemies. What's the motive? Not burglary."

"Some deluded person, imagining something," I said.

"No. It looked—how to put this. Intended. Sane."

I didn't know how chaos could look sane.

"He's been angry about something," she said.

"Gil's worked in the store all his life," I said. "He loves my dad."

"Black men have a lot of anger," she said. "I don't blame them for having a lot of anger. Maybe he wanted to buy out your father, but he couldn't afford to."

"You think he has a whole new personality, all of a sudden?" I said. "You wouldn't think this if he weren't black."

"Maybe he's a drug dealer," she said. She took off her bra.

"That's *really* racist," I said. "And besides—"

"Don't say that, Zo! You know me better than that." She bent to take off her panties, and walked naked to the bathroom, carrying a robe. She seemed to be taunting me with her nakedness. When she came out, she said, "Look, he's secretive. He seems angry. People sometimes just lose it—"

"He's not secretive," I said. "He keeps his personal life to himself, but so what?"

"It had to be him or the flower lady," Molly said. "The part-timers wouldn't be bothered. And if it was Doris, Gil knew about it."

"That's insane," I said again. I could not prove Gil had been home in bed when the store was vandalized. I thought of him sweeping up type with his long thin musician's hand the morning of the break-in. He was elegant; he looked dignified even on his hands and knees, in blue jeans that he wouldn't ordinarily wear to work. He too had been summoned in a hurry. He sat back on his heels and tried to sort the type. Until his recent silence, he'd continued to tease me for my interest in letterpress printing, despite my limited talent. With my clumsiness and occasional frustration, I was likelier than Gil to have scattered that type and spoiled those sheets.

The conversation left me sick with anxiety, unable to sleep, but somehow not surprised. Now that Molly had said it, I realized that I had known she might. Nothing quite like this had happened before, but it reminded me of a few incidents. Years ago, she flew to see her mother after an operation, and made accusations against a woman caring for her. None of the people on the scene—who sounded persuasive to me—agreed with Molly. More recent was the trouble with her boss at the California job. Apparently Molly had tried to place the blame for a mistake of her own on a recently hired young woman.

The filmmakers taught Julian to play jacks. He looked so different with short hair that I found myself speaking more formally to him. Long socks and knee pants were hot and uncomfortable, he informed us. Having the movie to talk about was lucky, because Molly and I could barely speak about the break-in. We reopened more quickly than I'd expected, and I spent a weekend, helped by Julian and Tony, sorting type, examining it, and replacing it in the cases. I taught them how to compare the metal shapes to make sure they were really from the same font. I wasn't sure Tony would understand what to do, but he caught on more quickly than Julian.

Not all the cases had been yanked out of the frame, and the task wasn't as hopeless as I'd thought at first. But I had to start over on the printing job for the book of children's poems, and it was just when preparation for teaching was claiming my attention. Meanwhile, as the filming grew closer, streets were closed and driving downtown became a series of detours. Nobody was allowed to drive within a block of our store, not that parking would be possible amid the trucks and trailers brought in by the film company. I worried about loss of business but couldn't fail to enjoy Julian's excitement, Tony's vicarious pleasure, and the old-fashioned sign that the filmmakers had hung. Molly didn't mention her suspicion again.

But I couldn't catch up on the big printing job. I wasted time with too many breaks, then hurried and made mistakes. I was able to work steadily only if I was rewarded with unmistakable progress. I wanted to finish early—to be done before the filming began—but I couldn't.

My father stayed away from the store. One afternoon I bought a few bottles of Foxon Park white birch beer, which he'd always liked, and drove to his house. It was cool and dim, with shades drawn. We drank birch beer in his kitchen.

"Dad, Gil didn't break into the store and damage it, did he?" I said at last.

"Of course not," said my father.

"Then what?"

"Molly's a wonderful girl. She makes me laugh. I watch her walk through the place thinking things up." I knew what he meant, and waited for what he'd say next. For a moment it seemed he'd stop there, but he didn't. "I think we made a mistake, Lorenzo," he said.

"You have to tell me what you're thinking," I said. "I can't protect Gil if you don't tell me." I thought of something else my father had said when he said that Gil had secrets: that he himself had secrets, and that I did, and Molly didn't. Molly held the secret of her unpredictable self, but did she have no secrets of the conventional sort? Some of my secrets had to do with Molly. I had not kept secret from her how I felt about the incidents in which I felt she'd been unfair in the past—far from it—but I'd kept secret how I counted and reconsidered them.

"And can you protect him if I do?" my father said, and I'd been so distracted by my own thoughts that it took a moment to remember that *him* referred to Gil. Dad tipped the bottle of Foxon Park to his lips, not slobbering or dripping—he was still my father—and set it on the floor.

The day before the shooting of the film, I had faculty meetings all day, but Molly and I went to the store after supper, leaving the boys at home, so we could do a little work. She'd been subdued while we ate.

We stayed late. Molly was busy in the front part of the store, working on a big offset job that included diagrams and maps. In a little more than two years she'd gone from being a marketer to being a marketer of printing to being a printer, if not an old-fashioned letterpress printer. Gil had taught her, I suppose. She had a better sense of how to put jobs together than I did. We often called in a graphic designer, but Molly had picked up design principles easily. Now she worked steadily in the other room, and my tension diminished in the pleasure of my own task. If I didn't hurry, my pages were done without trouble. When I tried to work quickly, I placed letters improperly and they didn't receive the ink as they should. Now crisp sheets emerged from the Vandercook. "The Man Who Lost His Umbrella," one of the poems was called, and I said the lines out loud:

> *A silly man lost his umbrella*
> *And he asked his dog*
> *"Did you see my umbrella?"*
> *And the dog wagged her tail.*

I'd been about to set this poem the day before the vandalism. For the first time, I thought I might be able to finish, and even finish on time. When Molly was ready to go, I talked her into staying a little longer. Then we turned off the lights and set the alarm.

No cars were parked on the block, and the surrounding streets were filled with trucks and trailers belonging to the movie company. We'd parked blocks away. We walked along Chapel and crossed the New Haven green, where a few homeless men slept on benches. The three famous churches were massive in the dark; chimes from city hall, beyond the churches at the edge of the green, rang out the quarter hour. Molly was silent; then she said, "I know what happened."

I didn't have to ask what she meant. "How do you know?"

"He told me."

"Gil?"

"He told me this afternoon."

"What did he tell you? He didn't do it!"

"No, you're right. He didn't personally do it." We crossed Elm Street and walked next to the library. Our car was halfway down the block.

Molly paused and then spoke in an expressionless voice. "Gilbert is gay. Or bisexual. His wife doesn't know, but for ten years he's been in a relationship with a man. He broke it off last month, and the vandalism was the man's revenge."

I could imagine that Gil might be gay, but I couldn't imagine him talking about it. "Gil said, 'I'm gay'?" I said.

"You think I'd make something like this up?" Molly said.

"No, no—I can't imagine him saying the words." It seemed darker than other nights, even in well-lit downtown New Haven.

She was silent again, and this time sounded resentful when she spoke. "He said, 'I've been in a liaison with a gentleman you do not know.'"

That I could imagine. "But he's only supposing that the man did it? He doesn't know?"

"He wouldn't say—and he wouldn't tell me anything about the guy, so there's nothing to say to the cops."

"So it's over," I said, as we reached our car—it was Molly's car. She hated being a passenger.

"No," said Molly. "No. I think I have to let him go."

"No, that's absurd," I said. It was so clear to me that it made no sense that for a moment I expected Molly would agree. I'd stopped outside the car, but she unlocked it and slid into the driver's seat, so I walked around to the passenger's side. She pulled out of the parking space.

"In a way it doesn't make sense," she said. "It wasn't exactly his fault. But I can't afford someone whose personal life would lead to something like this."

"You can't think this," I said. "It's impossible for you to think this."

She didn't answer, then after a silence said, "I hope the kids aren't still up. Julian has to be alert tomorrow."

"And you don't know for sure that it's true. Have you any idea what this would do to him? To his family? He's fifty-six years old."

"Let's talk about something else," she said. Then she said, "I'm not putting this business at risk, Zo. I'm just not."

We had to close the next day, when the scene near the store would be shot: nobody would be allowed on our block for hours. But since we were still behind in filling orders, Molly had decided that she and Gil and I, if we arrived early enough, could spend the day locked inside, catching up. Maybe we could even watch some of the moviemaking, and glimpse Julian playing jacks and running away. He was up early; before I was out of the shower, Molly had left to drive him downtown, calling to me that she'd see me at the store. I'd been awake much of the night. In the dark, I had finally said, "You may not do this," and from her pillow, sounding wide-awake, she'd said, "You may not tell me what I may not do." I asked myself what I'd do if Molly fired Gil, and I didn't know the answer. I needed to become someone I was not, someone who'd know what to say. It was too late.

Tony was supposed to spend the day with a friend, but he woke up insisting that he wanted to see Julian in the film. Then my father called. He asked me to take him to the store, even though it was closed—it would be the first time since the break-in—and when his voice became sharp, I agreed to take him, too. By the time we'd parked downtown, several blocks from the store, it was late morning.

Summer was ending, but the day was hot and the blocks seemed long. My father and Tony walked slowly, my father steady and silent, the gray cotton hat pulled low on his forehead, the brim tilted forward. Before we reached the store's block, I saw that a crowd had gathered behind a barrier at the corner, with an off-duty police officer.

Equipment filled the block, and there were more workers in ordinary clothes than actors with fedoras or boys in short pants, but we spotted Julian in his unfamiliar getup at the other end of the street. The filmmakers had brought in fake lampposts and antique cars. In the street before us, emphatic people conferred, argued, filmed, filmed again. The star and his pursuer ran, and the star fell forward, then got up and discussed something, then fell again—no gunshot noise—and this time he landed on his side, his hat next to him. An actress in a hat and high heels ran diagonally across the street toward him. Extras, including Julian, assembled, acted, retreated. Then they all did it at once: the leading man dashed in our direction, followed by the gunman, then he fell as Julian and the two other boys scurried; Julian sprinted across the street at an angle, just as the woman rushed past him, falling to her knees at the dead man's side, her bare arms flung above her head.

"It's her own fault," Tony said with some impatience, and I recalled overhearing Julian tell him the plot of the film: the star played a murderer, and his girlfriend had turned him in, even though she loved him.

I tried to convince myself that I could finish the letterpress job quickly. I tried to believe that Gil and Molly were working quietly together behind the store's glittering windows. Then my father said, "We should have sold the business."

At last I persuaded the police officer that my father was in danger of dehydration. Heads down, glared at by moviemakers who had stopped shooting but were still conferring, we made our way to Conte's Printing. The door was locked and I used my key, pushing Tony and my father ahead of me into the air-conditioning. Gil crossed the floor toward us, silent. He put the palm of his hand on the back of my father's head and pressed Dad's face into his own white shirt, like a parent protecting a child from seeing something terrible.

Of course, what had happened—what Molly had said—was not visible, yet the colors of objects seemed harsher, their edges sharp. Molly's back, in glaring blue-and-white stripes, was toward us.

"Mom?" Tony stepped forward. "Mom?"

Molly turned, looking at Tony, not me, and I understood that it was because she didn't want to find out—yet—how much she had lost. I couldn't look at her frightened face. I wanted love to be simple. I wanted to tell her how nimbly our son with his new haircut had darted across the street, how scared he seemed, how hard it was not to run toward him, stretching my arms out wide.

Sam Ruddick

Leak

I WAS TELLING Peyton about a friend of mine who'd seen a documentary on polar bears one day and quit his job in marketing the next; he'd moved to Alaska and gone to work for an environmental nonprofit, and I thought there must have been something wrong with him, because he'd always been so business-minded in the past, and the polar bear thing came out of nowhere.

I was on my back and Peyton was on her stomach, one leg bent so her foot was in the air, and at a little after two o'clock in the morning in the dark she looked like one of those three-page black-and-white fold-out ads in the front of *Vogue*—head on the pillow, high cheekbones, angular jaw, everything in shadow—and when I told her I thought maybe my friend was crazy, maybe it had something to do with his father being sick and his feeling like he couldn't do anything to help, she said you couldn't pin things down that way. She said it was like that sometimes. People just did things.

I smoothed a few strands of her hair with my finger, asked if she ever thought about leaving her husband. She closed her eyes and said, "No. Besides, suggesting divorce to a married woman you've been sleeping with for a couple months is like proposing to a single girl on the third date. I read that in *Cosmo*. Don't you read *Cosmo*?"

"Missed that issue," I said.

She touched my stomach, brought her face close to mine. "Anyway," she said. "I'm happy the way things are. How can I be unhappy when I can come over here and spend the weekend in bed with you?"

I knew she was stroking my ego, trying to change the subject, but it was working. I liked her. She was funny, and it was still new enough to be romantic. We'd met at the National Gallery. We were both crazy about Barnett Newman. She was nothing like Stacy, my ex-girlfriend. She wasn't broke, didn't work in a bar, didn't stay out drinking all night, so when she said spending the weekend in bed with me was enough to keep her happy, I thought to hell with it and kissed her.

Then someone knocked on the door.

"Company?" Peyton asked.

I shook my head, and whoever it was knocked again, louder this time—the way people knock when they're not going away— so I got out of bed and pulled on my jeans. Peyton sat up, looking concerned, holding the sheet over her chest with one hand, and I crept to the door, but when I looked through the peephole there was nobody there.

"Who is it?" Peyton whispered.

"Nobody," I said, and opened up to take a look around.

Stacy had been standing there out of sight, though, leaning against the wall to the side of the door, and before I could stop her she walked right in and started talking like it was perfectly natural for her to show up unannounced. "You would not believe the night I had," she said. "My boss is a cretin."

She made it all the way to the dining table before she saw Peyton, stopped for a second, then said "Hi" like it was no big deal and went into the kitchen. It was just an alcove, really, a tight white space carved into the wall. "You got anything to eat?" she asked. "I'm starving."

"Who's that?" Peyton asked, still whispering.

"Stacy," I said.

"The crazy one?"

Stacy poked her head out of the kitchen. "I'm not deaf," she said. "And I'm not crazy."

Peyton didn't say anything.

"Did he tell you I was crazy?" Stacy asked.

"Not in so many words," Peyton said.

Stacy ducked back into the kitchen, started opening cabinets, banging around. "All you got is pasta," she said, then raised her voice, calling out to Peyton. "All he ever has is pasta."

Peyton got out of bed, the sheet still covering her, then picked up her clothes and disappeared into the bathroom.

I stood in the entrance to the kitchen, looking at Stacy. She didn't look at me. She stood at the sink, filling a pot with water. She was wearing black jeans and a tight little T-shirt. The black beret, the dyed red hair in pigtails. I loved the pigtails, the little-girl thing. Lollipop, lollipop.

"Peyton's a looker," she said, hefting the pot of water from the sink to the stove. "You didn't tell me she was so pretty."

"What are you doing here?" I asked.

"Making pasta."

I didn't get a chance to tell her what was wrong with that answer before Peyton came out of the bathroom. She'd put her tan skirt back on, the cream-colored silk blouse. Usually it was just pretty, but now it seemed out of place. I was in jeans, Stacy was in jeans, and Peyton looked like she was going to a job interview. I mean, she'd come over that way, so there was nothing deliberate about it, and she probably would have preferred to be in jeans, too, but it was still weird, like an assertion of class. Not money, but style.

She took a seat at the dining table, where she had a clear view of Stacy, still in the kitchen. I walked over to her, put my hand on the back of her chair, and she looked up at me over her shoulder. I smiled. She didn't.

"You know your faucet's leaking?" Stacy asked.

"Hadn't noticed," I said.

"It's like Chinese water torture." She raised her voice again, like she had to shout to be heard above the din of a few drops of water. "You guys want some pasta?"

"I'm all set," Peyton told her.

"Stacy," I said. "You need to go home."

She turned to me like I'd insulted her. "I'm just gonna make something to eat real quick," she said. "Christ. Is that okay with you? Do you know what kind of night I've had?"

I was about to say I didn't give a fuck what kind of night she'd had, but Peyton spoke first. "Let her stay a minute, Oscar. After all, she's had a rough night."

They smirked at each other, and Stacy said, "Yeah, Oscar. I've had a rough night. Let me stay."

Peyton looked over her shoulder at me again, sternly this time, like she was a schoolteacher and I'd been caught passing notes. I was already in enough trouble, and she hadn't even read the thing. I'd have real problems, depending on what it said, and that was up to Stacy. Kicking her out would be as good as telling Peyton I was fucking her, which—in truth—had not been the case for several weeks.

So I sat down. I told Stacy, "Don't make a mess."

Stacy sat with us at the table while she waited for the water to boil. Peyton reached up, pulled the cord to the light on the ceiling fan, turning it on. I wished she hadn't.

"So what's going on here?" she asked.

Stacy said, "I had a lousy night at work. I wanted to meet you, anyway."

Peyton nodded. I'd told her about Stacy, but more as a thing of the past. She didn't know we were still talking. At least not that often. "You guys talk a lot?" she asked.

Stacy winked. "Don't worry. All he ever talks about is you."

Peyton wasn't buying it, though. She raised her eyebrows.

"We used to date," Stacy said. "On and off for years. Relationships like that are hard to let go of, you know? So we're still friends, but believe me that's it. I could *not* be with him like that again."

"You're not exactly helping my cause here," I told her.

In the kitchen, the water boiled over. It made a sound like static when it hit the stove. Stacy got up and went in. "You guys sure you don't want any?" she asked.

"I'm sure," Peyton said.

Stacy opened a box of bowtie pasta and dumped about half of it in the pot. "More for me," she said, then came back to the table and sat down. "Don't get me wrong. Oscar's a sweetheart, but you know how it is."

"No," Peyton said. "I don't."

Stacy shrugged. "Things kind of fizzled out. Like with you and your husband, I guess."

"Fizzled out?" I asked.

"You don't know anything about my husband," Peyton said.

"The passion's still alive?" Stacy asked.

Peyton stood up, grabbed her purse and keys. "I'm going home."

"Peyton," I said. "Wait a minute, will ya?"

I got up to follow her, but she was already out the door.

I looked at Stacy. "Fizzle-fizzle," she said.

The parking lot was full. All different kinds of cars, circles of light from the lampposts reflected in dazzling white on their hoods. The lot itself had been repaved in sections over the course of the past few months, and the colors reminded me of something out of a children's book; the blacktop too black, the yellow stripes too yellow.

Peyton didn't look back on the way to her car. She got in without saying anything to me. I leaned down by the driver's side door. She started the engine, sat there for a second, then rolled down the window. "Why did you start something with me if you still had something going with her?" she asked.

I started to say something but she cut me off, said "Never mind" and nearly ran over my foot backing out of her space. She didn't check behind her. Tires squealed and a black SUV smashed into the back of the car. It pushed her front end into the Chrysler parked next to her, the one right behind me. My legs would have been broken if I'd been standing a few inches to the left.

Car alarms went off all over the place. Peyton's car. The SUV. The Chrysler. The lady who'd been driving the SUV got out, started cursing and hollering. "What the fuck were you thinking?" All that. She was short, stocky. Gray hair. A white sweatshirt with a Christmas tree on it in the middle of June.

I looked all around, at the lights coming on in the windows up and down the building, at the clouds moving too quickly across the moon, taking it all in, standing firmly in the moment for the first time all night.

It took a couple hours to get everything sorted, the police reports and the tow trucks. An ambulance. Stacy heard the commotion and came out, started flirting with one of the cops. He was a young guy. Thin, with close-cropped hair. He looked like one of those army kids I'd seen on TV, the nineteen-year-olds patrolling Baghdad, getting blown to bits by car bombs and guys with grenades strapped to their chests. There was another cop questioning me, and he had to repeat every question because I kept looking over his shoulder at Stacy, chatting that kid up like she was going to get his number right there. If they'd been in a bar I wouldn't have put it past her to take him home, just to piss me off.

Peyton leaned against the side of the ambulance with her arms folded, the gray-headed lady inside, presumably on a gurney with a big collar on her neck, keeping it straight. She'd calmed down. She stopped yelling when they started giving her painkillers.

After a while the ambulance left, along with the cops, and the cars were towed away. It was just the three of us standing out there at four-thirty in the morning. The sky had cleared, no more clouds, just the moon, and it was too bright to see the stars.

"I'm calling George," Peyton said.

"Do you think that's a good idea?" I asked.

"You got a better plan?"

I'd been wanting her to tell him, but not like this. "You can stay here," I told her. "Stacy'll go home."

"Not unless you give me a ride," Stacy said. "I took the bus here from Pentagon Station. It's too late to catch one now. The Metro's closed, too."

"I'll just call George," Peyton said. "I want to get out of here."

I raised my voice more than I meant to when I asked, "Can't you spare me the drama? The last thing I need tonight is your fucking husband over here. He's gonna freak out, for Christ's sake."

"Oh, grow up," she said. "You think he doesn't know about you?"

"You told him?"

"I told him I wanted something on the side before I even met you," she said. "It's not like he hasn't had his share. I told you he didn't know because it made you feel good. You were getting such a kick out of being the bad boy."

"He loves that shit," Stacy said.

Peyton took out her cell phone and dialed. George must have answered on the first ring, because it wasn't more than a second before she was talking to him. "Hey hon," she said, her tone matter of fact, like she was going to ask him to pick her up at work, not her lover's apartment. "I need you to come get me."

I could hear him talking on the other end, but I couldn't make out what he was saying. "It was fun for a while," she told him. "But things went south. He's got a girlfriend."

George laughed. He was loud enough for me to hear him when he said, "You've got kind of a boyfriend yourself."

"Yeah, yeah," Peyton said. "Listen, though. I want to get out of here."

Stacy gave me a satisfied grin, like she'd won a bet, and George lowered his voice again. "No, honey," Peyton said. "There's a little problem with the car. I'll tell you about it when you get here, okay?"

Then she was giving him directions.

When she hung up, we went back upstairs, sat at my table again. The faucet was still leaking, a steady drip. "God, that's annoying," Peyton said. She went to the kitchen, turned the water on and off, trying to make it stop.

It wasn't long before George showed up. He knocked and Peyton answered, bag in hand. She was obviously disappointed when he came inside instead of taking her away, and I was shocked. Not because he came in. Because he was about five-two and maybe fifty years old, with a big gut and tight gray curls. Cheap blue slacks. His name embroidered in red on his shirt pocket. There were grease stains all over.

"Working late?" Peyton asked.

"We got this old Mustang," he said. "The transmission's kaput. I'm having fun with it."

I stood up and he extended his hand. "You must be Oscar."

I looked at his hand

"Oh," he said, "sorry," then went to the bathroom, left the door open while he washed the oil off. "I've always liked these little studio apartments," he said. "Great for a bachelor." Then he came back out and offered his hand again. We shook. "Nice to meet you," he said. "Peyton told me a little about you."

"What did she say?" I asked.

"She said you like the modern art. I never could understand that stuff myself. Looks like a bunch of scribble to me." He turned to his wife. "What happened to the car?"

"I wrecked the car," she said.

"How'd you manage that?"

"It's a long story. I'll tell you on the way home."

"Come on, now, Peyton," he said. "There's no reason to get prickly."

"Yeah, Peyton," Stacy said. "Lighten up."

"You're the girlfriend?" George asked.

"Yup."

"She used to be," I said.

"Used to be, used to be." He was still jovial, a regular Santa Claus. "You're a darling," he told her. "I love the little-girl look."

Stacy made a kissy face.

George made a face like he smelled something.

"What's the matter?" I asked.

He shushed me. "You hear that? What is that?" He stood there a minute, then followed his ears to the kitchen. "You know you got a leaky faucet?"

Peyton dropped her purse, slumped her shoulders and looked at the ceiling in surrender. "He knows," she sighed.

I walked over to the kitchen. George knelt down and opened the cabinet under the sink. "We've got to have a look at this," he said.

"That's really not necessary," I told him.

Peyton raised her voice. "Can we please just get out of here, George?"

George stuck his head in the cabinet. After a second he said, "This is an easy fix," pulled his head back out and looked up at me. "You got a toolbox?"

By that time Peyton was standing beside me in the entrance to the kitchen. "It'll just take a second," he told her.

The sleeve of her blouse brushed lightly against my arm, and I went to the closet to get the toolbox. My mother had given it to me when I moved out of my parents' house, nearly twenty years before, and I don't think I'd opened it but once or twice in all that time.

Wendell Berry

Nothing Living Lives Alone

I. FREEDOM

Andy Catlett was a child of two worlds. At his house down at
Hargrave, at the river mouth, going by car was taken for granted.
But at his Catlett grandparents' place, in the summer of 1945 and
for yet a few more years, there was not a motor-driven implement
or vehicle, except for the elderly automobile owned by Jess
Brightleaf and his family, who lived down the creek road on the
back of the farm. Andy's Grandpa Catlett, at eighty-one, less than
a year from his death, still rode horseback when he had any distance to go, though now he had to mount from the well-top. The
farmwork was still done by the Brightleaf brothers, Jess and
Rufus, and by Dick Watson, with teams of mules. They were good
mules too, as Grandpa Catlett would have added: mules well con-
formed and matched, well broke to work.

What he thought of as the town-world of automobiles Andy
had known from his first consciousness and was accustomed to,
though until the war's end and a little after, some farm people still
drove into Hargrave in horsedrawn wagons and buggies. Every

summer one of the last of those, a sweet old woman, as Andy's mother called her, with her nice grandson always in his Sunday clothes to come to town, drove her horse and buggy through the streets, peddling jams and jellies, vegetables from her garden, and fresh-picked wild berries.

But with no more deliberate choice than he had invested in the town-world, Andy had given his heart entirely to the older world of what his father, and Andy and his brother Henry also, would always call the "home place" as it was until the great alteration that followed the war. Until then it belonged to the motorless world of stones, streams, and soil, plants and animals, woods and fields, footpaths and wagon tracks, all of it infused still by his grandpa's still-excitable passion for good land, good livestock, good horses and mules, and good work.

The town of Hargrave, charmed by its highway and motor connections to everywhere else, thought itself somewhat worldly, but at the home place, with its broad open ridges falling away and steepening to the woods along Bird's Branch on one side and Catlett's Fork on the other, Andy felt himself in the presence of the world itself, in the world's native silence as yet only rarely disturbed by the sound of a machine, its darkness after bedtime unbroken by human light, its daylight as yet unsmudged, its springs and streams still drinkable. It was a creaturely world, substantial and alive. Even the rock ledges of the slopes, even the timbers and planks of the buildings seemed to him to be alive in the vital presence of the place. In those days he simply lived in it and loved it without premonition. Eventually, seeing it as it would become, he would remember with sorrow how it had been.

From the farmers he was kin to, and from others who were his influences, Andy learned that there was a difference between good and bad work, and that good work was worthy, even that it was expected, even of him. He wanted to work, to work well, to be a good hand, long before he was capable. By the time he became more or less capable of work, he had become capable also of laziness. Because he knew about work, he knew about laziness. Though he could not always resist the temptation to be lazy, he knew that laziness was what it was, and he was embarrassed by it even as he indulged in it.

His father, whom he knew familiarly, but also by reputation as Wheeler Catlett the lawyer, who had his law practice and other duties to attend to, had never been able to wean himself from farming—if he had ever tried to do so. As Grandpa Catlett got older, Wheeler had assumed increasing responsibility for the home place. And also, in partnership with his brother Andrew, he had acquired two other farms, which he carried on alone after Andrew's death in 1944.

Because he was a lawyer by profession, but a farmer by upbringing and by calling, Wheeler always had farming on his mind. He went to the farms before and after his day at the office, on Saturdays, on Sunday afternoons, and he would sometimes take a day off from the office to work with the cattle or the sheep, or to break a team or two of young mules. Or he would be up long before daylight, waking his sons to help, to meet a trucker at one of the farms to load a load of spring lambs, or of hogs, or, late in the fall, the year's crop of finished steers, for the trip to the Bourbon Stockyards in Louisville.

And so the first, the most continuous, and the dearest fabric of Andy's consciousness was provided by the home place, its life and work and the creatures, human and not-human, tame and not-tame, who lived there. And the home place belonged to the countryside around Port William and Port William itself, which was the native country of both his father's and his mother's families.

The home place, his father's home place, was about four miles, by road, from Port William. On one of the far corners of Port William stood the old house where his mother was born and grew up. At the houses of their Grandma and Grandpa Catlett and of their Granny and Granddaddy Feltner, Andy and his brother

Henry were as freely welcome and as much at home as they were in the house of their parents down at Hargrave, the county seat. But for Andy, the Catlett home place was the focus of his consciousness and affection because, of the three places, it was the most creaturely, the quietest, undisturbed by the comings and goings of even so small a center of trade as Port William. And it was at the home place that he was most free.

As he looks back across many years from his old age to his childhood, it seems to him that there was a time, from when he was eight or nine years old until he was fourteen, when he experienced intervals of a freedom that was almost absolute. This freedom came to him mostly in the neighborhood of the home place, mostly when he would be alone. Sometimes, when he was with his brother Henry and their friend Fred Brightleaf, they would be sufficiently free, by default of the watchfulness of their elders. They were capable then of exploits beyond the powers of a single boy. But sometimes they would get at cross-purposes, and would squander their freedom in arguments over what to do with it. Alone, Andy was free sometimes even of his own plans and intentions.

Grandpa and Grandma Catlett were the older of Andy's grandparents. He was freest at their place, maybe, because he got over the ground faster than they did, but also because they were not much inclined to worry about him. When he was with them he sometimes tried their patience, but he liked their company and their talk. Their memories went back almost to the Civil War, to a time long before the internal combustion engine, when the atmosphere of the Port William country would be pierced only occasionally by a steam whistle. For most of their lives the country had been powered almost entirely by the bodily strength of people and of horses and mules, and the people had been dependent for their lives mostly on the country and on their own knowledge and skills.

Without intending to do so, Andy learned much from watching his Catlett grandparents and from listening to them. From his grandpa he gathered knowledge of land husbandry, and of the proper conformation and good management of livestock. These were things that Grandpa Catlett passionately knew, and he enforced them in his grandson's mind by his naked contempt for anybody ignorant of them. From his grandma he became familiar with the economy of the household: the keeping and care of the old house, the uses and reuses of all the things that could be saved, and all the arts and refinements by which food made its passage from the ground to the plate.

From the house and barns and other outbuildings clustered on the hilltop, he passed beyond the supervision of his grandparents into the open fields on the ridges, or down into the woods on the steeper land along the creeks. On these travels he would often be alone, on foot or riding Beauty the pony. Sometimes he carried a cane fishing pole and a can of worms to the pond in the back field or to the holes along the creeks, coming home on his lucky days with strings of small perch or catfish that his grandma fried in batter. He might swim in the pond, which he was not supposed to do, or spend a long time watching the tumble bugs rolling their dung balls along the cow paths. He loved the mown fields and the croplands open to the sky. Even more, he loved the woods, where it seemed to him that every life was secret, including his own. Of the secret lives of the woods and the tall grasses he did not learn much, for he lacked the patience to sit still. But the place itself he learned so well that when he went to bed at night, then and for the rest of his life, he could see it all in his mind. In thought he could follow the paths and the wagon tracks. In thought he could walk over it and see how it looked from every height of the ground.

And there were hours and days when he hung about the men at their work, to watch, to listen, hoping to be given some bit of real work to do, sometimes proving able actually to help, but more likely than not told to watch himself or get out of the way, or he would be assigned to some drudgery that the men preferred to avoid: go to the spring or well, for instance, to bring back a fresh jug of water. But sometimes when he begged to drive a team, they would hand him the lines and then watch to see that he drove correctly and kept out of danger. And so he learned to do what he was capable of doing, and he imagined himself grown big and strong enough to cut swiftly and accurately with an ax, or to lift great forkfuls of hay onto the loading wagon, or to unload corn into the crib, the metal ringing as the mounded ears flew off the scoop.

As the men worked they talked, and their talk was wonderful. They told jokes and stories, some of which were full of grownup knowledge. Andy especially liked the talk of Rufus Brightleaf, who had a poetical and profane answer for everything.

One day, coming upon Rufus working alone, Andy asked, "Where's Jess?"

And Rufus replied without stopping or looking up, "He went to shit and the hogs eat him."

Or sometimes, when they had had a good day at work and he was feeling fine, Rufus would sing one of the songs of his extensive repertory. He would sing to the tune of "The Great Speckled Bird," raising his voice over the rattle of chains and wheels, maybe, as he drove a wagon home to the barn:

> *Did you ever see Sally make wor-ter?*
> *She could pee such a beau-ti-ful stream.*
> *She could pee for a rod and a quar-ter,*
> *And you couldn't see her a-ass for the steam.*

And he spoke of doctors who treated certain troublesome swellings with hairy poultices that never failed, healings that to Andy seemed veiled in a mystery almost biblical.

But rowdy as Rufus was, as he enjoyed being and was gifted to be, he was also a man perhaps of many small regrets and certainly of one great sorrow. His great sorrow was for his son whose death in a logging accident Rufus had witnessed, knowing on the instant that there was "not a thing I could do, not a thing." He had told Andy of this, as old Andy supposes, because he needed to speak of it to somebody, because he and the boy Andy were friends, and the boy was a listener. Knowing this, Andy was aware also that there were other hard things to know that came to Rufus's mind, causing a look to pass like a shadow over his face.

They were artists, the Brightleaf brothers, their work in all its stages beautiful to see. Like artists of other kinds, and like a considerable number of their neighbors in that country at that time, they held before themselves an ideal of perfection that every year they approached and every year inevitably failed and yet attempted again the next year, year after year.

They were of the kind known as "tobacco men," a title not bestowed upon every grower of tobacco, but only upon the most select, the best. In those days, just after the war when cigarettes had been standard equipment for the men fighting overseas, long before the proof of the unhealthfulness of tobacco, and tobacco's consequent decline in public favor and in quality, the premium at sale time was absolutely upon excellence.

The crop itself was in every way exceptional. It was intricately and endlessly demanding in the ways it was cultivated, handled, and prepared for market. In the time before tractors and chemicals, the tobacco crop was made by the work of mules and men and, when needed, women, the man-hours far exceeding the mule-hours. All crops then, of course, were dependent on such work, but tobacco was unique in the intensity, skill, and length of the work it required. Its production then, as Andy Catlett now thinks, looking back, involved higher standards and a greater passion for excellence than any other practice of agriculture, excepting only that of the better livestock breeders.

For the Burley tobacco of these parts, the crop year lasted from early spring, when the plant beds were burnt and sowed, until late winter, when at last the crop of the summer before would have been stripped, tied into "hands" according to grade, compacted in presses, loaded, hauled to market, and sold. The requirement for informed attention, care, judgment, and work was unremitting. Some of the work would be more or less solitary. But especially at the times of transplanting, harvesting, and stripping, crew work was necessary, and the crew was supplied by family members and hired help, both men and women, and by exchanges of work with neighbors. At these times the difficulty of the work was relieved, in some measure even compensated, by the sort of talk that people do for pleasure, the telling of jokes and stories, and by dinners at noon that were daily banquets, the food bountiful in variety and quantity, capably prepared, and joyfully eaten. Many a wife from then received and deserved the highest praise: "As good a cook as ever I ate after."

Jess and Rufus Brightleaf, and Jess preeminently, had a high reputation throughout that part of the country. They put their characterizing marks upon their crops at every stage. Their finished work on the warehouse floor would be recognized on sight by any bystanders who knew what to look for.

Often when Andy would be riding with his father through the fields, Wheeler would stop the car at some point of vantage to watch Jess Brightleaf at work in a tobacco patch, for Jess was a man worth watching. At his work he moved carefully, thoughtfully, with authority, and yet swiftly and gracefully, surrounded by his own work well done.

And always, a moment or two before putting the car into motion again, Wheeler would say quietly, "Beautiful, isn't it?"

"Yes," Andy would say. For it was in fact beautiful, and unforgettably so.

That was a good time for farmers. During the war and for several years after, farmers received prices that were something like just. And this, in expectation, brightened the mood of the work.

From their first year as tenants on the home place in 1939 until their last in 1948, Jess Brightleaf and his wife, by their work and their thrift, saved ten thousand dollars with which they bought a farm of their own.

II. IN THE OLD TIME

In his latter years Andy Catlett has tried to use appropriate hesitation and care in speaking, in any way particularly personal, of the diminishment of the world. He dislikes hearing old men, including himself, begin sentences with such phrases as "In *my* day" or "When *I* was a boy." But when he thinks of the freedom he enjoyed during the five or six years of his boyhood that were most active and carefree, he recognizes that he is setting up a standard of sorts by the measure of which the world must be seen to have diminished. It has diminished by the standard of a boy's freedom, but that freedom has diminished necessarily in association with other diminishments, both social and material.

His freedom then had little to do with home or school, but everything to do with a home landscape which was, as he can see now, an inhabited and a human landscape. On the farm of either set of his grandparents, he could walk within a quarter or half an hour from some spot in the woods where he imagined that no human had ever stood before to places where he knew he walked in the tracks of elders and companions, some of whom had died in his own time.

He could walk as quickly, moreover, from solitude that had lasted as long as needed into the company of men and women at work, who were doing work that they did well and even liked, that they expected to continue to do for the rest of their lives, in a place or a part of the country that they did not expect to leave. They were leading lives that were capable and settled. This was mainly true even of Jess Brightleaf's hired hand, Corky Dole, whom Jess paid off every Saturday night and bailed out of jail every Monday

morning. They knew their work. They did not dither. It was a settled culture, and there was a certain freedom for a child in that
alone.

It was hardly a perfect place or time. Like any of the past, it was
not a time that a person of good sense would consider "going back
to." But that time, to the end of the war and a while after in that
part of the world, had certain qualities, certain goodnesses, that
might have been cherished and enlarged, but instead were disval-
ued and discarded as of no worth.

Its chief quality can be suggested by the absence from it of a
vocabulary that in the last half of the twentieth century and the
beginning of the twenty-first would become dominant in the
minds of nearly everybody. Nobody then and there was speaking
of "alternatives" or "alternative lifestyles," of "technology" or "technological progress," of "mobility" or "upward mobility." The life
that Andy knew then in Port William and its neighborhood was
not much given to apologizing for itself. People did not call themselves, even to themselves, "just a farmer" or "just a housewife." It
required talk of an infinitude of choices endlessly available to
everybody, essentially sales talk, to embitter the work of husbandry
and wifery, to suggest the possibility always elsewhere of something better, and to make people long to give up whatever they had
for the promise of something they *might* have—at whatever cost,
at whatever loss. You might of course have heard somebody wonder toward the end of a long, hard, hot day of work, "You reckon
you'll ever get anywhere without changing jobs?" But that was
weariness and wit such as might come from anybody at any work
in the midst of the hardest of it. You might have heard the same
self-critical humor from somebody who had danced or coon-
hunted half the night before a hard workday. Andy has no record
of this time except his memory, but he does not remember that
anybody who spoke so of "changing jobs" ever spoke of the job he
wanted to change to.

Rather than alternative jobs or lives, the ordinary talk in barns or at row ends ran to the best remembered or imagined versions of things that were familiar: harvest dinners, capable mules or horses or hounds or bird dogs, days or nights of hunting or fishing, good crop years and crops, good days and good hands. Or they told jokes or stories in which there was an implicit recognition and acceptance of the human lot.

Such settled and decided people are parts of the world, as the unresting, never-satisfied seekers of something better can never be. The boy who wandered away alone into a new world newly discovered by himself could return to a familiar world communally known by people he knew who were at work or at rest in it. And in both worlds he was free. He was free not only to ramble at will and at large when he was beyond family supervision or had not been put to work, but he was free also in the company of Dick Watson, the Brightleafs, and any other grownups, who treated him as a child only when he was in the way, in danger, or in need of correction. Otherwise, they made no exceptions. They spoke to him as they spoke to one another, as a familiar.

Home to him, then, was a home countryside, one place with the limits of one place but limitlessly self-revealing and interesting, limitlessly to be known and loved. It was precisely in that limitlessness that he was free, a limitlessness inherent in the nature, the "genius," of the one place, free then of the litter of alternatives.

This was a freedom undoubtedly more apparent and available to a boy than to a man. But Andy would remember it. It would be the enabling condition and the incentive of his choice finally to leave off his wanderings and come home, to make his own life indistinguishable from the life of his place. And this was his choice, by the terms and standards of his time, to become "odd," as one of his most reticent old friends told him at last that he had chosen to be.

But the young Andy Catlett was free in another way that he did not know when he was young, that he has learned in all the time he has spent in growing old. In those years he thinks of now as the years of his freedom he was free of a fear that has since grown greater in every year he has lived. He was free of the fear of the human destruction of the world, a freedom that no child will again enjoy for generations to come, if ever again.

If Andy's regret for the loss of the old creaturely world of Port William in his childhood were only nostalgic or sentimental, then it would be merely a private feeling, properly to be ended by his death. His regret is considerable and worth talking about because it is applied to real losses, tangible and significant, some of which are measurable: the loss of the economic integrity and neighborly collaboration of rural communities, the loss of independent livelihoods, the loss of topsoil, the toxicity of air and water, the destruction by mining of whole mountains, the destruction of land and water ecosystems—so much destruction in the interests of machines, chemicals, and fuels to replace the people who have been displaced, by the same interests, from the home places of the world.

We can brush away the past, as we like to do and feel superior in doing, but the nightmare of Andy's old age is to *know*, wide awake, the destruction of many and of much not only pleasing and desirable, but of lasting value if they had lasted, and, for all we can yet know, necessary.

And suppose, to elaborate the nightmare, that we had decided even as late as 1950 to grant a proper stewardship and husbandry to the natural world. Suppose we had refused to countenance the industrialization of everything from agriculture to medicine to education to religion. Suppose we had not tolerated the transformation, in the official and then the public mind, of vocation to "a job," which is to say the transformation of the farmer, the tradesman, even the sharecropper (all subsistence-based) to an "employee" helplessly dependent on an employer and "the economy" and interchangeable with any other employee. Suppose we had not stood for the displacement of people who once functioned as parts of the creaturely world, working members of their places—the *quality* of their work always, of course, in question— to the "labor pool" and the placelessness of modern life.

Andy by now has lived and watched long enough to know the reality of the ongoing human destruction of the world. He knows that he himself is involved inescapably in its destruction. But he can remember, to further elaborate his nightmare, wandering in the woods or working in the fields early in the year, when he drank from wet-weather springs, the water cool and tasting of the ground, with no thought of chemical contamination. His experience of that time was decisive for him. It was luck, perhaps a blessing. It was an unaccountable gift, for the place and the way of life he learned then was in fact a sort of island: a small, fragile, threatened order in the midst of a world war and all its dire portent.

Freedom, then, existed. Andy knew so from his early travels and his early work in his home country. Along the way he learned too that freedom, when it happened, was an interval with responsibilities at either end. He knew long before he understood, or could choose to act on the knowledge, that neither freedom nor responsibility existed alone, or could exist alone very long, but that each depended on the other.

He was late in acting on that interdependability, partly maybe because of school, but certainly because he would remain a boy for a long time, a boy either in deference to the authority of grownups or in rebellion against it. His early experience of freedom, anyhow, prepared him poorly for school, and for prolonged enclosure of any kind. School, before it had taught him much else, taught him to be a critic, though it did not intend to do so, and though "critic" was not even a word he knew. He was in school when he made his first conscious objection to something he read in a book.

He read in a book (maybe it was a reader; maybe it was from the small library the teacher kept in her classroom) a story of two children, brother and sister, who visited their grandparents' farm where there was a wonderful woodland. The children played happily among the trees. They had a pet crow and a pet squirrel that accompanied them on their visits to the woods—and this, to Andy, was a charming thought, as was the thought of the beautiful woodland itself, as was the thought of the woodlands around Port William.

And then, without explaining why, the story told how the grandparents sold the trees to a logger, who cut them down. The logger cut them *all* down, every one of them. In proof there was a picture of the boy and girl standing in a field of stumps, and the crow and the squirrel perched on a stump apiece. The story then explained that, though the children and the crow and the squirrel would miss the woods, this was really not too sad because the woods would grow back again.

Until then, Andy had thought that anything printed in a book was true. And so it was a considerable shock to him when he realized that he knew—though he could not then have said *how* he knew: he knew from intuition and experience; maybe he knew, Heaven help us, by premonition—that the story had told a lie. The story was in fact too sad, it was a story of great loss and sorrow, and it could say nothing to make itself happy. To know that grownups, even writers and teachers, were questionable did not smooth Andy's way through his formal education.

III. A TIME OUT OF TIME

The old man, Andy Catlett, does not believe that the mind of any young creature is a blank slate. But he knows without doubt that young Andy Catlett, in the years of his boyhood, was being formed. He was being in-formed. He was being shaped, and this was his dearest education, as a creature of his home place, his home country, by his growing knowledge of it. He was sometimes deliberately taught by his grandparents, his father, and the other elders who in one way or another were gathered around him. He was learning by their example, instruction, and insistence the ways of livestock, of handwork, of all in the life of farming that would make him, beyond anything else he might become, a countryman. But he was also shaping himself, in-forming himself, by knowledge of the country that he got for himself or that the country itself impressed upon him.

In the winter of 1947, after Grandpa Catlett died, Grandma Catlett wintered in a room in the Broadfield Hotel down in Hargrave. And then, early in April, when Elton Penn came in his truck to load her and her spool bed and her bureau and her rocking chair to take her home, Andy loaded himself and his bundle of clothes and books and went home with her. Now, as Andy thought, as she allowed and maybe encouraged him to think, her ability to live at home depended on him. He took a deep pleasure in the sense of responsibility that filled him then, and he was steadily dutiful and industrious. Grandma was cooking as always on the woodstove, and in the mornings, sometimes all day, they still needed fires for warmth. Andy kept the kitchen supplied with firewood, and carried in coal for the stove in the living room. When the cow freshened, Andy did the milking, night and morning. Later, Grandma said, they would need a garden, of course, and Andy would need to help with that.

On school day mornings, after he had done his chores and eaten breakfast, he got himself out to the road in time to catch the school bus. But he had a little initiative in this. Because he was considered an occasional or temporary rider of the bus, he apparently was not officially expected by the driver. And so if he got to the road ahead of the bus, he would put up his thumb. If he failed to catch a ride for himself, then he rode to school on the bus. This was a freedom he cherished, and he told nobody about it. The people who gave him rides also apparently kept his secret. He shirked his lessons, antagonized his teachers, stored up trouble for himself. On days of no school, as long as he showed up for meals and did his chores, and as soon as he was out of sight of the house, he was free.

One warm spring Saturday afternoon, when he had fished his way from pool to pool down Bird's Branch and had caught nothing, he came to a large, dry, flat rock. He propped his fishing pole against a tree and lay down on the rock. The rock was unusually large and flat and smooth, and he felt that something should be done about it. And so he stretched out on it for some time, looking up into the treetops of the woods. He was no longer on the home place then, but had crossed onto the more or less abandoned back end of a farm that fronted in the river valley. He was at the mouth of a tributary dell known as Steep Hollow, whose slopes you could not climb standing up. The woods there was an old stand of big trees. Whether because of the steepness of the ground or the dubious benevolence of neglect, the stand had never been cut. But now, remembering it, he is obliged to remember also that a few years later it was cut, and is forever gone.

The woods floor was covered with flowers, and the tree leaves were just coming out. Andy's eyes were quick in those days, and he could see everything that was happening among the little branches at the top of the woods. He saw after a while, by some motion it made way up in a white oak and not far from the leafy globe of its nest, a young gray squirrel that, except for its tail, appeared to be no bigger than a chipmunk.

The squirrel was just loitering about, in no hurry, and Andy studied it carefully. The thought of catching and having something so beautiful, so small, so cunningly made, possessed him entirely. He wanted it as much as he had ever wanted anything in his life. He knew perfectly that he could not catch a mature squirrel. But this one being so young and inexperienced, he thought he had half a chance.

The tree was one of the original inhabitants of the place. It had contained a fair sawlog in the time of Boone and the Long Hunters. By now it was far too big to be embraced and shinned up by a boy, or a man either, and its first limb was unthinkably high. But well up the slope from the old tree was a young hickory whose first branch Andy could shinny up to, and whose top reached well into the lower branches of the oak. Andy was maybe a better than average climber, and he had spent a fair portion of his life in trees. He was small for his age, and was secure on branches too flimsy for a bigger boy.

He went up the hickory and then into the heavy lower limbs of the oak. The climbing was harder after that. Sometimes he could step from one thick limb to another up the trunk. Sometimes he had to make his way out to the smaller branches of one limb, from there into the smaller branches of the one above, and from there back to the trunk again. Finally he was in the top of the tree, a hundred or so feet from the ground. Just above him was the little squirrel, more beautiful, more perfect, up close than it had looked from the ground. The fur of its back and sides was gray but touched, brushed over, with tones of yellowish red and reddish yellow, so that against the light it seemed surrounded with a small glow, and the fur of its underside was immaculately white. Its finest features were its large, dark eyes alight with intelligence and the graceful plume of its tail as long as its body.

Andy knew with a sort of anticipatory ache in the inward skin of his hands and fingers what it would feel like to catch and hold this lovely creature and look as closely at it as he wished. He climbed silently, and slowly from one handhold and foothold to another, up and out the little branches that held him springily and strongly until he was within an easy arm's reach of the squirrel. He reached almost unmovingly out, and at the approach of his hand, the squirrel leapt suddenly and easily to another branch. It did not go far, but the small branch it was now on belonged to a different limb from the one Andy was on. And so he had to go back to the trunk and start again.

About the same thing happened for a second time. The almost-catchable little squirrel waited, watching Andy with a curiosity of its own, until it was almost caught. This time it ran a little farther out on its limb and leapt onto a branch of another tree, another oak. Now Andy had to climb a long way down to find a limb that crossed to the second tree, make his way out to limbs still affording handholds and footholds, limber enough to lean under his weight until he could catch a limb as strong in the other tree, swing over, go to the trunk of that tree and up and out to the highest branches, where again he almost caught the squirrel.

That was the way it happened so many times he lost count. The squirrel seemed to wait for him, watching him with interest, imaginably even with amusement, taking its rest while Andy laboriously made his approach, and then at the last second, without apparent fear, seemingly at its leisure, leaping beyond reach, never far, but always too far to be easily approached again. In fact, Andy and the squirrel must have been at about the same stage of their respective lives: undoubting, ignorant, fearless, curious, happy in the secret altitudes of the treetops and the little branches, neither of them at all intimidated by the blank blue sky above the highest branches, the outer boundary of both their lives.

It was a time out of time, when time was suspended in constant presence, without past or future. It began to move again only when the squirrel finally leapt onto the snag of a dead tree and disappeared into an old woodpecker hole.

And then it was late in the day, past sundown, and Andy was still high up among the tall trees. He had not thought of getting back to the ground for a long time, and from where he had got to he was a long time finding a way. The trunks were too large to grip securely and were limbless from too high up. He finally made his way to a grapevine, and slid down it slowly to ease the friction on his hands and legs. When he stood finally on the ground again, it seemed at first to rock a little as if he had stepped down into a boat. He was sweating, his hands and arms and legs bark-burnt and stinging, and he was a long way from home. He recovered his fishing pole, now deprived of its charm and the sense of adventure he usually invested in it, and started back.

When the screen door slammed behind him and he stepped into the back porch, his grandma opened the kitchen door.

"Where," she said, drawing the word out, "on God's green earth have you been?"

"Fishing," he said, which was true as far as it went.

But he was late. He was too late. It was getting dark. In coming back so late he had betrayed not only her trust but his own best justification for staying out there in the free country with her and not in town.

"Oh," he said, "I'll go milk right now. I'll hurry. I won't be long."

She said, "*I* did it."

So while he had been up in the treetops with the squirrel, forgetful of the time of day and where he was, she alone had done the evening chores and milked the cow. She said no more. She left him, as she would have put it, to stew in his own juice, which he did. He would not forget again, and he would not forget the lesson either.

Nor would he forget for the rest of his life his happiness of that afternoon. What would stay with him would not be his frustration, his failure to catch the squirrel, but the beauty of it and its aerial life, and of *his* aerial life while he tried to catch it among the small, supple branches that sprang with his weight as if almost but not quite he might have leapt from one to another like the squirrel, almost but not quite flying.

He had not wondered how, if he had caught the squirrel, he would have made his way back to the ground. It would take him several days to get around to thinking of that. The heights of that afternoon he had achieved as a quadruped. From where he had got to he could not have climbed down with his two feet and only one hand. If he had caught the squirrel, he would have had to turn it loose.

Christine Sneed

The First Wife

1.

The famous do resemble the unfamous, but they are not the same species, not quite. The famous have mutated, amassed characteristics—refinements or corporeal variations—that allow their projected images, if not their bodies themselves, to dominate the rest of us.

If you are married to a man whom thousands, possibly millions of women believe themselves to be in love with, some of them, inevitably, more beautiful and charming than you are, it is not a question of if but of when. When will he be unfaithful, if he hasn't been already? It isn't easy, nor is it as romantic as the magazine photographers make it look, to be the wife of a very famous, memorably handsome man. There are very few nights, even when you are together, when you don't wonder what secrets he is keeping from you, or how long he will be at home before he leaves for another shoot or another meeting in a glamorous city across one ocean or the other, with some director or producer who rarely remembers your name. Marriage is a liability in the movie business, despite the public's stubborn, contradictory desire to believe that this particular marriage is different, in that it will endure, even prosper, with children and house-beautiful photo essays in *Vogue.*

There were always so many others lurking about, hoping to take my place, if only for a few days or hours. It was like being married to the president of an enormous country where nearly everyone was offering him sexual favors, ones he really wasn't scorned by anyone but me for accepting.

2.

He married me in part because I wasn't famous, not as famous as he was, in any case. He was the beauty in our household, and I was not the beast but the brains. I wasn't ugly or plain, and I remain neither ugly nor plain, but in college, when for a while I fantasized strenuously about becoming an actress, it soon became clear to me that I liked making up the characters more than playing them. I also realized early on that men age much better in Hollywood than women do. My husband will never be old in the same way that I will be. Even if my fame were as great as his, I would be called an old woman much sooner than he an old man. But I will never be as famous as he is, and although he can be blamed for many things, this isn't one of them.

How did it end? Before I say what it was like to be courted by him, to fall in love, however briefly or genuinely, I prefer to talk about the end because it is rarely ever given its due. It is the film-maker's and the writer's most reliable trick to seduce us with the details of a marvelous and improbable coupling while hinting darkly that things did not end well, that some tragedy or tragic character flaw in one or both of the principals brought on a heart-breaking collapse. And when the collapse comes, it is rarely given more than a few pages, a few sodden minutes at the end of the film.

My husband was Anders Gregory, and this is and has always been his real name. It is regal-sounding, I suppose, a name that demands our attention or at least a moment's pause. His father was French, his mother Swedish, he their only son, the one masculine bloom raised in a garden of sisters. He and his sisters got along well enough most of the time, but he was the favorite—a fact their parents did little to disguise, despite the three daughters' spectacular scholastic and athletic achievements. Anders was bookish, quiet and sheltered during early adolescence, but then he became handsome and, in time, the best-looking man in the room. He attracted the heated attention of his sisters' friends and, in time, the attention of one of their fathers who was a film producer.

"If I'd met Anna's father even a couple of years earlier than I did, I bet I wouldn't have become an actor," Anders told me not long after we met. "If I'd been seventeen instead of nineteen, I probably would have rolled my eyes and been a sarcastic jerk to him. I was the kind of dork who smoked alone in his room with his Doors albums and Kerouac novels. I used to spend a lot of time wondering if Jim Morrison and I would have been friends."

I laughed. "You did not."

"Of course I did. Every punk I knew was like that where I grew up."

"You would have found your way to L.A. eventually. Especially since you were only an hour and a half away."

He shook his head. "No, I'm telling you, it wouldn't have happened. Bakersfield is like another planet. It was luck, nothing else."

His rise was fast and without real difficulty, a fact he admits to most people because he thinks it adds to his appeal. There is no odor of desperation about him, no stories of violent hand-wringing or sobbing before the security gate of some powerful director or casting agent's Bel Air mansion. He embodies the most glittering American dream—the version that dictates that success is one's birthright and should come easily. Americans romanticize struggle and hard work but do not, in fact, like to work hard.

It was January when our marriage split open, which didn't mean much because we lived in Southern California, in Laurel Canyon, and it hadn't taken me long to prefer it to my snow-choked hometown of Minneapolis. "You probably knew this was coming," he said. He wasn't lying next to me or sitting across from me at the dinner table, avoiding my gaze. He didn't have to look at me at all because he said these words over the phone. I hadn't seen him in three weeks. He was in Canada filming a movie about caribou hunters, and I'd heard that he was with another woman. She wasn't in the movie and she despised cold weather, but I knew she was up there with him. We had friends in common, this woman and I. The film industry really is a small world, its tributaries and rivers and landmasses all mapped out by our mentors, our adversaries, our lovers past and future.

"I didn't think this would happen so soon," I said.

He hesitated. "You don't sound upset."

"I am upset."

"You don't sound like it."

"I'm not going to yell at you, not over the phone. I want you to come home and talk to me about this in person. Ask Jeff for a couple of days off. Tell him I'm sick, that I'm in the hospital. Tell him to shoot some of the scenes you're not in."

"I'm not going to lie. He could easily check."

"Then tell him that your wife of five and a half years has asked that you come back and talk to her before you try to divorce her."

There was a tense pause. "Try to divorce you? What do you mean by 'try'?"

I hung up on him. When he called back, I didn't answer. He called me sixteen more times that night, maybe even twenty-six—I can't remember the precise number, but I didn't answer any of those calls, each new sequence of rings sounding more and more desperate and enraged. I didn't turn off the phone because it felt better to hear his distress than to sit in stunned silence. There was no prenuptial agreement; we had talked about it, but the idea had deeply embarrassed both of us. He had ignored the advice of his friends and his agent before our wedding because, again, he believed in success, not failure. He also thought that as a writer of literary screenplays, of character-driven political and romantic satires, I was not as interested in money as other people were. He was right, but I was interested in revenge.

I wanted him to come home and tell me to my face that he was leaving me for another woman. As you can see, I wanted to make it difficult for him.

3.

When you are thirteen, a recent initiate into the tragicomedy of adolescence, you imagine yourself marrying the boys whose dazed or beaming faces greet you from the dog-eared pages of teen magazines. You imagine yourself marrying your girlfriends' older brothers, those with driver's licenses and beginners' mustaches and possibly an alarming tattoo or two they have tried to hide from their parents. You imagine yourself, after the prom or on the night they propose, being deflowered by these boys, both the famous and unfamous ones. You peer at your face in the mirror for hours after school and worry about your nose and cheekbones and slightly crooked teeth. You know yourself to be pretty enough, but probably not beautiful. Your legs are bony, or else they are too fat—you unwillingly, helplessly, wear the evidence of a loving mother's after-school cupcakes and cookies and Friday night deep-dish pizzas.

Anders Gregory is only three and a half years older than I am. He was a senior in high school when I was a freshman, and from a young age, he did not carry with him the sense that he would be famous, as many other stars apparently do. The same night that he had talked about serendipity, he told me that he had planned to become a structural engineer and design vast, intricate bridges; he had always liked science and math. He was not a spendthrift, not in the hysterical fashion that many famous people are. There was never any fear of bankruptcy because he did not insist on having seventeen vintage Rolls-Royces in storage or a large staff of servants who all lived in his palatial home. We had a cook and a housekeeper who each worked four days a week. Someone came to do our landscaping; someone else came to take care of the pool. This is, of course, the manner in which many people live in the wealthier towns and cities of the world. I loved Anders and did not want to lose him. I thought that I might be able to forgive him if he appeared at the foot of our bed the morning after his call from Alberta and proclaimed that he had spoken too soon, that he had made a mistake.

4.

I know that contradictory examples do exist. Paul Newman and Joanne Woodward's long marriage was astonishing, but people forget that he left his first wife to marry her. If Joanne had been his first, I'm not sure it would have lasted.

I wonder about Elizabeth Taylor, hardly an example of spousal fidelity, but nonetheless—would she have stopped at three, if her beloved third husband, Michael Todd, hadn't died in a plane crash a year after their marriage, in a plane he had named *Lucky Liz*? Or would Richard Burton's appearance have been inevitable, their own two marriages and divorces, and the 69-carat diamond he bought for her at Cartier, also inevitable?

5.

Other men I have had relationships with have not been as famous as Anders, but hardly anyone on earth is. He is in an exclusive club, the .001 percent of the world's population with instantly recognizable faces. The members are musicians, miscreants, politicians, movie stars: Mick Jagger, Cher, Che Guevara, Hillary Clinton, Bozo the Clown.

I was seeing someone else when I met Anders, one of my former graduate school classmates who was trying to earn a living as an actor. His name was James, as in Jesse, he liked to say, not Henry, which confused most people who heard this because James was his first name, not his last. By the time we started dating, he had been hired to act in a few commercials and had also had nonrecurring parts on four or five TV shows. He was funny and a little strange and often unpredictable in that he might tell me to meet him for dinner at a nice restaurant where he would show up wearing a police uniform and handcuff me to him. We would walk into the restaurant and he would tell people that it was all right, I wasn't dangerous, no cause for alarm. He loved attention, and not surprisingly, I did too. I liked him quite a lot, though I couldn't imagine that we had a real future. He was probably depressive and sometimes would descend into days-long funks when he didn't get a callback, but most of the time he was sexy, spontaneous, enthusiastic. As far as I was concerned, we were having fun. We made each other feel less lonely, and in a big city, especially one like Los Angeles, this isn't so easy to do. Ordinary people feel lonely in a way that the famous do not, and despite how it might seem to those who do not live in southern California, there are so many more ordinary people than movie stars sitting in traffic jams or buying their coffee beans and wheat bread at Vons.

6.

What happened is nothing new or surprising: Anders left me for a popular actress, one he had met on the set of his fourteenth feature film. The film flopped, which pleased me. Before I married him, other people's failures had rarely made me happy, but under his unobservant gaze, I turned petty, often mean. The actress was his lover in the flop, and I'd known as soon as he told me that she had been cast to play the female lead that things I could not hope to control were going to occur. She was impossible to dismiss. It wasn't only her beauty and fame, both greater than mine, or her age, which was less than mine. She is the type of person who cares about causes. She cares about them publicly, but genuinely, I will admit. She has raised and donated sizable sums of money for the construction of schools and hospitals and women's shelters in countries I had never previously considered visiting, let alone donating any portion of my earnings to. Hers, somehow, is a voice that people in power, here and abroad, listen to. For more than any other reason, I dislike her because she reminds me that I am not good and kind enough, that my causes are laughable because few extend beyond my front door. I am aware that most people live their lives the same way that I do—no one is more important to us than ourselves—it is simply the nature of our species, of any species, I suppose, but this thought is not a comfort.

We had one phone conversation, accidentally, while Anders and I were in the process of divorcing. She picked up his cell phone one morning, probably forgetting to look at the display to see who was calling. But I also wonder if she saw my name in the liquid crystal, and for a wild, breathless second she needed to know the words that I'd been saving up to say to her.

We both froze when we heard each other's voice. I finally mumbled, "I guess Anders isn't free?" I couldn't even pretend that I didn't recognize her voice.

"He's not here." There was something in her tone I couldn't pin down—shame? Or only wariness?

"When will he be back?"

"I'm not sure. A few hours maybe?"

If I'd been capable of organizing a coherent thought, I would probably have said something unforgivable to her then, something she would remember and worry over, possibly for the rest of her life. Something that she would think was true, even if it wasn't—that she had no talent; that he would cheat on her too if he hadn't already; that he was cheating on her now with me.

I only asked her to tell him to call me back, my heart beating so hard I was sure that it would have burst from my chest if my breastbone hadn't been there to hold it down.

The caribou movie was his sixteenth feature film. It ended up doing very well, its box office receipts respectable, the director and one of the costars winning prestigious awards. I didn't go to see it. Anders did not appear at the foot of our bed the morning after his break-up phone call. He did not appear in person at our home until two and a half weeks later, during a scheduled hiatus in the film's production. Instead, he sent emissaries, three of his closest friends, one at a time, to tell me how embarrassed and regretful he was, how he hoped we could both be reasonable, how he hoped I'd eventually understand and forgive him. Coward, I said. Stupid fucking cowardly bastard. I wanted him to fall through the Canadian ice. I wanted him to get frostbitten. I hoped that certain crucial body parts would fall off. I said these childish things to anyone who would listen, and at first there were many people who did.

Then, within four days, the news of our collapse began to appear in the papers, a big headline in a few of the sleazier ones, in falsehood-riddled articles with the most unflattering pictures of me they could find—ones where my eyes were half-closed or I appeared to be snarling, ones where I looked drunk but wasn't at all. Anders looked angelic, innocent, desirable—the onus, somehow, on me—I had driven him into the arms of a more beautiful and worthy woman. In some photos, her head was superimposed onto pictures where my head had actually been—Anders with his arm around my waist, whispering in my ear, kissing my cheek, looking the adoring husband; his hand at the small of my back, his body leaning protectively toward mine. These were old pictures, ones from our courtship and first year of marriage. I wanted to sue these sleaze rags but knew that it would be wasted time and money. The pictures and the stories were already out there. Nothing could be done to take them back.

7.

"No." When I thought about it, I realized this was a word we had said to each other often.

We didn't have any children. Nor did we adopt. We had thought that we would do one or the other, possibly both, but after two years, then three more, it hadn't happened. There was always a bigger, more important movie to make, more time to be spent apart, another topic that I hoped to research, another screenplay to adapt or write. I had known after year four that it wouldn't happen. I had stopped wanting a baby as much as I had at the beginning, and he had stopped talking about becoming a father. There was, at least, no vicious custody battle to add to the war over our finances.

"You didn't earn any of this money that you're trying to take from me," he said not long before the divorce was set in motion, angry that I wasn't going to settle for four million in cash and the house in Laurel Canyon, leaving him the New York co-op and the Miami villa and over sixty-seven million in stocks and other more liquid assets. "You have your own fucking money, Emma."

"I know that," I said, "but I'm not the one leaving you for someone else."

He exhaled loudly. "You know that I'm really sorry this has happened."

"That's hard for me to believe."

"You don't have to believe me, but it's true anyway. I don't want us to be enemies. Maybe we could eventually be friends."

I snorted. "Sophie would love that."

"She'd understand."

"I really doubt that, Anders. Not everyone wants the same things you want."

When the outrage and jealousy dissipated, there was only abjectness. I knew in those moments that I would have taken him back. I knew that I would never be as close to another man like him. Whether or not I wanted to admit it, he was extraordinary, and being with him had made me feel as if ordinary concerns, ordinary disappointments and sorrows, had less to do with me than with other people. That is what celebrity signifies more than anything else—it is the apparent refutation of the banal.

"How can you still care about him?" asked one friend, a divorced woman herself. "After all of the things he's done to humiliate you? You have more self-respect than that, don't you?"

"I don't know," I said, because maybe I didn't. I had the idea, obscenely childish and predictable but one that could have been a very potent kind of revenge, of writing a book about our marriage. In a self-righteous fever, I wrote ninety pages before I knew that I didn't have the will to finish it. By this point in our separation, Anders doubtless considered me a hardened opportunist, but I was not completely unhinged. In spite of my bitter, lingering feelings of betrayal, I knew that it would be better for me to retain my self-respect and the notions of decency that had been ingrained in me by my Midwestern upbringing: you do not let people know what you're thinking, especially if your thoughts are uncharitable; you do not profit (emotionally or financially) at other people's expense; you do not intentionally hurt the people you care for or once cared for very much.

I missed him fiercely at times and awoke in the middle of the night, my face damp with tears, wondering if I could win him back. The clock on the bureau ticked unyieldingly, its answers all in riddles. After several nights in a row of this, I couldn't bear the sound of its ticking and threw it away.

Friends, my parents, my one sibling (an older brother who liked

Anders quite a bit), thought that if nothing else, I should have been relieved that the pain and anxiety and implacable jealousy were ending: the innumerable days during our marriage when I had been at home, trying to work, picturing him having a very good time with the other cast members in a film that was shooting in Moscow or Key West or Nairobi or Paris or Kuala Lumpur, picturing all of the fans who hoped to get close to him, to smile at him and be smiled upon in return, the fans who wanted to touch him, hold his hand, look him directly in the eye and then go home to remember this one-minute interlude for the rest of their lives.

As I saw it, he was always off somewhere, living the best days of his life. If I went with him on a shoot, I wasn't precisely welcomed, by him or by anyone else working on the film. I was a potential fuck-it-upper, though some people were kind and decorously curious about my current writing projects. Anders needed to concentrate, memorize his lines, rehearse, get into character, which I understood but resented. I wanted love, physical proof that he needed only me—an outrageous and absurd desire.

N.B.: No one who marries someone famous knows precisely what will happen to his or her self-esteem. If you are famous too, there is even more potential for competition, for keeping track of who is more adored, who is getting better roles, more media attention, more critical acclaim and money. You might search fan sites, fruitless and stupid as this would be, to determine who your far-flung enemies are, who has proclaimed the most ardent love for your husband, who plans to act on it as soon as possible. Despite how pitiful these sites and their custodians are, you feel corrosive jealousy. You want to go through the fan mail that arrives at the studio before your husband sees any part of it, throw most of the letters away, threaten with bloody bodily harm those who have sent lewd photos, written bad erotic poetry: "I Want to Suck Your Dick for Sex Days Straight, Mr. Gregory."

If they all weren't so stupidly earnest, it might have been funnier.

8.

After seven months of bickering, we settled for much more than four million in cash, for more than the Laurel Canyon house, and after we both signed the papers, we didn't speak again for two and a half years, not until our paths overlapped at a fund-raiser for an AIDS research foundation that his second wife had insisted he attend with her. He married her a year after leaving me, this time each of them signing prenuptial agreements. Five months later, they were parents.

I'm not sure why I did it, but I started seeing a married man. He had been a friend for a number of years, one I had always been mildly attracted to but hadn't done anything to encourage. His name was Otik, a Czech man who directed commercials and music videos. Barring the gambling addiction, he wanted to be Dostoyevsky. I had read some of the novel he was writing before I became his lover and it impressed me, though it wasn't likely to be published—there was nothing American about it, no levity in its pages, false or otherwise. I did not see how it could possibly sell here. I didn't tell him this and I turned out to be wrong. When his book sold, *The Monk's Arsenal,* he sent me three dozen roses—red, yellow, and pink. I tore off the tissue paper and felt the heated rush of tears because this was something Anders had done during our first two or three years together. Enormous bouquets with quotes from Keats or Shakespeare scribbled onto the cards would arrive for no reason. I liked to imagine the people in the flower shop, the young girls who took the order from Anders's assistant, knowing that this Anders was *the* Anders and wondering if they would ever be loved by a famous man who could give them everything they desired.

I met Anders when I was in graduate school at UCLA where I spent four fevered months in my second year writing a screenplay for him. In a moment of bravado, I sent it to him. And then, as if it were an elaborate, waking dream, he called a dozen weeks later and said that he loved it, he wanted to meet me, he was so flattered and impressed. I was twenty-seven, prematurely cynical about love, but then suddenly every woman I knew hated me.

We met for lunch on Olvera Street, his bodyguard waiting outside on a chair the restaurant owner smilingly set by the entrance for him. I couldn't speak for the first several minutes without laughing nervously. My face was flushed, my legs unreliable, my palms so sweaty my napkin became damp. I was terribly lonely and had wanly hoped for someone like him for a long time. It was why I had moved from Minneapolis to California—I had the same dream as millions of other hopeless people—to be discovered and declared worthy by someone far above me in stature.

He was tall, taller than I was by several inches, and smelled like he had just stepped from his bath. His hair was longer than I had last seen it—in a film that had been released a couple of months earlier, one in which he had appeared naked and raving over a brother's death—and he touched my arm several times as he told me that he already had a director and a couple of producers interested and they were probably going to film my screenplay if I would allow them to. They would buy it from me, of course, for a fair price. I shook my head, incredulous. "It's a gift," I said. "I couldn't possibly make you pay for it."

He laughed. "If someone offers you money for your work, you take it. Rule number one. Maybe the only rule in L.A. Do you act, too?"

I was smiling so hard that my face hurt. "I wouldn't dream of it," I said.

He touched my arm again. People in the restaurant were leering at us. I could feel them trying to decide what was going on, who I was. How in the world had I arrived at this table? Why not them? "Really?" he said. "I thought everyone did."

I couldn't tell if he was being ironic, but I didn't think he was. "I'd rather direct," I said, hoping he'd laugh. More than feeling his hands on me, I wanted to make him laugh. Other women, prettier ones, probably couldn't, not being clever enough.

Instead, he winked. "It's always one or the other. Often both."

They paid forty-two thousand for my screenplay, more money than I had earned in a year, two years, probably, at that time in my life. The film, *Two Things You Should Know*, was a success. Later I learned that I could have gotten a lot more if I had tried to sell it through an agent, but Anders and his backers hadn't really needed to pay me anything. The film made money, sold overseas to European and Asian distributors, won a few big awards in the U.S. Suddenly, I had become someone kind of important. I wrote a sequel a year or so later, *Two More Things You Should Know*, that wasn't bad, but it wasn't ever produced. By then, Anders was being sought out by the Italian-American directors he had always fantasized about working with.

For a while, we were friends, nothing more, and met from time to time for lunch or dinner; we talked on the phone and went to parties where we knew we would see each other. I was in love with him from the beginning, more or less, but didn't admit it to myself. I felt an immense, heart-heavy gratitude toward him; he was, it seemed, responsible for my life becoming what I had long hoped it would. He appeared to care about me, too, and not just because the film I had written for him was the first one in which most of the better-known critics took him seriously.

I told myself that I didn't want to get involved with him. I could see that he had every woman's ardent attention wherever he appeared. From what I knew of him, he did not date any one woman for more than a few months. He was as restless as many famous men seem to be—there are so many options, so many willing participants. If you don't feel the pressure to make one momentous choice, you don't—it is easier to make a number of small choices, to keep making them.

But I loved that he liked me, that he kept track of me, sent me gifts, called occasionally. I knew that it was better to be his friend than his short-lived lover. But after *Two Things* debuted, a year after he had finished filming it, he bought me an expensive German car because the film was such a remarkable success.

After Anders delivered the car, he started to court me. I didn't know it was a courtship, but to most others, especially to James, my depressive boyfriend, it was obvious. "You're being obtuse," he said. "Or else you're just lying. I can't believe you can't see what he's up to."

"He has so much money that I'm sure it's not a big deal to buy me a car."

"No, probably not, but the gesture is the big deal. You don't buy a car for someone you don't expect something from in return. How often does he call you now?"

I looked at him, feeling his unease, his desire to give up on me, but he didn't want to, and I didn't want him to either, not yet. His lips were very red right then, as if he'd been pressing them together hard. He was an attractive guy, a tall, sturdy man, and had played high-school basketball well, something he was still proud of. I liked his long limbs and solid frame, his tangled dark hair. I liked, too, that other women noticed him.

"Not that often," I said, which was a lie. Anders was calling me every few days. Sometimes he wanted me to read a script, which I always did, scorning most of them. But mostly he wanted to talk and flirt. He told me he didn't know anyone else like me, and of course this was the best compliment I could imagine, aside from "I can't live without you," which of course he never said. "He's just thanking me again for the screenplay."

"He paid you for it."

"He's still just my friend." I had never told him that I'd written the screenplay specifically for Anders. It would have been a stupid, possibly cruel, thing to do.

James rolled his eyes. "If that's what you want to call it."

9.

He asked me to marry him when he was sitting next to Tom Petty on *The Tonight Show* sofa. Petty had just played two songs, talked to Jay for a few minutes, and then Anders came out wearing a beautiful shirt, one made of indigo linen that I had bought for him during a trip to Chicago a few months earlier. They talked for several minutes before Jay, with his friendly squinting smile, asked him about his love life. Anders smiled back and said, "Everything's going well. But it'll be even better if Emma, my girlfriend, says yes to my marriage proposal."

Jay looked at Anders, blinking several times, and said, "Have you asked her? Are you telling me that you asked her and she said she wasn't sure?"

Anders shook his head. "Actually, I'm asking her now. I hope she's watching."

The audience started shrieking and hooting and kept it up until the producers broke for a commercial. I was over at my friend Jeanie's house, another transplant from the Minneapolis area, and hadn't been watching as attentively as I usually did when Anders appeared on TV (it was later, after I saw a recording of the program, that I memorized every detail of Jay and Anders's exchange), but when I heard my name and realized what was going on, I started shaking so hard that Jeanie had to hold both of my hands for several minutes before getting up to pour us both a large glass of wine and then another. Very soon my cell phone began to ring without stopping for most of the night. Friends from home, my parents and other relatives, were calling to congratulate me, to weep and exclaim with me. I could not believe that he wanted to marry me and I suppose I should have paid attention to this disbelief, but who says no when someone you love, famous or no, asks you to marry him?

Soon after his proposal, a few of my friends started to show their jealousy and doubt but tried to pass it off as bracing skepticism, meant only to make me think.

One friend from home said, You'll always have money now. What's the point of you working anymore? Why don't you go with him when he's shooting his movies and try to have fun?

A second friend said, What about all his gorgeous ex-girlfriends? Is it really over with all of them? How would you even know for sure?

A third friend said, Is he actually going to go home with you for Christmas and family reunions?

Someone else, my brother's girlfriend, said, Will it be an open marriage?

10.

Anders's favorite childhood jokes:

> What did the dog say when its owner played too hard with it?
> Ruff ruff.
> Why don't witches like to clean the floor?
> Because their broom sticks.

For a while I thought that he didn't take himself too seriously. After all, he could easily have ignored the script I'd sent to him, never bothered to meet me in person to tell me that he liked it and wanted to buy it. He could have had his agent contact me instead. He could have gotten swept up in the cult of his own fame and completely left everyday life behind.

I suppose it was inevitable that he would meet another woman who interested him more than I did, one who did the same work he did, who understood all of the lurid fan mail and faraway meetings and the sheer exhaustion he felt on some days simply being who he was.

11.

James did not say that he hated me when I admitted to my feelings for Anders. For one thing, he was a little in awe of him. He might even have hoped that somehow he would benefit from my new, fantasy relationship, that I would feel guilty and ask Anders to go out of his way and introduce James to directors or casting agents. He was probably even more talented than Anders was, and for a while, I thought that he would succeed—it might have been on television rather than in film, but his success did not seem at all far-fetched. His depression, his self-sabotaging tendencies, his impatience and manic intensity, however, conspired to keep him from the success he had hoped for.

This is something few people talk about in Hollywood, or anywhere else, despite how obvious it is: most people don't succeed as actors simply because they can't handle the near-constant rejection that confronts most beginners. Rejection is the relentless, powerful hazing that disables ninety-seven out of a hundred talented people. No one tells you that for your first two hundred auditions, you would be lucky to land one or two parts, minor ones at that. No one says this because it is stories like Anders's that have convinced most of us that it should be easy, and if it isn't, if you're not immediately chosen and declared the next Cary Grant or Robert De Niro or Meryl Streep, then you're just not good enough.

12.

Otik, the married man I started seeing after my divorce, never asked what it had been like for me to be with Anders, whether I expected to be as happy again, or as miserable. He did not care to know, nor did he seem concerned that his own life was not as glamorous as Anders's, at least not in the same highly visible way.

He was a dozen years older than I was, and, due in part to the close relatives and friends he had lost to various wars and self-destructive habits, he was unimpressed by the things that impress most of us.

He said a few things at the beginning of our affair that I thought did have to do with Anders, though he was never named.

"Certain events that happen to us," he said, "we spend a lot of time trying to forget, or else we try to live as if they are about to happen again, even when we know they won't."

Immediately I felt defensive. "I don't live in the past," I said.

"That's not what I'm saying, Emma. I don't mean you in particular. It's something I've been thinking about a lot lately. My wife is dependent on me for things she believes I provide for her but I don't. Half of what we see isn't really there."

I didn't believe she was as needy or as deluded as he made her sound. She ran a Montessori school and had been raising two children on her own before meeting Otik. She intimidated me with her direct gaze, her air of always knowing the answer before anyone else. "She seems very grounded to me," I said.

He shook his head. "She doesn't have a lot of confidence in herself. She thinks that I keep her life from falling apart."

Along with Dostoyevsky, he idolized Milan Kundera. I think this was part of the problem. Not that I didn't like Kundera too, but in addition to their celebratory sexiness, his books had a surreal fatalism to them, as did Otik himself, and sometimes when we were together, it seemed as if I were facing a grinning cement wall. "I don't feel like that," I said. "I know what you do and don't provide for me."

"I'm not worried about you. Your sentimentality is well-disguised."

"Thanks."

He laughed. "That's a compliment. Most people can't wait for the chance to tell you what's wrong with them."

13.

As a lover, what was Anders like? Was I too nervous to enjoy it the first time? Or was it so extraordinary to be alone with him, naked in his embrace, that it was the best time of my life?

These are a few of the questions my less discreet friends have asked.

Whether or not they realize it, these are also the questions all the people who read celebrity magazines ask themselves about the featured couples as they turn the pages. *What could it possibly be like for them . . . ? Is each time always the best time?*

I have heard that a man in New York, a clever guy with social influence and connections, holds parties meant to seem like old-fashioned salons where he and his friends discuss questions such as, Do people who can afford it deserve to have more than one or two kids? Is sushi a big con? Is sex overrated?

My answer to that last question is a qualified no. The actual physical rewards of sex, because they are so often inconsistent, probably are overrated, but its emotional heft, its implicit statement that another person desires you, possibly more than anyone else, if only in that moment, is, in a way, unrivaled. I loved sleeping with Anders because he was there—perilously close, and in those moments, no one else was as close to him as I was.

The first time was at my home, not his, and I wasn't ready for it, not amply perfumed or dressed in something ridiculous and remarkable. He came over unannounced, and it was raining and February and the previous day had been Valentine's Day. He had sent me a card, and flowers, and four pounds of Swiss chocolate. He had been in New York that day, doing publicity for his latest project, apparently dateless. When he appeared at my front door, his hair was damp, his face tired but smiling; he asked if he could come in, if he could stay for a while, possibly for good?

This isn't real, I kept thinking all that night and the next morning. This is a joke, isn't it?

Kevin Wilson

A Birth in the Woods

H E HAD BEEN WARNED that there would be blood.
Caleb's mother had told him in their daily lessons, "No
one is actually hurt. Blood doesn't necessarily mean pain." She
showed him a drawing of a baby floating in space, connected to
the placenta. "The baby may be bloody when it comes out, but it
isn't bleeding. We'll wash him off, wash the sheets and towels, and
you won't even remember it." Since his parents had decided that
Caleb, six years old, would assist with the birth, he found an
unending list of questions for his mother to consider. When he
asked if there had been a lot of blood when he was born, his
mother shook her head. "You were easy," she said. "You were so
easy."

His father whittled a block of wood into a duck for the unborn
baby before he took his penknife and dug it into the tip of his
thumb. When the blood rose to the surface of the skin and trickled down his father's hand, Caleb looked away, nauseated. His
father swung him around, softly, and held up the sliced thumb.
"It's just blood," he said. "It gets out sometimes and that's not the
worst thing in the world." Caleb held out his hand, and his father

made a quick slice into the boy's own thumb. When the blood bubbled up, Caleb and his father laughed. "Blood's nothing to worry about," his father said, and Caleb felt safe, another lesson learned. His father regarded the half-whittled duck, now streaked with brown-red blood, and threw it into the woods surrounding their cabin, the expanse of trees so dense for miles in every direction that it seemed to Caleb that no one else in the world existed. "Don't show your mother what we've done," his father said, and Caleb nodded. He wondered how long he would have to wait until he could retrieve the duck for himself.

This was how Caleb was taught, by what was around, the things closest to him, which did not include other children or adults. When the potatoes had come into harvest, his mother had shown him how to use one to power a clock. She did not explain the principle behind this, seemed bored in fact by the particulars, and was intent only on showing Caleb the strangeness of the world. She sliced worms in half, and they watched for weeks as one of the halves grew into a new worm.

"Does this work with people?" he asked.

"No, never," she said quickly.

"Sometimes, actually," retorted his father, who then smiled, pleased to have the chance to make trouble.

"That's not true," said his mother, and then thought about it for a few seconds. "No," she said again, assured of her answer.

Caleb placed his finger on the worm and watched the animal bend and curl from his touch.

He was learning to read, slowly, without much progress, though his mother seemed pleased. "The Browning Method of Typographical Comprehension and Reading," she would proudly say as she held the pamphlet for Caleb to see. She would show him a letter from the deck of flashcards; they were up to *L* in the alphabet, a ninety-degree angle, a thumb and index finger extended. Once he had the letter, he was given a book, something random from a garage sale or one of her old college texts. He was to search the book for that single letter and circle it each time it appeared. He would scan the lines of each page for the shape of the letter, the space it occupied within a word. He had noticed how an *E* looked slightly different next to a *C* than it did to a *D,* the open mouth of the *C* inviting the *E* closer, while the *D* bowed out, pushing the *E* into the next letter. She never showed him a word, never touched a line of letters and made the sound of their joining. "When will I be able to read, though?" he would ask her, his hands smeared with ink. "Soon enough," she would say. He did not believe her, but he had no choice. He needed her to tell him the things he would know.

Now there was the baby involved, about to arrive. His mother's stomach was huge. The unmistakable bulge seemed to suggest that she was growing shorter each week. Her belly was a thing she always cradled with both hands while she walked, as if she were afraid of injuring something with it instead of the other way around. She would weigh herself and then laugh, stepping off the scale as the arrow zipped back to zero, before Caleb could read the weight.

"You didn't tell me your weight," he complained, but she would walk away, giggling.

"It's broken," she would say. "It's certainly not working correctly."

One night, when the baby shifted and pressed against his mother's spine, she cried out and then instantly tried to pretend that she had been singing a song.

"Maybe we could go to the doctor," his father said. "Just a little preliminary visit."

"The baby is going to be big," she said. "Why pay a doctor to solve that mystery for us?"

When his father mentioned the hospital a second time, his mother frowned. "We decided, Felix. We decided that we would make a world apart from the world. We can't give up on that every single time things seem difficult."

Caleb put his hand on her stomach and felt the baby kick twice, his mother wincing each time.

When she had first explained to Caleb about the baby, the fact of it, she had sat down beside him on the floor and swept the math sticks, individually carved blocks the length and width of a finger which he used to add and subtract, out of the way. "We're going to put math on hold for a while," she said. "For the next few months, we'll focus on science. Biology. Caleb?" He had picked up one of the math sticks and was rubbing his thumb across the smooth grain of the wood, but he put it back down. She smiled. He was learning. "We're going to have another baby," she said. "You're going to be a brother."

"What?" he said, still trying to understand.

"A baby. A little boy or girl."

"When?" he asked.

"Soon," she said. "Six or seven months."

"Why?" he asked.

"Because your father and I thought we would all be happier with another person in the house, someone else to be a part of our family."

"Where?" he asked, moving along the questions he had been taught to ask when he did not know exactly what was happening.

"Right here," his mother answered. "Right here in the house."

She had worked to teach him the how of this baby, but it was difficult. She used hand gestures, stick figure drawings, biological terms like *ovaries* and *sperm*. Caleb still did not understand, though he nodded sometimes just to make her happy.

"I know," she said. "It doesn't make a lot of sense, does it?" He nodded. "I think maybe I know a way to help you understand exactly what happens," she said. "A way to learn."

Later that night, he could hear his parents as they argued in their room.

"No," his father said as he tried to keep his voice from rising. "Jenny, I am not going to do that."

"He wants to understand, Felix. He wants to know how it works."

"There are things he can learn from us and there are things he can learn on his own. We can't teach him everything."

"We can," she said. "You just don't want to."

"I guess not," he said, and then they were quiet.

Caleb got out of his bed and crawled to his parents' room. He looked through the open crack of the door. His mother rested her head on his father's chest, and he stroked her hair. "You're a good teacher," he told her. "He'll understand eventually."

"I am a good teacher," she said, softly.

The next morning, Caleb's mother told him that she had talked to his father last night and they had realized that they weren't entirely sure themselves how a baby came to be. "In some ways," she said, "it's a mystery, and mysteries can be just as wonderful as knowing."

It was evening. Snow fell heavily in the mountains and ice formed and then shattered, scraping along the tin roof of the house. His father had gone to the shed to collect wood for the stove. Even inside the cabin, Caleb could see his own breath. His mother breathed in short, rapid bursts and the dense air hovered around her. "It's close," she said, "it's nearly time."

He was prepared for the baby. His mother wanted him to be near in order to observe what was happening, to be a part of the procedure.

"We're all making this baby," she said. "Each one of us is doing our part."

While his father brought wood into the house and fed it into the stove, and his mother held the baby inside her and timed her contractions as the spasms shot across the surface of her face, Caleb placed new batteries in the flashlight and tested the brightness. He would hold the flashlight steady and direct the light toward the place where the baby would come, to help his father see the head when it emerged. He threw the light into the corners of the room and stared at the wide spot of light and how it illuminated the walls, the wood beams that his father had placed together to make the house. He swung the flashlight around on himself and stared directly into the light until his mother called out for him to focus on his work. He turned toward her figure, but all he could see was the leftover imprint of light, pure brightness, and it took several seconds before he could make out his mother, heavy with the baby and watching him.

While she sat on the sofa with her legs pulled up to her chest, his father laid down a plastic sheet over the mattress, then one of the fresh bedsheets.

"The same thing," his mother panted, "do it over."

"I did all this the last time and the boy came out fine," his father said. He placed another plastic sheet over the bed, followed by the final bedsheet. Caleb watched him and forgot his own work, which was to tape two copies of *The Guinness Book of World Records* together and place them in a sack. They had told him several times that the books were to keep his mother's hips raised, an important task. He carefully edged the newly made book—taped together, unable to be opened and read—into the sack, trying hard not to rip the paper. His work did not seem nearly as interesting as the sheets, the bed, the place where everything would happen.

"Why do you need two plastic sheets?" Caleb asked. Neither parent answered, focused on their own concerns. Blood, he thought. It had to be blood.

"It's happening," his mother said calmly, her breathing unaltered. A puddle of liquid collected on the floor and seeped between the slats of the wood, and his father ran over with a clean linen nightgown for her to change into. "Look away, Caleb," his father shouted, but his mother laughed. "It doesn't matter. It's going to happen soon, Caleb," she said as she slipped out of her nightgown and held her arms over her head. Though he had seen her naked before, Caleb turned and looked at the wall, embarrassed about the water that had pooled at her feet. "Once the membrane ruptures," she continued, "something irreversible has occurred. You'll see. The baby will be here soon."

The woodstove was burning full now. The windows fogged over, and somewhere deep in the woods, trees began to snap in half. The room was filled with empty plastic bags, bowls, and pillows. Cotton towels, steaming and sterilized, had been pulled from the oven, and smelled faintly of smoke. Next to the bed, the nightstand was covered with gauze and sanitary pads, everything a perfect, brilliant white. Caleb rubbed a hole in the fog on a window, stared out into the darkness at the expanse of ice and snow, and turned back to the sheeted bed, empty and white. On the edge of a wooden chair hung the still-wet nightgown. He noticed the reddish coloration that dotted it. His mother had told him about it. She had called it "bloody show," but she had said she would tell him when it happened and she hadn't. He was about to ask her about it when his father called for his help in moving his mother. She seemed calm, but her hands were shaking. Caleb wanted the baby to come.

He held his mother's left hand while his father stood on her right side and helped her to the bed. Without any apparent effort, his father lifted her into his arms and gently placed her on the bed. Her belly wobbled and she turned onto her side to face Caleb, who again placed his hand inside hers. "Soon," she said, and grimaced as she squeezed his hand.

Though they had insisted that he would help deliver the baby, his parents kept sending Caleb farther away from the bed to do various tasks. He went to the upstairs closet for a heating pad, though the house was already sweltering and dry with the heat from the fire. His father would hand him a pillow and send him into another room to shake the dust off it. When his mother complained of the heat, he took a plastic bag and stepped into the cold outside. His boots crunched the ice. With a wooden spoon, he broke up the snow and scooped it into the open bag before he finally twisted it shut. When he came back inside, he heard his father say, "I just don't like this weather, all this ice." He stopped talking when he saw Caleb, who held the already melting snow in his hands. "Bring it over here, son," he said. His mother's face was red and splotchy from the heat and the waiting, and Caleb hurried to the bed and placed the bag against her forehead.

"That feels nice," she said. She turned from Caleb and said to his father, "See? The snow helps."

His father sent him back outside for more. Each time he returned, his mother looked more and more exhausted. Her face was wrinkled with confusion.

"It's taking too long," she said as she rolled softly from side to side.

There were already seven bags of now-melted snow on the floor of the room, but his father asked him to go outside again. The bags reminded him of the time his father had returned from town with a plastic bag that held two goldfish and how quickly, almost instantly when they were placed in the waiting fishbowl, they had died. Caleb thought that moving them out of the bag had killed them but his parents assured him this was not true.

His mother moaned in pain, and his father pushed him toward the door. He was beginning to trust the word of his parents less and less with each minute that passed without the baby's arrival. His hands were numb but he plunged them into the snow again.

Back in the house, the heat stung his face. His mother struggled to sit up, but the weight of her belly dragged her back down.

His father wiped the sweat from her face and arms with a wash-cloth. A contraction traveled through her body and she screamed, the sound strangled and broken but loud. His parents continued to shift and reposition themselves, unable to settle into the thing that was happening. He had been so easy and now they were making something difficult and it was hard for Caleb not to be angry with his parents. The snow melted and spilled out of the bag, but he did not put it down. He was unsure of how to proceed, and he could only wait until his parents told him what was next.

His mother relaxed for a moment, the time between contractions. In the brief space of calm, both of his parents finally noticed his presence, and their faces became unlined and assured.

"Come closer," his mother said, and Caleb placed the bag of melted snow on the floor and went to her. He wanted to touch her stomach, but he couldn't do it, did not want to cause her any more discomfort. "It's hard right now, but it will get easier," she said, and Caleb only nodded, afraid to speak.

His father went to the kitchen and returned with a jar of honey. "You need this," he said to her as he unscrewed the jar, "for your strength." Caleb reached out his hand for the jar, wanting to help. He took the wooden wand from inside the jar, sticky on his fingers, and drizzled honey onto his mother's tongue. She smiled and then nodded for more. He did this three times, until she held up her hand. "It's coming," she said. "We need to get ready." She grabbed the bedsheet in both hands, waiting for the contractions, and Caleb wanted to run back outside, into the cold and quiet and darkness, but he stayed beside his mother and waited for the baby to come.

She screamed again, though Caleb could not hear the sound, only a humming as he stared at his mother's open mouth and closed eyes. He could hear only the tree limbs as they crashed to the ground, the fire in the stove, the sound of his heartbeat. She screamed yet again and squeezed his hand tightly. The tips of his fingers all met at the same point, and the pain in his hand opened his ears to the sound of his mother, who now whimpered as the next contraction came.

"Okay," his father said, and crouched between her legs. "We're getting close. Stay calm."

Caleb remembered the flashlight, which was at the foot of the bed. "I need to hold the flashlight," he told his father, who again looked surprised to find him in the room.

"No," his father said, "you stay with your mother, hold her hand, give her honey and water. I don't want you over here." His mother nodded, squeezed his hand again, though her eyes were still closed.

"But the flashlight," Caleb whined, unwilling to give up his job.

His father grabbed the flashlight and dragged an end table close to the bed. He turned on the flashlight and directed it toward Caleb's mother. "See?" his father said. "This will work fine," and Caleb instantly felt unnecessary; he was ashamed that his job could be performed by a table, that he was not going to learn anything from this.

It was still snowing outside and filling up the space around the house until they were the only people left on earth, three of them crowded together, the fourth still to come. The air was hot and used up, ragged. His mother was breathing strangely now. The air left her body only to be sucked quickly back in, over and over. Her belly was stretched tight, to the point that the skin seemed to vibrate. Caleb was simply a hand to be held, a presence, as his mother never opened her eyes, only breathed and pushed and screamed when it became too much. It felt like seconds, though an hour had passed. Time was mixed up in the repetition of the actions, the darkness and snow outside, the fire in the house, the baby.

It was coming now, no stopping it. His father called for her to push and his mother tried, her hand barely able to squeeze Caleb's any longer. "Something's wrong," she kept saying, but his father seemed not to hear her, only ever asking her to keep pushing, to breathe, to bring this baby into the world. He shouted again for her to push, and she screamed back at him as the pain shook her, and Caleb held on. His body pulled farther and farther away from his hand and deeper into his heart, and he held his breath until he could not last any longer and had to take another huge gulp of air. He closed his eyes and even when his father said, "Here it comes, one more time," he did not open them. Even when his mother screamed with such force that her voice gave out. Even when his father whispered, "Oh, good Lord," and the baby made its first sound, howling itself into existence, Caleb remained shut off from the things around him.

When Caleb did open his eyes, the baby was still howling, its tiny lungs powering its body, as if sound were what kept it alive, and all he saw was what he had been told to expect. On the sheets, on his father's hands and shirt, on the baby, or what he thought was the baby. Blood.

His mother was now quiet. The baby overpowered all the other sounds in the room. As Caleb listened more closely, the sound alternated between a high-pitched and insistent howl and a low, rumbling moan. His mother let go of Caleb's hand, and though he tried to hold on, eventually he let her go. His father moved quickly. He cut the cord, and a thin line of blood spurted across his face. He put the placenta in a bowl, where the mass seemed to move like a beating heart. The baby was now on a pillow on the floor, and it wriggled and barked, its body bluish-red. Caleb stayed near his mother. Though her breathing was regular again, her skin was pale, and his father shouted for him to help.

Caleb didn't move but then his father shouted again, "Goddamn it, Caleb, hand me the towels. Goddamn you." Caleb lifted the stack of towels from the table and brought them to his father. On this side of the bed, he could fully see the blood on the sheets as it spread farther and farther out. At the sight of it, so much,

Caleb felt dizzy. He got lighter, and then threw up on himself, clear and tasteless. His father didn't seem to notice and kept working. He pressed the towel against Caleb's mother, and a small red blot appeared on the clean white fabric and then, so painstakingly slow that it seemed a trick of the eye, grew larger. His father said, "Goddamn it, goddamn it," the words quick like a succession of sneezes.

Caleb's mother finally spoke, hoarse and raspy words forced out of her body. "I want my baby." The baby still screamed, the reason for all of this, now forgotten on the floor, the blood all they could focus on. His mother squeezed her legs together to hold the towel in place and Caleb's father lifted the baby. He gasped as he held it in the light and then said, "Something's wrong, isn't it? The baby, this isn't right."

Caleb watched the new thing, large and substantial in his father's hands. It was a baby, but it was covered all over in dark black hair, which was slicked with blood and mucus. It had a long, bearlike snout and its fingers were mashed together into useless claws. It growled, and its furry hands reached up toward the ceiling and batted at his father's face. Caleb realized now that it was not his brother, not a baby, but an animal, a creature, something wild. It was something inside their house that should not be there.

His mother continued to motion for the baby, and his father, dazed, disconnected from what he was holding, placed it on her chest. She held on to it, stroking its face. "My baby," she said. "It's my baby."

"Jenny," his father said, his voice now quiet but anxious with what he had to say. "It won't stop. I can't make it stop."

She touched his father's face, kissed him. "It will be okay. This is our baby, Felix. We have our baby."

"We have to take you to a hospital. Something's wrong. The baby needs a doctor, too; there's something wrong with him."

His mother kept yawning, her eyelids heavy. "We can't go. We're here—we have to stay here."

"Jenny."

"Go find help."

His father went back to the foot of the bed and removed the towel, which was now heavy with blood, and threw it to the floor. "Jenny," he said again, crying now, pleading with her. With the baby still resting on her chest, she fell into a half sleep. The baby tried to wriggle out of her grasp, but she held on to him.

His father pressed a new towel tight against her. Caleb stared at the bloody towel, twisted and curled on the floor. His mother was dying, he now realized; the baby had brought something else with it, slow and painful.

"I'm taking you to a hospital," his father said finally. As he walked toward her, he tripped over the towel, and it uncoiled, showing slashes of white cotton patterned against the blood. He moved to pick her up, but she moaned in pain.

"No," she panted. "Don't do that. I don't think I can move, Felix."

His father touched her forehead, which left a streak of blood. It looked like a lowercase *j* to Caleb, sweeping over and up with a dot, before it mixed with the sweat on her forehead and became nothing, only blood. "I'll be back as soon as I can," he said. She nodded, closed her eyes, and nuzzled the baby.

Caleb's father threw on his jacket and took the flashlight from the table. His hands shook so hard that the beam of light jittered across the room before he finally turned it off. Caleb was afraid of him, of the look on his face, but he did not want to be left in the house. "Can I come with you?" he asked, but again his father did not seem to hear him. Caleb pulled at the arm of his jacket. "What about me?" he asked.

"You watch over them," his father said, and now tears were spilling down both cheeks. "Keep them safe."

His father started the truck, and the engine clacked and then hummed with power. He rolled down the window and told Caleb,

"I'll be right back. I'll come back with help, and we'll fix this and we'll all be okay." But he was still crying and Caleb could hardly listen anyway. "Okay?" his father repeated. Caleb nodded and the truck backed out of the driveway, onto the road that led to town, which was nearly obscured by the snow. Ice crunched underneath the wheels, and the truck crept at such a slow pace that it seemed like it might be going in reverse.

Caleb went back inside and leaned against the window, afraid to go back to his mother and the baby. He felt the possibility of his father's never returning move down his spine—that he would drive into town and keep going into the next town and the next, until home and the new baby, the strange thing he'd made, were only a memory.

The truck slid down the road and made the first curve. There was the sharp sound of the brakes tapping on and off, and the headlights were steady on the road in front of it. Caleb rubbed the fog from the window and watched as the truck headed into the next curve, nearly out of view, and then he heard the brakes dig in, and the wheels skidded across the ice. Too fast, it seemed, still going, around the bend and disappearing from view, the lights gone, the brakes still squealing, and then, for one brief second, silence, the snow falling. Then a crash, loud and jarring, and the sound of metal twisting, the world giving up its shape.

Caleb ran beneath the dinner table and hid himself under a white sheet. His mother called out for him, but he didn't answer, could not bear to go to her. "Caleb?" she asked again, her voice so soft. "I'm sorry, honey. I didn't know it would be like this." The baby started again. Its cries were now empty of anger or confusion, merely a noise to fill the house. He could hardly hear his mother, but he refused to move from under the table. Instead he strained his ears to the sound of her. "Take care of him, Caleb. This is your brother and I want you to be a good brother and make sure he's safe. I need you to watch over him until your father comes back. Will you do that, Caleb?"

He didn't answer, pulled the sheet tighter around him.

She was crying now. "Caleb? I'm so sorry."

He waited for her to speak again but there was only silence, interrupted by the occasional sound of the baby's whimpers and cries. Caleb closed his eyes and pretended to be asleep, waited for her to come to him, to lift the sheet off and carry him to bed. With every minute that passed, he grew more tired, lulled by the nearly imperceptible sound of snow freezing, turning into ice.

The fire had all but burned itself away, and the house was growing cold. Caleb did not want to move. He willed his body to stop shaking, but the cold was getting inside of him. When he finally stirred, pushing one of the chairs out of the way as he crawled from under the table, the baby heard the sound and gave a small cry and then stopped, as if waiting for a reply. Caleb walked to the stack of wood and removed a piece. The weight was heavy in his tired arms. He opened the door to the stove and slid the piece into the waning fire, watched the wood slowly ignite around the edges and hold the flame. As he warmed his hands, he looked toward the bed, where his mother was still and quiet. He moved a step closer and saw the baby shivering under its soft coat of black fur; it had fallen from his mother's hands onto the bed and had pulled its limbs tightly against itself.

When Caleb touched his mother, he knew that she was dead. He could not explain the feeling except to understand that his mother's arm felt lifeless, that nothing was left to move through it. He quickly pulled his hand away and stared at her calm face. He took a washcloth and wiped the streak of blood from her forehead. While the baby softly moaned and kicked in its sleep, Caleb cleaned each of his mother's fingers, scrubbing the nails until they were spotless. He kissed her cheek and his lips tingled until he looked down at the baby, the only other thing alive in the house.

He poked at the baby, trying to jab it awake. The fur on its head was soft, but the hair on its body was like steel wool, rough and bristly and flecked with blood. The baby finally stirred and immediately began howling, its mouth a perfect *O*, though Caleb was not yet up to that letter in the alphabet. To him, the mouth was a circle, around and around and around, with nothing but a sound coming out. The sound echoed through the house and hung in the fire-warmed air. This thing had killed his mother. It had come in the dead of night and left his mother hollowed out and empty.

Caleb placed his open palm over the mouth of the baby. He pinched the baby's snoutish nose closed with his thumb and fore-finger. The muffled sound traveled through his arm, thrummed against his elbow. He could feel the anger inside the baby and he clamped down harder as he felt its lungs shrink with the effort to fight back. He could end it right now, could snuff the baby in mid-scream and hide it in the woods. Perhaps it wasn't meant to live long, was strangely twisted up inside and could not last on its own. Its breath stumbled and sputtered against the closed door of Caleb's hand. A few seconds more.

But he couldn't continue. He didn't want the baby and what it had created, but he could not take the easy steps to end it; he remembered his mother's plea for him to protect his brother. He took his hand from its mouth and the baby sucked in air, pulled the world into its lungs. The scream returned; the baby's claws curled up in rage. Caleb lifted the baby into his arms and pulled the heavy weight close to his chest. He sat on the floor and held his brother in his arms, allowed him to fight and scream and scratch the air until he had tired himself out. Caleb took the honey from the nightstand and removed the wand from the jar. The baby sucked on the end like a pacifier, his first food in the world. When it was gone, Caleb pried the wand loose. The baby had a small tooth, malformed and gray, on the top left side of his mouth. Caleb touched it with his finger and found the edge sur-prisingly sharp. The baby clamped down and Caleb removed his finger just in time. He dipped the wand into the honey again and fed the baby this way for the next few minutes; after each feeding, he would wipe the sticky excess from his mouth to keep him clean. The baby was his brother and they were alone in what was left of the night, pitch-black and cold except for the tiny space their bodies occupied. Caleb reached into his pocket and produced the duck his father had whittled, with its dark blood. He placed it between the baby's paws and the baby twitched as he sniffed the blood that had soaked the duck before he was ever born. The object seemed to further calm him, and Caleb continued to steady the duck as it constantly threatened to slip out of the baby's grasp. As if teaching him a lesson, Caleb softly quacked and then shook the duck so gently that it would not frighten his brother. "Duck," Caleb said, though the word sounded as if it were from a language that had died out hundreds of years ago. He knew it meant absolutely nothing to anyone but him.

The baby curled against Caleb's shirt and squirmed to find comfort, unable to sleep. His body left a damp, bloody imprint on the fabric. Caleb would watch over him.

When the front door opened the next day and the morning sun spilled into the room, there was Caleb, stained with blood, and the newborn baby, finally asleep in Caleb's arms, all that was left of the day before.

Hisham Matar

Naima

MY MOTHER DID NOT like the heat. I never saw her in a swim-suit or in sudden surrender closing her eyes at the sun. The arrival of spring in Cairo would set her off planning our summer getaways. Once we spent the holidays high up in the Swiss Alps, where my body stiffened at the sight of deep hollow chasms emp-tied out of the rocky earth. Another time she took us to Nordland, in northern Norway, where the splintered peaks of austere black mountains were reflected sharply in the unmoving waters. We stayed in a wooden cabin that stood alone by the shore and was painted the brown of withered leaves. Around its roof hung a gutter as wide as a human thigh. Here whatever fell from the sky fell in abundance. There was no other man-made structure in sight. Some afternoons, Mother disappeared and I would not let on to Father that my heart was thumping at the base of my ears. I would keep to my room until I heard footsteps on the deck, the kitchen door slid-ing open. Once I found Mother there with hands stained black-red, a rough globe dyed into the front of her jumper. With eyes as clean as glass, wide, satisfied, she held out a handful of wild berries. They tasted of a ripe sweetness I found hard to attribute to that landscape.

One night, fog gathered thickly, abstracting the licks and sighs of the northern lights. You need adulthood to appreciate such horror. An anxious heat entered my eight-year-old mind and I curled up in bed, hoping Mother would pay me one of her night visits, kiss my forehead, lie beside me.

I woke up several times believing that Naima was there. She was our maid, and had been since before I was born, before my parents left our country and moved to Egypt. In winter, when the sky got dark early and Mother worried about her making the long commute home, Naima would sleep on my bedroom floor. I would watch her lying on her side, facing the skirting board, her leg bent with the tight determination of a tree branch. Her devotion had always seemed muscular, too intense, but now I yearned for it; I wished that she had come with us, or even that I had been left behind with her in Cairo.

In the morning the still world returned: the innocent waters, the ferocious mountains, the pale sky dotted with small, newborn clouds. I found Mother in the kitchen, warming milk, a glass of water on the white marble counter beside her. Not juice, tea, or coffee but water was her morning drink. She took a sip and with her usual insistence on quiet muffled the impact of the glass on the marble with the soft tip of her little finger. Any sudden sound unsettled her. She could conduct an entire day's chores in near-silence.

It should not have been difficult for me to speak, to say the usual "Good morning, Mama," but at times she seemed impenetrable, as if contained within an invisible structure. I sat at the table, where, when the three of us gathered at mealtimes, Mother would occasionally glance at the fourth, empty chair as if it signaled an absence, something lost. She poured the hot milk into a cup for me. A sliver of steam brushed the air then disappeared beside her neck.

"Nuri, habibi," she said, speaking my name the way she often did, with careful affection, "why the long face?"

She took me out onto the deck that stretched above the lake. The air was so brisk it stung my throat. I remembered what she had said to Father in the car when the naked mountains of Nordland first came into view: "Here God decided to be a sculptor; everywhere else he holds back."

"Holds back?" Father had echoed. "You talk about him as if he's a friend of yours."

In those days Father did not believe in God. He often greeted Mother's references to the divine with irritated sarcasm. Perhaps I should not have been surprised when, after Mother died, he now and again voiced a prayer; sarcasm, more often than not, hides a secret fascination.

Was it the romance of wood fires, the discretion of heavy coats that attracted my mother to the northern and unpeopled places of Europe? Or was it the impeccable stillness of a fortnight spent mostly sheltered indoors with the only two people she could lay claim to? I have come to think of all those holidays, no matter where they were, as having taken place in a single country—her country—and of the silences that marked them as her melancholy. There were moments when her unhappiness seemed as elemental as clear water.

After she died, it soon became obvious that what Father had always wanted to do in the two weeks off that he allowed himself every summer was to lie in the sun all day. So the Magda Marina, a small hotel in Agamy Beach, near Alexandria, became the place where he and I spent that fortnight. He seemed to have lost his way with me; widowhood had dispossessed him of any ease that he had once had around his only child. When we sat down to eat he either read the paper or gazed into the distance. Whenever he noticed me looking at him he would fidget or check his watch. As soon as he finished eating, he would light a cigarette and snap his fingers for the bill, not bothering to check whether I had finished, too.

"See you back in the room."

He never did that when Mother was alive.

Instead, when the three of us went to a restaurant, they would sit side by side facing me. If we were all engaged in a conversation, she would direct most of her contributions toward me, as if I were the front wall of a squash court. And when his unease led him to play the entertainer she would monitor, in that discreet way of hers, my reactions to his forced cheerfulness or, if he could bear it no longer, to his silences. With Mother's eyes on me I would watch him observe the other patrons or stare out at the view, which was often of some unremarkable street or square, no doubt daydreaming or plotting his next move in the secret work I never once heard him talk about. At these moments it felt as if he were the boy obliged to share a meal with adults, as if he were the son and I the father.

After Mother passed away, he and I came to resemble two flat-sharing bachelors held together by circumstance or obligation. But then, at the most unexpected moments, a tenderhearted sympathy, raw and sudden, would rise in him, and he would plunge his face into my neck, sniff deeply and kiss, tickling me with his mustache. It would set us off laughing as though everything were all right.

At the Magda Marina, he spent his time sunbathing and reading fat books: one on the Suez Crisis, one a biography of our late king, with his portrait on the cover. Whenever Father acquired a new book on our country—the country my parents had fled, the country I had never seen, yet continued to think of as my own—he would immediately finger the index pages.

"Baba, who are you looking for?" I once asked.

He shook his head and said, "No one."

But later I, too, searched the indexes. It felt like pure imitation. It was not until I encountered my father's name—Kamal Pasha el-Alfi—that I realized what I was looking for. Kamal Pasha, those books said, had been a close adviser to the king and one of the few men who could walk into the royal office without an appointment.

Whenever the young monarch was in one of his anxious moods—perhaps suspecting his end to be near—it was Kamal Pasha el-Alfi who was called to ease his fears. In these books my father was also described as an aristocrat who, having been forced into exile by the revolution, had moved "gradually but with radical effect" to the left. I read these things about my father before I could understand what they meant. And if I came to him with my questions he would smoothly deflect them: "It was all so long ago."

I rarely persisted, because I knew that he was being true to Mother's wishes.

"Don't transfer the weight of the past onto your son," she once told him.

"You can't live outside history," he argued. "We have nothing to be ashamed of. On the contrary."

After a long pause she responded, "Who said anything about shame? It's longing that I want to spare him. Longing and the burden of your hopes."

I recall how sometimes, during the edgeless hours of the afternoon, I would use Mother's hip for a pillow. I would listen to the steady rhythm of her breath, the pages of her book turning. If I fell asleep, the sound would become a lazy breeze rustling a tree, or a broom brushing the earth. I hold the memory of her collarbone. I used to reach for it the way a rock climber would a sturdy ledge. I recall also her hair, strands as thick as strings. I would stretch one across my forehead, or on my tongue, and feel it tighten like a blade. None of this would distract her from her reading. I would watch the wide blossom of her eyes scanning the lines, those same eyes which grew keen whenever I caught her standing behind a heavy curtain in a game of hide-and-seek or when I revealed to her a luminous butterfly I had captured. How quickly her cheeks would redden then. She would speak, a warm whisper, before laughter flexed her throat. She was as close as I ever came to having a sister.

And then there were those cruel, sudden gaps, the clearings where she stood alone, not knowing how to return. How her eyes would wilt, looking at me as if acknowledging someone she half knew. Sometimes at night I would wake up and find her there, studying my face. She would force a smile and depart, quietly closing the door behind her, as if I were not hers. Other times she would lie beside me, our two heads sharing one pillow. Her pale thin fingers, which never seemed to match her strength, were like frozen twigs. She would tuck them between my knees or, if I was lying on my back, slide them behind my lower back, the place that is still hers.

But if I was ill it was Naima who would not leave my bedside. Mother would occasionally come in and stand at the foot of the bed, clearly concerned but awkward, as if she were intruding on a private moment. Once I confronted her about this. I babbled and stuttered, and she held me and said, "I know, it breaks my heart, too. But we mustn't see it this way. We are all lucky. We must count ourselves lucky."

In her last year, her silences grew deeper and more frequent. Some days she did not leave her room. When she called, she called only for Naima, who also called her Mama.

"Of course, Mama"; "Straightaway, Mama."

Naima would often be sent to the pharmacy for aspirin, sleeping pills, painkillers.

So old and persistent did Mother's unhappiness seem that I had never stopped to ask its cause. Nothing is more acceptable than what we are born into.

I remember the last night.

It was late evening. Naima had already changed out of her house galabia and into the hard fabric of her black dress, a veil wrapped tightly around her head, revealing the delicate shape of her skull. The familiar carrier bag hung on her wrist, containing one or two but never more than three pieces of fruit, the round forms pressing against the plastic. At Mother's instruction, every evening Naima had to go to the large fruit bowl that sat at the center of the long dining table and take home those guavas, apricots, or apples which had passed their prime. Naima resisted and would often argue that the fruit was still good. Her resistance baffled me because I knew that on her birthdays Naima's parents were able to give her only an apple or a handful of mulberries.

Now she stood there, silent and hesitant, at Mother's door. She brought her hand up but did not knock.

"When she wakes up," she whispered, "tell her I went home. See you tomorrow."

She must have detected that I did not want her to go, because she stopped and asked, "Did you brush your teeth?"

When I looked up from the sink I saw her in the mirror, standing outside the bathroom, her hands clasped against her waist, like a person in prayer. Her Nubian face looked even darker than usual. I followed her to the door and stood barefoot on the cold marble. She studied her foggy reflection in the long, narrow glass window in the lift door and with nervous hands tucked away stray hairs. She never stopped dreading the long journey home. On the occasions when she spent the night with us, she would carry out her tasks in the house with renewed enthusiasm, insisting on dusting the bookshelves again, cleaning the bathrooms one more time, all the while cracking jokes at which no one laughed. The silences that followed these jokes always turned her cheeks a deep shade of purple.

"Go on now, you will catch a cold."

But I did not move until the lift arrived because, regardless of her words, I knew she welcomed my attachment. There was always some elusive way in which Naima showed that she needed confirmation not so much of my attention as of my loyalty, as if she feared I might, one day, betray her.

I waited for Father and only once dared walk into their room. Mother lay on her side and did not move when I touched her ear.

I went to my room and stood on my desk chair facing a photograph that Mother had recently taken of herself. She was the one who had had it framed and had hung it there. Her eyes stared out unflinchingly, but her jawbones were slightly out of focus, as if she was emerging from a cloud. I liked it because her face was nearly life-size. I did not know then why Mother looked better in photographs taken before I was born. I do not mean simply younger but altogether brighter, as if she had just stepped off a carousel: her hair settling, her eyes anticipating more joy. And in those photographs you could almost hear a kind of joyful music in the background. Then, after I arrived, it all changed. For a long time, before I knew the truth, I thought it was the physical assault of pregnancy that had claimed her cheery disposition.

Occasionally it would reemerge, this happy outlook, awakened by a memory from the past, as when she told the story of Father slipping and landing on his bottom on one of the steep alleyways in Geneva's Old Town.

"His back white with snow," she said, barely able to speak because of her laughing. "Calling my name as he nearly tripped up the Christmas shoppers."

Father's face changed, a solemn expression suggesting that he might be taking offense, which of course made the whole thing funnier. "I nearly broke my neck," he finally said.

"Yes, but your father has always been an excellent navigator," she said, and they both exploded into laughter.

I do not recall ever being so happy.

I woke up to Father repeating, "Savior, Savior," and the sound of his reaching, anxious steps.

I stood in the doorway of my bedroom, my eyes weak against the blazing chandelier in the hall. Other people were there, two men in white. They held the front door open as Father rushed toward them, Mother slack in his arms. Her long, disheveled hair trembled with every step he took. One of her dangling feet seemed to swing more rapidly than the other. I ran after him, down the stairs. I remembered him once daring me to a race down those stairs, saying that he could descend the three flights faster than it would take me to go down in the lift. When the lift landed on the ground floor, he had pulled the door open, trying not to let his breathlessness show, his eyes sparkling with satisfaction. But now, when he saw me following, he stopped.

"Nuri."

His eyes were red. Mother lay silent in his arms, her eyelids hard as shells. I paused for a moment, and the two men in white overtook me.

"Nuri," he shouted, and the two men looked at me. The expressions on their faces are still a source of horror.

I climbed back up, stopping at every landing, looking down the stairwell. Then I stood on our balcony, my hands gripping the cold metal balustrade above my head. I watched him carry her to the ambulance. One of her breasts was almost out of the gray satin nightdress. When the men in white tried to take her, Father shook his head and shouted something. He laid her on the stretcher, straightened and covered her body, caught the fall of her hair, wrapped it like a belt around his fist, and then tucked the bundle beneath her neck. A siren started up. Father walked back into the building, past the still figures of Amm Samir, the building's porter, and his sons. Early light was just breaking, and they, too, must have been startled out of sleep. Somehow they did not seem surprised, as if they expected such a calamity to befall "the Arab family on the third floor." The Nile flowed by strong and indifferent. There was hardly a wind to flutter the bamboo grasses that covered its banks. The leaves of the banana trees hung low, and the heads of the palms seemed as heavy as velvet.

I heard the door of the apartment slam shut.

"Where are they taking her?"

He kneeled before me so his face was level with mine. "She

needs to rest. For a while . . . in hospital," he said, and stopped as if to stifle a cough.

"Why? We can take care of her here. Naima and I can take care of her. Why did you let them take her?"

"She will be back soon."

He smelled of cigarettes, of other people. He looked as if he had not slept at all. I followed him into their room. Her form was still stamped into the mattress. Father's side was undisturbed. The room had the air of a place that had witnessed a terrible confrontation, a battle lost.

Father spent most of the subsequent days at the hospital. Never having had to look after me, he was now continuously asking Naima whether his son had eaten or if it was bedtime yet.

"Has he bathed? Make sure he brushes his teeth."

I was suddenly spoken of in the third person. I had become a series of tasks. I could tell that Father was irritated by having to bear such domestic responsibility. And every time I cried for the mother from whom I had never before been separated, he looked at once fearful and impatient.

"Naima," he would call, louder than necessary.

I asked to be taken to the hospital.

"The doctors are doing everything they can. There is nothing more any of us can do."

"Then why do you spend the whole day there?"

I watched his anxious eyes.

Two days later, he took us to visit Mother. At a set of traffic lights, a boy, possibly my age, although his thinness made him look younger, tapped on my window. Around his arm hung necklaces of jasmine. He was wearing a red patterned T-shirt that reminded me of one I used to wear.

Rigid with shyness, Naima asked, "Could we buy some? Madam loves jasmine."

Although Naima did not address Father directly, the question was clearly intended for him. She was often wary around him. She would usually send me to ask whether it was coffee or tea that he wanted, if he was expecting anyone for lunch, or if there was anything else he needed before she left. Father rolled down his window, and the thick heat of the day spilled in. The boy ran to him. Father bought the whole bunch, his eyes lingering on the boy's T-shirt. He handed the jasmines to Naima and rolled up his window. His eyes now were on the rearview mirror, trying to catch a last glimpse of the boy.

Naima fingered the necklaces in her lap.

"You will get them knotted doing that," I said, and immediately regretted it as she looked nervously at the rearview mirror.

"Aren't those the clothes we gave Ibn Ali?" Father asked.

Relieved, Naima looked back. We watched the boy run between the cars and vanish.

"Yes, Pasha," she said. "It looks like the same T-shirt."

Ibn Ali was one of the orphanages Father visited, often taking Naima and me with him, to deliver food or clothes or make a donation. There was also Abd al-Muttalib and Al Sayeda Aisha and Al Ridha.

"Don't let it upset you," Naima told him. "No matter what you do, you can't stop them working."

"But so young," he said.

"Not much younger than I was," she said softly, and after too long a delay.

Naima gripped my hand tightly as we went deeper into the maze of neon-lit corridors. The jasmines were slung neatly around her other arm. The odor of the hospital was so unforgiving that every so often she would bring the cloud of white flowers to her nose. I tugged, and she let me do the same. Father was already a few meters ahead. With every step he took, the leather heels of his shoes were striped by the neon light.

We found Mother lying under a cold blue lamp. The bedcovers were folded beneath her arms, one wrist was encircled by a yellow plastic bracelet, and a constant bleeping hammered the silence.

Naima placed the jasmines at the foot of the bed and covered her face.

"Did I not tell you . . ." Father said, pulling her out of the room.

I was alone with Mother. I wanted to lift the flattened pillows, puff them up. Her skin had turned ashen. Her eyes were shut with an outrageous finality, a moisture lingering where the eyelids met. I thought of touching her, and the impossibility of it frightened me. My mind returned to a distant memory. I was four or maybe five. She was getting ready for a party. I was crouched beneath the chiffonier, beside her feet: black high heels, stockings a color that made her skin look powdered. A thin fluorescent line hovered above where the black suede of the shoe met the stockings. An optical illusion. I traced it, erasing and redrawing the light with my finger. Then she moved. I looked up, smiling, thinking I had tickled her, but she was only leaning closer to the mirror in order to scrutinize the exactness of her lipstick line.

Father was right: there was nothing any of us could do here.

A few days later Father came home from the hospital earlier than usual. He went straight to his room. I stood outside his door for a minute or two, then knocked.

"Not now, Nuri," he said, his voice uneven.

After a few minutes, I heard the sound of running water in his bathroom. I remembered what Mother used to tell him whenever she found him in a bad mood: "Take a cold shower. It's what the Prophet, peace and blessings be upon him, used to do whenever he received bad news." And I remembered Father shaking his head. But that was when he was in no need of God. When he got out of the shower he called for Naima.

"Shut the door behind you. Where is Nuri?"

"Ustaz Nuri is in his room," she said, even though she saw me standing outside the door and forced a smile before walking in.

He began whispering. A few seconds later I heard her give a short scream. Had he placed a hand on her mouth?

For the rest of that day Naima's fingers trembled.

Her eyes filled with tears when I asked, "Are you all right? Are you ill? Shall I pour you a glass of cola?"

Every hour or so she would come to ask, "Has your father spoken to you yet?"

Father stayed in his room, talking on the telephone.

At sunset he called me in.

"Sit down. Let me see your hand." After a few seconds he said my name, then the words "Mama will not be coming home."

After another pause he spoke again.

"She will never be coming back."

I pulled my hand away. I did not believe him. I insisted that he take me to the hospital.

"She is no longer there."

He restrained me, carried me to my room, and locked the door behind us. Outside, Naima cried, begging to be let in. Father opened the door and with astonishing tenderness pulled her to his chest and kissed her head. He held me, too, and began muttering that from here on life was never going to be the same, that God had felled his only tree and shelter. I searched but could not find a tear in either of his eyes. This should not have surprised me, for I had never seen Father cry.

The following day, seventy-five wooden chairs, the sort most commonly found in Egyptian cafés, with a profile of Nefertiti printed on the seat, arrived. The porter, Amm Samir, and his silent children carried two huge speakers up the stairs. They slid off their slippers at the door, and, their stiff bodies swaying momentarily beneath the weight, placed the speakers, each taller than Father, in the middle of the hall. The angle at which they were left facing each other suggested a quarrel. Then the porter and his children carried every piece of furniture that was in the reception hall into the dining room. Armchairs were capsized over the dining table, and their cushions stuffed beneath. I watched Amm Samir's dark, hard feet sink into the rug. Each toenail curved forward into the thick wool. Each joint was crowned with a little gray stone of skin, and each heel was like the battered end of a club. At what point, I wondered, will his sons' feet look like this? Noticing me, Amm Samir placed a heavy hand on my head and, after a second's hesitation, kneeled down and kissed my forehead. He looked at Father. And Father, choosing to give Amm Samir the approval he requested, said, "Thank you." With lowered heads, the sons followed Amm Samir out.

Urgency and grief had rendered Father, Naima, and me nearly equal. Together we arranged the chairs. And at one point Father asked Naima her opinion.

"Where shall we put the speakers?"

"By the entrance," she said, embarrassed, and when he hesitated she pressed on. "But that is where they are always placed, Pasha."

"Perhaps in your district," he said.

The possibility of a smile brushed both of their faces.

"But it's people's duty to attend, Pasha. It wasn't I who set the custom."

"Enough. Lift," he said, and together they carried the speakers to where she had suggested, placing one at either side of the entrance.

We pushed the chairs against the walls in conspiratorial silence. When we were done, we stood in the middle of the room, and I hoped that there would be something else for us to do, but then Father disappeared into his room, and Naima returned to the kitchen.

The front door was left open. The reception hall began to resemble a waiting room. Not knowing where to go, I sat and counted the chairs, which now stood in a rectangle. The first time I came up with seventy-four. On the second attempt I had seventy-seven. Only the fourth or fifth time around did I get seventy-five. Then I saw our next-door neighbor walk out of the lift. He did a double take. The Koran was not playing yet, so he may have thought we were preparing for a party. But something about me must have suggested bad news. I went to Naima in the kitchen, and the man followed behind me.

"Greetings, Ustaz Midhaat."

"What happened?"

"Madam passed away," Naima told him, and, just as she did, tears appeared in her eyes.

Ustaz Midhaat looked at me now with eyes as wide as coffee cups. I moved behind Naima.

A few minutes later he returned with his whole family. Father came out dressed in a white galabia. He wore a galabia only to bed, and so he looked as if he had wandered out from a dream. He sat beside our neighbor, saying almost nothing, his cheeks covered in stubble. Naima served them unsweetened black coffee and asked me to pass around a plate of almonds. Then Father waved to me to come.

"The Koran, turn on the Koran," he whispered.

By the afternoon more neighbors had arrived, people we hardly knew, and by nightfall the place was packed with silent mourners. I had never seen our house so full yet so quiet. Naima was joined by an army of servants, lent by neighbors, whom she managed with a new authority.

I took the lift up to the roof to escape. The city stretched in all directions. It hummed and clanked like an engine in the night. The streets coiled into knots here and there. Not even the Nile tempered it. If I could I would have erased it, wiped it clean. I have never before or since experienced such a careless desire for violence. Then I felt a presence behind me. Naima, even with her endless duties, had noticed my absence.

In the morning my mother's three siblings, Aunt Souad, Aunt Salwa, and Uncle Fadhil, arrived from our country. I had never met them before, but recognized them from photographs. My aunts kept remarking how brave I was and how unusually long my eyelashes were, and teased me about my Cairene accent, my skin. They said that because I was darker than Father and Mother I was really the son of my great-grandfather, who was, by all accounts, nearly as dark as I am. They tickled my toes, hugged me when I laughed, dug their faces into my neck and inhaled deeply before kissing. At night, they took turns lying beside me, telling stories that usually included a mention of the waterfalls or pomegranates or palm trees of our country. If in the night I went to get a drink of water, one of them would appear behind me, asking whether I was all right.

They sweetened my name to Abu el-Noor, calling it out whenever they saw me daydreaming. The slightest hint of contemplation worried them. If I was in the bathroom for a little longer than usual, I would hear one of my aunts whisper, "Abu el-Noor, habibi, are you all right?"

Father let his beard grow. It surprised me how heavily streaked with gray it was; he was only thirty-nine and the hair on his head was completely black.

Once, Uncle Fadhil embraced him, speaking solemnly and with a hint of urgency. Father eventually began nodding in a resigned sort of way, his eyes still on the ground.

Another time the door of his bedroom was ajar, and I saw him cornered by my two aunts.

"He is unusually aloof for a boy his age," Aunt Salwa was saying.

"Let us take him back. He will grow up among his cousins," Aunt Souad added.

"We will bring him up as our own," Aunt Salwa said. "This way, when the country comes back to us, he can play a role."

After a long pause Father spoke. "I could not do that to Naima. She would never forgive me."

Long ago, when Naima was ill with bilharzia, Father, at Mother's insistence, brought me to visit her. It took about an hour to reach the maze of her neighborhood by car. But, as our driver, Abdu, was keen to tell Father, the journey on public transport took at least an hour and a half.

"Three hours' round trip, Pasha."

Father did not react.

Every time Abdu rolled down his window to ask someone for directions, the pedestrian would lean down and study our faces. Eventually we found Naima's street. It was so narrow that the car could barely fit through.

"Careful," Father said in a near-whisper, while holding on to the handle above his window.

"Don't worry, Pasha," Abdu replied, also in a whisper.

Raw sewage meandered down the middle of the road, passing between the wheels. Father asked Abdu to roll up his window, but by then the stench had already entered the car. Above us clothes-lines sagged under the weight of laundry and veiled most of the sky. Every so often Abdu had to press the horn, which sounded like an explosion in the narrow street. People had to find door-ways to stand in, and even then we had to pass ever so slowly, almost brushing against their bodies. I watched a buckle, a detail of fabric, the occasional child's face. These people who lined the road stood still and kept their arms by their sides. I was sure that from that angle they could see my bare knees on the beige leather upholstery.

Naima, her seven siblings, and her parents lived in a two-bedroom apartment in a four-story building that was covered in flaking red paint with the words *Coca-Cola* repeated across it.

Abdu waited with the car. Children preceded Father and me up the stairs, announcing our arrival and occasionally stopping to look back, giggle, and elbow one another before running up again. On each landing small paper bags sat bulging with rubbish, many of them punctured or torn. Flies the size of bees weaved lazily around them.

"Don't touch," Father said, and I immediately pulled my hand off the railing and placed it in his open palm. He did not let go until we were at the door of the apartment.

Naima's father, who was a security guard at one of the museums, met us on the landing in his uniform. He looked worried. The mother cried when she saw Father, then was ordered by her husband to go and make tea. There was hardly any furniture in the living room. One carpet, the size of a prayer rug, lay in the center of the tiled floor as if concealing an imperfection or some secret passage. Naima lay on a mattress in a corner. I sat beside her. She took hold of my hand. My skin burned in her grip. She neither smiled nor cried, but stared at me with a peculiar gentleness, as if I were a kind of nourishment.

"Nothing, really," the father said. "Her mother spoils her. She's just after attention." Turning toward Naima, he asked loudly, "Aren't you?"

She did not respond.

"She will be up in no time," he told Father, anxiety making him blink his eyes.

"She should take as long as she needs," Father told him. "We only came to wish her well."

The mother returned with a plate and placed it on the rug: crumbled feta and sliced tomato submerged in the pee yellow of cotton oil. She stopped for a moment and looked at Naima and me.

"Isn't that right, Umm Naima?" the father said. "You spoil your daughter."

She waited a few seconds before speaking.

"She loves him like a son," she said to Father.

"Yes," he told her.

Although Naima would not let her eyes leave my face, she had taken note of this exchange. I squeezed her hand. I thought of saying something. Instead, I placed my palm on her cheek. She held it there. I thought perhaps the relative coolness of my skin was a comfort to her. But then tears welled in her eyes.

"Come, girl, don't be afraid," her father said, fear detectable in his voice.

And just as suddenly Naima's tears vanished.

The parents insisted that we eat. Father shook his head. I wished he were better able to conceal the frown on his face. Naima's father handed us loaves of bread. Mine was hard and speckled with flour stones. The mother poured a thick black liquid, and when I asked what it was the father said, "Tea, of course," and I was convinced I had offended him. About two centimeters of the powdered leaf sat in the base of the glass. Father kneeled down, broke a small piece off his loaf, and dipped it in the solitary dish on the floor.

"There, thanks very much."

I bowed all the way down, feeling the blood gather in my head, and kissed Naima's hot forehead.

Uncle Fadhil seemed to have come to Cairo mainly to accompany the women. As a man, he faced the greatest risk of retaliation for visiting his "backward, traitor" relatives. He mostly sat smoking. Whenever I sat next to him he would squeeze my skinny upper arms and say, "Flex."

Three days after they arrived, he told my aunts it was time to go. "Just in case the authorities think we are enjoying ourselves," he said, weariness curling his eyebrows.

Naima and I stood watching Amm Samir and his eldest son, Gamaal, fasten the luggage on the roof rack. We waved when the car pulled away, then went back upstairs. When I was in my room, surrounded by the smell of my aunts, I wept.

Our apartment struggled to resume its original character. Naima moved soundlessly, cleaning the indifferent surfaces, preparing our joyless meals. I felt a tremor whenever I heard the clang of pots in Mother's kitchen. Father seemed awkward and nervous around me. The beard was gone, and now he spent most of his time out or in his room. Naima no longer slept at her home but on the floor in my bedroom. There was an abstract urgency in the air.

The arrival of Hydar and Taleb, old friends of Father's who, after the revolution, had settled in Paris, rescued us. Hydar brought his wife, Nafisa, who raised her voice every time she addressed me.

Father gave up his room to Hydar and Nafisa. When they resisted, he said, "Listen, ask Nuri, I hardly sleep there. I prefer the couch. Honestly."

Then he insisted that Taleb take my bed.

"This man knew you before you were born."

Taleb blushed, nodding.

I slept on the floor, in Naima's place, and she slept in the kitchen.

Mother had not liked having guests, particularly these guests, and this had been a recurring source of disagreement between my parents. But now Father and his friends could stay up drinking whiskey until the early hours. I would hear Taleb getting into bed. I think if he had not tried so hard to be quiet he might have made less noise. His breath would quickly fill the room with the chemical smell of alcohol.

I could not help but feel that Mother's coldness toward Father's old Parisian friends was somehow part of a general unease that marked my parents' relationship to Paris. They almost never talked about their time in that city. And on the rare occasion that Mother did speak about how I came to be born there she would always begin by telling me how Naima came to work for the family. I did not then understand how this detail mattered at all to the story.

She told me how she and Father had gone to Cairo expressly to employ a maid. And how, on the two-day drive back to our country, thirteen-year-old Naima had hardly stopped crying. But every time they had tried to turn back she objected.

"At one point, she began begging us to go on, so we continued."

Perhaps mistaking my silence for disapproval at the maid's young age, Mother said, "I wanted someone young, to get used to our ways, to be like a daughter." Then she stopped and looked at her fingers, and only when she glanced up again did I realize that tears had been gathering in her eyes.

Eighteen months after my parents employed Naima, our king was dragged to the courtyard of the palace and shot in the head. Father was a government minister by this stage and, instead of risking ill treatment, detention, or even death, he decided to flee to France. Naima was the last to step onto the boat, right behind my parents, pulled on board by Abdu the driver. They all stood watching the coast drift away, the smoke rise.

When the boat arrived in Marseilles, Taleb was standing at the dock waiting for them. Was he smiling, was he sucking at the end of a cigarette, did he wave? Mother did not like to talk about Taleb.

"Why? Is he a bad person?"

"No, not at all."

It never seemed like anger that she felt toward him. More like shame. And I think she thought of Paris and the time in Paris in the same way. So I was eager to ask Taleb, to find out what had happened after they arrived.

"Poor Naima could hardly stand," he said. "She had been throwing up the whole way. But your mother was determined. She didn't want to stay in Marseilles. I never understood that. She didn't even want to rest the night. She insisted we go directly to the train station and get on the first train for Paris."

I pictured her marching ahead and imagined Father behind her, glad for her stubbornness, glad that someone at least knew what to do next.

"And how was she on the train?"

"Who? Your mother? Like the Sphinx. I told jokes, but they were obviously bad ones."

"And Naima and Abdu? Did they go back to Egypt?"

Here Taleb looked at me as if I were suddenly standing a long way away. He seemed to consider the distance and whether it was wise to cross it.

"Abdu went back from time to time, but Naima didn't, of course."

"Where did they stay?"

"In Paris."

He seemed to have lost interest in the conversation. I thought of how to bring him back.

"Uncle Taleb?"

"Yes."

"How long have you lived in Paris?"

"Since university. Too long."

"Do you like it?"

"What does it matter? It seems to like me."

"Did Mama and Baba stay with you?"

"No, I found them an apartment in the Marais. Not ideal, but close to the hospital. A nice place, but a big step down from what they were used to."

"Not a hotel?"

"Six months is too long for a hotel. And in the end they stayed a year."

"Really?" I said. "I always thought they were there only a couple of months."

"You breathed Parisian air for the first eight months of your life. You will be ruined forever."

I liked Taleb. Unlike Nafisa's, his sympathy was not patronizing. He took me to places I had never been. One afternoon, as I followed him through the arches of Ibn Tulun Mosque, I asked him, "Uncle Taleb?"

"Yes."

"What did my mother die of?"

He stopped and looked at me in that way again but said nothing.

Late one night, he on the bed, I on the floor, the room as black as a well and filling up with the smell of whiskey, Taleb suddenly spoke.

"Some things are hard to swallow," he said.

I recalled a dog in our street that had choked on a chicken bone. It wheezed and coughed and then eventually lay on its side and surrendered, blinking at me.

"You must know, regardless of anything, about her great humanity," he said, the word utterly new to me. I repeated it in my mind—humanity, humanity—so that I could look it up later. "She never ceased to be tender with Naima, who was innocent, of course. Ultimately, everyone is innocent, including your father."

After a long silence, just when I suspected he had fallen asleep, Taleb spoke again.

"You have no idea what he was back home. It's difficult, looking at him now, to believe that he is the same person and that the world is the same world. And he wanted someone to inherit it all."

The following day Taleb, Hydar, and Nafisa flew back to Paris. And although Naima changed the bedsheets, I could still smell Taleb's head on my pillow. I asked Naima to replace it.

"Why?" she said, and pressed the pillow against her face. "It's perfectly clean."

Karl Taro Greenfeld

Mickey Mouse

AFTER OUR TRIUMPHANT WINTER, the pink-white cherry blossoms already budding on mossy branches, the first cicadas buzzing in the late afternoons, our Empire's prospects boundless, our fleets triumphant, our soldiers valiant, our Divine Emperor infallible, I received in my third-floor office on our deserted campus a visitor, my former classmate Kunugi.

He was dressed in a three-piece tweed suit, worsted wool from London, with a paisley pocket square peeking over the selvage and a gold watch chain dangling from another cavity into the fabric. He had always been a dandy, and now, in his new prosperity, in his high office, with his surfeit of imperial spoils, he could afford such finery. He shook an English cigarette from a box and lit it with an American lighter.

I had been seated at my drafting table, working on some pen and ink sketches, and as the ink was still wet I did not cover the illustration before answering the door. Kunugi immediately crossed the room and inspected the drawing, a mother and son, each tightly bundled in a kimono, walking on a country road, first snow falling. The mother was carrying a military uniform bound in white string. My first attempt had them walking with a crippled soldier hobbling on crutches, still in uniform but with one leg missing. In this version, I had tried it without the soldier, and it was more effective, his absence implied.

This does not inspire, Kunugi observed as he exhaled. He offered me a cigarette.

I did not smoke, not since I had had tuberculosis in my twenties. But I reached out for one.

Take the whole pack, he said, we seized warehouses full in Singapore.

I looked at the package, black and gold, an elaborate coat of arms, lions on hind legs facing off under Roman lettering.

It's just a sketch, I explained, pointing to my drawing.

But Kunugi had already moved on.

We have a problem, he declared.

I removed a cigarette and searched on my drafting table for a box of matches until Kunugi held out his lighter.

I coughed the first time I tried to inhale, but the tobacco tasted delicious, so I inhaled again and felt the pleasant, still-familiar dizziness brought on by the nicotine.

Mickey Mouse, he began, is on the list of enemy characters.

This did not surprise me.

I thought back to when Kunugi and I had both been students here together. He had been among the best in our department, winning several student prizes and even gaining entry into the Nikka group, his canvases hanging next to those of renowned artists. His affectation then had been a beret, a pipe, bodkin trousers—and now look at him. We had been rivals for the same professor's attention, and even shared stylistic similarities—work that I now can see was our naive imitation of impressionism. We rarely interacted despite being intensely aware of one another. Shortly before graduating, I had abandoned that derivative form of painting, moving into uncomfortable territory as I searched for more individual expression. Kunugi continued in the faux European vein, and when he was invited to the Nikka group, I was so jealous I couldn't bear to say hello to him at the show.

I lost touch with Kunugi after university, as I continued to paint, even winning a small scholarship that allowed me to live in Paris for a few months and on my return securing a prestigious gallery show in Asakusa. Kunugi must have stopped painting, for I never saw his name among the lists of entries to various contests and prizes that we all vied for. I heard from a classmate that he had taken over his family business, something to do with fabrics and patterns. His name reappeared in my life a year ago at the bottom of a letter addressed to several dozen of us explaining that in voluntary accordance with the National Mobilization Law, the *Weekly National,* the liberal magazine publishing my illustrations, had suspended publication. I suspected I would lose my position at the university as well. Instead, I was to lose my livelihood by attrition. I was reduced to one class of four students, all of them physically unfit for active duty, for which I was allowed to keep my office. For income, I took on a few private students, pampered children of officials who only wanted to paint in the traditional style, no foreign subjects or influences.

Kunugi, I recalled, had always had bushy eyebrows. Now, he still had the long, slender face, but he must have plucked his eyebrows, for he had only a spider's leg–shaped brow over each of his narrow eyes. He had a mustache the shape and size of the German dictator's.

Would you like tea? I asked, taking up my kettle and feeling the side of it for warmth. I would have to refill it from the communal tap in the hall.

He shook his head and removed a silver flask of brandy.

We need you, he explained, pulling out the cork stopper and taking a sip.

Me?

He held out the flask. I took a small nip.

He continued: To come up with a cartoon character, like Mickey Mouse, only Japanese. But as entertaining as Mickey Mouse! We want to make cartoons better than the Americans. We can make wonderful Japanese films, but we have failed to come up with any entertainment between the news and the films. We can't show these disgusting foreign cartoons.

He took back the flask. So you, Ohta-kun, you will work on a new cartoon character, a Japanese cartoon character that will make our pure race forget all about enemy characters.

He had thought of me because of the work I had done for the *Weekly National,* my caricatures and illustrations, what I considered my minor work but that had turned out to be the only work of mine that anyone knew. That kind of cartoon had come easily to me, pen and ink, bold lines, simple figures; I could capture a street scene or a rural village in three dozen strokes. But I knew nothing about animated characters.

Kunugi left me a card with the name and address of the Information Bureau, a consolidation of various government offices under the aegis of the Home Ministry in Kasumigaseki. When I turned up, I saw that I was actually at the old Communications Ministry, which had now been turned into a branch of the military. I presented my card to the vast guard kiosk, where soldiers in crisp green uniforms stood before a gray-painted sheet metal wall with small green and red blinking lights shaped like tiny, nippleless breasts. They took my card and my identification card, filled out a form on onionskin paper, and rolled that into a leather-capped bamboo tube which they dropped into a pneumatic cylinder beside them. With a shhhhhoooop, the bamboo tube was sucked away. And I stood waiting.

There was a thumping sound and one of the guards opened the returned tube, removed the onionskin, and read out my name, saying I was to go to an office on the second floor.

I found the office, slipped off my shoes, entered, bowed, and said my name. I looked up discreetly and saw through a thick haze of tobacco smoke a half dozen men in civilian clothes seated at desks in the vast, open room. I shuffled over to the desk that faced all the other desks, where the bucho would sit in a civilian office, which this seemed to be. I said my name and a man with a round face, small nose, sideburns, and eyeglasses looked up at me over his steel-frame rims.

Ohta, I said.

Ebitsubo, he said. He had a protuberant fleshy growth on the side of his forehead. The skin flap was angled slightly downward and looked like a tiny dolphin trying to jump out of his head.

I explained that Kunugi had told me to report here, that I was to be given more instructions. Ebitsubo studied the card I gave him.

I've never done this before, I explained.

He looked surprised. Really?

I bowed. My mistake. I've drawn, of course, and drawn cartoons. But never an animated cartoon.

Don't worry, he assured me. First, come up with the character. When you do, our writers will help you with appropriate scenarios.

He indicated this room full of men leaning back in their chairs and smoking. The writers, presumably all underemployed now that their magazines and newspapers had voluntarily suspended publication.

He removed a key on a string from around his neck and opened his top drawer, taking out some tickets which had Prince Konoe's face on them. I had never seen these before.

Are these some kind of money? I asked.

He shook his head. They were vouchers, I could exchange them for certain goods.

Food?

He shook his head.

Art supplies. Paint. Paper.

He told me I could also work here, if I liked.

I told him I had my own office, at the university. But could I get additional ration coupons?

He said no, that could not be arranged.

We were advancing everywhere, in Burma, the Dutch East Indies, New Guinea; Manila had fallen.

My office in an old stone building on the Geidai campus was always cold. I had a kerosene heater but couldn't find any fuel for it, so I was reduced to burning charcoal in a ceramic kiln that emitted a terrible stench and gave me frequent headaches. After looking through historical material in my almanacs, the Heian period Kozanji Temple scroll with its anthropomorphic frogs and rabbits became my inspiration. I had proposed a dozen characters, including a tanuki, a badger, a deer, a pair of monkeys, and a sympathetic ape in a samurai headdress. Ebitsubo had rejected them all; I had not even heard from Kunugi. But as long as I worked on this project, I continued to receive my vouchers, and could exchange these at a poor rate for food coupons or could sometimes trade them for currency that I used to buy food from the street vendors. I spent most of my time using my new art supplies to work on my own drawings, street scenes I observed: an old woman in prayer before a street corner shrine, boys watching soldiers, a Korean selling sweet potatoes from a metal drum.

I had come down to the Azabu area to purchase more charcoals, paint, ink, and paper. The woman who ran the art supply store didn't seem happy about the vouchers, and explained she wouldn't make change for them. I agreed and took my supplies, wrapped in rice paper and twine.

Vendors were selling black market goods from wooden crates: Manchurian oranges, Vietnamese peaches, and salted fish from Korea. One well-fed man even had a dozen bars of Dutch chocolate for sale, terribly expensive; all of this, I assumed, the spoils. I pulled my padded cotton coat tight around me and made my way to the Keihin line. The first two trains each had just one car that wasn't reserved for the military and were immediately over-whelmed with passengers. As I waited on the platform under a cloudy spring sky, I was surprised by a loud and vigorous whining, like the amplified howl of a cat. I looked at my fellow passengers, and then, at once, we all realized what this was: an air raid siren.

We did not know where we were supposed to go, so we stepped back from the platform and began briskly walking in the general direction of the exit. As we were waiting at the top of the stairs, we heard quick, short, sharp percussive thumps, like the cylindrical fireworks we used to ignite in the summer. There were a few screams, and then from behind me I felt a shove and then sud-denly the space around me filled up with other people's shoulders, elbows, and hips as we were pushed down the stairs. Ahead of me, I saw a head disappear as someone must have fallen, and then as I was jostled I felt beneath my feet soft contours of a human body. I continued with the mass of people until we were all in the tun-nel below where we stood, now noticing that after those first few explosions, they had ceased. We had panicked for nothing.

A few days after the Honshu bombing, the first time in history that our homeland had been attacked by foreigners—a dozen or so criminal American bombers—Kunugi came to see me again.

He now wore a crisp-looking military uniform, khaki, with shiny bronze medals and badges on the front and a cap on his head with a five-point star insignia inside an imperial cross.

I asked him about a rumor I had heard: that much of the uni-versity would soon be closed down. Only the hard science depart-ments would remain open. The rest of the faculty and student body would enlist or voluntarily go to work in factories.

He didn't answer. Instead, he said I had to redouble my efforts. Morale was low after the bombing.

I would offer you tea, I said, but I don't have any.

He made a perfunctory bow. I heard from Ebitsubo you haven't come up with anything satisfactory.

I told him I had been trying, but that this wasn't my natural form, cartoon animals. Perhaps you should find someone else, I suggested.

He slapped me.

Do your duty, he shouted, for your Emperor.

My cheek stinging, I quickly opened a folder and showed him some of my characters, careful to hide my personal work. I showed him my latest effort, a cat who wears a military uniform and flies a fighter plane.

Kunugi lit a cigarette and flipped past my army cat, and before I could stop him he came to a drawing I had done of the scene on the train station stairwell during the bombing, the terrified faces, the guilty looks we all shared down in the tunnel. He paused at the drawing and then turned back to my militarized feline.

This isn't bad, he said, bring it to Ebitsubo and see what he says. Here, he handed me real ration coupons. Keep working.

To save money, I walked the six kilometers from my office to Kasumigaseki to show my army cat to Ebitsubo. He was now alone in the vast office. Not only were the writers gone, but so were their chairs and desks, all of it, the men and material, apparently requisitioned for the war effort.

He looked at my latest illustrations.

I stood in the empty office. Who was going to write these stories? I wondered. Who would produce them?

You're just like the rest, Ebitsubo said.

That surprised me: the rest? There were others working on this project?

Your character is well rendered, attractive, and anthropomorphic, but he lacks a certain cuteness, something that makes you root for him. Mickey Mouse is successful because you want him to overcome obstacles. A cat is a lazy predator who sleeps all day. A mouse is seen as industrious.

He had a point. Perhaps I can just draw a mouse? I suggested.

The others have tried, Ebitsubo explained, cheap copies that only remind you of Mickey.

No, I would have to come up with something more compelling.

We had lost numerous ships, aircraft, and airmen at some speck of an island near Hawaii, though the whole engagement was presented as a success because we had taken two frigid little specks off Alaska. Paper, paint, ink, all the supplies I still had access to were now so scarce that I could trade them for rice, tea, flour, soy sauce, and cabbage and still have enough to work on my own illustrations. Without the vouchers from special branch, I would have starved.

I was forced to leave my office when the university did shut down. And like most of the remaining faculty, I received my draft papers. I was surprised the army would take a forty-three-year-old with a spot on his lungs. I removed my boxes and what remained of my supplies, setting them on a cart with wooden wheels I had borrowed from the janitor, who himself had enlisted. I rolled what I could across to my Ueno flat, just one room with a kitchen.

Kunugi summoned me one morning, a runner in uniform showing up at my flat, panting and handing me a note ordering me to appear.

When I did report to Kunugi's office, a vast, third-floor suite of a downtown hotel that had been requisitioned by his special branch, he asked me about my work, how much longer would I need?

Behind him was a scroll by Kyoto artist Hashimoto Kansetsu, frolicking monkeys on a cypress tree. In the warm breeze, the monkeys were undulating at me. In the alcove below the monkeys were what looked like very good examples of Tang dynasty pottery figures and an elaborate, gold laquerware box.

I told him I had been drafted. That I had just a few days.

Before I reported at the prefectural army headquarters, I spent two days moving several crates of my illustrations back to the cellar beneath my old office building on campus, a huge, damp stone-walled space that was to have doubled as our bomb shelter. Already, the campus had a deserted feeling, as the unkempt gardens were starting to go a little wild. Within a few months, the grounds would be put to use for agriculture, neat little rows of vegetables growing where students had once crossed the courtyards.

The lieutenant who looked at my draft notice seemed disappointed at the medical report he had in front of him. The doctors had correctly ascertained the weakness of my lungs, which had been even more depleted by my taking up smoking again.

We can't do much with you, he said, at your age, in your condition. You're not suitable for the front.

I nodded. That was fine with me. I had heard, however, that those deemed unfit for fighting were sent to even worse units, diggers, builders, pavers, units fed minimal calories and assigned the work unfit for the warriors.

The lieutenant went through his files and then looked again at my letter. He seemed surprised by what he found.

There has been a special action, he said, you've been assigned to special branch. Maybe they can make some use of you. (Kunugi? I wondered.)

And so he stamped my forms, told me to report within twenty-four hours to Fort Akagi for my military training, and gave me a coupon for a meal at the commissary.

I survived the war, spending a few months continuing my feckless attempts to come up with a comical yet inspiring cartoon character under the auspices of Kunugi and Ebitsubo. I kept trying until the special branch was disbanded in 1943. (Another artist, a painter from Kyodai, had in the meantime come up with *Inu Nora,* the stray dog who joins the army and becomes a hero.) I lost touch with Kunugi, and without his tutelage, I worried that I would be given arduous duty. Instead, I was assigned by the military to help design currency for occupied territories before that program too was ended, and I worked the last year of the war in a munitions factory in Kawasaki until that was bombed. I spent the last few weeks of the war living in a trench just outside Yokosuka naval base, subsisting on the food the naval officers discarded, ferns we gathered, and pine needles we battered and roasted.

Kunugi, whom I had come to think of as the ultimate survivor, was ordered to command a unit in Okinawa. But somehow, through connections, he was able to postpone that duty until after the island fell to the Americans.

I heard a few months after the capitulation that Kunugi had been killed in the Tokyo firebombings during the spring of 1945.

After the war, I retook my position on campus, though now teaching illustration instead of painting. I had a different office, this one on the first floor, a perpetually damp room that smelled of mold and cat urine, but it came with a small stove so it could be heated up to an almost bearable temperature in winter. My health was fading, my lungs wheezing like leaking bellows, and I could no longer walk the many kilometers across the city that I used to. But I was so happy to be teaching again, to have students who were eager to learn figure drawing, illustration, and rendering. Our university had merged with a music college, and I only had a dozen lice-infested candidates that first year of the occupation, enrolled as much for the free lunch as for the education, but then every year a few more students joined as we shook off our long, artless Imperial nightmare.

Our old university buildings were made of stone, and so had

come through the firebombings while the surrounding neighborhoods charred to cinders. Miraculously, my crates of work were charred but had survived. A few years later, when there was some interest in looking back at how we lived during the conflict, a prominent Ginza gallery arranged a show of my wartime illustrations. I was grateful they sent a car for me, a rarity in those days, and when I arrived, I was astonished at the crowd. Nearly a hundred attendees, and a few newspaper reporters were there to interview me.

Near the end of the evening, when I was tired and seated on a bench near the front of the gallery, an old woman approached me, short gray hair tied up beneath a *furoshiki,* her slender body wrapped in layers of gray and brown cotton and wool. Up close, I could see she had fine features, almond-shaped eyes, a small, shapely nose, the kind of sharp characteristics that a few years ago would have been described approvingly as "pure Japanese."

She said my name.

I nodded.

She said she was Kunugi's widow and that she was pleased that I was showing my work.

My husband often spoke about you as classmates.

I bowed slightly.

He said you were a real artist. He said it was important that a real artist like you survive the war.

She looked around the gallery. I expected her to compliment my work.

But she had already told me what she came to say.

Ann Packer

Things Said or Done

"**B**Y THE WAY," my father says, "I'm probably dying."
Except for sleep, we've been together nonstop for the last
thirty hours, ever since we met at the Hartford airport yesterday
morning, but he has chosen this moment to unburden himself: this
moment, when we're carrying folding chairs through a windowless
corridor in a neighborhood community center in Berkeley, California. Well, I'm carrying folding chairs, my elbows sticking out as the
bottoms of the chair backs dig into my curled fingers, while he is
empty-handed, strolling back toward the storage room.

"Sure, ignore me," he calls when I don't respond.

"You're probably dying," I call back.

Up ahead, the once homely rec room is growing more festive
by the minute. Three young women with bare feet wind garlands
of flowers up the frame of a makeshift gazebo, and five neat rows
of chairs are arranged on the linoleum floor, with a center aisle for
the bridal procession.

"My piss smells like raw meat," he calls. "Plus I'm always tired.
I'm thinking kidney disease."

"Sounds right," I call back.

I enter the room and set the chairs down for a moment. In the dry California air, my hair, which is curly enough, frizzes with static, and I find a clip in my pocket and pin a section away from my face. Beyond the grimy clerestory windows puffs of cloud float across the sky. It's a crisp September day, auspicious for a wedding. The groom is my middle-aged brother, the bride a very pretty twenty-three-year-old girl who was until recently an intern in his lab at the University of California. Her name is Cressida, but on the plane yesterday my father began referring to her as "Clytemnestra," and because I made the mistake of objecting, he won't give it up.

Cressida's mother directs me to start row number six with my chairs. Like her daughter, she is tall and long-limbed, and she's as calm and unfussy a mother of the bride as I've ever seen. According to my brother she is fifty, a year younger than I, but somehow I feel as if I am by far the less mature of the two of us, probably because in this context she is all mother, whereas I don't have children—unless you count my father.

I head back to the storage room, expecting to find him, but he seems to have vanished. Cressida's younger brother, a high school senior with sleepy eyes, has discovered a cart with wheels, and I help him load a dozen chairs onto it and dispatch him down the corridor, glad for a moment of solitude. We've been working since nine o'clock, an early call after a rehearsal dinner that lasted till well after midnight. Like the wedding, the rehearsal dinner was arranged and catered by Cressida's family, though they allowed my father and me to make a gift of the wine. It took place in their backyard, where a giant paella was served at picnic tables crowded with jars of daisies. There were about forty of us, family and close friends, and toward the end of the night Cressida's mother made a point of telling me how sorry she was that my mother wasn't arriving until today, which was nice but didn't conceal—in fact, communicated—her bafflement that a retired librarian who lives alone could be too busy to spend a full weekend at her son's wedding. It isn't busyness, though, it's history: decades of it, beginning with my mother's decision to leave my father when I was sixteen. She had, for twenty years, tried to hold him together, but there were just too many pieces of him for that, and now she keeps a steady and inviolable distance.

"Ha," he says, appearing in the doorway with his hands on the hips of his baggy khakis—pants so old a wife would not allow them and a daughter shouldn't, but I can't do everything. "There you are. That woman, the mother, is about to tell us to take a meditation break!"

"That woman."

"Meditation and/or stretching. That's what it said on her list."

I frown to show I can't believe he looked at her list, though of course I can believe it.

"Sasha," he says, "she left it lying on the piano. I'm supposed to walk right by that?"

"As a matter of fact you are. Where were you just now?"

"Went to see a man about a hearse."

This is an old family joke—it means he was in the bathroom. He claims it started as a misunderstanding of mine, that as an appealingly morbid little girl I heard "hearse" when someone on a TV show said he needed to see a man about a horse. I don't remember this, but if it happened I'm sure I only pretended to mishear, that the apparent "mistake" was a calculated move to please him. Beginning when I was very young, he conferred specialness on me and then required that I earn it, and I was only too happy to comply, dividing my efforts between precocity (memorizing at age seven the prologue to *The Canterbury Tales,* for example) and fussiness (insisting on two thick foam rubber pillows for sleep every night; refusing ever to wear green). We lived in tacit agreement that I could be anything but ordinary. Like him, I was to breathe only the rarefied air of the never-quite-satisfied, and the more difficult I was, the more entranced he became. Which is not, it turns out, the best preparation for life. Or marriage, as my ex-husband would certainly attest.

"Anyway," my father says, leaning against the storage room door and peering with apparent fascination at the back of his forefinger, "it can't be good."

"Your finger."

"My health! Something's wrong. My piss smells like chocolate."

"I thought it was raw meat," I say, but then Cressida's brother returns with the empty cart, and my father gives up both the promise of a minor skin injury and the opportunity to be offended by me, both so he can lay a trap for the boy. Feigning nonchalance, he asks what's next on the schedule.

"Schedule?" the boy says.

"What do we do after the chairs are in place?"

"It's fine," I interject. "We're happy to do whatever."

"Yeah, but there must be a schedule," my father says. "A *list*."

"I don't know," the boy says. "My dad just got here with the programs, I can ask him."

"The programs!" My father glances at me: this is getting better and better. "What is this, a concert?"

"Well, they're not really programs. More sort of souvenirs? With photos and poems and stuff?" The boy shrugs. "They're nice."

At the word "poems," I turn my back on my father and begin loading chairs on the cart. Long ago, in another lifetime, he was a professor of English, and he still has proprietary views on what should be called poetry and what should be called—well, not poetry. I hope if I don't look at him he'll keep his mouth shut.

"Oh, um," the boy says, face reddening, "now that I think about it—my mom's going to try to get everyone to do partner massages."

I shoot a murderous look at my father and say, quickly as I can, "She wants to make sure we don't work too hard. That's thoughtful."

The boy glances over his shoulder and leans forward. "Do you mind not telling Peter? I told Cress I wouldn't let my parents do anything dumb, and—you know."

"Sure," I say. "No problem."

He pushes the cart away, and now I have to look at my father again: he is grinning triumphantly, showing off his crooked yellow teeth. "What did I tell you?" he says. "Partner massages! Only in California!"

"That's what you told me."

And told me and told me. We're staying at a bed-and-breakfast that offers—unexpectedly, I admit—an afternoon class in self-massage, and after my father made the obligatory joke about how we used to call that masturbation, he declared that in no bed-and-breakfast anywhere else in the country would there be anything offered in the afternoon but sherry or tea. Then we discovered there was a clothing-optional hot tub in the backyard, and it was as if he'd won the lottery. The thing is, we lived in California once ourselves, and his scorn can't erase the fact that he thought of it as paradise when it was his.

My father is not an easy person in the best of circumstances, but he's especially cantankerous when he has to see my mother. It's been thirty-five years since she left him, but I remember it vividly: his heartsick weeping, his enervation, his despair. He was supposedly job hunting at that point, having been "let go" by the Connecticut boarding school where he'd gone when higher education didn't work out, but after the initial shock of her departure he abandoned his search and hung around in his pajamas all day, waiting for me to get home from school. "Come talk to me," he'd plead as soon as I entered the house, and he'd lead me to the study, where he'd been sleeping since she left, on the hard foam pallet of a Danish modern sofa. While I perched on a sliver of windowsill, he'd sit behind the desk and ask if I thought she'd ever come back, or even, incredibly, why she'd left, as if he'd been away for the bulk of their marriage and needed me to tell him what had happened. (He wasn't away. Years later, in that cultural moment when the words "present" and "absent" cast off their classroom meanings and entered the crowded realm of the psychological metaphor, I joked to friends that if only my father had been *more* absent, things might have worked out between him and my mother.)

As we continue arranging chairs, I keep an eye on him, half for damage control and half to monitor his mood. The bride and groom were banned from the proceedings, and at noon the rest of us—assorted relatives and friends, my brother's troop of graduate students—are offered a break and a snack and are instructed that this setup help is the only gift we are allowed to give the couple. "A little late telling us," my father says, but under his breath, and I'm grateful he didn't say it louder. I'm even more grateful that no massages were suggested, partner or otherwise.

I'm recruited to help with flowers, and I join a group stuffing blossoms into every size, shape, and color of vase imaginable. My mother will like the unfussy, inclusive mandate of this wedding, the leggy perennials, the homey appetizers I saw in the community center fridge. Her flight is due to land at three-forty, which is cutting it close even for her. Surprisingly, she will be staying at the same bed-and-breakfast as my father and I, a mark of resignation, or maybe indifference.

I'm putting a bunch of white roses into a glass jug when my father comes over and says he's not well and needs to rest.

"So sit down," I say.

He looks at the ceiling, as if there might be someone up there to recognize my boorish insensitivity. "I have to *lie* down. Right now."

"*Right* now?"

"I'm telling you, I'm not well."

He looks fine, but I know better than to argue. I make our apologies to Cressida's parents and lead the way to the car. Other people throw parties; my father throws emergencies. It's been like this forever. When I was a kid I thought the difference between my father and other parents was that my father was more fun. It took me years to see it clearly. My father was a rabble-rouser. He was fun like a cyclone.

Peter found the B&B, which is on a quiet street in a residential neighborhood and looks very much like an ordinary Berkeley house: painted a bold burnt orange, its front yard landscaped with birch trees and a slate pathway. Inside, the owners' private area is to the right; the breakfast room is straight ahead, already set for tomorrow with a basket of tea bags on the communal table and more of the stiff beige napkins we used this morning (made of bamboo, we were told); and to the left are the guest quarters, down a hallway that is still hung with photographs of the teenagers who once occupied these rooms.

The whole drive from the community center my father complained and sighed, insisting he really didn't know what was wrong, only that something was, but by the time we reach his room he's feeling "a little bit better," and I leave him. There are two more rooms, a very small one next to my father's and a larger one at the end of the hallway, and the proprietor insisted I take the larger one since I'm staying three nights and "the other lady" is staying only one. This means that tonight my parents will go to bed with only a thin wall between them, closer than they've slept in decades.

I'm more tired than I realized, and when I add up the transcontinental flight yesterday, the incredibly late night given that we were on eastern time, and the work of schlepping chairs all morning, I think it's no wonder he wanted to lie down—I do, too. I close the blinds and take off my shoes and stretch out on the bed. There's a separate guesthouse in the backyard, occupied this weekend by a couple from Melbourne, and I hear their voices and the occasional splash as they soak in the hot tub.

I'm just drifting off when my cell phone buzzes with a text. *Viens,* my father has written, as if the French will somehow mask the imperiousness.

I find him not lying down or even sitting but pacing between bed and window. "What's wrong?"

"This Clytemnestra. Do you suppose she thinks we're rich?"

"Uch, Daniel," I say. "I was lying down."

"You're so blasé. My son is getting married."

"And?"

"And I don't want him to get hurt again."

This is an allusion to Peter's romantic history, with its long fallow periods and terrible ecstasies, though it is of course an allusion to my father's, as well. Last night, staring across the picnic table at Peter, I caught a glimpse of the boy he was at thirteen, when his family fell apart, and I thought it made sense, how late he was marrying: he'd waited till he was older than our father was at the time his marriage ended. What this means, though, is that he's old enough to be Cressida's father, and I worry about the strains of gratitude in his voice when he talks about her.

"Also," my father says, "it makes me feel old."

"This is a *happy* thing," I tell him. "You should feel young—most people are a lot younger when their children marry. You were only fifty-whatever when I got married."

"And look how that turned out."

"You know, you can think stuff like that and choose not to say it."

"I was heartbroken about your marriage."

"As opposed to my divorce."

"That's not fair," he cries, but he's smiling now, a coy, aren't-I-a-naughty-boy smile. The truth is he has never been a fan of anyone I've dated.

Now he says, "You didn't take me seriously this morning about my health," a classic kvetcher's bait and switch. I don't respond and he says, "Are you saying you did?"

"I'm not saying anything."

"I noticed!"

"What does the doctor think?"

"I haven't been," he says. "She'll order a scan, I'll be like one of those suitcases at the airport."

I say she might ask a question or two first, but he ignores me, looking off into the distance and caressing his chin. He says, "Have you ever thought about this? They have CAT scans and PET scans, but CAT scans aren't a kind of PET scan—there's a taxonomy problem. CAT scans should be a kind of PET scan, and there should be other PET scans, too—DOG scans, which would be, you know, Diagnostic Oldfart Geriatricography. And RAB-BIT scans, Retired Alterkoker Bladder . . ."

I let myself drift as he continues. I think of this sort of thing as The Daddy Show, and long ago, when I was a little girl, I enjoyed it. In fact, there was a time when he staged a literal show every night before I went to bed, and it was the highlight of my day. Once I was under the covers but still sitting propped against my pillows, he put on finger puppets—a felt Daddy-O-MacDaddy on his left forefinger, a felt Sasha-the-Pasha on his right—and the two of them bopped through literature and history as narrated by my father, joining in the Norman Conquest, acting out parts of *Twelfth Night,* never an idle evening until I was ten or eleven and began making excuses about being tired or having homework. After that, he retired the puppets, but to this day he has not stopped performing.

"Did you see that *New Yorker* cartoon," he is saying, "with the rabbits in the living room, sitting with their legs crossed holding martini glasses? I thought of a *much* better caption than the one they had. It should have said—"

"If you think you're sick," I say, "you need to go to the doctor."

"But I'm scared."

He looks scared, and I give him what I hope will seem like a sympathetic smile. I *am* sympathetic—somewhat, and more for the hypochondria than for whatever ails him—but the algebra of our relationship means it's hard for me to offer compassion when that's so clearly what he wants.

"Seriously," he says. "It's time I told you this. I'm scared, but it's not death I'm scared of, it's dying. It's pain. Will you promise me no pain? I'm not asking you to do me in, just a very fast morphine drip."

"Dan, you're way ahead of yourself."

He looks down his giant, beaky nose at me. "Excuse me for having the bad manners to tell my daughter how I feel." He glares, and I can't decide what to say next. If I were he, I'd try to bump him out of it with a family joke—his joke, which is itself a reaction to his mother, the legendary Moomie Horowitz (as if there could be two Moomies, but that is what we called her), who was one of the great complainers of all time. If dissatisfaction was a virtue in our family, endless talking about it was to take unforgivable advantage of one's good fortune, and whenever my brother or I whined or moaned about something, my father would tell us: Beware the family curse. Beware the Horowitz horror!

We face each other, I perched on the bed, he on the chair. He is, in fact, getting on: his bright blue eyes are hazed by cataract clouds, and his hair, once as red and curly as mine, is beige and cut so short that it clings to his scalp in tiny disheveled patches, looking like nothing so much as a helmet of brown rice. He will fall ill someday, whether he's ill now or not, and someday he will be gone. I have imagined the time after, with its cavern of sadness, and I know that even his most irritating foibles will acquire, in recollection, a kind of charm, and that grief will have its way with me again and again.

I say, "I'm sorry you're scared."

He shrugs, and I go to the window and watch the Australians in the hot tub, their bodies so submerged I can't tell whether they've taken the clothing option or not. They are talking and smiling, and at one point the husband puts his hand flat on top of the wife's head, an oddly tender gesture. They look to be in their sixties; at breakfast this morning they said they'd both just retired and were taking their first ever trip away from Australia.

A mile from here, my brother is alone in his apartment—doing what, I don't know. How do you spend your wedding day if you are one of the sweetest and most solitary people on the planet? He is a man so overwhelmed by his own heart that he arranged a sabbatical the last time he fell in love, an entire year away, effectively guaranteeing that his beloved would meet someone else during his absence and move on. It's extraordinary to me that he is getting married.

"Maybe if you went to the doctor with me," my father says, and I turn and tell him I'd be happy to—which I'd have said five hours ago if only he'd asked. I suggest we both lie down for a while, and when he agrees I return to my room.

The next thing I know, I'm waking in a strange bed to the sounds of my mother on the other side of the wall. I hear the zip of her suitcase, the slide and clatter of plastic hangers moving along a bar. If my father is awake, he can hear this, too. I last saw her about eighteen months ago, when I drove from western Massachusetts, where I live, to Old Lyme, Connecticut, where she'd just finished remodeling her cottage. On that particular trip I didn't stop in Hartford to see my father—I visit at least once a month, often more—but even so I felt what I always feel, that in the most literal of ways, as in all others, he is between us.

I wash my face before I go knock on her door. We chat for a few minutes, exchanging travel stories, marveling at the weather. She tells me I look great, and I tell her she looks great, which she does, in her proudly unkempt way: her nearly white hair hangs past her shoulders, thick and flyaway; and she's unapologetically frumpy in a mid-calf calico skirt and running shoes. She gave up vanity the way other people give up sugar, and her arms and hips and stomach are as soft and plump as bread dough.

"Fat, anyway," she says cheerfully. "I hope I won't embarrass Peter."

"He can't wait to see you," I say, which is surely true, though not something he said to me.

"Where's Dan?"

I point at the wall dividing her room from my father's. "He's a little under the weather," I say in a low voice.

Her face betrays nothing, neither concern nor skepticism; for thirty-five years she has been the very embodiment of the correct way to behave with your children after a divorce. In my twenties, I tried to get her to open up: "It's been ten years," I said. "I'm an adult, we can talk." This was just after my divorce, and I guess I wanted to dish with her, but she wouldn't budge.

"What's Cressida like?" she says now, backing up and sitting on the bed. She puts her hands together and holds them between her knees, a gesture I've known forever.

I fill my mother in about Cressida and her family and then move on to last night's party, leaning a little harder than I should on how welcoming everyone was and how much fun we all had. "They're big hikers," I say. "After the thing tomorrow they're going to take us on a hike." This, too, is unkind: I happen to know that my mother is on an early flight—booked, she claims, before she knew there would be a brunch.

She smiles, ignoring or maybe not even noticing what I've really said. She tells me that last time she was here she and Peter spent a glorious afternoon at Mount Tam. "It was fantastic," she says. "I still remember the view."

From my father's room comes a loud cough, a cough that could have been produced for one reason only, to remind us of his existence. I don't think he can hear what we're saying, just the sound of it, but I have no doubt he's using every gram of concentration to determine from our pauses and cadences how we are getting along. With him, I generally pretend that my mother and I are closer than in fact we are, whereas with her I pretend that he and I are not as close as we are, or rather that we have one of those healthy parent-child relationships characterized by mutual affection and respect, not mutual suspicion and resentment. I think I've done a better job convincing him than her.

"So," she says, glancing at her watch, "we've got half an hour?"

I look at my watch and say, "Wow, that's right."

And here is more pretending: we are both acutely aware of the time, the strain, the welcome need to part so we can dress.

At 5:35 I leave my room and go to the front hall, where I told both my parents I would meet them. I made sure to say we would all three be meeting—no surprises—but even so I've been careful to arrive first. While I wait, the Australians appear in matching blue sweatshirts, each with the word "VICTORY" in giant letters across the front. "We're going to a baseball game," the husband says, rhyming "game" with "lime." "In our team colors." "Our football team," the wife says, and then together they say, "Soccer, that is." They laugh and she says, "Have a lovely time at your brother's wedding. September's the best time to get married in Australia— it's our spring, you know."

They head off, and I think of my own short-lived marriage, which also began in September, at my fiancé's family's reform temple in suburban New Jersey, since I had neither synagogue nor intact family of my own. We had met in college, broken up after graduation, and then found each other again and mistaken famil- iarity for love. After we married we had some fun traveling together, but once we tried to settle down I began picking at him over tiny annoyances—because the big annoyance, the fact that he wasn't paying enough attention to me, was too unreasonable for me to recognize at that point, let alone communicate. When I wasn't picking at him I was picking at the rest of mankind, going on and on about some slight, a minor social disappointment, an achievement inadequately rewarded. I was twenty-five, I thought it was just a matter of time before people shaped up and started acting as I wanted. Such is the lot of the narcissist's child, to inherit her parent's umbrage over the world's indifference.

And here is the narcissist, looking dapper in a light brown suit and paisley necktie, and loafers with tassels. "She's a little late," he says, glancing at his watch.

"A minute," I say. "Actually forty-five seconds."

"Well, but she's not here yet."

"You look spiffy."

He adjusts the knot of his necktie, smooths his lapels. "And she's . . ."

"Great," I say.

We stand here for an eon of seconds, until my mother's footsteps sound, then we both turn to look at her. She has pinned up her hair and put on lipstick and a sapphire caftan, and she looks marvelous. I hear my father suck in a mouthful of air. "Joanie," he says. "Always a pleasure."

She kisses the air above his shoulder. "What an occasion, hmmm?"

I always think I can finesse these situations—the last was maybe seven years ago, when I received an award at the college where I teach—but in the event I am clumsy and fall back on false hurry. "Right, let's get going," I say, and I leave the house ahead of them and have the car doors open before either has made it to the sidewalk.

The community center parking lot is only half full, and we find Cressida's father and brother greeting people at the entrance. During the car ride, my father went on and on to me about the book he's reading, offering an elaborate critique of its faux Faulknerian dreaminess and moral vacancy, and my mother, once I've introduced her, says she wants to find Peter and vanishes.

"She's certainly haughty," my father says.

"Don't," I say.

Some people I recognize from the party last night come up to say hello, and we talk to them, and then to the next group, and soon it is time to go inside. In our absence this afternoon, the rec room was even further transformed, and it is stunning now, with gauzy drapes covering the walls and dozens of flower arrangements creating a lovely chaos of color.

The programs are lying on the chairs. They have Peter's and Cressida's names in calligraphy on the front, along with today's date. My father opens his and flips through the pages. "They've got e. e. cummings," he says. "And Rumi."

"Could be worse," I say, knowing he wishes it were.

My mother appears and sits with us, sliding her bag, a large silver brocade satchel that's oddly capacious for a social event, under her chair. She tells us she found Peter standing with some of his graduate students in the courtyard. "He looks beautiful," she says, eliciting an offended sigh from my father, I don't know why.

"Did you get a chance to talk?" I ask, remembering the morning of my wedding, when my mother told me she wanted time alone with me and then said in the gravest voice imaginable that her only regret about leaving my father was the message it sent me and Peter about the impermanence of love. "The thing is," she said, "it's up to you, how long it lasts. You get to choose, the two of you together." These words, despite their wisdom, did not in the end make a difference for me and my ex-husband, but I imagine they might for Peter and Cressida, if at some point a difference needs to be made.

"He was with other people," she says. "I just gave him a hug."

Then Peter appears before us, looking, in fact, quite beautiful, in a greenish gray suit and a soft white shirt with no collar. He is tall and skinny, my brother, with high cheekbones from our mother and our father's narrow shoulders. His hands are at his sides, and, holding his arms steady, he looks at us and swings his fingers up and down in an almost imperceptible wave. He got his hair cut today; his ears are pink and vulnerable. We rise from our seats to watch Cressida and her father come up the aisle, and when I look back at Peter, I see that he is wearing the kind of giant grin that just takes over sometimes, when nothing exists but how happy you are.

For the next several minutes tears leak from my eyes, and I'm grateful for the tissues my mother passes me, a fresh one as soon as she sees that the last is sodden. On my other side, my father simply lets his face get wet, and finally a tear splashes onto his program, briefly magnifying a few letters before they thicken and begin to slide down the page.

The reception is at the back of the room, spilling into the courtyard, and my father and I mill around with wine and then wine plus appetizers passed on trays by a small army of teenage girls. He stays at my elbow, volunteering very little of his own conversation but occasionally annotating mine with opinions and contempt. It's not till he heads off to use the bathroom that I search out my mother, whom I find with Cressida's mother, the two of them clasping hands.

"I didn't know your mother was an artist," Cressida's mother says when she sees me. "She's so talented." To my mother she says, "You've got to show her the one of Cress and Peter."

I understand now why my mother brought such a big bag: she's been sketching. It's true, what Cressida's mother said: she is very talented. When I was young, hardly a guest came over whom she didn't capture in a quick sketch, and she drew us—Peter and my father and me—over and over again. After she left him, my father spent days studying the portraits hanging around the house, as if what she'd seen in each of us might reveal whatever it was he'd missed in her. Then one day he took them all down and put them in a large envelope, and for the next few years, until he had the house painted so he could sell it and move somewhere smaller, there were shadow portraits everywhere, faint gray smudges outlining empty rectangles.

My mother hands her sketchpad to me, opened to one of the newlyweds. Cressida is lovely, but in this drawing my mother has discovered something else, and it's a revelation. Cressida and Peter are standing alone together, in front of one of the panels of gauze, and her fingertips are curled onto the waistband of his pants, a gesture not of sexual play or possession, but of reassurance. With her hair spiraling past her shoulders and her pretty collarbones reflecting the diffuse light, she looks at my brother with what I can describe only as faith.

I flip the pages, see sketches of Cressida's delighted mother and distracted father, of her brother pulling at the collar of his shirt. Then suddenly there I am, together with my father: we're standing in a corner, each of us with a glass of wine held bouquet-style, at low chest level with both hands. He looks sad and dazed, and I look—how can I describe this?—like a not unattractive middle-aged woman with overly curly hair who has just sucked on a wedge of lemon.

"God in heaven," I say.

"What?" my mother replies.

"Who's this charmer?"

Cressida's mother has turned to talk to someone else, and my mother moves to my side for a better look. "You look lovely. Beautiful and serious."

I hand the sketchpad back to her.

"You do," she says, looking down at the sketch, "see, through here," and she runs her finger along the charcoal lines of my forehead and temple, bisected by a short coil of hair.

"Listen," I say, "I should find Dan," and I leave and head for the hallway to the bathrooms, thinking I shouldn't've just walked away but also that she won't mind, may in fact prefer it, because now she can continue sketching. She's like a shy teenager with a guitar: her sketchbook helps her connect with other people while keeping her at a safe, busy distance.

I run into my father as he's leaving the men's room. He sees me and says, "Red meat, if you want to know, and speaking of which: Are they having a real dinner? Because I can't stand around eating things off toothpicks all night. It's a wedding, shouldn't there be a skimpy piece of salmon with my name on it somewhere?" I open my mouth to respond, but he continues: "It's not like they're poor.

That house was worth a million if it was worth a penny. What about a cold bread roll? What about salad with candied walnuts and too much balsamic vinaigrette?"

"It's not a sit-down kind of reception," I say.

"Obviously."

Back in the rec room, he stops walking and falls into silence. I stand beside him, aware that he could be on the verge of an unpleasant slide.

"Nice what they did with the room," I say.

He grimaces. "Where's Joanie? Has she left already? I wouldn't put it past her."

"She's around. I was just talking to her."

"And why are there no tables? All those chairs from earlier, what are we supposed to do—go sit in rows?"

"Dan."

"What?"

This could be a mistake, but I say it anyway: "Beware the Horowitz horror."

For a long moment it could go either way, but at last he grins, and I relax a little. He chuckles and says, "That made you laugh, you and Peter. But mostly you. Do you know, I used to think of you as my child and Peter as your mother's? Not that you should tell him that, of course."

"Not to worry."

"I feel bad about it. Do you think he knew?" He gives me a sidelong look. "Never mind, he knew, he knew. Ah, God, regret." He falls silent again, and I think it would be a good idea to move on, into the party, out to the courtyard—somewhere. But just as I'm about to suggest this, he proclaims:

> *Things said or done long years ago,*
> *Or things I did not do or say*
> *But thought that I might say or do,*
> *Weigh me down, and not a day*

> *But something is recalled,*
> *My conscience or my vanity appalled.*

"Yeats?" I say.

"Isn't it marvelous?"

"Such a lovely view of maturity."

"But it's true, not a day goes by. Which is worse, do you suppose?"

"Which what is worse?"

"Appalled conscience or appalled vanity?"

I think for a moment. "Appalled conscience for me. For you it's appalled vanity."

He barks out a laugh. "Well, that appalls my vanity right there."

"And that," I say, "appalls my conscience."

He laughs at that, and I begin to laugh, too, and it takes root: we're giggling like children. We laugh and laugh, and my father flaps his hand in front of his face as if he were trying to put out a fire. Then I have a memory, from the year we spent in California. My father had been denied tenure at Yale and had a temporary appointment in the English Department at Stanford. I was thirteen. One evening shortly after we arrived, the four of us went into San Francisco and happened to stroll past a fancy French restaurant just as a well-dressed couple came out and were about to step into the backseat of a waiting taxi. Before they could get into the car, the door to the restaurant opened again, and a waiter rushed out, calling after them and holding in his upturned palm a tinfoil swan. "Your gâteau," he cried, and the couple took the package and thanked him and got into the taxi. Nothing, a nothing moment, slightly amusing, but for the entire rest of the evening and the weeks or maybe months following, that scene split us into parts: my father and me into sick hilarity, my mother into eye-rolling exasperation, my brother into bored indifference. "Your gâteau" with an empty palm held skyward—that was all it took, one of us saying it to the other, my father to me or I to him, and each time we fell into great convulsions of laughter.

I don't mention it, though. The memory actually slows my laughter, stops it. That year in California. If, as the saying goes, adolescence is not a developmental stage but a diagnosis, then I had a life-threatening case of it. Along with the requisite parental dethroning—okay, *paternal* dethroning; that was the year I could not bear my father—there was lying, promiscuity, drug use. For years afterward it was as if I were recovering from a stomach flu and could eat nothing but dry toast and applesauce: I was obedient, cautious, the least likely teenager on earth to cause her parents a moment of concern.

My father is looking at me, and I take his hand and interweave my fingers with his. We stand in silence. As if my teenage rejection of him weren't enough, he was terminated at Stanford after that one year. And the next two were terrible, the fallen university professor discovering how entirely different and difficult it was to teach high school. It wasn't until after my mother was gone that he finally landed, at a small organization dedicated to promoting the work of Wallace Stevens, Hartford's hometown poet. It barely paid a living wage, but he stayed with it—gradually and in the end gratefully arriving at the point in life when you understand there are no great changes ahead. When he retired, a few years ago, he was given a plaque inscribed with these words from the great poet himself: "After the final no there comes a yes / And on that yes the future world depends."

"You're a good girl," he says to me now, and I tell him, "Shhh, be quiet," but he keeps going. "You've given me so much. So much."

"You've given me a lot, too."

He squeezes my hand. "Don't worry, I won't ask you for a list."

"Dan. What am I going to do with you?"

"Throw me in the oven with some garlic and parsley."

This is another old family joke and I smile, but suddenly I'm tired and want this—the conversation, the reception, the weekend—to be over. He exhausts me, there's no getting around it.

He says, "I still think there isn't enough food at this thing."

"Let's find some more."

I pull my hand free of his and look around to see what's available, but at that moment my mother walks up, and so we stay put. Her lipstick has rubbed away, and she's begun to look weary.

"Having a nice time?" I ask her.

"It's lovely. Cressida's very smart."

My father straightens his back, lifts his chin.

"She knows her own mind," my mother continues, ignoring or unaware that he's peeved. "That's unusual in someone so young."

"Knows it?" my father says crisply. "Or thinks she knows it? And how could you decide which without being the expert yourself?"

My mother lifts one shoulder. She turns slightly, putting herself in quarter profile to us. The room is warm, and she plucks her caftan away from her chest several times.

"We've been talking," he tells her, "about regret."

She waits.

"And which is worse, guilt or humiliation. Which is it for you?"

"Sorry, Dan," she says, "I'm not biting," and she heads off without a pause, without even a glance back at us.

I don't look at him, but I can feel him bristling. I'm in awe of her rules of nonengagement. She's so detached and consistent. And yet not entirely avoidant, not as avoidant as I expected. Is this new, or does my memory misrecord her, so that each time she surprises me a little? She stayed at the B&B. Rode with us in the car. Sat with us for the ceremony. She returns and returns, as true and indifferent as the moon.

"What chicken shit," he says.

The teenage girls who were passing trays earlier have disappeared, but one of them left a platter of aram sandwich spirals on a table, and I say, "Look, let's grab some of those."

"I was just making conversation," he grumbles.

"You were baiting her. It was obnoxious."

He presses his lips together and looks away as I load several sandwiches onto a small plate. "You know I'm right," I say. "Now come on," and I hold out the food.

He frowns and picks up a piece. "What is it?"

"Just eat it," I say, and he takes a bite, and the whole thing promptly unrolls, releasing a few strips of turkey, a sodden length of lettuce, and a blob of tomato, all of which land on his suit jacket.

"For Christ's sake," he exclaims, brushing at the mess and creating several trails of mayo on his lapel. "Damn it. Look at me."

I set the plate on the table and grab a napkin. As I dab, I attempt to make consoling noises, which just escalate his anger, and he cries, "Fuck!" loud enough so that the people closest to us fall silent. "Fuck," he yells again, "*fuck*," and now it's the whole room, silent until the silence itself becomes the objectionable sound and people begin to talk again.

My father stalks away, and I shield my face with my hand, mortified. Why didn't I head him off before he tried to provoke her? Or better yet, why didn't I walk away when she did? I feel someone touch my shoulder and look up to find Peter at my side, frowning, his cheeks ghosted with the kiss marks of well-wishers.

He says, "God, I'm sorry."

"*You're* sorry."

"We didn't want you to get stuck with him tonight."

"*Ma nishtanah halailah hazeh mikol haleilot?*" I ask, the first of the four questions posed on Passover—"Why is this night different from all other nights?"—and he bursts out laughing.

"Wait," I say, "she's not Jewish, is she? Cressida?"

"You can't believe I remember it?"

"It's been a few decades."

"I've been to the odd seder over the years," he tells me, and then we say, simultaneously, "*Very* odd," as if Dan were operating us like a puppeteer from wherever his pique took him.

"We're so glad you're here," he says, and I think I'm not losing a brother, *he's* losing a personal pronoun. This is a sour little thought, but I can't help myself.

"We're glad to be here," I say. "You know that."

My father sits on a folding chair directly in front of the gazebo where the ceremony took place, the set of his shoulders telling a story of boundless indignation. My mother stands against the wall, alone with her sketchpad, her pencil moving quickly over its surface. For a while I mill around, and then I join her and see that she's drawing not people but flowers. "Aren't the lantana pretty?" she says, but after another stroke or two she closes the sketchpad.

"Don't let me stop you."

"No, I'd rather talk." She smiles at me. "I want you to know that I have regrets."

"It's okay."

"No, I want to say this. I have regrets, but only one about leaving your father."

"I know," I say. "You regret the message it sent me and Peter about the impermanence of love."

She looks puzzled.

"No?"

"No."

"That's what you told me on my wedding day. What's your one regret?"

"How interesting," she says. "I suppose that was what I felt, for a long time." She reaches up and touches her earlobe, a nervous habit I remember from long ago.

"And now?"

She takes a deep breath. "Now I regret that you ended up in a caretaker role. I regret," she says, looking deeply into my eyes, "that because of my choice to leave him, that role was available for you to take."

I'm surprised by this—shocked, actually; I never knew she felt this way and can't believe she is saying so—but while all kinds of responses crowd my mind, the one I speak sounds hollow and is, in certain ways, beside the point. I say, "He isn't that bad. He's lived a good life."

And she says, "What about you?"

My entire body warms under the heat of her regard. What *about* me, and why ask now? For years we've been so careful, my mother and I, around the great disappointment that is my circumscribed life, always in concert in our efforts to keep the identity of the draftsman—or, rather, the draftsmen—out of sight. Shall I tell her about the tiny pleasure of tending my herb garden, about the excessive thanks I get from the colleagues to whom I make small gifts of dried thyme? Shall I tell her about the relief I feel now that the "introductions" I am sometimes offered to unattached men have devolved from awkward dinner parties to quick e-mails? Shall I tell her about the unexpected delight of a good TV show, especially a drama that unfolds over many episodes and encourages the blocking out of an entire evening each week for three or even six months? Or shall I tell her that my father's piss smells like raw meat?

The look on her face is classic Joanie, an unlikely mix of impassive and caring. I shrug, deciding to stay quiet—if you could call such inertia a decision—and she raises her eyebrows ever so slightly.

Just then there's a chiming sound from the far side of the room, and I turn to see Peter and Cressida in front of a table bearing a magnificent four-tiered wedding cake. Cressida has a knife in one hand and a wineglass in the other. "Hello," she calls out, and then, louder, "*Hello,*" her voice a good-size bellow that for some reason pleases me deeply. I step closer to them.

"First," she says, "we want to thank you all for being here. And second, as far as this thing on the table behind us goes, did you really think I was going to let my mother bake oatmeal cookies?"

Everyone laughs and applauds, and then there are toasts, and speeches, and finally the cake is wheeled away to be sliced and served. When I finally look back over my shoulder, my mother is gone. My father is still seated, but he is no longer the only one; chairs have been pulled this way and that, into small and large circles, into pairs. His shoulders are curved now, his head is down.

A passing girl offers me a piece of wedding cake. I lift the plate to my face and breathe in the sugary sweetness, then spot my mother near the back of the room. I approach her, extending the plate on my palm when I get close and lifting it high.

She smiles a slightly puzzled smile. "That's something. What is that? I've forgotten."

My father would be cackling by now. I lower the plate but keep it extended. "Wedding cake. We can share it."

She raises her palm, mimicking the way I held the plate. "No, it's something from Stanford. That year."

" 'Your gâteau.' "

"That's right, 'Your gâteau.' That was so silly." She smiles again, but after a moment a sober look comes over her face and she says, "You know, I came close to leaving him that year—I thought about it constantly. I think I would have if it hadn't been for that boy, that friend of yours, remember? From around the corner?"

I shake my head.

"You don't remember?"

I'm thinking: Then? Then you thought of leaving? That early? This is the kind of information that derails entire histories—the family equivalent of moving the start date of the Vietnam War back a decade, say, thereby throwing off your memory of everything that happened before and since. "Remember who?" I say.

"That boy. Your friend."

"A boy would've been a friend of Peter's."

"No, he was yours. And his mother had left his father, and I felt so sorry for him, such a forlorn, lost child. All I could think was, I can't do that to my kids. It took me three years to figure out that if I wasn't doing it *to* you, then I could do it."

I nod. This is more than she's said to me on the subject in thirty-five years, and I don't really want to hear about it, not now. I don't feel like listening; earlier, I didn't feel like talking. Is this what I do with my parents? Want what I can't have and then once I can have it, stop wanting it?

She reopens her sketchpad. "I should get them as they're saying good-bye," she says, and I look over and see Peter and Cressida at the door, hugging their guests.

Across the room is my father, looking at me. It's long past time for me to begin the process of restoring him to himself. I start toward him, and once he sees I'm finally coming he looks away, like a timid girl at a school dance, afraid to jinx the approach of a suitor.

Miroslav Penkov

East of the West

I T TAKES ME thirty years, and the loss of those I love, to finally arrive in Beograd. Now I'm pacing outside my cousin's apartment, flowers in one hand and a bar of chocolate in the other, rehearsing the simple question I want to ask her. A moment ago, a Serbian cabdriver spat on me and I take time to wipe the spot on my shirt. I count to eleven.

Vera, I repeat once more in my head, *will you marry me?*

I first met Vera in the summer of 1970, when I was six. At that time my folks and I lived on the Bulgarian side of the river, in the village of Bulgarsko Selo, while she and her folks made their home on the other bank, in Srbsko. A long time ago these two villages had been one—that of Staro Selo—but after the great wars Bulgaria had lost land and that land had been given to the Serbs. The river, splitting the village in two hamlets, had served as a boundary—what lay east of the river stayed in Bulgaria and what lay west belonged to Serbia.

Because of the unusual predicament the two villages were in, our people had managed to secure permission from both countries to hold, once every five years, a major reunion, called the *sbor*. This was done officially so we wouldn't forget our roots. In reality, though, the reunion was just another excuse for everyone to eat lots of grilled meat and drink lots of *rakia*. A man had to eat until he felt sick from eating and he had to drink until he no longer cared if he felt sick from eating. The summer of 1970, the reunion was going to be in Srbsko, which meant we had to cross the river first.

This is how we cross: Booming noise and balls of smoke above the water. Mihalaky is coming down the river on his boat. The boat is glorious. Not a boat really, but a raft with a motor. Mihalaky has taken the seat of an old Moskvich, the Russian car with the engine of a tank, and he has nailed that seat to the floor of the raft and upholstered the seat with goat skin. Hair out. Black and white spots, with brown. He sits on his throne, calm, terrible. He sucks on a pipe with an ebony mouthpiece and his long white hair flows behind him like a flag.

On the banks are our people. Waiting. My father is holding a white lamb under one arm and on his shoulder he is balancing a demijohn of grape rakia. His shining eyes are fixed on the boat. He licks his lips. Beside him rests a wooden cask, stuffed with white cheese. My uncle is sitting on the cask, counting Bulgarian money.

"I hope they have deutsche marks to sell," he says.

"They always do," my father tells him.

My mother is behind them, holding two sacks. One is full of *terlitsi*—booties she has been knitting for some months, gifts for our folks on the other side. The second sack is zipped up and I can't see what's inside, but I know. Flasks of rose oil, lipstick, and mascara. She will sell them or trade them for other kinds of perfumes or lipsticks or mascara. Next to her is my sister, Elitsa, pressing to her chest a small teddy bear stuffed with money. She's been saving. She wants to buy jeans.

"Levi's," she says. "Like the rock star."

My sister knows a lot about the West.

I'm standing between Grandma and Grandpa. Grandma is wearing her most beautiful costume—a traditional dress she got from her own grandma, which she will one day give to my sister. Motley-patterned apron, white hemp shirt, embroidery. On her ears, her most precious ornament—the silver earrings.

Grandpa is twisting his mustache.

"The little bastard," he's saying, "he better pay now. He better."

He is referring to his cousin, Uncle Radko, who owes him money on account of a football bet. Uncle Radko had taken his sheep by the cliffs, where the river narrowed, and seeing Grandpa herding his animals on the opposite bluff, shouted, *I bet your Bulgars will lose in London,* and Grandpa shouted back, *You wanna put some money on it?* And that's how the bet was made, thirty years ago.

There are nearly a hundred of us on the bank and it takes Mihalaky a day to get us all across the river. No customs—the men pay some money to the guards and all is good. When the last person sets his foot in Srbsko, the moon is bright in the sky and the air smells of grilled pork and foaming wine.

Eating, drinking, dancing. All night long. In the morning everyone has passed out in the meadow. There are only two souls not drunk or sleeping. One of them is me, and the other one, going through the pockets of my folks, is my cousin Vera.

Two things I found remarkable about my cousin: her jeans and her sneakers. Aside from that, she was a scrawny girl—a pale, round face and fragile shoulders with skin peeling from the sun. Her hair was long, I think, or was it my sister's hair that grew down to her waist? I forget. But I do recall the first thing that my cousin ever said to me:

"Let go of my hair," she said, "or I'll punch you in the mouth."

I didn't let go because I had to stop her from stealing, so, as promised, she punched me. Only she wasn't very accurate and her fist landed on my nose, crushing it like a plain biscuit. I spent the rest of the sbor with tape on my face, sneezing blood, and now I am forever marked with an ugly snoot. Which is why everyone, except my mother, calls me Nose.

Five summers slipped by. I went to school in the village and in the afternoons I helped Father with the fields. Father drove an MTZ-50, a tractor made in Minsk. He'd put me on his lap and make me hold the steering wheel and the steering wheel would shake and twitch in my hands, as the tractor plowed diagonally, leaving terribly distorted lines behind.

"My arms hurt," I'd say. "This wheel is too hard."

"Nose," Father would say, "quit whining. You're not holding a wheel. You're holding Life by the throat. So get your shit together and learn how to choke the bastard, because the bastard already knows how to choke you."

Mother worked as a teacher in the school. This was awkward for me, because I could never call her "Mother" in class and because she always knew if I'd done my homework or not. But I had access to her files and could steal exams and sell them to the kids for cash.

The year of the new sbor, 1975, our geography teacher retired and Mother found herself teaching his classes as well. This gave me more exams to sell and I made good money. I had a goal in mind. I went to my sister, Elitsa, having first rubbed my eyes hard so they would appear filled with tears, and with my most humble and vulnerable voice I asked her, "How much for your jeans?"

"Nose," she said, "I love you, but I'll wear these jeans until the day I die."

I tried to look heartbreaking, but she didn't budge. Instead, she advised me:

"Ask cousin Vera for a pair. You'll pay her at the sbor." Then from a jar in her nightstand Elitsa took out a ten-lev bill and stuffed it in my pocket. "Get some nice ones," she said.

Two months before it was time for the reunion I went to the river. I yelled until a boy showed up and I asked him to call my cousin. She came an hour later.

"What do you want, Nose?"

"Levi's," I yelled.

"You better have the money," she yelled back.

Mihalaky came in smoke and roar. And with him came the West. My cousin Vera stepped out of the boat and everything on her screamed, *We live better than you, we have more stuff, stuff you can't have and never will.* She wore white leather shoes with a little flower on them, which she explained was called an Adidas. She had jeans. And her shirt said things in English.

"What does it say?"

"The name of a music group. They have this song that goes '*smooook na dar voooto.*' You heard it?"

"Of course I have." But she knew better.

After lunch, the grown-ups danced around the fire, then played drunk soccer. Elitsa was absent for most of the time, and when she finally returned, her lips were burning red and her eyes shone like I'd never seen them before. She pulled me aside and whispered in my ear:

"Promise not to tell." Then she pointed at a dark-haired boy from Srbsko, skinny and with a long neck, who was just joining the soccer game. "Boban and I kissed in the forest. It was so great," she said, and her voice flickered. She nudged me in the ribs and stuck a finger at cousin Vera, who sat by the fire, yawning and raking the embers up with a stick.

"Come on, Nose, be a man. Take her to the woods."

And she laughed so loud even the deaf old grandmas turned to look at us.

I scurried away, disgusted and ashamed, but finally I had to approach Vera. I asked her if she had my jeans, then took out the money and began to count it.

"Not here, you fool," she said, and slapped me on the hand with the smoldering stick.

We walked through the village until we reached the old bridge, which stood solitary in the middle of the road. Yellow grass grew between each stone, and the riverbed was dry and fissured.

We hid under the bridge and completed the swap. Thirty levs for a pair of jeans. Best deal I'd ever made.

"You wanna go for a walk?" Vera said after she had counted the bills twice. She rubbed them on her face, the way our fathers did, and stuffed them in her pocket.

We picked mushrooms in the woods while she told me things about her school and complained about a Serbian boy who always pestered her.

"I can teach him a lesson," I said. "Next time I come there you just show him to me."

"Yeah, Nose, like you know how to fight."

And then, just like that, she hit me in the nose. Crushed it, once more, like a biscuit.

"Why did you do that?"

She shrugged. I made a fist to smack her back, but how do you hit a girl? Or how, for that matter, will hitting another person in the face stop the blood gushing from your own nose? I tried to suck it up and act like the pain was easy to ignore.

She took me by the hand and dragged me toward the river.

"I like you, Nose," she said. "Let's go wash your face."

We lay on the bank and chewed thyme leaves.

"Nose," my cousin said, "you know what they told us in school?"

She rolled over and I did the same to look her in the eyes. They were very dark, shaped like apricot kernels. Her face was all speckled and she had a tiny spot on her upper lip, delicate, hard to notice, that got redder when she was nervous or angry. The spot was red now.

"You look like a mouse," I told her.

She rolled her eyes.

"Our history teacher," she said, "told us we were all Serbs. You know. Like, a hundred percent."

"Well, you talk funny," I said. "I mean you talk Serbianish."

"So you think I'm a Serb?"

"Where do you live?" I asked her.

"You know where I live."

"But do you live in Serbia or in Bulgaria?"

Her eyes darkened and she held them shut for a long time. I knew she was sad. And I liked it. She had nice shoes, and jeans, and could listen to bands from the West, but I owned something that had been taken away from her forever.

"The only Bulgarian here is me," I told her.

She got up and stared at the river. "Let's swim to the drowned church," she said.

"I don't want to get shot."

"Get shot? Who cares for churches in no-man's-water? Besides, I've swum there before." She stood up, took her shirt off, and jumped in. The murky current rippled around her shoulders and they glistened, smooth, round pebbles the river had polished for ages. Yet her skin was soft, I could imagine. I almost reached out to touch it.

We swam the river slowly, staying along the bank. I caught a small chub under a rock, but Vera made me let it go. Finally we saw the cross sticking up above the water, massive, with rusty feet and arms that caught the evening sun.

We all knew well the story of the drowned church. Back in the day, before the Balkan Wars, a rich man lived east of the river. He had no offspring and no wife, so when he lay down dying he called his servant with a final wish—to build, with his money, a village church. The church was built, west of the river, and the peasants hired from afar a young *zograf,* a master of icons. The master painted for two years and there he met a girl and fell in love with her and married her and they too lived west of the river, near the church.

Then came the Balkan Wars and after that the First World War. All these wars Bulgaria lost, and much Bulgarian land was given to the Serbs. Three officials arrived in the village; one was a Russian, one was French, and one was British. East of the river, they said, stays in Bulgaria. West of the river from now on belongs to Serbia. Soldiers guarded the banks and planned to take the bridge down, and when the young master, who had gone away to work on another church, came back, the soldiers refused to let him cross the border and return to his wife.

In his desperation he gathered people and convinced them to divert the river, to push it west until it went around the village. Because according to the orders, what lay east of the river stayed in Bulgaria.

How they carried all those stones, all those logs, how they piled them up, I cannot imagine. Why the soldiers did not stop them, I don't know. The river moved west and it looked like she would serpent around the village. But then she twisted, wiggled, and tasted with her tongue a route of lesser resistance—through the lower hamlet she swept, devouring people and houses. Even the church, in which the master had left two years of his life, was lost in her belly.

We stared at the cross for some time, then I got out on the bank and sat in the sun.

"It's pretty deep," I said. "You sure you've been down there?"

She put a hand on my back. "It's okay if you're scared."

But it was not okay. I closed my eyes, took a deep breath, and dove off the bank.

"Swim to the cross!" she yelled after me.

I swam like I wore shoes of iron. I held the cross tightly and stepped on the slimy dome underneath. Soon Vera stood by me, in turn gripping the cross so she wouldn't slip and drift away.

"Let's look at the walls," she said.

"What if we get stuck?"

"Then we'll drown."

She laughed and nudged me in the chest.

"Come on, Nose, do it for me."

It was difficult to keep my eyes open at first. The current pushed us away so we had to work hard to reach the small window below the dome. We grabbed the bars on the window and looked inside. And despite the murky water, my eyes fell on a painting of a bearded man kneeling by a rock, his hands entwined. The man was looking down, and in the distance, approaching, was a little bird. Below the bird, I saw a cup.

"It's a nice church," Vera said after we surfaced.

"Do you want to dive again?"

"No." She moved closer and quickly she kissed me on the lips.

"Why did you do that?" I said, and felt the hairs on my arms and neck stand up, though they were wet.

She shrugged, then pushed herself off the dome, and laughing, swam splashing up the river.

The jeans Vera sold me that summer were about two sizes too large, and it seemed like they'd been worn before, but that didn't bother me. I even slept in them. I liked how loose they were around my waist, how much space, how much Western freedom they provided around my legs.

But for my sister, Elitsa, life worsened. The West gave her ideas. She would often go to the river and sit on the bank and stare, quietly, for hours on end. She would sigh and her bony shoulders would drop, like the earth below her was pulling on her arms.

As the weeks went by, her face lost its plumpness. Her skin got grayer, her eyes muddier. At dinner she kept her head down and played with her food. She never spoke, not to Mother, not to me. She was as quiet as a painting on a wall.

A doctor came and left puzzled. "I leave puzzled," he said. "She's healthy. I just don't know what's wrong with her."

But I knew. That longing in my sister's eyes, that disappointment, I'd seen them in Vera's eyes before, on the day she had wished to be Bulgarian. It was the same look of defeat, scary and contagious, and because of that look, I kept my distance.

I didn't see Vera for a year. Then, one summer day in 1976 as I was washing my jeans in the river, she yelled from the other side.

"Nose, you're buck naked."

That was supposed to embarrass me, but I didn't even twitch.

"I like to rub my ass in the face of the West," I yelled back, and raised the jeans, dripping with soap.

"What?" she yelled.

"I like to . . ." I waved. "What do you want?"

"Nose, I got something for you. Wait for——and——to—— church. All right?"

"What?"

"Wait for the dark. And swim. You hear me?"

"Yeah, I hear you. Are you gonna be there?"

"What?"

I didn't bother. I waved, bent over, and went on washing my jeans.

I waited for my folks to go to sleep and then I snuck out the window. The lights in my sister's room were still on and I imagined her in bed, eyes tragically fixed on the ceiling.

I hid my clothes under a bush and stepped into the cool water. On the other side I could see the flashlight of the guard, and the tip of his cigarette, red in the dark. I swam slowly, making as little noise as possible. In places the river flowed so narrow people could stand on both sides and talk and almost hear each other, but around the drowned church the river was broad, a quarter mile between the banks.

I stepped on the algae-slick dome and ran my fingers along a string tied to the base of the cross. A nylon bag was fixed to the other end. I freed the bag and was ready to glide away when someone said, "This is for you."

"Vera?"

"I hope you like them."

She swam closer, and was suddenly locked in a circle of light.

"Who's there?" the guard shouted, and his dog barked.

"Go, go, you stupid," Vera said, and splashed away. The circle of light followed.

I held the cross tight, not making a sound. I knew this was no joke. The guards would shoot trespassers if they had to. But Vera swam unhurriedly.

"Faster," the guard shouted. "Get out here."

The beam of light etched her naked body in the night. She had the breasts of a woman.

He asked her something and she spoke back. Then he slapped her. He held her very close and felt her body. She kneed him in the groin. He laughed on the ground long after she'd run away naked.

All through, of course, I watched in silence. I could have yelled something to stop him, but then, he had a gun. And so I held the cross and so the river flowed black with night around me and even out on the bank I felt sticky with dirty water.

Inside the bag were Vera's old Adidas shoes. The laces were in bad shape, and the left shoe was a bit torn at the front, but they were still excellent. And suddenly all shame was gone and my heart pounded so hard with new excitement, I was afraid the guards might hear it. On the banks I put the shoes on and they fit perfectly. Well, they were a bit too small for my feet—actually, they were really quite tight—but they were worth the pain. I didn't walk. I swam across the air.

I was striding back home, when someone giggled in the bush.

Grass rustled. I hesitated, but snuck through the dark, and I saw two people rolling on the ground, and would have watched them in secret if it weren't for the squelching shoes.

"Nose, is that you?" a girl asked. She flinched, and tried to cover herself with a shirt, but this was the night I saw my second pair of breasts. These belonged to my sister.

I lay in my room, head under the blanket, trying to make sense of what I'd seen, when someone walked in.

"Nose? Are you sleeping?"

My sister sat on the bed and put her hand on my chest.

"Come on. I know you're awake."

"What do you want?" I said, and threw the blanket off. I could not see her face for the dark, but I could feel that piercing gaze of hers. The house was quiet. Only Father snored in the other room.

"Are you going to tell them?" she said.

"No. What you do is your own business."

She leaned forward and kissed me on the forehead.

"You smell like cigarettes," I said.

"Good night, Nose."

She got up to leave, but I pulled her down.

"Elitsa, what are you ashamed of? Why don't you tell them?"

"They won't understand. Boban's from Srbsko."

"So what?"

I sat up in my bed and took her cold hand.

"What are you gonna do?" I asked her. She shrugged.

"I want to run away with him," she said, and her voice suddenly became softer, calmer, though what she spoke of scared me deeply. "We're going to go west. Get married, have kids. I want to work as a hairstylist in Munich. Boban has a cousin there. She is a hairstylist, or she washes dogs or something." She ran her fingers through my hair. "Oh, Nose," she said. "Tell me what to do."

. . .

I couldn't tell her. And so she kept living unhappy, wanting to be with that boy day and night but seeing him rarely and in secret. "I am alive," she told me, "only when I'm with him." And then she spoke of their plans, hitchhiking to Munich, staying with Boban's cousin and helping her cut hair. "It's a sure thing, Nose," she'd say, and I believed her.

It was the spring of 1980 when Josip Tito died and even I knew things were about to change in Yugoslavia. The old men in our village whispered that now, with the Yugoslav president finally planted in a mausoleum, our western neighbor would fall apart. I pictured in my mind the aberration I'd seen in a film, a monster sewn together from the legs and arms and torso of different people. I pictured someone pulling on the thread that held these body parts, the thread unraveling, until the legs and arms and torso came undone. We could snatch a finger then, the land across the river, and patch it up back to our land. That's what the old folks spoke about, drinking their rakia in the tavern. Meanwhile, the young folks escaped to the city, following new jobs. There weren't enough children in the village anymore to justify our own school, and so we had to go to another village and study with other kids. Mother lost her job. Grandpa got sick with pneumonia, but Grandma gave him herbs for a month, and he got better. Mostly. Father worked two jobs, plus he stacked hay on the weekends. He no longer had the time to take me plowing.

But Vera and I saw each other often, sometimes twice a month. I never found the courage to speak of the soldier. At night, we swam to the drowned church and played around the cross, very quiet, like river rats. And there, by the cross, we kissed our first real kiss. Was it joy I felt? Or was it sadness? To hold her so close and taste her breath, her lips, to slide a finger down her neck, her shoulder, down her back. To lay my palm upon her breasts and know that someone else had done this, with force, while I had watched, tongue swallowed. Her face was silver with moonlight, her hair dripped dark with dark water.

"Do you love me?" she said.

"Yes. Very much," I said. I said, "I wish we never had to leave the water."

"You fool," she said, and kissed me again. "People can't live in rivers."

That June, two months before the new sbor, our parents found out about Boban. One evening, when I came home for supper, I discovered the whole family quiet in the yard, under the trellis. The village priest was there. The village doctor. Elitsa was weeping, her face flaming red. The priest made her kiss an iron cross and sprinkled her with holy water from an enormous copper. The doctor buckled his bag and glass rattled inside when he picked it up. He winked at me and made for the gate. On his way out, the priest gave my forehead a thrashing with the boxwood foliage.

"What's the matter?" I said, dripping holy water.

Grandpa shook his head. Mother put her hand on my sister's. "You've had your cry," she said.

"Father," I said, "why was the doctor winking? And why did the priest bring such a large copper?"

Father looked at me, furious. "Because your sister, Nose," he said, "requires an Olympic pool to cleanse her."

"Meaning?" I said.

"Meaning," he said, "your sister is pregnant. Meaning," he said, "we'll have to get her married."

My family, all dressed up, went to the river. On the other bank Boban's family already waited for us. Mother had washed the collar of my shirt with sugar water so it would stay stiff, and now I felt like that sugar was running down my back in a sweaty, syrupy stream. It itched and I tried to scratch it, but Grandpa told me to quit fidgeting and act like a man. My back got itchier.

From the other side, Boban's father shouted at us, "We want your daughter's hand!"

Father took out a flask and drank rakia, then passed it around. The drink tasted bad and set my throat on fire. I coughed and Grandpa smacked my back and shook his head. Father took the flask from me and spilled some liquor on the ground for the departed. The family on the other side did the same.

"I give you my daughter's hand!" Father yelled. "We'll wed them at the sbor."

Elitsa's wedding was going to be the culmination of the sbor, so everyone prepared. Vera told me that with special permission Mihalaky had transported seven calves across the river, and two had already been slain for jerky. The two of us met often, secretly, by the drowned church.

One evening, after dinner, my family gathered under the vines of the trellis. The grown-ups smoked and talked of the wedding. My sister and I listened and smiled at each other every time our eyes met.

"Elitsa," Grandma said, and laid a thick bundle on the table, "this is yours now."

My sister untied the bundle and her eyes teared up when she recognized Grandma's best costume readied for the wedding. They laid each part of the dress on its own—the white hemp shirt, the motley apron, the linen gown, festoons of coins, the intricately worked silver earrings. Elitsa lifted the gown, and felt the linen between her fingers, and then began to put it on.

"My God, child," Mother said, "take your jeans off."

Without shame, for we are all blood, Elitsa folded her jeans aside and carefully slipped inside the glowing gown. Mother helped her with the shirt. Grandpa strapped on the apron, and Father, with his fingers shaking, gently put on her ears the silver earrings.

I woke up in the middle of the night, because I'd heard a dog howl in my sleep. I turned the lights on and sat up, sweaty in the silence. I went to the kitchen to get a drink of water and I saw Elitsa, ready to sneak out.

"What are you doing?" I said.

"Quiet, *dechko*. I'll be back in no time."

"Are you going out to see him?"

"I want to show him these." She dangled the earrings in her hand.

"And if they catch you?"

She put a finger to her lips, then spun on her heel. Her jeans rasped softly and she sank into the dark. I was this close to waking up Father, but how can you judge others when love is involved? I trusted she knew what she was doing.

For a very long time I could not fall asleep, remembering the howling dog in my dream. And then from the river, a machine gun rattled. The guard dogs started barking and the village dogs answered. I lay in bed petrified, and did not move even when someone banged on the gates.

My sister never used to swim to the Serbian side. Boban always came to meet her on our bank. But that night, strangely, they had decided to meet in Srbsko one last time before the wedding. A soldier in training had seen her climb out of the river. He'd told them both to stop. Two bullets had gone through Elitsa's back as she tried to run.

This moment in my life I do not want to remember again:

Mihalaky in smoke and roar is coming up the river, and on his boat lies my sister.

There was no sbor that year. There were, instead, two funerals. We dressed Elitsa in her wedding costume and laid her beautiful body in a terrible coffin. The silver earrings were not beside her.

The village gathered on our side of the river. On the other side was the other village, burying their boy. I could see the grave they had dug, and the earth was the same, and the depth was the same.

There were three priests on our side, because Grandma would not accept any Communist godlessness. Each of us held a candle, and the people across from us also held candles, and the banks came alive with fire, two hands of fire that could not come together. Between those hands was the river.

The first priest began to sing, and both sides listened. My eyes were on Elitsa. I couldn't let her go and things misted in my head.

"One generation passes away," I thought the priest was singing, "and another comes: but the earth remains forever. The sun rises and the sun goes down, and hastens to the place where it rises. The wind goes toward the west, toward Serbia, and all the rivers run away, east of the west. What has been is what will be, and what has been done is what will be done. Nothing is new under the sun."

The voice of the priest died down, and then a priest on the other side sang. The words piled on my heart like stones and I thought how much I wanted to be like the river, which had no memory, and how little like the earth, which could never forget.

Mother quit the factory and locked herself at home. She said her hands burned with her daughter's blood. Father began to frequent the cooperative distillery at the end of the village. At first he claimed that assisting people with loading their plums, peaches, grapes into the cauldrons kept his mind blank; then that he was simply sampling the first rakia which trickled out the spout, so he could advise the folk how to boil better drink.

He lost both his jobs soon, and so it was up to me to feed the family. I started working in the coal mine, because the money was good, and because I wanted, with my pick, to gut the land we walked on.

The control across the borders tightened. Both countries put nets along the banks and blocked buffer zones at the narrow waist of the river where the villagers used to call to one another. The sbors were canceled. Vera and I no longer met, though we found two small hills we could sort of see each other from, like dots in the distance. But these hills were too far away and we did not go there often.

Almost every night, I dreamed of Elitsa.

"I saw her just before she left," I would tell my mother. "I could have stopped her."

"Then why didn't you?" Mother would ask.

Sometimes I went to the river and threw stones over the fence, into the water, and imagined those two silver earrings, settling into the silty bottom.

"Give back the earrings," I'd scream, "you spineless, muddy thief."

I worked double shifts in the mine and was able to put something aside. I took care of Mother, who never left her bed, and occasionally brought bread and cheese to Father at the distiller's. "Mother is sick," I'd tell him, but he pretended not to hear. "More heat," he'd call, and kneel by the trickle to sample some *parvak*.

Vera and I wrote letters for a while, but after each letter there was a longer period of silence before the new one arrived. One day, in the summer of 1990, I received a brief note:

Dear Nose. I'm getting married. I want you at my wedding. I live in Beograd now. I'm sending you money. Please come.

There was, of course, no money in the envelope. Someone had stolen it on the way.

Each day I reread the letter, and thought of the way Vera had written those words, in her elegant, thin writing, and I thought of this man she had fallen in love with, and I wondered if she loved him as much as she had loved me, by the cross, in the river. I made plans to get a passport.

Two weeks before the wedding, Mother died. The doctor couldn't tell us of what. Of grief, the wailers said, and threw their black kerchiefs over their heads like ash. Father brought his drinking guiltily to the empty house. One day he poured me a glass of rakia and made me gulp it down. We killed the bottle. Then he looked me in the eye and grabbed my hand. Poor soul, he thought he was squeezing it hard.

"My son," he said, "I want to see the fields."

We staggered out of the village, finishing a second bottle. When we reached the fields we sat down and watched in silence. After the fall of Communism, organized agriculture had died in many areas, and now everything was overgrown with thornbush and nettles.

"What happened, Nose?" Father said. "I thought we held him good, this bastard, in both hands. Remember what I taught you? Hold tight, choke the bastard, and things will be all right? Well, shit, Nose. I was wrong."

And he spat against the wind, in his own face.

Three years passed before Vera wrote again. *Nose, I have a son. I'm sending you a picture. His name is Vladislav. Guess who we named him after? Come and visit us. We have money now, so don't worry. Goran just got back from a mission in Kosovo. Can you come?*

My father wanted to see the picture. He stared at it for a long time, and his eyes watered.

"My God, Nose," he said. "I can't see anything. I think I've finally gone blind."

"You want me to call the doctor?"

"Yes," he said, "but for yourself. Quit the mine, or that cough will take you."

"And what do we do for money?"

"You'll find some for my funeral. Then you'll go away."

I sat by his side and laid a hand on his forehead. "You're burning. I'll call the doctor."

"Nose," he said, "I've finally figured it out. Here is my paternal advice: Go away. You can't have a life here. You must forget about your sister, about your mother, about me. Go west. Get a job in Spain, or in Germany, or anywhere; start from scratch. Break each chain. This land is a bitch and you can't expect anything good from a bitch."

He took my hand and he kissed it.

"Go get the priest," he said.

I worked the mine until, in the spring of 1995, my boss, who'd come from some big, important city to the east, asked me, three times in a row, to repeat my request for an extra shift. Three times I repeated it before he threw his arms up in despair. "I can't understand your dialect, *mayna,*" he said. "Too Serbian for me." So I beat him up and was fired.

After that, I spent my days in the village tavern, every now and then lifting my hand before my eyes to check if I hadn't finally gone blind. It's a tough lot to be last in your bloodline. I thought of my father's advice, which seemed foolish, of my sister making plans to go west, and of how I had done nothing to stop her from swimming to her death.

Almost every night I had the same dream. I was diving at the drowned church, looking through its window, at walls no longer covered with the murals of saints and martyrs. Instead, I could see my sister and my mother, my father, Grandpa, Grandma, Vera, people from our village, and from the village across the border, painted motionless on the walls, with their eyes on my face. And every time, as I tried to push up to the surface, I discovered that my hands were locked together on the other side of the bars.

I would wake up with a yell, the voice of my sister echoing in the room.

I have some doubts, she would say, *some suspicions, that these earrings aren't really silver.*

In the spring of 1999 the United States attacked Serbia. Kosovo, the field where the Serb had once, many centuries ago, surrendered to the Turk, had once again become the ground of battle. Three or four times I saw American planes swoop over our village with a boom. Serbia, it seemed, was a land not large enough for their maneuvers at ultrasonic speed. They cut corners from our sky and went back to drop their bombs on our neighbors. The news that Vera's husband was killed came as no surprise. Her letter ended like this: *Nose, I have my son and you. Please come. There is no one else.*

The day I received the letter I swam to the drowned church, without taking my shoes or my clothes off. I held the cross and shivered for a long time, and finally I dove down and down to the rocky bottom. I gripped the bars on the church gates tightly and listened to the screaming of my lungs while they squeezed out every molecule of oxygen. I wish I could say that I saw my life unwinding thread by thread before my eyes, happy moments alternating with sad, or that my sister, bathed in glorious light, came out of the church to take my drowning hand. But there was only darkness, booming of water, of blood.

Yes, I am a coward. I have an ugly nose, and the heart of a mouse, and the only drowning I can do is in a bottle of rakia. I swam out and lay on the bank. And as I breathed with new thirst, a boom shook the air, and I saw a silver plane storm out of Serbia. The plane thundered over my head and, chasing it, I saw a missile, quickly losing height. Hissing, the missile stabbed the river, the rusty cross, the drowned church underneath. A large, muddy finger shook at the sky.

I wrote Vera right away. *When Sister died,* I wrote, *I thought half of my world ended. With my parents, the other half. I thought these deaths were meant to punish me for something. I was chained to this village, and the pull of all the bones below me was impossible to escape. But now I see that these deaths were meant to set me free, to get me moving. Like links in a chain snapping, one after the other. If the church can sever its brick roots, so can I. I'm free at last, so wait for me. I'm coming as soon as I save up some cash.*

Not long after, a Greek company opened a chicken factory in the village. My job was to make sure no bad eggs made it into the cartons. I saved some money, tried to drink less. I even cleaned the house. In the basement, in a dusty chestnut box, I found the leather shoes, the old forgotten flowers. I cut off the toe caps and put them on, and felt so good, so quick and light. Unlucky, wretched brothers. No laces, worn-out soles from walking in circles. Where will you take me?

I dug up the two jars of money I kept hidden in the yard and caught a bus to town. It wasn't hard to buy American dollars. I returned to the village and laid carnations on the graves and asked the dead for forgiveness. Then I went to the river. I put most of the money and Vladislav's picture in a plastic bag, tucked the bag in my pocket along with some cash for bribes, and with my eyes closed swam toward Srbsko.

Cool water, the pull of current, brown old leaves whirlpooling in clumps. A thick branch flows by, bark gone, smooth and rotten. What binds a man to land or water?

When I stepped on the Serbian bank, two guards already held me in the aim of their guns.

"Two hundred," I said, and took out the soaking wad.

"We could kill you instead."

"Or give me a kiss. A pat on the ass?"

They started laughing. The good thing about our countries, the reassuring thing that keeps us falling harder, is that if you can't buy something with money, you can buy it with a lot of money. I counted off two hundred more.

They escorted me up the road, to a frontier post where I paid the last hundred I'd prepared. A Turkish truck driver agreed to take me to Beograd. There I caught a cab and showed an envelope Vera had sent me.

"I need to get there," I said.

"You Bulgarian?" the cabdriver asked.

"Does it matter?"

"Well, shit, it matters. If you're Serbian, that's fine. But if you're a *Bulgar,* it isn't. It's also not fine if you are Albanian, or if you are a Croat. And if you are Muslim, well, shit, then it also isn't fine."

"Just take me to this address."

The cabdriver turned around and fixed me with his blue eyes.

"I'm only gonna ask you once," he said. "Are you Bulgarian or are you a Serb?"

"I don't know."

"Oh, well, then," he said, "get the fuck out of my cab and think it over. You ugly-nosed Bulgarian bastard. Letting Americans bomb us, handing over your bases. Slavic brothers!"

Then, as I was getting out, he spat on me.

And now, we are back at the beginning. I'm standing outside Vera's apartment, with flowers in one hand and a bar of Milka chocolate in the other. I'm rehearsing the question. I think of how I'm going to greet her, of what I'm going to say. Will the little boy like me? Will she? Will she let me help her raise him? Can we get married, have children of our own? Because I'm finally ready.

An iron safety grid protects the door. I ring the bell and little feet run on the other side.

"Who's there?" a thin voice asks.

"It's Nose," I say.

"Step closer to the spy hole."

I lean forward.

"No, to the lower one." I kneel down so the boy can peep through the hole drilled at his height.

"Put your face closer," he says. He's quiet for a moment. "Did Mama do that?"

"It's no big deal."

He unlocks the door, but keeps the iron grid between us.

"Sorry to say it, but it looks like a big deal," he says in all seriousness.

"Can I come in?"

"I'm alone. But you can sit outside and wait until they return. I'll keep you company."

We sit on both sides of the grid. He is a tiny boy and looks like Vera. Her eyes, her chin, her bright, white face. All that will change with time.

"I haven't had Milka in forever," he says as I pass him the chocolate through the grid. "Thanks, Uncle."

"Don't eat things a stranger gives you."

"You are no stranger. You're Nose."

He tells me about kindergarten. About a boy who beats him up. His face is grave. Oh, little friend, those troubles now seem big.

"But I'm a soldier," he says, "like Daddy. I won't give up. I'll fight."

Then he is quiet. He munches on the chocolate. He offers me a block that I refuse.

"You miss your dad?" I say.

He nods. "But now we have Dadan and Mama is happy."

"Who's Dadan?" My throat gets dry.

"Dadan," the boy says. "My second father."

"Your second father," I say, and rest my head against the cold iron.

"He's very nice to me," the boy says. "Yes, very nice."

He talks, sweet voice, and I struggle to resist the venom of my thoughts.

The elevator arrives with a rattle. Its door slides open, bright light out of the cell. Dadan, tall, handsome in his face, walks out with a string bag of groceries—potatoes, yogurt, green onions, white bread. He looks at me and nods, confused.

Then out comes Vera. Bright speckled face, firm sappy lips.

"My God," she says. The old spot grows red above her lip and she hangs on my neck.

I lose my grip, the earth below my feet. It feels then like everything is over. She's found someone else to care for her, she's built a new life in which there is no room for me. In a moment, I'll smile politely and follow them inside their place, I'll eat the dinner they feed me—*musaka* with *tarator*. I'll listen to Vladislav sing songs and recite poems. Then afterward, while Vera tucks him in, I'll talk to Dadan, or rather he'll talk to me, about how much he loves her, about *their* plans, and I will listen and agree. At last he'll go to bed, and under the dim kitchen light Vera and I will wade deep into the night. She'll finish the wine Dadan shared with her for dinner, she'll put her hand on mine. "My dear Nose," she'll say, or something to that effect. But even then I won't find courage to speak. Broken, not having slept all night, I'll rise up early, and, cowardly again, I'll slip out and hitchhike home.

"My dear Nose," Vera says now, and really leads me inside the apartment, "you look beaten from the road." *Beaten* is the word she uses. And then it hits me, the way a hoe hits a snake over the skull. This is the last link of the chain falling. Vera and Dadan will set me free. With them, the last connection to the past is gone.

Who binds a man to land or water, I wonder, if not that man himself?

"I've never felt so good before," I say, and mean it, and watch her lead the way through the dark hallway. I am no river, but I'm not made of clay.

John Berger

A Brush

I WANT TO TELL YOU the story of how I gave away this *Sho* Japanese brush. Where it happened and how. The brush had been given to me by an actor friend who had gone to work for a while with some Noh performers in Japan.

I drew often with it. It was made of the hairs of horse and sheep. These hairs once grew out of a skin. Maybe this is why when gathered together into a brush with a bamboo handle they transmit sensations so vividly. When I drew with it I had the impression that it and my fingers loosely holding it were touching not paper but a skin. The notion that a paper being drawn on is like a skin is there in the very word: *brushstroke*. The one and only touch of the brush! as the great draftsman Shitao termed it.

The setting for the story was a municipal swimming pool in a popular, not chic, Paris suburb, where, from time to time, I was something of an habitué. I would go there every day at 1:00 p.m., when most people were eating, and so the pool was not crowded.

The building is long and squat, and its walls are of glass and brick. It was built in the late 1960s, and it opened in 1971. It's situated in a small park where there are a few silver birches and weeping willows.

From the pool when swimming you can see the willows high up through the glass walls. The ceiling above the pool is paneled, and now, forty years later, several of the panels are missing. How many times when swimming on my back have I noticed this, while being aware of the water holding up both me and whatever story I'm puzzling over?

There's an eighteenth-century drawing by Huang Shen of a cicada singing on the branch of a weeping willow. Each leaf in it is a single brushstroke.

Seen from the outside, it's an urban not a rural building, and if you didn't know it was a swimming pool and you forgot about the trees you might suppose it was some kind of railway building, a cleaning shed for coaches, a loading bay.

There's nothing written above the entrance, just a small blazon containing the three colors of the tricolor. Emblem of the Republic. The entrance doors are of glass with the instruction POUSSEZ stenciled on them.

When you push one of these doors open and step inside you are in another realm that has little to do with the streets outside, the parked cars, or the shopping street.

The air smells slightly of chlorine. Everything is lit from below rather than from above as a consequence of the light reflected off the water of the two pools. The acoustics are distinct: every sound has its slight echo. Everywhere the horizontal, as distinct from the vertical, dominates. Most people are swimming, swimming from one end of the large pool to the other, length after length. Those standing have just taken off their clothes or are getting out of them, so there's little sense of rank or hierarchy. Instead, everywhere, there's this sense of an odd horizontal equality.

There are many printed notices, all of them employing a distinctive bureaucratic syntax and vocabulary.

THE HAIR DRYER WILL STOP 5 MINUTES BEFORE CLOSING TIME.
BATHING CAPS OBLIGATORY. COUNCIL DECREE AS FROM MONDAY
JAN. 5, 1981.

ENTRY THROUGH THIS DOOR FORBIDDEN TO ANY PERSON WHO
IS NOT A MEMBER OF STAFF. THANK YOU.

The voice embodied in such announcements is inseparable from the long political struggle during the Third Republic for the recognition of citizens' rights and duties. A measured, impersonal committee voice—with somewhere in the distance a child laughing.

Around 1945 Fernand Léger painted a series of canvases about *plongeurs*—divers in a swimming pool. With their primary colors and their simple, relaxed outlines these paintings celebrated the dream and the plan of workers enjoying leisure and, because they were workers, transforming leisure into something that had not yet been named.

Today the realization of this dream is further away than ever. Yet sometimes while putting my clothes in a locker in the men's changing room and attaching the key to my wrist, and taking the obligatory hot shower before walking through the footbath, and going to the edge of the large pool and diving in, I remember these paintings.

Most of the swimmers wear, as well as the obligatory bathing cap, dark goggles to protect their eyes from the chlorine. There's little eye contact between us, and if a swimmer's foot accidentally touches another swimmer, he or she immediately apologizes. The atmosphere is not that of the Côte d'Azur! Here each one privately pursues her or his own target.

I first noticed her because she swam differently. The movements of her arms and legs were curiously slow, like those of a frog, and at the same time her speed was not dramatically reduced. She had a different relationship to the element of water.

The Chinese master Qi Baishe (1863–1957) loved drawing

frogs, and he made the tops of their heads very black, as if they were wearing bathing caps. In the Far East the frog is a symbol of freedom.

Her bathing cap was ginger-colored and she was wearing a costume with a floral pattern, a little like English chintz. She was in her late fifties and I assumed was Vietnamese. Later I discovered my mistake. She is Cambodian.

Every day she swam, length after length, for almost an hour. As I did too. When she decided it was time to climb up one of the corner ladders and leave the pool, a man, who was himself swimming several tracks away, came to help her. He was also Southeast Asian, a little thinner than she, a little shorter, with a face that was more carved than hers; her face was moonlike.

He came up behind her in the water and put his hands under her arse so that she, facing the edge of the pool, sat on them and he bore a little of her weight when they climbed out together.

Once on the solid floor she walked away from the corner of the pool toward the footbath and the entrance to the women's changing room, alone and without any discernible limp. Having noticed this ritual a number of times, I could see, however, that, when walking, her body was taut, as if stretched on tenterhooks.

The man with the brave carved face was presumably her husband. I don't know why I had a slight doubt about this. Was it his deference? Or her aloofness?

When she first came to the pool and wanted to enter the water, he would climb halfway down the ladder and she would sit on one of his shoulders, and then he would prudently descend until the water was over his hips and she could launch herself to swim away.

Both of them knew these rituals of immersion and extraction by heart, and perhaps both recognized that in the ritual the water played a more important role than either of them. This might explain why they appeared more like fellow performers than man and wife.

Time went by. The days passed repetitively. Eventually when

she and I, swimming our lengths, crossed each other for the first time going in opposite directions, with only a meter or two between us, we lifted our heads and nodded at each other. And when, about to leave the pool, we crossed for the last time that day, we signaled Au Revoir.

How to describe that particular signal? It involves raising the eyebrows, tossing the head as if to throw back the hair, and then screwing up the eyes in a smile. Very discreetly. Goggles pushed up onto the bathing cap.

One day while I was taking a hot shower after my swim—there are eight showers for men, and to switch one on there are no taps, you press an old-fashioned button like a doorknob, and the trick is that among the eight there's some variation in the duration of the flow of hot water until the button has to be pressed again, so by now I knew exactly which shower had the hot jet that lasted longest, and, if it was free, I always chose it—one day while I was taking a hot shower after my swim, the man from Southeast Asia came under the shower next to mine and we shook hands.

Afterwards we exchanged a few words and agreed to meet outside in the little park after we'd dressed. And this is what we did, and his wife joined us.

It was then that I learned they were from Cambodia. She is very distantly related to the family of the famous Prince Sihanouk. She had fled to Europe when she was twenty, in the mid-seventies. Prior to that she had studied art in Phnom Penh.

It was she who talked and I who asked the questions. Again I had the impression that his role was that of a bodyguard or assistant. We were standing near the birch trees beside their parked two-seater Citroën C15 with a seatless space behind. A vehicle much the worse for wear. Do you still paint? I asked. She lifted her left hand into the air, making a gesture of releasing a bird, and nodded. Often she's in pain, he said. I read a lot too, she added, in Khmer and in Chinese. Then he indicated it was perhaps time for them to climb into their C15. Hanging from the rear mirror above the windshield I noticed a tiny Buddhist dharma wheel, like a ship's helm in miniature.

After they had driven off I lay on the grass—it was the month of May—beneath the weeping willows and found myself thinking about pain. She'd left Cambodia after Sihanouk had been ousted with the probable help of the CIA and in the year when the Khmer Rouge under Pol Pot had taken over the capital and begun the enforced deportation of its two million inhabitants to the countryside, where, living in communities with no individual property, they had to learn to become New Khmers! Nearly a million of them didn't survive. In the preceding years Phnom Penh and its surrounding villages had been systematically bombarded by U.S. B-52s. At least a hundred thousand people died.

The Khmer people, with their mighty past of Angkor Wat and its gigantic, impassive stone statues that later were abandoned, damaged, marauded, and so acquired a look of suffering. The Khmer were, at the moment she left her country, surrounded by enemies—Vietnamese, Laotians, Thais—and were on the point of being tyrannized and massacred by their own political visionaries, who transformed themselves into fanatics so that they could inflict vengeance on reality itself, so they could reduce reality to a single dimension. Such reduction brings with it as many pains as there are cells in a heart.

Gazing at the willows, I watched their leaves trailing in the wind. Each leaf a small brushstroke.

Today Cambodia is one of the poorest countries in Southeast Asia, and 75 percent of its exports are manufactured in sweatshops producing garments for the brand-name rag trade multinationals of the West.

A group of four-year-old kids ran past me up the steps and through the glass doors. They were going to their swimming lessons.

The next time I saw her and her husband in the pool I

approached her when she had finished one of her lengths and asked if she could tell me what it was that caused her pain. She answered immediately as if naming a place: polyarthritis. It came when I was young, when I knew I had to leave. It's kind of you to ask.

The left half of her forehead is a little discolored, browner than the rest, as if the leaf of a frond, once placed on her skin there, had slightly stained it. When her head is thrown back floating on the water, and her face looks moonlike, you could compare this little discoloring to one of the so-called seas on the moon's surface.

We both trod water and she smiled. When I'm in water, she said, I weigh less, and after a little while my joints stop hurting.

I nodded. And then we went on swimming. Swimming on her front, as I have said, she moved her legs and arms as slowly as a frog sometimes does. On her back she swam like an otter.

Cambodia is a land that has a unique osmotic relationship with freshwater. The Khmer word for homeland is *Teuk-Dey*, which means Water-Land. Framed by mountains, its flat, horizontal, alluvial plain—about a quarter of the size of France—is crossed by six major rivers including the vast Mekong. During and after the summer monsoon rains, the flow of this river multiplies by fifty! And in Phnom Penh, the river's level rises systematically by eight meters. At the same time, to the north, the lake of Tonle Sap overflows each summer to five times its "normal" winter size to become an immense reservoir, and the river of Tonle Sap turns round to run in the opposite direction, its downstream becoming upstream.

Small wonder then that this plain offered some of the most varied and abundant freshwater fishing in the world, and that for centuries its peasants lived off rice and the fish of these waters.

It was on that day while swimming during the lunch hour at the municipal swimming pool, after she had said the word *polyarthri-*

tis, pronouncing it as if it were a place, that I thought of giving her my *Sho* brush.

The same evening I put it into a box and wrapped it. And each time I went to the pool I took it with me until they turned up again. Then I placed the little box on one of the benches behind the diving boards and told her husband so he could pick it up when they left. I left before they did.

Months passed without my seeing them because I was elsewhere. When I returned to the pool, I looked for them but could not see them. I adjusted my goggles and dived in. Several kids were jumping in feetfirst, holding their noses. Others on the edge were adjusting flippers on their feet. It was noisier and more animated than usual because by now it was the month of July, school was over, and the kids, whose families couldn't afford to leave Paris, were coming to play for hours in the water. The special entrance fee for them was minimal, and the lifesaving swimming instructors maintained an easygoing discipline. A few regulars, with their strict routines and personal targets, were still there.

I had done nearly twenty lengths and was about to start another when—to my astonishment—I felt a hand firmly placed on my right shoulder from behind. I turned my head and saw the stained moon face of the onetime art student from Phnom Penh. She was wearing the same ginger-colored bathing cap and she was smiling a wide smile.

You're here!

She nods, and while we are treading water she comes close and kisses me twice on both cheeks.

Then she asks: Bird or flower?

Bird!

Thereupon she lays her head back on the water and laughs. I wish I could let you hear her laugh. Compared with the splashing and cries of the kids around us, it is low-keyed, slow, and persistent. Her face is more moonlike than ever, moonlike and timeless.

The laugh of this woman, who will soon be sixty, continues. It is unaccountably the laugh of a child—that same child whom I imagined laughing somewhere behind the committee voices.

A few days later her husband swims towards me, asks after my health, and whispers: On the bench by the diving boards. Then they leave the pool. He comes up behind her, puts his hands under her arse, and she, facing the edge of the pool, sits on them while he bears a little of her weight, and they climb up and out together.

Neither of them waves back to me as they have on other occasions. A question of modesty. Gestural modesty. No gift can be accompanied by a claim.

On the bench is a large envelope, which I take. Inside is a painting on rice paper. The painting of the bird I chose when she asked me what I wanted. The painting shows a bamboo, and perched on one of its stems a blue tit. The bamboo is drawn according to all the rules of the art. A single brushstroke beginning at the top of the stalk, stopping at each section, descending and becoming slightly wider. The branches, narrow as matches, drawn with the tip of the brush. The dark leaves rendered in single strokes like darting fish. And last the horizontal nodes, brushed from left to right, between each section of the hollow stalk.

The bird with its blue cap, its yellow breast, its grayish tail, and its claws like the letter W, from which it can hang upside down when necessary, is depicted differently. Whereas the bamboo is liquid, the bird looks embroidered, its colors applied with a brush as pointed as a needle.

Together, on the surface of the rice paper, bamboo and bird have the elegance of a single image, with the discrete stencil of the artist's name stamped below and to the left of the bird. Her name is L—.

When you enter the drawing, however, and let its air touch the back of your head, you sense how this bird is homeless. Inexplicably homeless.

I framed the drawing like a scroll, without a mount, and with great pleasure chose a place to hang it. Then one day, many months later, I needed to look up something in one of the Larousse illustrated encyclopedias. And, turning the pages, I happened to fall upon the little illustration it contained of a *mésange bleue* (blue tit). I was puzzled. It looked oddly familiar. Then I realized that, in this standard encyclopedia, I was looking at the model—the two Ws of the blue tit's claws were, for instance, at precisely the same angle, as were also the head and beak—the exact model that L— had taken for the bird perched on the bamboo.

And again I understood a little more about homelessness.

Yiyun Li

Kindness

1.

I am a forty-one-year-old woman living by myself, in the same one-bedroom flat where I have always lived, in a derelict building on the outskirts of Beijing that is threatened to be demolished by government-backed real estate developers. Apart from a trip to a cheap seaside resort, taken with my parents the summer I turned five, I have not traveled much; I spent a year in an army camp in central China, but other than that I have never lived away from home. In college, after a few failed attempts to convince me of the importance of being a community member, my adviser stopped acknowledging my presence, and the bed assigned to me was taken over by the five other girls in the dorm and their trunks.

I have not married, and naturally have no children. I have few friends, though as I have never left the neighborhood, I have enough acquaintances, most of them a generation or two older. Being around them is comforting; never is there a day when I feel that I am alone in aging.

I teach mathematics in a third-tier middle school. I do not love my job or my students, but I have noticed that even the most meager attention I give to the students is returned by a few of them with respect and gratitude and sometimes inexplicable infatuation. I pity those children more than I appreciate them, as I can see where they are heading in their lives. It is a terrible thing, even for an indifferent person like me, to see the bleakness lurking in someone else's life.

I have no hobby that takes me outside my flat during my spare time. I do not own a television set, but I have a roomful of books at least half a century older than I am. I have never in my life hurt a soul, or, if I have done any harm unintentionally the pain I inflicted was the most trivial kind, forgotten the moment it was felt—if indeed it could be felt in any way. But that cannot be a happy life, or much of a life at all, you might say. That may very well be true. "Why are you unhappy?" To this day, if I close my eyes I can feel Lieutenant Wei's finger under my chin, lifting my face to a spring night. "Tell me, how can we make you happy?"

The questions, put to me twenty-three years ago, have remained unanswerable, though it no longer matters, as, you see, Lieutenant Wei died three weeks ago, at forty-six, mother of a teenage daughter, wife of a stationery merchant, veteran of Unit 20256, People's Liberation Army, from which she retired at forty-three, already afflicted with a malignant tumor. She was Major Wei in the funeral announcement. I do not know why the news of her death was mailed to me except perhaps that the funeral committee—it was from such a committee that the letter had come, befitting her status—thought I was one of her long-lost friends, my name scribbled in an old address book. I wonder if the announcement was sent to the other girls, though not many of them would still be at the same address. I remember the day Lieutenant Wei's wedding invitation arrived, in a distant past, and thinking then that it would be the last time I would hear from her.

I did not go to the funeral, as I had not gone to her wedding, both of which took place two hours by train from Beijing. It is a hassle to travel for a wedding, but more so for a funeral. One has to face strangers' tears and, worse, one has to repeat words of condolence to irrelevant people.

When I was five, a peddler came to our neighborhood one Sunday with a bamboo basket full of spring chicks. I was trailing behind my father for our weekly shopping of rationed food, and when the peddler put a chick in my palm, its small body soft and warm and shivering constantly, I cried before I could ask my father to buy it for me. We were not a rich family: My father worked as a janitor, and my mother, ill for as long as I could remember, did not work, and I learned early to count coins and small bills with my father before we set out to shop. It must have been a painful thing for those who knew our story to watch my father's distress, as two women offered to buy two chicks for me. My father, on the way home, warned me gently that the chicks were too young to last more than a day or two. I built a nest for the chicks out of a shoe box and ripped newspaper, and fed them water-softened millet grains and a day later, when they looked ill, aspirin dissolved in water. Two days later they died, the one I named Dot and marked with ink on his forehead the first one to go, followed by Mushroom. I stole two eggs from the kitchen when my father went to help a neighbor fix a leaking sink—my mother was not often around in those days—and cracked them carefully and washed away the yolks and whites; but no matter how hard I tried I could not fit the chicks back into the shells, and I can see, to this day, the half shell on Dot's head, covering the ink spot like a funny little hat.

I have learned, since then, that life is like that, each day ending up like a chick refusing to be returned to the eggshell.

I was eighteen when I entered the army. Lieutenant Wei was twenty-four, an age that I now consider young, though at the time she seemed much older, a lifetime away from me. The day I arrived at the camp, in a midsize city plagued by hepatitis and pickpockets, I came with a single half-filled suitcase. The army had sent an extensive list of supplies that would be issued to us: toothbrushes and towels and washbasins, mess kits, thermoses to be shared among a squad, uniforms for all seasons—we used to joke that, had the army known the sizes of our bras, they would have ordered them too, dyed the same green as our socks and underpants.

A few men and women in uniform loitered under a tree. I had taken a night train, making a point of leaving home and arriving at the camp at the earliest time allowed. My father had seen me off at the train station, shaking my hand solemnly through the open window when the train whistled its signal of departure; my mother had not come, citing illness, as I had known she would.

After I registered, a woman officer, about a head taller than I was, her hair cropped short, introduced herself as Lieutenant Wei, my platoon leader. She had on a straw-colored uniform shirt buttoned to the top, dark green woolen pants, and a crimson tie. I did not cringe under her severe stare; I had lived, until then, beneath the unrelenting eyes of my mother. Decent if not strikingly beautiful—sometimes during a meal she would study my face and comment on it; in the evenings when my father was working the night shift, she would remark on my adequately developed curves. I had learned that if one remained unresponsive in those situations one could become transparent; when my mother's eyes peeled off my clothes piece by piece they would meet nothing underneath but air.

After I changed into my uniform, Lieutenant Wei ordered me to mop the barracks. Yes, I replied; yes, Lieutenant, she corrected me. Yes, Lieutenant, I replied readily, and she looked at me for a long moment, then turned around as if disgusted by my lack of defiance.

I was the first one of our platoon to have arrived, and I walked through the aisles between the bunk beds, studying the names taped to the metal frames. The company was housed in a three-story building, with each platoon occupying a long floor and bunk beds lining both walls, separated into four squads by wash-stands and desks. I would be sharing a bunk bed with a girl named Nan: We each had a white sheet, underneath which was a thin straw mattress; a quilt and a blanket, both dark green, folded as though they were sharply cut tofu. There was no pillow, and soon we would all learn to wrap up our outside clothes—dresses and shirts that were forbidden in the barracks—into pillows at night. Next to my bed was a window opening to the courtyard, where trees whose names I had yet to learn stood in a straight line, their branches pointing upward in a uniform manner.

Lieutenant Wei came back later and ran a palm over the floor. Do not think this is your home, she said, adding that I'd better prepare to shed a few layers of skin. When she ordered me to mop the floor again, I replied, "Yes, Lieutenant."

"Louder," she said. "I can't hear you."

"Yes, Lieutenant."

"I still can't hear you," she said.

"Yes, Lieutenant," I said.

"You don't have to yell in my face. A respectful and clear reply is all we need here."

"Yes, Lieutenant," I said. She stared at me for a long moment and said that a soldier shed sweat and blood but never tears. I waited until she left before I dried my face with my sleeve. It was my father's handshake through the open window that I had cried for, I told myself, and swore that I would never again cry in the army.

2.

A dream has occurred repeatedly over the past twenty years, in which I have to give up my present life and return to the army. Always Lieutenant Wei is in the dream. In the early years she would smile cruelly at me. Didn't I tell you that you would be back? The question was put to me in various ways, but the coldness remained the same. The dreams have become less wicked as the years have gone by. I'm back, I tell Lieutenant Wei; I always knew you would come back, she replies. We are older, having aged in my dreams as we have in real life, the only remnants of a previous life among a group of chirrupy teenage girls.

These dreams upset me. Lieutenant Wei's marriage, two years after I had left the army, and her transfer to another city, which would know her only as a married woman and later a mother, and then would see her die, must have wiped her history clean so she could start collecting new memories not about young, miserable girls in the camp but about happy people who deserved to be remembered. I never showed up in her dreams, I am certain, as people we keep in our memories rarely have a place for us in theirs. You may say that we too evict people from our hearts while we continue living in theirs, and that may very well be true for some people, but I wonder if I am an anomaly in that respect. I have never forgotten a person who has come into my life, and perhaps it is for that reason I cannot have much of a life myself. The people I carry with me have lived out not only their own rations but mine too, though they are innocent usurpers of my life, and I have only myself to blame.

For instance, there is Professor Shan. She was in her early sixties when I met her—but this may be the wrong way to put it, as she had lived in the neighborhood for as long as my father had. She must have watched my generation grow up, and studied every one of us before singling me out—I like to imagine it that way; you see, for a lonely woman, it is hard not to make up some scenario that allows her to believe herself special in some minor way.

Professor Shan was in her early sixties and I was twelve when she approached me one September evening. I was on my way to the milk station. "Do you have a minute?" she asked.

I looked down at the two empty bottles, snuggled in the little carrier my father had woven for me. He had painted the dried reed different colors, and the basket had an intricate pattern, though by then the colors had all paled. My father had a pair of hands that were good at making things. The wooden pegs he put on the foyer wall for my school satchel and coat had red beaks and black eyes; the cardboard wardrobe had two windows that you could push open from the inside, a perfect place for me to hide. He had built my bed too, a small wooden one, painted orange, just big enough to fit in the foyer alongside the wardrobe. We lived in a small one-room unit, the room itself serving as my parents' bedroom, the foyer my bedroom; there was a small cube of kitchen and a smaller cube of bathroom next to the foyer. Later it occurred to me that we could not afford much furniture, but when I was young I thought it was a hobby of my father's to make things with his own hands. Once upon a time he must have made things for my mother too, but from the time my memory begins, their bedroom had two single beds, my father's bare and neatly made and my mother's piled with old novels, perilously high.

"Do you have a minute? I am asking you," the old woman said again. I had developed a look of distractedness by then, and she was not the most patient woman.

I was on the way to the milk station, I stammered. "I'll wait for you here," she said, tapping on the face of her wristwatch with a long finger.

When I was out of her sight I took my time examining the trees by the roadside, and the last blossoming wildflowers. The line at the milk station was long, and that was what I told her when I reported back to her late. I addressed her as Teacher Shan, and she corrected me, telling me to call her Professor Shan. She led me up flights of stairs to her flat on the fifth floor. It did not occur to me that there was anything odd about this. The only thing my mother had warned me about, when I had had my first period a month earlier, was not to spend time alone with a man.

Professor Shan's place, a one-room unit also, seemed more crowded than ours even though she lived there by herself. Apart from a table, a chair, and a single bed, the room was filled with trunks: dark leather ones with intricate patterns on the tops and sides, wooden ones with rusty metal clips, and two matching trunks—once bleached but by then more yellow than white—made of bamboo or perhaps straw, I couldn't tell which. On each trunk there were books. She moved a pile of books to make a spot for me to sit on her single bed, and then took a seat in the only chair in the room. Up to that point I had not studied her, but I realized now that she was a beautiful woman, even at her age. Her hair, grayish white, was combed into a tight bun, not a single strand running loose. Her face—the high cheekbones, the very prominent forehead, and the deep-set eyes—reminded me of a photograph of a female Soviet pilot in my textbook. I wondered if Professor Shan had some mixed blood. It was a secret joy of mine to study people's faces. I must take after my mother, who, apart from studying my face at meals—the table placed between the two beds in my parents' bedroom—rarely took a bite. Sometimes, waiting for us to finish eating, she would comment on the people passing by outside our window: *Oily and puffy as fresh fried dough,* she described a woman living a floor above us; the man next door had a long and bitter-looking face, like a cucumber.

My mother was the prettiest woman I had known until then, with almond-shaped eyes in a small, heart-shaped face, a straight and delicate nose, and, as I later learned from her collection of romantic novels from the early 1900s, a cherry-petal mouth. When she grew tired of watching the world, she would study her own face in an oval mirror that she kept close to her all day long. "A princess trapped in the fate of a handmaiden," she would say to no one in particular. My father, eating silently, would look up at her with an apologetic smile, as if he were a parent responsible for his child's deformed body.

My father had married late in his life, my mother early, he at fifty and she at twenty. Two years later they had me, their only child. When I was in elementary school, other children often mistook him for my grandfather, but perhaps that was because he had to be a parent to my mother, too. Together my mother and I made my father grow old fast. You could see that in his stooped back and sad smile.

"Do you always let your mind wander in front of your teachers?" Professor Shan asked, though I could see the question was more an amusement than a criticism. In her youth, she must have been more beautiful than my mother. I wondered what my mother would think, if she knew my opinion. One thing I was certain of was that my mother would not get along well with Professor Shan, eccentricity being both women's prized possession.

I was aware of Professor Shan's existence as much as I was aware of the other people in the neighborhood: If you live in one place long enough, you do not need to seek gossip and rumors; stories, all sorts of tales, will come to find you. Even for a family like ours, with a mother who rarely talked to people and a father who was, in my mother's words, *quiet as a dead log,* stories would come in eavesdropped form while I waited in lines—and it seems that I spent my childhood perpetually in lines, waiting for eggs, cooking oil, meat, soap, milk, and other rationed goods, waiting to pay the rent and utilities, waiting to get my mother's prescription filled at the pharmacy. That was where I had first heard bits and pieces of Professor Shan's story, even before I met her: She had taught high school English in another district before her retirement. She had a son and a daughter, who, after graduating from college, had both vanished, reappearing every once in a while as visitors from America. People could not agree on how they had managed to leave the country, though the most reasonable explanation was that Professor Shan had relatives on her mother's side who had fled to the States. Once upon a time there had been a husband, a much friendlier person than Professor Shan, but he had disappeared, too, and it was said that he had been sent to the American relatives just as their children had been; it was also said that he had taken up with a younger woman and started a Chinese restaurant with her in New York City, which might be true, as he was never seen in the neighborhood again.

In any case, sitting in Professor Shan's room on that first day, I could not imagine that the place had once been occupied by a family. There were no framed photographs or letters bearing foreign addresses, and the room, packed with the trunks, seemed too small even for Professor Shan by herself. She studied me while I looked around the room, then picked up an old book and turned to a random page. "Read the line to me," she said. The book was the first one in a series called *Essential English,* which Professor Shan had used to learn English fifty years ago. The page had a small cartoon of a child on a seat, the kind one would find in a luxury theater. In the cartoon, the child, who was not heavy enough to keep the seat from folding back, smiled uncertainly on his high perch, and I felt the same. I had entered middle school earlier that month, and had barely learned my alphabet.

When I could not read the caption, Professor Shan put the book back with the other volumes, their spines different colors that were equally faded. "You do know that you are not your parents' birth daughter, don't you?" She turned and faced me. "And you do know that no matter how nicely they treat you, they can't do much for your education, don't you?"

I had not doubted my blood until then—I knew that my parents were different from most parents, but I had thought that it was their age difference, and my mother's illness. Moyan: My mother sometimes said my name in a soft voice when my father was not around, and I would know that she had some secrets to tell me. A man can have children until he is seventy, she would say; a woman's youth ends the moment she marries. Moyan, do not let a man touch you, especially here and here, she would say, gesturing vaguely toward her own body. Moyan, your father would get you a stepmother the moment I died, she would say, narrowing her eyes in an amused way; do you know I cannot die now because I don't want you to live under a stepmother? In one of these revelatory moments she could have said, Moyan, you were not born to us; we only picked you up from a garbage dump—but no, my mother had never, even in her most uncharitable moment, said that to me, and in fact she kept the secret until her death, and for that alone I loved her, and love her still.

"If your parents haven't told you this, someone else must," Professor Shan said when I did not reply. "One needs to know where she came from, do you understand?"

In my confusion I nodded. I am fortunate to be slow in responding to news—I have avoided much drama in my life, as the impact, if there is any, comes much later, in solitary meditation.

"I was an orphan myself." Slowly, over the next three years, her story would come in full. Her mother, a woman who had stayed unmarried to take care of her own aging parents, had inherited their small china shop when they died; by then she was too old to get married. She went to a Shanghai orphanage in the deadly winter of 1928 and adopted the only girl who was not suffering pneumonia. She named the young girl Shan Shan; she had no family name, as there was not one she could claim. McTayeier School for Girls, the best school in Shanghai, was where Professor Shan had been educated, the school's name spelled out for me to remember, "The McTayeierans," the song she and her classmates had sung at school gatherings, sung to me. In her early twenties, Professor Shan had been hired by a teachers college but was fired when her dubious history was discovered. People who think they know their own stories do not appreciate other people's mysteries, Professor Shan explained; that is why people like you and me will always find each other. Those words, first said to me in the early days of my visits, are what made me go back to her every day at five o'clock.

She read to me. She scoffed at my English textbook, and told me to start on the first volume of *Essential English*. She never checked my progress, and after a while I realized it did not make any difference to her that I only looked at the illustrations. Instead she read her collection of novels to me. We began with *David Copperfield,* she sitting in the only chair in the room, I on the bed. Intimidation kept me focused at first, as sometimes she would look up sharply in mid-sentence to see if my eyes were wandering to the trunks, or the trees outside. I worried that she would find me a fraud and dismiss me. I did not like her or dislike her yet, but I was in shock, unable to process the fact that I was not related by blood to my parents, and Professor Shan's reading voice, with a melody that was not present when we talked, was soothing in a way that my mother's voice never was. Professor Shan would read long passages, stopping only when she seemed pleased, and then translate for me. Her translation seemed shorter than the original English, but even those brief Chinese words gave me a joy that I did not get elsewhere—she used phrases that belonged to a different era, a language more for the ancients than the living, and before long I began to mimic her. I had never been a talkative person, but now I had even fewer words, for the ancients had the most efficient ways of saying things. My schoolmates found it laughable but I persisted, ignoring teenage slang for a mixture of language used in ancient poetry and eighteenth-century romance novels. My father, who was not an educated person, did not seem to find it odd, perhaps having little idea how education could change one's speech, but my mother, more than once, studied me after my father and I exchanged some words. I knew I had invaded her territory—after all, she was the one who read ancient poetry and centuries-old novels to pass the time. She could not make up her mind about how to accept my change, I could see, just as I could not make up my mind about the news of her not being my birth mother.

3.

By our third week in the army everyone in my squad had received a letter from home; a few had received additional letters from their friends. Without fail all of them cried when they read them. Ping, the youngest among us, fifteen and a half, doubtless a genius to have graduated high school that young, read aloud her father's letter between sobs: "After you registered and went into the barracks, Baba cried on the way to the train station. The night train from Wuhan to Beijing was fully packed, and Baba stood for eighteen hours, but that, compared to Baba's little darling's suffering in the army, was nothing. I have the calendar on my wall, and every morning I mark a day off, knowing it is one day closer to our reunion."

I was the only one, by the fourth week, not to have received a letter. "Are you sure you don't want to write to your parents again?" asked Nan, who stood next to me in line for the formation drill and slept in the bunk bed above me. "Your last letter might have got lost, and they might not have the address to write to you."

I shook my head. I had sent a postcard to my parents the first week, saying nothing but that I had arrived safely. My father was not the type to write a letter, and secretly I was relieved that my father was not like Ping's, who would continue sending letters filled with unabashed words of love, which Ping never hesitated to share. My mother might write me, on a whim, a letter filled with quotations from ancient poems, but then again, she might have decided to cut me out of all communications.

At the end of the week I was summoned to Lieutenant Wei's room. It was a Sunday, and we had the morning off from drills. She motioned for me to take the only chair, and I moved it away from her before sitting down in the middle of the room. There was a single bed on my left, with an army-issue quilt, blanket, and sheet. There was no pillow on her bed, and I wondered if she wrapped up some old clothes as we did at night, or if she had a pillow hiding in her closet. On the wall next to the bed were a few framed photographs. A black-and-white one stood out. A young girl, thirteen or fourteen, looked away with a smile, as if she had been teasing the photographer. "That was taken the summer before I enlisted," Lieutenant Wei said as she studied me. "Have you been out to town yet?"

"No, Lieutenant," I said. She only had to check her chart to know that I had never requested one of the two-hour permits to visit town on Sundays.

"Why? The town is too small for someone from Beijing to visit?"

I thought about the question, which, like all questions put to us by an officer, could have many traps. There was no particular reason, I said. I could have said that I wanted to give the opportunity to the other girls, who were more eager to have the two hours of freedom, but that would have led to more questioning. I had learned, in the past few weeks, that an officer's friendliness was not to be trusted. Lan, a girl whose hometown was in the same province as Lieutenant Wei's hometown, once had an amicable chat with Lieutenant Wei at a drill break, but five minutes later, when Lan made the mistake of turning right when the rest of us turned left, Lieutenant Wei ordered her to leave the formation and do a hundred turn-lefts. Even worse, Lan was to give herself the drill command, and by the time she reached thirty, her voice was choked by her tears. Lieutenant Wei, while the rest of us watched with anxiety, told Lan that if she did not make the command clear and loud to all who were witnessing her punishment, it would not count. Similar incidents had happened to others: A girl was ordered to stand in the middle of the mess hall during a meal after she had laughed at a joke told quietly to her by a squad mate; another girl was asked to read a self-criticism in front of the company because she had claimed the food from the mess hall was better suited for feeding pigs than human beings. These punishments were measured out not only by Lieutenant Wei and the other junior officers, but also by Major Tang, the commander of our company, who, as the only male officer, liked to storm through the barracks for unannounced inspections.

When I did not reply, Lieutenant Wei changed the topic and said that she had heard that I hadn't yet received a letter from home. I wondered who had reported this to her, but perhaps this was how the army worked, details about our lives recorded by informants among us. My parents are not the type to write letters, I said.

"Is that a problem for you?"

"A problem, Lieutenant?"

"Would you like to phone them?" Lieutenant Wei said. "I could arrange for you to make a phone call to your parents if you wish."

My parents did not own a telephone. The nearest public telephone was a few blocks from our building, guarded by a brusque middle-aged woman. A message would be taken but would not be delivered until the end of the day; she was paid as a government worker, her salary at a set level, so she rarely inconvenienced herself to deliver even the most urgent messages. Once in a while when the residents filed complaints, she would for a week or two put the callers on hold and send her teenage son around the neighborhood. "A phone call for number 205," he would call out in front of a building, his voice no longer a child's but not yet a grown man's. He was said to be slow, so no school would admit him, and he spent his days, if not as a companion to his mother, then running around the neighborhood and intimidating young children with incoherent ghost stories. My mother would never respond to such a boy calling our flat number in that manner, nor would she be willing to make a trip to the phone booth to call me back.

I told Lieutenant Wei that there was no need to make a call, as my parents did not have a telephone at their place.

"And a neighbor? A friend living nearby?" Lieutenant Wei said. "Anyone who could receive a phone call on their behalf so they know you are well?"

The only telephone number I knew—though I had never used

it—was Professor Shan's. It was written on a slip of paper, in her neat handwriting, and taped on the red telephone next to her single bed. I had studied the number many times while she was reading a long passage, and after a while I could not get it out of my mind.

There is no one I could call, I said when Lieutenant Wei pressed me again. She studied my face as if trying to decide if I was lying out of defiance. She retrieved a file folder from a drawer, and pages rustled under her impatient fingers. I looked out the window at the evergreen trees, wishing to be one of them. I loved trees more than I loved people; I still do. Few creatures are crueler than human beings, Professor Shan had said once; we had been standing side by side next to her fifth-floor window, looking down at people busy with their late-afternoon lives. I can guarantee you, Professor Shan said, pointing to the weeping willows by the roadside, every one of those trees is more worthwhile than the people you'll get to know in life; isn't it a good thing that once you are bored by people you still have trees to watch?

"Your father's work unit? Can you call him there?" Lieutenant Wei said. "But of course we'll have to arrange for you to call during the weekdays to catch him at work."

She was reading my registration form, where I had put down "service" for my father's occupation, along with the name of the department store where he worked night shifts. I wondered if she was calculating my parents' ages, as the registration form asked for their birth information, too.

There was no need to call him, I replied. My parents were not the type who would begrudge the army for not giving them sufficient information about my well-being.

Lieutenant Wei seemed not to notice the hostility of my words. "Your mother—what kind of illness does she have?"

When I had entered elementary school I had been instructed by my father to put down "retired early from illness" for my mother's occupation. What kind of illness? the teachers would

ask. What did she do before she became ill? At first I did not know
how to answer, but by middle school I became an expert in deal-
ing with people's curiosity—she was a bookkeeper, I would say,
the most tedious and lonely job I could come up with for her;
lupus was what had been troubling her, I would explain, the name
of the disease learned in fifth grade when a classmate's mother had
died from it. I thought about what kind of tale would stop Lieutenant Wei from pursuing the topic. In the end I said that I did
not know what had caused her disability.

The earliest I could remember people commenting on her illness was when I was four. I was standing in a long line waiting for
our monthly egg ration when my father crossed the street to buy
rice. What kind of parents would leave a child that small to hold
a place in line? asked someone who must have been new to the
neighborhood, and a woman, not far behind me, replied that my
mother was a mental case. *Nymphomania* was the word Professor
Shan had used, and it was from her that I had learned the story of
my parents' marriage: At nineteen, my mother had fallen in love
with a married man who had recently moved into the neighborhood, and when the man claimed that he had nothing to do with
her fantasy, she ran into the street calling his name and telling
people she had aborted three babies for him. They would have
locked her up permanently had it not been for my father's marriage proposal. My father, who people had thought would remain
a bachelor for life, came to my mother's parents and asked to take
the burden off their hands. Which would you have chosen for
your daughter had you been a mother, Professor Shan asked me,
an asylum or an old man? She'd told me the story not long after I
had become a regular visitor to her flat. I had stammered, not
knowing how to pass the test. Professor Shan said that it was my
mother's good fortune that her parents had given her up to a man
who loved her rather than to an asylum; love makes a man blind,
she added, and I wondered if my father's misfortune was transparent to the world.

Later I would realize that my family—my father's reticence, my mother's craziness, and my existence as part of their pretense of being a normal married couple—must have been gossip for the neighborhood, and their story, sooner or later, would have reached me, but when I left Professor Shan's flat that day, I resented her heartlessness. We were only fifty pages into *David Copperfield,* and I could have easily found an excuse not to go to her flat again, but what good would it have done me? I was no longer my parents' birth child, and their marriage, if it could be called a marriage, was no doubt a pitiful one.

Lieutenant Wei closed the file folder. She seemed, all of a sudden, to have lost interest in my case. She looked at her wristwatch and said that since there was still an hour until the end of the day, meaning eleven o'clock, when drills started, I might as well use the time wisely and go water and weed our platoon's vegetable garden.

Today I would give anything for a garden, but the only space I can claim now is my flat. It's on the north side of the building, so the only sunshine I get is slanted light for an hour in the evening. My father used to keep pots of green plants on the windowsill, but they have long since withered and found their way to the trashcans. Today I would give anything for a garden—perhaps not as big as the one we used to have in the army, as it would be pure greed to ask for that, but a small patch of earth. At eighteen, though, I had not the urge to nurture anything. "The garden was weeded and watered yesterday, Lieutenant," I said.

"Are you telling me that I have given you a worthless order? How about the pigs? If you think the vegetables grow without your contribution, maybe you could put some efforts into cleaning the pigsties."

The pigs, not yet fully grown, were kept at the far end of the camp. There were five pigs for each company, and the conscripts in the cooking squad had told us that the pigs were to be butchered at the end of our year for the farewell banquet. Other than the five pigs, we saw little meat. Once in a while Ping would devise an extensive plan to sneak a pig out of the camp, find a willing butcher to kill it, and another willing soul to cook it; the scheme grew more detailed and vivid, but it was only talk, for the sake of passing time.

I said it was not our squad's turn to take care of the pigs. Most shared duties—grounds-keeping around the barracks, gardening, helping the cooking squad prepare meals for the company, feeding the pigs and cleaning the pigsties, cleaning the toilet stalls and the washing room—were rotated among the four squads in the platoon, and apart from the kitchen duties, during which we could sneak extra food to our table, they were dreaded and carried out with aversion.

"I see that you haven't learned the most basic rule about the army," Lieutenant Wei said. "This is not the civilian world, where one can bargain."

4.

The civilian world slowly crept in on us, in the form of letters from old school friends and packages of chocolates from parents, memories of childhood holidays and teenage expeditions, and, in my case, Professor Shan's voice, reading D. H. Lawrence, her tone unhurried. *Well, Mabel, and what are you going to do with yourself?* When I closed my eyes at the shooting range I could hear her voice, and the question, posed from one character to another, now seemed to request an answer from me. Or else: *To her father, she was The Princess. To her Boston aunts and uncles she was just "Dollie Urquhart, poor little thing."*

The point of a boot kicked my leg, and I opened my eyes. I was not in Professor Shan's flat, released momentarily from responsibility by her voice, but facedown, my elbows on sandbags, my right cheek resting on the wooden stock of a semiautomatic rifle. The late October sunshine was warm on my back, and two hundred yards away the green targets, in the shape of a man's upper body, stood in a long line. Two magpies chattered in a nearby tree, and the last locusts of the season, brown with greenish patterns, sprang past the sandbags and disappeared into the yellowing grass. I shifted my weight and aligned my right eye with the front and rear sights. The training officer did not move, his shadow cast on the sandbags in front of me. I waited, and when the shadow did not leave to check on the next girl, I pulled the trigger. Apart from a crack, nothing happened—it would be another two weeks before we would be given live ammunition.

"Do you think you got a ten there?" asked the training officer.

"Yes, sir," I said, still squinting at the target.

He sighed and said he did not think so. Try again, he said. I held the rifle closer so that the butt was steadied by my right shoulder. I had noticed that people, once put into an army, become two different species of animal—those who were eager to please, like the most loyal, best trained dogs, and those who, like me, acted like the most stubborn donkeys and needed a prod for every move. I looked through the sights and pulled the trigger.

"Much better," the training officer said. "Now remember, the shooting range is not a place to nap."

Shooting practice was one of the few things I enjoyed in the army. Major Tang showed up occasionally to inspect us, but since aiming was one thing we had to practice on our own, he had little patience for staying at the shooting range for hours. The three platoon leaders, including Lieutenant Wei, sat in the shade of ash trees and chatted while two of the shooting officers for the company, who liked to sit with them, told jokes. Our officer, older and more reticent, sat a few steps away and listened with an indulgent smile. The two girls on my right talked in whispers, and now and then I caught a sentence; they were discussing boys, analyses and guesses that I did not bother to follow. On my left, Nan hummed a tune under her breath while maintaining a perfect shooting position. I was amazed at how soldierly she could act, her posture perfect in formation drills, her impeccable bed-making winning her titles in the internal-affairs contest. Anyone could see her mind was elsewhere, but the military life seemed to provide endless amusements for her; she never misbehaved, and she was among the few who hadn't received any public humiliation. I turned my head slightly, still resting my right cheek on the stock but looking at Nan rather than the target. Her uniform cap was low on her eyebrows, and in the shadow of the cap she squinted with a smile, singing in a very low voice.

"The Last Rose of Summer," she told me when I asked her about the song during the break. Nan was a small girl and looked no more than thirteen years old. She had joined a famous children's choir when she was six, and when the other children her age had entered middle school and left the choir, she had remained because she liked to sing, and she could still pass for a young child. When she reached sixteen, the choir changed its name from "children's choir" to "children and young women's choir." She'd laughed when she told us about it. Would she go back to the choir? one of the girls had asked her, and she'd thought for a moment and said that perhaps after the army she would have to find some other hobbies. One could not possibly remain in a children's choir all her life, she'd said, though she seemed to me the kind of person who could get away with anything she set her heart on. I could imagine her still singing at twenty or thirty among a group of children, looking as young and innocent as them— though this I did not tell Nan. We were friendly toward each other, but we were not friends, perhaps the only two in our platoon who hadn't claimed a close friend eight weeks into the military life. I did not see the need to have someone next to me when I took a walk around the drill grounds after dinner for the fifteen minutes of free time; nor did I need to share my night-watch duty with a special friend, so I was often paired with leftover girls from the other platoons—girls like me who had no one to cling to— and it suited me well to spend half a night with someone as quiet as I was in the front room of the barracks, dozing off in two chairs set as far apart as possible.

Nan was a different case. She was friendly with everyone, including the officers and the conscripts in the cooking squad, and was courted by quite a few girls hoping to become her best friend. You could see that she was used to such attention, amused even, but she would not grant anyone that privilege. Even our squad leader, who had become a favorite of the officers with her increasingly militant treatment of us, was unwilling to assign the most dreadful duties—cleaning the toilets, or the pigsties—to Nan. A less gracious person than Nan would have been the target of envy, yet she seemed untouched by any malignancy.

One girl, overhearing our conversation, asked Nan to sing "The Last Rose of Summer." Nan stood up from where we were sitting in a circle and flicked dried grass and leaves from her uniform. Her voice seemed to make breathing hard for those around her; her face, no longer appearing amused, had an ancient, ageless look. I wondered what kind of person Nan was to be able to sing like that—she seemed too aloof to be touched by life, but how could she sing so hauntingly if she had not felt the pain described in those songs?

The shooting range was quiet when Nan finished singing. A bumblebee buzzed and was shooed away, and in the distance, perhaps over the hills where a civilian world could not be seen, a loudspeaker was broadcasting midday news, but we could not hear a word. After a while, a girl from another platoon who had sneaked away from her squad to join our circle begged Nan to tell us something about her trips abroad. Apart from Nan, none of us had traveled abroad—none of us had ever had a legal reason to apply for a passport.

I could not decide if Nan was annoyed or pleased by such requests, but she never failed to tell some tales: singing in front of a Vienna palace, learning tap dancing from an American teenager on a cruise ship, taking a long train ride across Siberia in February on her way back to China from a European tour, the whole time stuck in a carriage with girls eight or nine years younger. She had learned chess from the choir director on that train ride, she said, while the young children sang and clamored, and a doll-like girl, not yet seven, had played violin for hours like an oblivious angel.

"How old is your choir director?" the girl from the other platoon asked.

Nan shrugged and began another tale about the Macedonian folk songs they'd had to learn because of a detour. I noticed that this was her way of not answering questions she found unpleasantly nosy or uninteresting. Even though Nan kept smiling, you could see that the girl who had asked the question was ashamed of her blunder. In fact, there was so much pain and yearning in the girl's face that I turned to look at the officers under the ash trees, Lieutenant Wei massaging the nape of Lieutenant Hong's neck, and the two young shooting officers competing with exaggerated gestures to talk to another platoon leader. From where we sat, twenty meters away, they looked young and ordinary, their laughter distant but their happiness tangible. After a moment the older shooting officer looked at his wristwatch and, almost apologetically, blew the whistle to signal the end of the break.

At night, when I could not sleep, I thought about other people and their pain. I wondered, for instance, what kind of pain could be found in Nan's heart that gave such unbearable sadness to her songs, but she was the most imperturbable person I had met, and if she could be connected to any pain, it would be what she inflicted on others, perhaps against her will. I thought about the girls who vied for her attention, often with open animosity toward each other; they had become transparent in their longing, but I did not know what more they could ask from Nan. She shared her songs and her stories; she treated everyone kindly. Would they be lying in their beds, wondering if Nan had ever known pain? But why would one want to access another person's pain, when there is enough in one's own life? In the barracks there was much love in the air—boys left behind in the civilian world were missed and written long letters; boys met in the camp were discussed, sometimes with giggles, sometimes less gleefully; more subdued was the longing between the girls that manifested itself as a competition to become best friends. *People don't know what they are doing and saying. They chatter-chatter, and they hurt one another, and they hurt themselves very often, till they cry.* At night I tried to remember Professor Shan's voice when she read her favorite story to me, and when I was not sure if I remembered the exact words, I turned on my flashlight and reread the story under the quilt. *But don't take any notice, my little Princess.*

We had spent ten months with *David Copperfield*, slowly at first, two or three pages a day, and later five or six pages. I don't remember at what point I had begun to understand what was read to me, in bits and pieces of course; it must be similar to the moment a child first understands the world in words, when what is spoken to her has not yet taken on a definite meaning, but she becomes more confident each day that there is a message behind those jumbled sounds. I told my parents that I had been visiting Professor Shan, as she had agreed to tutor me with my schoolwork, a lie that my father had not questioned and my mother had not bothered to listen to. I did not tell Professor Shan that I had begun to understand her, but surely she saw the change: Perhaps my eyes wandered less often to the trees outside the window, or perhaps my face betrayed an eagerness where before was only ignorance. In any case, two-thirds into the novel she stopped translating for me. Neither of us talked about this change of routine. I was quiet, still intimidated by her, though I had begun to look forward to the hour spent in her flat. She had not begun to tell me her stories—that would come later. I had not begun to share her attachment to books—that too would come later, much later, perhaps only after I had stopped visiting her. Still, her fifth-floor flat, where life did not seem to be lived out in the measuring of rice and flour or the counting of paper bills and coins, at least during the time I was there, became a place that no other place could be: Strangers, closer to my heart than my neighbors and acquaintances, loved tragic and strange loves and died tragic and strange deaths, and Professor Shan's unperturbed voice made it all seem natural. Looking back, I wonder if it was because of my limited understanding of the language that all tragedies became acceptable to me. Perhaps all that time I was imagining a different story than the one read to me.

After *David Copperfield,* we read *Great Expectations.* Then *The Return of the Native* and, later, *Tess of the d'Urbervilles.* It was during *Jude the Obscure* that she began to tell me her story, in fragments I would piece together later. Sometimes the story came at the beginning of the afternoon, sometimes when she took a break from reading the novel to me. She never talked long about herself, and afterward we did not discuss it. I had become less nervous around her; still, I did not talk much about my life at school or at home—intuitively I knew she had little interest in the life I lived outside the hour in her flat. Only once did I ask her advice, about where to go for high school. I was not an excellent student, though decent enough to do well in entrance exams. She asked me my choices of schools, and when I listed them for her, she answered that they were all good schools, and it rather did not matter, in her opinion, where I went. In the end, I chose the school farthest from our neighborhood, a decision that later proved convenient when I had to come up with an excuse to stop visiting Professor Shan.

5.

I turned out to be excellent at shooting. I was one of the few who scored all tens in our first live-ammunition practice, and when we marched back from the shooting range, I was displayed in front of the company along with three other girls with a red ribbon pinned to my chest. Major Tang called the four of us budding sharpshooters and gave a speech that ended with the slogan "My gun follows my orders, and I follow the Communist Party's orders."

"That slogan," said Jie, one of the other sharpshooters. "Don't you think it sounded so . . . off-color?"

"What do you mean?" I asked.

"You're too innocent for this discussion." Jie laughed, but a few days later she sought me out. "Do you read English?"

Apart from the officers and the conscripts in the cooking squad, all of us were able to read some English, since we had studied it in high school, and I said that to Jie. "I know that, of course," she said. "I'm asking you if you could read an English novel for me."

I had never talked to anyone about Professor Shan, and I did not memorize English vocabulary during the free time, as some of the other girls, who had their hearts set on going to America after college, did. I replied vaguely that I could try, and after dinner the next day Jie approached me with a copy of *Lady Chatterley's Lover*. "It was once a banned book," she told me with hushed excitement, and asked me to promise not to let the secret out to anyone. "My boyfriend sent it to me. Don't lose it. He went to great trouble to find a copy."

The book, a poorly xeroxed copy, was wrapped in an old calendar sheet, the words small and smudged. "Don't look like I'm corrupting you. You're old enough to know these things." In a lower voice Jie told me that there were many colorful passages in the novel, and could I mark all the passages describing sex between the man and the woman for her? I blushed at the words she used—*zuo-ai*, doing love, an innocent yet unfortunate mistranslation of the English phrase *making love*. Jie said she didn't have the patience to read the book herself, and told me if I wanted to I could skip pages as long as I did not fail to mark what she should be reading.

Jie was an outgoing girl, loud and confident, fond of crass jokes. Perhaps the fact that I did not have someone to reveal her secret to was behind her reasoning; or she might have simply pitied me for my naïveté about the world, and thought of me as someone in need of enlightenment. In any case, I did not ask her for an explanation—it was easier to let people have their opinions than to convince them otherwise.

At night I covered my head with the quilt and pointed the light from my flashlight onto the pages. I was sixteen when Professor Shan began to read the stories of D. H. Lawrence to me; it was the fall I entered high school. My favorite author, she said of Lawrence, but did not say more. It became clear to me—and I tried not to show my disappointment—that we would not return to Dickens or Hardy, at least not for a long while. She pointed out the novels she would read to me after we finished with the two volumes of Lawrence's stories: *The White Peacock, Sons and Lovers, The Rainbow, Women in Love.* Her eyes seemed to gleam unusually as she laid out her plan. I wonder whether she had been waiting for that moment ever since I had begun visiting her. Were Dickens and Hardy only a preparation for Lawrence? Was she waiting for me to grow older, or to become better with English, so that I could understand Lawrence?

That fall, milk was no longer rationed, but our family could not afford it, as I needed lunch money for the high school canteen. Every day I rode out of the school gate at quarter to four, the earliest possible time, and cycled across a district and a half to get to Professor Shan's flat at quarter after five. I did not go home to report to my parents first. My father, on a longer night shift now, would leave for work around five, and it mattered little to my mother when I returned home—my father left a cooked meal for us, which my mother rarely touched. She was becoming even thinner, ghostly hollows around her cheeks, and she lay in her bed and read ancient romance novels for hours.

There was a woman who was beautiful, who started with all the advantages, yet she had no luck. She married for love, and the love turned to dust. Professor Shan began reading to me as soon as I arrived. Sometimes she would lay snacks on the table—a few biscuits, half an orange, a handful of roasted chestnuts—but she herself never ate anything when I was around, so I did not touch the food either.

I did not like Lawrence, and my mind began to wander to other things. I had enjoyed Dickens, who talked to me at times in a wordy manner as I imagined a grandparent would. I had never met my father's parents, and my mother's parents had washed their hands of her, so I was only a stranger to them. I had loved Hardy, and had dreamed of the countryside in his books—black-and-white dreams in which everything looked slanted as if in a woodcut print—but this may have had more to do with the joy of finding myself able to understand English. I dared not show that I was annoyed by Lawrence. I had lived with a mad mother all my life and found madness, which seemed prevalent in the stories read to me now, the most uninteresting topic. I tried to suppress a yawn and let my mind wander to a man whose name I did not know and whose face had begun to haunt me. The man lived on the second floor of Professor Shan's building and had a young daughter named Nini. "Nini's Papa" was how I greeted him. He did not use my name—he had never asked me for it, so perhaps he did not know mine either—and he called me Nini's Sister, as if I were connected to his daughter by blood.

I now know his name, as he has become one of the most renowned flutists in the nation. I have seen his face on posters, and read in newspapers and magazines the story of his success after years of hardship, about his childhood spent as an orphan with distant relatives, serving in his teens as an apprentice to a blind folk musician whom he then had buried while traveling across south China, about his years of playing in the street for small change, his failed marriage and estranged daughter. The articles called him "a figure of inspiration." He has not aged much in twenty-five years, though he looks less melancholy, more at ease with the world. I imagine his students in the conservatory having youthful crushes on him, love that has long been due him. Sometimes I wonder if he still remembers me, but the moment the thought occurs to me, I laugh at myself. Why should he think about someone who is a reminder of his humiliation? Only those who live in the past have space in their hearts for people from the past; the man surely has enough success to savor only the present, with many people to occupy his heart, perhaps far too many.

Nini's father had married into the flat on the second floor. Having no place of his own and, worse, no job, made him a laughingstock, or, rather, his wife. It was said that she had fallen in love with him when she saw him play his flute in the park, a near beggar who, the neighbors used to say, "must have a short circuit in his brain to think of himself as an artist." Much to her parents' chagrin, she made up her mind to marry him and support him while he tried his luck getting into the National Conservatory. A year later they had a daughter, and his in-laws, with whom he and his wife shared the two-bedroom flat on the second floor, refused—unlike most grandparents—to take care of the baby. Nini's mother worked as a clerk in a government agency, and while she was away, Nini's father could be seen walking the baby around the neighborhood. It must have been disheartening for a man, once homeless, to be made homeless again, during the daytime, along with his child, but as a young girl I did not sense the agony of his situation. Rather, I was envious of his freedom, not belonging to a school or a work unit, and I wished to be his companion during his long hours of aimless wandering.

Nini was just learning to speak when I first began to visit Professor Shan. I was not the kind of well-raised child who knew to compliment a woman on her new dress or a father on his adorable daughter, but whenever I saw Nini and her father in the late afternoons, often playing in the small garden across the narrow lane from Professor Shan's building, I would greet them. I praised the girl for the stick she held in her hand, or the pebbles she gathered into a pile. Her father thanked me, speaking on her behalf, and it became a habit for both of us to speak through his daughter. "Nini, have you had a good day with your *baba*?" I would ask her.

"Tell your sister that we've had a good day," he would reply, and even later, when Nini was older and chose not to acknowledge either of our existences, we would still use the girl as an intermediary to exchange words.

I never saw Nini's father play the flute. He had a gaunt look by the time I entered high school: Where there had once been a smile, there was now only a distracted look, his hair gray before its time, his back beginning to stoop. He spent less time with Nini then—the girl must have been accepted by her grandparents, as a few times I saw them walk her to a preschool. I wondered what he would do with his time now that Nini was in school. When I walked past their flat on the way to Professor Shan's, I studied the green wooden door, the paint peeling off at the edge, a child's doodle by the doorknob. I imagined the world behind the door, what Nini's father, when he unlocked the door, would have to brace himself to face. At night I tried to remember his face and his voice, but hard as I tried, I was never able to recall enough details to make him a real person.

On an early November afternoon, when I was locking my bicycle in front of Professor Shan's building, Nini's father appeared quietly from around the corner.

"How are you, Nini's Papa?" I said when he did not speak. "Did Nini have a good day?"

An old woman exited the building and gave a meaningful glance toward him before calling out to her grandchildren to come in and do homework. In a low voice, Nini's papa asked if he could talk with me for a few minutes.

I followed him to the small garden. It was one of those mild autumn days, the last before the harsh winter would begin. The sun, half setting, was pinkish orange in the cloudless western sky, which was warm orange and pink and magenta.

The man stopped by a trellis of wisteria, the flowers long gone, the last leaves hanging on to the vine. "I want to let you know that I will be leaving the neighborhood tomorrow."

I nodded, as if I had known it all along and was not surprised by the news. The streetlights, whitest blue, blinked to life with a collective buzzing.

"Nini's mama and I signed the divorce papers today," he said.

I had known Nini's mother for as long as I could remember. She was fifteen years older, ordinary in all ways but for her marriage. She was too old to be part of my generation, but not old enough to become one of those ubiquitous women we called "auntie," who claimed the right to yell at any child from the neighborhood, so our paths had never crossed. It occurred to me that I had never, despite all the time I spent imagining his life, thought of her as someone dear to him. I wondered if she had been forced to divorce him by her parents, or if she had, at long last, joined the world in condemning him as a useless man.

"I was waiting for you to come back from school," he said. "You've always been kind to me, and I want to have a proper farewell."

"Where will you be tomorrow?"

He looked lost at the question, and then said that there were ways for a man to manage.

"Will you still try to get into the conservatory?"

Perhaps he would, he said, but such things were not up to him. One should not give up, I said eagerly, quoting an old saying about fate allowing what is allowed, but it is one's responsibility to fight for what one wants before it's decided by fate. He smiled, and I recognized the derision. I must have sounded childish to him, but when he spoke, his derision was directed at himself. He had fought more than his share of fights against fate, he said; perhaps he should be a warrior rather than a flutist.

I tried to find other words of comfort, but it was enough of an effort to hold back my tears. He was about to say something when a sanitation worker, sweeping a pebble path nearby, began to whistle a love song from a Romanian film from the fifties. We both turned to look at the man. I wondered, for a moment, if my father, mopping the floor of the empty department store in the middle of the night, hummed old love songs to himself.

"Will you let me know when you get into the conservatory?" I asked after the sweeper had moved on.

Nini's father raised his eyes as if startled by the question. Professor Shan is waiting to tutor me, I said.

He hesitated and held out a hand to shake mine. I wished I had more to say to him, and he to me. I took his hand; as soon as our fingers touched we both let go. "Farewell, Nini's Sister," he said.

"Farewell, Nini's Papa," I said.

Neither of us moved. A bicycle bell chimed and was followed by other chimes, none of them urgent—a child must have been walking past the bicycle shed and felt the urge to test all the bells. "Farewell, Nini's Papa," I said again.

He looked at me, and I wondered if he would come closer, and if I should push him away if he did. I wanted to ask him if he would miss me as I would him; I wanted to ask him if away from this sad neighborhood we could see each other again. But the love that was not yet love, the questions that were not asked thus never answered—in retrospect, I wonder if it was all mere fantasy in a lonely teenager's heart. But there were things to be accounted for: the farewell that a man thought necessary for a girl he barely knew, the silence while listening to a stranger's whistling, the hand that was raised to wipe my tears but that had paused midair and then patted my head. Be good, he said, and walked away into the dark shadows of the trees.

I was no more than ten minutes late when I got to Professor Shan's flat. She opened the door before I knocked and looked at me quizzically. There was a traffic accident in Peace Road, I said, and she led me into the flat without acknowledging my lie. When she turned the pages to the place we had ended the day before, I stared at the yellow tassel on the bookmark. The man's fingers had been cold to the touch; I clasped my hands together, and my palms felt feverish.

Professor Shan stopped reading. "You seem to have trouble focusing today," she said, and replaced the bookmark in the book, putting it back where it belonged on top of a leather trunk.

I mumbled, but she waved in dismissal and told me to help myself to the fruits and biscuits she had laid out on the table. She walked to the only window in the room and parted the curtains. I wondered if she spent her days, when I was not around, studying the world from her fifth-floor window; and if she had caught me talking to Nini's papa, on that day or previously.

"When one is young, one thinks of love as the most important thing," Professor Shan said, still facing the window. "It's natural if you think so, though I do hope you've learned a few things from the books I've read to you. One could waste one's life pursuing a flower in the mirror, a moon in the river, but that is not what I want to see happen to you."

I looked at the back of her head, the impeccable bun that was pulled a little higher than an old woman's, so that she looked like a ballerina, with her straight back and long pale neck, and when she turned around, for a moment her face looked cold and marble-like in the light. "The moment you admit someone into your heart you make yourself a fool," she said. "When you desire nothing, nothing will defeat you. Do you understand, Moyan?"

6.

I was caught by Lieutenant Wei one night reading *Lady Chatterley's Lover*. I was close to finishing the novel; perhaps one more night would do. I had bracketed every sex scene and marked it with an arrow in the margin of the page, though I was not enjoying the novel myself. Duty propelled me to continue reading and, on top of that, curiosity about what Professor Shan might say about each of the characters. Toward the end I was overtaken by fatigue. Perhaps that was what made me less alert to the creaking of the barracks door. When Lieutenant Wei lifted the quilt from my head, I had barely enough time to hide the book under the makeshift pillow of bundled clothes.

"What are you hiding from me?" Lieutenant Wei asked in a low voice.

The early December night air was cold on my warm face, which must have looked flushed in the glare of her flashlight. I fumbled under the bundled clothes without lifting my head from the pillow. When I found the right book I raised it to the light. Lieutenant Wei grabbed it and told me to get dressed and report to her room in two minutes.

When I was certain that she had gone back to her room, I checked under the clothes again. Jie's book was safe there, and I decided that I would smuggle it back to her first thing in the morning.

The confiscated book—a collection of Lawrence's short stories—was lying open on Lieutenant Wei's desk when I entered her room. She signaled for me to sit down on her chair. "What's the book about?" she asked.

"A lot of things, Lieutenant."

"Like what?"

"Men and women, Lieutenant," I said. "And children."

"What about them?"

What about them? I thought about the question and wondered what kind of punishment Lieutenant Wei would give me. The only time I had come to her notice was when I scored perfect marks during shooting practice. It was one of those useless talents you don't ask for in life. Still, at practice I aimed and pulled the trigger with the utmost concentration, my mind calm; the caretaking of the rifle—disassembling it and laying the parts at perfect angles on a sheet of newspaper, then cleaning them with a soft rag and putting them back together with precision, all while the training officer timed us on his stopwatch—gave me immense satisfaction.

"Are they romantic stories?" Lieutenant Wei asked.

I would not call them romantic, I replied. What would you call them, then? she asked, and I said they were stories about mad people.

"Are they worth breaking the rule of internal affairs?"

"Not really, Lieutenant."

"Are you lying?"

"No, Lieutenant," I said.

Lieutenant Wei picked up the book, ready to tear the pages. I wished I could plead with her that the book was a present from a dear friend, but the truth was, I had always known that I would be punished for having it: Apart from the volumes of *Essential English*, which I had little interest in reading, Professor Shan had never allowed me to take a book away from her flat; I had stolen the stories of Lawrence when I decided not to go back.

"I can see you're lying," Lieutenant Wei said. She closed the book and studied the cover. "Do you want the book back?"

"No, Lieutenant."

"Why not?"

"They are unworthy stories, Lieutenant," I said.

She stared at me, and I tried to look as blank as I imagined I had in front of Professor Shan when I told her, a few days after the departure of Nini's father, that my schoolwork no longer allowed me to spend time with her. For the briefest moment Professor Shan had looked disappointed, or perhaps even hurt. One has to do what she thinks suits her best, she'd said, and I mumbled that the coursework was heavier than I'd expected. I had wished to leave her with the impression that I would return once the summer holidays began, but she must have seen through me. She told me to wait and then left the room. I still cannot understand what I did next; I quietly took one of the story collections of Lawrence—the one we had just finished—and slipped it into my book satchel. A moment later, Professor Shan returned with a bar of Lux soap, which had just begun to be imported, the most expensive and most luxurious soap. It was wrapped in a piece of peach-colored paper with a beautiful woman printed on it, and I recognized the fragrance that I had always connected with her flat. Be good to yourself, she said, and before I could think of words of gratitude or apology, she waved for me to leave and told me to close the door behind me.

The soap and the book had traveled with me to the army. At night I slept with them, sometimes opening the book to a random page and imagining Professor Shan's voice reading it. I had seen her around the neighborhood a few times after that, and she acted as if we had never known each other. I wondered then—and wondered again in the army—why she did not confront me about the stolen book. Could it be that she had stopped reading the stories after I left, so never realized her loss?

When Lieutenant Wei asked me if I was certain that I did not need the book, I replied that as far as I cared, the book could be tossed into the garbage can at this very moment.

Lieutenant Wei said that in that case, she would keep the book for herself. I wanted to remind her that she did not read English. "Who knows? Maybe one day I can learn English, too, so I can read the book myself," she said, as if she had read my mind. "What do you think? Will I be able to read the book after I learn English?"

"I don't know, Lieutenant," I said.

"How long did you study English before you could read the book?"

The digital clock on her desk said quarter to midnight. I wondered how long she would keep me. A few years, I said, and shifted in the chair.

"A few years is not that long," Lieutenant Wei said. "Maybe you can start teaching me now. Will I be able to read a little English by the time you leave?"

I did not know what kind of trap she was setting. A few of the girls from the platoon had become friendly with Lieutenant Wei, but I did not see the point of befriending an officer.

"I've had reports that you have received letters from your parents, is that right?" Lieutenant Wei asked.

"Yes, Lieutenant," I replied. My father had written twice, both letters brief, saying that he and my mother were well and that they hoped I was, too.

"Why are you unhappy?"

"Unhappy, Lieutenant?"

"What's bothering you?"

"I don't understand the question, Lieutenant."

"Did you break up with your boyfriend?" Lieutenant Wei said.

"I have never had a boyfriend, Lieutenant," I said. I would rather she had ripped my book and sent me back to the barracks with a week of cleaning duty at the pigsties.

"When I enlisted," Lieutenant Wei said, "my boyfriend saw me off at the train station and then sent a letter to the training camp to break up with me. The first letter I got in the camp. I was much younger than you are now. I was fourteen and a half. He was eighteen, and he did not have the courage to say it to my face. You think it's the end of the world, but it is not. The army is a good place to sort these things out."

I wondered if other girls, for different misdemeanors, were kept hostage at odd hours in this room and informed of the love history of Lieutenant Wei. It was ludicrous of her, I decided, to think that any unhappiness could be explained by a breakup; more ludicrous if she thought she could, by recounting her own story of triumph over heartbreak, lessen other people's pain.

"Apparently you have no interest in this discussion about feelings," Lieutenant Wei said.

"I do my best to summarize my feelings in my ideological reports, Lieutenant," I said. Every Sunday night, we read our weekly reports at the squad meeting. I always began mine that in the past week I had kept up my faith in Communism and my love of our motherland; I filled the rest of the page with military and political slogans that not even Major Tang could find fault with. I had been criticized by our squad leader for being insincere in my reports, so I learned to add personal touches. "In the past week I have continued my efforts to understand the invincibility of Marxism," and "In the coming week I will work on *The Communist Manifesto.*"

Lieutenant Wei sighed. "I'm not talking about the feelings in your ideological reports."

"I don't have much feeling about most people, Lieutenant," I said. There had not been a boyfriend and perhaps there never would be one—the man who had not wiped away my tears under the wisteria trellis had later done so, repeatedly, when my memories were revised into dreams, and he who had chosen not to claim the love had left no space for others to claim it: In high school there had been a boy or two, like there is a boy or two for most girls during those years, but I had returned their letters in new envelopes, never adding a line, thinking that would be enough to end what should not have been started.

Without a word Lieutenant Wei put the book in her drawer. I wondered how Professor Shan would have felt had she known that her beloved book had fallen into the hands of someone who, in her mind, was ill-educated. I felt a slight, vindictive joy, directed both at Professor Shan and at myself.

I saluted Lieutenant Wei's back when I was dismissed, but before I opened her door she told me in an urgent tone to come back. We stood in front of her window, huge flakes of snow falling in the windless night. In a hushed voice, as if it were a secret that we needed to keep between us, she said without turning to me, "You know, I've never seen real snow."

7.

The snow continued falling the next morning, bringing a festive mood to the camp. It was the first snow many of the locals had ever seen, and the weatherman had forecast a record storm, more snow than in one hundred and twenty years, if not longer. The officers' orders came as though from a faraway land, their shrill whistles making our military routines muffled. At formation drill, we marched with less resolve, the ground becoming more and more plush by the hour. A huge snowman was erected in front of the mess hall by the cooking squad, his straw hat almost touching the eaves; a squad of smaller snowmen was installed next to the pigsties, in perfect formation.

The wind picked up in the evening, and by the next day the snow was more of a concern than a marvel. It did not stop until the end of the third day. The temperature had fallen sharply. There was no heating in the camp, and most of the pipes were frozen. The cooking squad, who kept the big stove burning, managed to have running water in the kitchen, and each of us was rationed a basin of water. In the mornings we broke the ice on the surface to clean our faces.

Ping was the first in our squad to develop frostbite, which in a day or two affected all of us, on our cheeks and ears, hands and feet. None of us, after days of marching in the snow, had dry shoes or socks.

The snowstorm had turned us quiet; talking seemed to require extra energy that we did not possess. On the evening of the third day, while we were waiting for the dinner whistle, Ping reread her father's letter from the previous week—the snowstorm had stopped the post, and the weekly letter from Ping's father, precise as clockwork, had not come—and announced that she was not crying not because there was nothing to cry about, but because tears would do more damage to her already swollen cheeks. Nan smiled, then sang us a folk song in which a girl named Little Cabbage loses her mother during her infancy and goes on to suffer a long and painful life under the reign of a cruel stepmother and spoiled half brother.

"We Little Cabbages should unite and take our fates into our own hands," Ping said after Nan finished the song. "I have an idea: We should pair up and share beds at night."

The most miserable time of the past few days had been crawling under the ice-cold quilt. Most of us went to bed wearing layers of clothes. Still, a small shift in position would cause one's arm or leg to come into contact with the cold sheet; we dared not move in our sleep, and as a result woke up with cramped muscles.

Ping began telling a story that she said she had read in *Reader's Digest*. A priest, having arrived in the Canadian wilderness, was assigned a young local girl as a guide for his journey to his post, and when the two were stranded in a shed by a snowstorm, the girl discovered that she had forgotten to bring a flint and tinder. At night, it was so cold that they were in danger of freezing to death, so the girl suggested that they sleep together to keep each other warm. "Of course the priest, who had never been close to a young woman, fell in love when the girl wrapped them up together in a blanket. He never reached his destination but married the girl. Years later, she told him that she had lied—a local girl, she would never have forgotten the flint and tinder," Ping said, for a moment looking alive and happy. "Imagine that!"

Lieutenant Wei might not allow us to share beds, our squad leader said. Why not? Ping asked, and said that Lieutenant Hong had begun sleeping in Lieutenant Wei's bed. "They're cold, too."

"How did this discovery occur?" Nan asked, and winked at me as if she and I had access to some secret knowledge that was denied Ping. She was on the way to the restroom a couple of nights ago, Ping said, when she saw Lieutenant Hong sneak into Lieutenant Wei's room. "They didn't see me, of course," Ping said. "But think about it. It makes sense, no? Two bodies are better than one in this cold weather."

Two girls whose beds were across the aisle nodded at each other and asked the squad leader to pair them up. The squad leader said that she would have to report to Lieutenant Wei, and five minutes later returned with the official permission. Should we draw lots every night? Ping asked, becoming more excited about her idea. We could spend the day guessing whom we would sleep with at night, she said; suspense would make the time go faster.

Nan watched the squad with amusement. I waited, and when she did not say anything, I said that I could not bed with another person.

"Why?" asked Ping.

I would not be able to sleep, I said.

"But think about how warm it would be," Ping said. "One can't possibly sleep well in this cold."

I shook my head, and said that under no condition would I share a bed with another person.

"You're aware"—the squad leader looked at the other girls before turning to me—"that if we've made the decision collectively, you should honor it."

I could feel the other girls' animosity. I had made myself into a hedgehog, with its many arrows, which could neither protect itself nor frighten its enemies, sticking out ridiculously.

"I'll sleep alone, then, too," Nan said.

"But it's not fair," Ping said. "I don't understand why some people feel they have the right to be special."

People make fools of themselves in this or that way—Professor Shan's words came back to me later that night, when I tried to stay still under the ice-cold quilt; *neither you nor I are exempt,* she had said, *but we do our best, do you understand?*

The snow stopped the next day. The city, having no means to deal with the snow, had been paralyzed by the storm. The afternoon drills were called off, and when we arrived at the city center, with shovels and pickaxes, most of the roads were covered by frozen snow that had been packed hard by wheels and feet. "Soldiers," announced a general who drove past us in a Jeep with Major Tang, speaking through a megaphone. "You've been fed by the army, and now it's time to prove your value to the army."

The city, where proprietors of small shops called out to passersby for business, and peddlers fought to sell fruits and other goods, as I had found out during my only Sunday visit, was vacant. The streetlamps were scarcely lit, perhaps to conserve energy. A few early stars flickered in the sky, which was a smooth dome of deep blue. Once in a while a bus, empty and lit dimly from inside, rattled past us, and we would stop our pickaxes and shovels to watch the wheels leave hard tracks in the newly loosened snow.

"What do you mean you can't finish?" Major Tang yelled at Lieutenant Wei, when she reported to him, an hour into cleaning, that she worried we had been assigned too much. The night wind cut into our cheeks as if with a thin blade, but more dispiriting than the pain was the endless road. "The word *impossible* does not exist in the military dictionary. Now, Lieutenant, do you and your soldiers have the courage to face the challenge from nature?"

"Yes, Major," Lieutenant Wei replied.

Major Tang told us that dinner would be ready only when the road was cleared. "Now let's sing a song to boost our morale," he said, and ordered us to sing "The Marching Song of the Red Women Warriors."

An hour and then two hours later, the platoon still saw no hope of finishing the road. Ping threw her shovel onto the hard snow and began to cry. Our squad leader tried to hush her, but halfway through her sentence, she was choked by tears, too. I leaned on the handle of the pickax and watched a few of my squad mates join in the crying, their world complicated only by the most superficial dilemmas.

Lieutenant Wei came toward our squad, and without a word grabbed the pickax from my hands and lifted it over her head. The ground shook when the pickax hit the hard snow, and more girls stopped shoveling. Lieutenant Wei looked possessed, her jaws tight, her arms brandishing the pickax with mad force. Ping stopped crying and, shivering, hid behind another girl. Nan shook her head before picking up the shovel again, trying to pry loose the snow that Lieutenant Wei's pickax had cracked.

It was after midnight when we returned to the barracks. Nan said that she had changed her mind, and she wanted a bedmate too. "I won't do it," I said when my squad mates looked at me, and I said it again to Lieutenant Wei. The lights-out bugle blew, the drawn-out tune seeming to take forever to reach the end. *She had no great desire to live,* I remembered from one of Lawrence's stories, underlined twice with red pen by Professor Shan. I wondered if she had thought that she, too, lacked a great desire to live, but that must not be the case: People who do not cling to life perish, one way or another. As far as I could see, Professor Shan would live forever in her flat, watching with all-seeing eyes those who peopled her books; perhaps she was thinking of me at this very moment, shaking her head at my follies.

I climbed into bed before Lieutenant Wei left the barracks, and turned my back to my squad.

8.

In late January, three days after the Lunar New Year, I left home to return to the army. I did not tell my parents that there was still another week until the holiday leave ended, nor did I inform anyone at the camp of my decision to return early.

"Would you like me to see you off at the train station?" my mother asked when I came into her bedroom to say good-bye. She was leaning against a stack of pillows on her bed, an old novel, its pages yellow and fragile, resting on her chest as if her hands were no longer strong enough to lift the book. She had become less careful with her looks, strands of hair going astray, pajamas worn all day long where before she had always dressed herself at dawn;

she looked frailer, too. On the day I returned from the army, she had seemed happy to see me.

There was no need, I replied. My father, standing in the doorway with a duffel bag in his hand, waited for us to finish our farewell. In the duffel bag he had packed, heads to ends, two dozen pickled eggs, wrapped up neatly in four columns of newspaper. I had told him not to bother with the eggs, but he had insisted that I looked ill-fed.

"So, you are doing well in the army?" my mother asked.

I said that all was well. I had noticed, upon returning, that my mother would sometimes make an effort to chat with me, but her interest was fleeting, and she was easily tired or bored by me; so eventually we settled into the old mode, conversations between us polite and formal. My father, too, seemed to cling to my presence more than before: In the mornings when he returned home from the night shift, he would pick up two pieces of fried bread from the street peddler and watch me eat them before they turned cold. The previous day he insisted on accompanying me when I went to the stores to buy a few things for the camp, looking away when I asked the clerk for sanitary napkins.

Had they missed me while I was gone? I could not tell. My parents had always been quiet around each other, simple household communications transmitted not by words: My father, upon returning from work in the morning, would brew the tea and then hand a cup to my mother, who would by then have groomed and dressed herself; when breakfast was ready, he'd place her plate first on the table, and she would join us without having to be reminded, though she rarely touched the food. My father would nap from mid-morning to early afternoon, and my mother left the flat when he slept. I never knew where she went, but she always came back and rested in bed when my father got up to finish the day's chores. When she became weaker, she no longer took long walks when my father napped. They must have talked to each other, but mostly there was silence between them, a comfort more than a reason for resentment. I believe, to this day, that despite its cruelty, fate granted them the best companions they could have asked for in a marriage: They knew what they needed from each other, and they did not request what they could not have.

My mother told me to come closer to her bed. My father nodded at me in a pleading way, and she told me to bend over so she could have a good look at my face. She touched my cheeks where the frostbitten skin was now puffy and tender, with a yellowish hue, which gave my face the look of a rotten apple. "Look what they did to you," my mother said, as if she had noticed it for the first time.

The frostbite is getting better, I said, and then asked my father if it was time for us to go.

"Things get better. Or else they get worse," my mother said. "You should learn to take care of your face. You are prettier than you let yourself believe."

I don't mind looking ugly, I said.

"You should know that you can't possibly be ugly, because you are my daughter." She was almost inaudible.

Later I wondered if she meant that she would not have adopted a homely-looking baby, or if, perhaps, on a whim, she wanted to claim my blood connection to her. She seemed to have other things to say, but I said good-bye, and she only laughed lightly. Typical for a young girl to be in a hurry, she said, and then waved for my father and me to leave her alone.

Neither my father nor I talked on the bus ride to the train station. He looked older, moving more slowly than I remembered. Men his age should be thinking about retirement, but I knew he could not retire before I could support them. I felt guilty about escaping home and leaving the burden of my mother to him. How was he managing while I was not home? I asked him as we waited in the long line at the boarding entrance. He seemed surprised by my question. Nothing much to manage, he replied, and said that things were as they always were. This talk, neither here nor there, left us embarrassed, and I could see his relief when we finally boarded the train. He lifted my suitcase to the luggage rack and carefully stored the duffel bag with the eggs under my seat. Be well, then, he said, shaking my hand, again solemnly. I told him not to wait for the departure of the train, knowing he would not obey my wish. When the whistle blew, he stepped off the train and waved behind the gray and grimy window when the train inched forward, and I waved back once, thinking perhaps we were the loneliest family in the world because we were meant to be that way.

No one questioned my lie when I arrived. The camp was empty, no rushing steps on the staircase for the early morning training, no singing contest before meals so that Major Tang could determine which platoon would enter the mess hall first. The senior officers, who had families at the compound across the street, showed up once a day, and only when they were present did the junior officers—Lieutenant Wei and the other two platoon leaders, the company supply officer, and the clerk—assume a military appearance.

I began to eat with the cooking squad in the kitchen so that the officers would not be reminded of my presence. The conscripts, boys my age or younger, had joined the army to seek a future that was otherwise not available to them. I knew there were girls who were particularly close to the cooking squad—whether for friendship or an extra bite or two I could not decide. Before, I had talked to the conscripts only when our squad was on cooking duty, so I worried that they would resent a stranger, but they seemed happy that I—or perhaps any girl for that matter—chose to eat with them. They told jokes, making fun of people that I had never met, or of one another, and I tried my best to smile, since I knew they were doing it for my sake.

After each meal, I followed the two conscripts on duty to the pigsties, and then to the vegetable garden, which did not require a lot of work at this time of the year. None of us had things to rush to, so we made the outings last as long as we could. The boys took turns pushing the handcart, slowly so the slopping swill would not spill out of the buckets; at the beginning I asked to help, but they were gallant and never let me. Their jokes continued on these trips, but soon bits and pieces of their secrets surfaced. It did not take me long to figure out that each of them was in love with a girl from the company, but theirs was the most hopeless kind of love, as they would continue their lives in the army, and we would be gone by summer. When the boys began to confess, I did not ask questions or make comments; all they needed was someone not in their position to listen to them, so I did. None of the girls being dreamed about was me, though the conscripts did not seem to sense any awkwardness in confessing to a girl they had collectively dismissed as undesirable.

I wished this life could go on forever. When the swill was poured into the trough, white steam rose into the chilly air, and the pigs, already snorting with impatience, pushed against one another—but sooner or later, satisfied by a good meal, they would calm down. The conscripts cleaned the trough and then the sties, and the pigs found their favorite spots to lie in the sun. The pigs' needs were simple, their happiness easily granted; the boys were in pain, but still they joked, their dreams laughable to their companions and themselves alike. If I climbed atop the low brick wall of the pigsties, I could see the shooting range, and the hill beyond that was turning yellowish green. The earth in the vegetable garden softened every day, and soon another planting season would begin, but when harvesttime came, we girls would be back in the civilian world. If I focused on the joyful squeals of the pigs, I could pretend my parents did not exist; in the sun-filled vegetable garden, who were Professor Shan and Nini's father but phantoms in one's fantasies?

The night before the other girls returned from leave, Lieutenant Wei found me in the barracks. Apart from brief greetings, she had left me alone the past few days, and I wondered if my early return was an inconvenience. Sometimes I could hear, from the hallway, her voice along with the other officers. One night a few male officers from the boys' companies had visited, and their laughing and singing had not ended until after midnight.

"So, I see you're getting yourself ready ahead of time," Lieutenant Wei said. She examined the barracks, which I had been cleaning daily.

"Yes, Lieutenant."

"Did you have a good leave? Was your family well?"

"Yes, Lieutenant."

"Why did you come back early, then?"

"I misremembered the date, Lieutenant," I said.

Perhaps I was disappointing her with my insistence, but disappointment can occur only where there is something to hope for in the first place. I had no hope to offer her.

"I see that you've spent a lot of time with the cooking squad," she said.

"They are kind to let me help, Lieutenant."

"But I want to remind you to keep things simple regarding them."

"I don't understand, Lieutenant."

"Of course you do," she said. "Don't you know that you do a bad job acting dumb?"

"I consider my behavior soldierly around the cooking squad, Lieutenant."

"You don't have much feeling toward those poor boys, is that what you're saying? To tell you the truth, you're not my concern. You could suffer the most horrible thing and I wouldn't give a damn. But have you ever thought about the boys? They won't have your future. When you're back in the city they will still be here. You don't mess with other people's lives and then disappear. But how can you understand other people's pain, you city girl, full of yourself?"

We had been polite around each other since the snowstorm, and I thought we would go on maintaining that formality. If the boys of the cooking squad were in pain, I was not the one who'd caused it, I wanted to defend myself, but I knew Lieutenant Wei was talking about herself more than the conscripts. I did not give my future much thought, though other girls made it obvious, with their talk about college life and occasionally about going abroad, that we girls had futures worthy of our suffering in the army. I wondered if I could make Lieutenant Wei feel better by telling her about my parents, whom I had run away from, or about Professor Shan, whom I longed to visit again but for reasons I did not understand could not allow myself to, or Nini's father, whom I would never see again. But animosity is easier to live with than sympathy, and indifference leaves less damage in the long run.

9.

In early April we set out on a monthlong march across Mount Dabie, hailed by Major Tang as the revolutionary cradle of our Communist nation. The expedition, planned to boost our Communist morale, was nevertheless a welcome alternative to our daily drills, and to the long hours we spent sitting in ideological seminars.

Never would I have a more memorable time than the month I spent in the mountains, though I wonder, when I say this, if it appears so only because it is our nature to make a heaven out of places to which we can never return. But if I close my eyes and hum the songs that we sang on the road—"The Red Azaleas," "The Warsaw Marching Song," "The Song of the Communist Youth," "Under the Shining North Star"—I can see us again, lining up on the first day at the drill grounds, waiting for the lorries to arrive and transport us from the camp to an army depot in the mountains. *Don't we look like giant snails bearing our homes on our backs?* I remember Ping's comment—each of us carried, bundled tightly in a plastic sheet, a bedroll and a set of uniforms for changing, a heavy raincoat, two pairs of shoes, a satchel with towels, a cup, a toothbrush and toothpaste, and a canteen, all arranged as compactly as possible so the items would not become more of a burden than they were. Turtles, Nan corrected Ping, and went on to tell a joke about turtles, though hard as I try now, I can remember only the laughter around her after she finished the joke.

We were jostled in the covered lorries, for hours it seemed, on the winding mountain road, and our excitement was slowly replaced by exhaustion. On a particularly uneven stretch of road, Nan stood up from where she was sitting on her bedroll, and worked loose the rope that bound the two roof tarps together. Lieutenant Wei, who was sitting at the other end, ordered her to sit down. Nan looked out the gap for a long moment and then retied the tarps as best she could. "If the lorry missed a turn, we would die together," she said to no one in particular, and began to sing in English: *If you miss the train I'm on, you will know that I am gone. You can hear the whistle blow a hundred miles.*

Her voice was more sorrowful than ever, though there was a smile on her face. Lieutenant Wei seemed to be as stricken as we were, even though she could not understand what Nan was singing. When the song ended, we listened to the tree branches scratching the tarp and pebbles bumping off the wheels of the lorry. I wondered why sadness seemed to roll off Nan as raindrops roll off a lotus leaf, without leaving any trace; I wondered how one could acquire as unaffected a soul as she had.

We stayed in the army depot that night, the last time during the journey we would be sleeping in bunk beds—later we would sleep on the unpaved dirt floors of village schools, and in the meeting halls of People's Communes from the fifties that were no longer in use, and in the field, our whole squad squeezed together in a small patch of space. I would soon learn to let my defenses down, but on that first night, when the mountain air chilled our bones and made our teeth chatter, I again refused to share a bed with a squad mate.

At three o'clock in the morning, I was shaken awake for my night-watch duty. I wrapped myself in a quilt and went into the yard, and took my position under the brick wall. The night was clear and cold, the stars so close that one could almost reach them by raising a hand. An owl hooted and was answered by another, and I remembered the story—one of the few my father had told me—about the owls that carried the message of death: They would spend each night counting the hairs in a person's eyebrows, and when they finished counting at daybreak, that person would die. When the owl hooted again, I shivered and rubbed my eyebrows, as my father had done for me when I was little, so the owls cannot count your eyebrows, he had said, his gentle touch on my eyebrows a comfort.

Jie, the other girl on night duty, shone her flashlight at me from where she was sitting at the foot of a tree. I clicked on my flashlight and waved back. A minute later she trotted over. "Are you cold?" she said.

"Yes."

"Are you afraid?"

"No."

"Are you lonely?"

Jie arranged her quilt around her and said she would sit with me, and I did not remind her that, if we were discovered, we would both get into trouble. We sat back to back, leaning onto each other, both huddled with our machine guns, though we had not been supplied with ammunition. Jie had behaved casually around me since the winter, and I wondered if it was natural for friendship to be formed out of shared secrets; she was the closest friend I had ever had.

"If some bad guys came, we could do nothing," Jie said.

"We'd whistle and then run," I said, searching my quilt for the whistle I had been supplied along with the gun.

Jie laughed lightly and asked me if I realized the irony of our hugging guns that would not shoot. I don't understand, I said, though I did; Jie was fond of telling me off-color jokes, as if my reading *Lady Chatterley's Lover* for her had qualified me to hear all the secrets she said she could not share with the others.

"Have you ever been in love?" Jie said.

"No," I said.

"Sometimes you miss someone so much that all of a sudden you can't remember how he looks or sounds," she said, and asked if I had ever experienced that.

I thought about Nini's father, whose face I could call up if I wanted to, though I rarely did; I thought about Professor Shan, whose voice came more easily to me than her face.

"My boyfriend and I—we did it in the winter."

"Like they did in the novel?" I asked.

Jie told me not to believe anything I'd read in that book. "You think you will remember every moment, every detail, but the truth is, I can't remember much about it. Can't even remember how long we were at it."

How could one forget such things? I could recall many details of the afternoons in Professor Shan's flat, the last sunshine of the day slanting in from the window, her fingers slowly turning the pages, a cricket chirping from under one of the old trunks; I had not forgotten a single word that Nini's father had said to me on the night of his divorce.

"Let me ask you—if two people love each other, doesn't it mean that every minute of one's life matters to the other?"

I had never loved someone, I said, so I would not know. Jie said that in that case, she was asking for directions from a blind person. Her boyfriend was not interested in her life in the army; he saw it as a nuisance that kept them apart for a year. "But won't you remember tonight fifty years from now?" Jie asked. "I wish he'd remember these things with me. Two heads are better than one."

"In bed," I said. Jie laughed and said she did not know I could be naughty. It was a pity that I was in his place, I said, and Jie told me not to make fun of her. I was sad that she did not understand I meant it: She and I would drift apart once we left the army; we were not close, not even real friends. I would not be the one to carry the memory of tonight for her.

I wished her boyfriend were here; I wished too that someone other than Jie were next to me, someone who one day would share the memory of the mountains with me. The wish, illogical as it was, persisted into the following days when we marched in the mountains. It was sunny in those days, the sky blue, red azaleas wild on the cliffs. If one looked up, one could see the long line of green figures ahead, disappearing and then reappearing along with the winding road, and when one quieted her steps momentarily, the singing of the companies behind would drift uphill. In the valleys, there were creeks, and sometimes a river, and there was always a lone fisherman sitting in the shade of his wide-brimmed straw hat, and a long-legged white egret nearby, neither disturbing the other. When the mountains were replaced by rolling hills we knew that we were approaching a village: First came the fields of purple milk vetch that unfolded like giant rugs, white and yellow butterflies busying themselves in and out of the lavender blossoms; closer to the village, there were rice paddies, and water buffaloes with barefooted boys sitting astride them; once in a while a sow would spread herself across the narrow road that led into the village, a litter of piglets pushing against her. Small children chased after us, calling us Auntie Soldiers and begging for candies. Even the youngest ones knew not to eat them right away—they gingerly licked the candies and then wrapped them up so they would last days, perhaps even weeks. Feeling guiltily privileged compared to the children, we competed to offer them treats, but sooner or later we would leave them behind and march on until dusk fell, when smoke could be seen rising from the field kitchen in the valley.

Walking comforted me. I marched alone and did not join the

chorus when the platoon was singing; here in the mountains, walking was the only thing required of me, and for hours I would be left undisturbed, my mind empty of troubling thoughts. Never before had I loved the world as I did then, the sunshine and the spring blossoms, the new trees in the woods, and the lizards in the grass. Even the daily ritual of blister popping—in our satchels each of us carried a sewing needle, and in the evenings the brigade doctor would pass out cotton balls soaked in alcohol so we could sanitize the needles and pop the blisters on our feet—brought me an odd sense of liberation. There was a joy in knowing the realness of one's body: the sting when a blister was pierced; the heaviness in one's arms where the blood was pulled down by its own weight after a day of marching; the exhaustion in one's limbs lying down on the floor of a village school; the moment of uncontrollable shivering when one left the cluster of warm bodies for night-watch duty, the coldness seeping in.

10.

We arrived at a town called Seven-Mile Plain after one of the longest marching days, covering thirty-two kilometers—across two rivers, over mountains, and through valleys. It was the fifteenth day, halfway through our journey, and when we limped into the town's only elementary school, the full moon was already in the eastern sky, golden with a red hue. The cooking squad had set out in the schoolyard one of the most extravagant meals we would have on our journey: stir-fried eels, marinated pork with snow peas, tofu and vegetable soup, and, to our surprise, a bottle of local beer for each of us.

In a very long toast, Major Tang summarized every day of the journey, squinting at times, trying to read the map he held. Is he already drunk? Ping mumbled, eyeing the basins of food on the ground that would soon have a layer of fat congealing on their surfaces.

A free night was announced after dinner, and we were told that bedtime would be called an hour later. That generosity, along with the beer from dinner, created a festive mood. Girls walked in twos and threes in the schoolyard, which was a sizable plot that went uphill until it reached a fence. Locust trees, decades old, surrounded it, with clusters of cream-colored blossoms hanging heavily between branches, their sweet fragrance growing more intense as the night progressed. Under one of the oldest trees a group of girls sang a love song from an old movie.

I walked to the school gate and was disappointed to discover that it was padlocked. Before I turned around, someone stepped from the dark shadow of the high wall and called to me.

It was a boy in uniform, and he asked me if I knew Nan. I thought of denying it, but he said he had seen me at drills and knew that I was in Nan's squad. He told me his name and which company he was from, and then asked me if I could pass a letter to Nan.

"Where are you staying?" I asked, and the boy said that his company was stationed for the night in the middle school across the street.

"And you can leave the schoolyard freely?" I said.

The boy smiled and said he had jumped the wall. I thought about him outside the school gate, waiting to catch a glimpse of Nan. When he asked me again if I could pass on his letter, I said that Nan had too many admirers to care about a letter from a stranger. The boy appeared crestfallen, and I refrained from asking him why he had never imagined other people falling in love with the girl of his dreams. "Here," he said, passing a green bottle through the gap in the metal gate. "You can have this if you help me."

He had put a bottle of local yam liquor in my hand. Under the crudely drawn trademark of a phoenix was a line that proclaimed it the fiercest drink west of the Huai River, with a 65 percent alcohol concentration.

"I only drank a little," said the boy eagerly. "It's almost full to the top."

"What do I do with it? Pour it on my blisters?"

He seemed perplexed at my joke, and I wondered if his courage had come from the drink, which had made him as much a fool as his love had. I did not know why I had accepted his present. I had given my ration of beer to a conscript in the cooking squad—I had never touched alcohol in my life, nor had I ever seen it around our flat. I took a stroll around the schoolyard, and when I couldn't locate Nan, I sat down in the farthest corner of the yard, under an old locust tree, its bulging root the perfect seat. *What dissolves one's sorrow but a good drink?* It was one of my mother's favorite quotations from an ancient poem, even though she had never touched a drop. I uncapped the bottle, wiped its mouth carefully, took a gulp, and was immediately choked to tears.

After the burning sensation in my chest became less of a torture, I took another mouthful, all the while aware of my intention to pour the liquid out and discard the bottle, though I never did gather the resolution. When Lieutenant Wei approached me, much later it seemed, I recognized her footsteps. I hesitated, and did not stand up to salute her.

"What are you doing here?" she asked. "You missed the bedtime whistle."

It occurred to me that I had heard some muffled steps, and later that the schoolyard had become quiet, but I had not once thought of my obligation to report to the classroom for bedtime. I did not hear the whistle, I replied. I wondered if the officers were conducting a search for me; and perhaps in my daring confusion I even asked the question aloud, since Lieutenant Wei snatched the bottle from my hand and said I should be grateful that she did not report me missing. "What would happen if you reported me?" I asked. I stood up, trying to steady myself by leaning onto the tree trunk. The world seemed sharper, as if a hand had retraced the edge of everything: the moon, the dark shadows of the trees,

Lieutenant Wei's frown, my bottle in her hand. "Would I be punished in any way that you think would make me repent?"

"You're drunk."

Perhaps so, I said.

"Is anything the matter?" she asked, her voice softening. "Can I help you?"

Anything the matter? I laughed and said that the trouble was, I did not know a single thing that could be called *the matter*. How do you unravel a mess of yarn when you don't even see the yarn? I said, realizing that I must sound ridiculous.

Lieutenant Wei asked if she could have a drink. I nodded. She took a sip of the liquor, then passed the bottle to me. Let us drink like good friends, she said. I took a gulp and poured the rest of the liquid on the root of the locust tree. "We are not meant to be friends," I said to Lieutenant Wei.

"Not for once?" she asked.

I could not tell if her tone was a pleading one. "I was not yet given a life when you were born; when I was born you were old already," I said.

"I don't understand," Lieutenant Wei said.

Of course she would not understand. When I was in elementary school, I had once discovered a handmade bookmark in one of my mother's old novels, a few lines of an ancient folk song written in my mother's neat handwriting: *I was not yet given a life when you were born; when I was born you were old already. How I wish I had not come this late, but death has placed mountains and seas between you and me.* I had thought, at twelve, that my mother had written out the lines for my father, and I had cried then for them, thinking that she was right, that one day death would come for my father long before it was her time. Later I realized that it was not for my father but for a married man that she had written those lines out; I did not know who the other man was, but I knew he must be younger than my father. Still, with a wife and children, and without any affection to spare for my mother, he must have been as unreachable as death would have made him.

"Why are you unhappy?" Lieutenant Wei said when I did not speak. Placing a finger under my chin, she lifted my face slightly toward the moon. "Tell me, how can we make you happy?"

I now know that it was out of innocent confidence that Lieutenant Wei asked those questions. She was twenty-four then, a sensible and happy person. There are people, I now know, who have been granted happiness as their birthright, and who, believing that every mystery in life can be solved and every pain salved, reach out with a savior's hand. I wish I had replied differently, but at eighteen, I was as blind to her kindness as she was to my revulsion at any gesture of affection. "Why don't you give me a happiness drill right at this moment?" I said. "There is nothing we can't achieve in the army, isn't that right, Lieutenant?"

The rainy season began the next day, and it rained on and off for the rest of our journey. The mountain road was muddy, and the bedrolls on our backs, despite our heavy raincoats, inevitably got damper each day, "good for nothing but cultivating mushrooms," as Nan drily observed one night. Wildflowers by the roadside drooped in the storms, but even if they had not, we would not have regained the impulse to decorate our buttonholes with them. The officers stopped ordering us to sing, and sometimes we walked for an hour or two without talking, the only noise coming from the rustling of our raincoats, the rain falling on the tree leaves, and our footsteps in the soft mud.

I avoided Lieutenant Wei as much as she avoided me, though strangely, when we sat down in an open field at breaks, I would watch the rain fall off my visor, and hope for the chance to talk to her again. Stop being an idiot, I scolded myself; still, I found myself involuntarily searching for her when we set up camp in the evenings.

The rain stopped on May Day, and the sky lit up, the purest blue I had ever seen. We ended the marching early, at midday, and stationed ourselves in a place called Da-Wu—*nirvana*—an unusual name for an impoverished mountain town. There were only two days left in our journey, but before we returned to the camp, there was to be a field exercise that night. Da-Wu, once a model town, which had spent more than it could afford building intricate air-raid shelters and tunnels outside of town as preparation for the Sino-Soviet war, provided the perfect site.

We set out at eight, the third platoon to use the training site. On the way there we met the other platoon of girls, marching and singing as if returning from a most exhilarating game. The assignment was simple—two squads were to face each other in a meeting engagement, and the squad leaders were to lead their soldiers to annihilate the enemies. Each of us got two rounds of ten blanks, and when we reached the entrance to a network of tunnels, Lieutenant Wei whistled, the signal to begin.

The musty tunnel, unused but by the most adventurous children perhaps, smelled sulfuric from the encounters of the previous platoons. We stumbled our way through, the flashlight of the squad leader the only light. Someone giggled when she bumped into the person ahead of her, and Ping, in a loud whisper, wondered if there were rats or bats rushing to find shelter from us. It was as if we were returned to our childhood for a war game in the schoolyard, and the machine guns only added to the excitement, since as children the most we could do was use a tree branch as a weapon, or shape our hands into pistols.

After fifteen minutes, we exited the tunnel and stepped into a long trench. Across the dark field we heard rustling, so our squad leader ordered us to find shooting positions in the trench. No more than five minutes later we had emptied our rounds of ammunition into the emptiness between us and our enemies, the metallic explosions shrieking in our ears and lighting up the field just long enough for us to see the smoke dispersing. What a fun game! a girl shouted before she fired the last bullet. There was clapping on the other side of the battleground in reply.

When we gathered again, Lieutenant Wei asked us to report on the battle. I killed ten and injured five, Ping yelled out, and soon it became a boisterous competition. When the clamor quieted down, Lieutenant Wei said, Let me show you something, and led the platoon down a different road back to town.

We stopped at a trench on the other side of the battleground. Hundreds, perhaps thousands of fireflies twinkled, lighting up the tall, slender grasses in the trench. No one spoke. We had killed as many times as we had been killed, yet we had never been as alive as we were on that beautiful night in May.

"In memory of tonight, I'm going to ask someone to sing a song for us," Lieutenant Wei said. Many girls turned to Nan, and she handed her machine gun to the girl standing next to her. Lieutenant Wei shook her head at Nan and turned to me. "Can you sing a song for the platoon?"

I could not read Lieutenant Wei's face. "I'm not good at singing, Lieutenant," I replied.

"That is not a problem for us," Lieutenant Wei said. "All we need is for you to step up and sing."

Some of the girls gazed at me sympathetically, others were perplexed. They must have been wondering what wrong I'd committed to earn myself this punishment. When I still did not move, Lieutenant Wei raised her voice and ordered me to step out of the formation, her voice no longer patient.

At eighteen I entered the army fresh and young, and the fire-red stars on my epaulets shone onto my blossoming youth, I sang flatly. It was the first marching song we had been taught back in the fall. Lieutenant Wei ordered me to stop. "Sing us a civilian song," she said.

"I don't know any civilian songs, Lieutenant."

"Do you need me to find someone to teach you a song at this very moment, Comrade Moyan?" Lieutenant Wei said.

"I am a slow learner, Lieutenant."

"There is nothing we can't achieve in the army," Lieutenant Wei said. "We'll stay here all night waiting for you to learn a song and sing it for us, if that has to be the case."

When I began to sing again there was a ripple of unease. "It Is a Shame to Be a Lonely Person" was the song, called by Major Tang the product of a corrupt and lost generation. Halfway through I saw Jie roll her eyes, unimpressed by my foolish stubbornness; Nan watched me, puzzled. What would Professor Shan have said if she had seen me then, singing and crying in front of people who deserved neither my song nor my tears? *One's fate is determined by what she is not allowed to have, rather than what she possesses:* Professor Shan's words came to me then, her only comment after reading me a Lawrence story called "The Fox."

11.

A military Jeep was waiting for me when we returned to the meeting hall where we had set up camp for the night. Major Tang, who was exchanging small talk with the driver, informed me that I was to leave immediately for the train station at the county seat. Three hours earlier a telegram had arrived at the camp, which the driver now produced from his pocket, the thin green slip of paper smelling of cigarette smoke. *Mother passed away please return,* sent by someone whose name I did not recognize. My father, unable to leave my mother alone, must have sent someone to the post office in his place. I imagined the stranger spelling out the message; when words of condolence were offered he must have said, Thank heaven it was not his daughter who would be getting the telegram.

I brought only my satchel with me. There was no time to say farewell to anyone, as the driver had orders to make sure I caught the last night train to Beijing. We arrived just as the train was leaving the station, so the driver, ignoring my suggestion that I could spend the night in the station and catch the first train in the morning, sped down a country road that for the most part ran parallel to the train tracks until his Jeep overtook the puffing engine. At the next station, a small one with neither a waiting area nor a ticket booth, the driver insisted on waiting with me and seeing me board the train safely. The only other passenger on the platform was a dozing old man, leaning on a thick tree branch he used as a walking stick; at his feet were two heavy nylon bags and a bamboo basket. He stirred when he heard our steps. The driver asked him where he was going, but the old man, not understanding the question or perhaps too deaf to hear it, mumbled something in some local dialect before dozing off again. Soon the train arrived, and the driver helped the old man up the steps and then passed him his bags. I went for the basket, and only then did I discover the small child, wrapped in an old blanket and sleeping inside, one finger curled under her smiling face.

I lifted the basket gingerly, and the child shifted her head, heaved a sigh, but did not wake. Someone—a conductor perhaps—took the basket from me. The driver said something about "the poor child," but I did not hear him clearly enough to reply. Once I boarded the train, the driver pulled the metal door and closed it behind me. When I looked at him from the window in the door, he saluted me and waited until the train began to move before putting down his hand.

I waved at him. I did not know if he could see me through the dark night and smoky window, though he did not move, standing straight and watching the train leave. When I could no longer see him I leaned against the cold metal door, the loneliness I had learned to live with all of a sudden unbearable. I did not know the driver's name, nor had I gotten a close look at his face—but for years to come I would think of his salute, a stranger's kindness always remembered because a stranger's kindness, like time itself, heals our wounds in the end.

My father looked like a very old man, his eyes hollow, his hands shaking constantly, the grief too heavy. He had turned seventy the day before my mother's death—a suicide, I had guessed at once, though he did not tell me what she had done. It was from neighbors that I found out—she had hanged herself in the bedroom. Anybody else would have broken that curtain rod with her weight, but of course your mother was so skinny, an old woman said to me, as if my mother's only misfortune was that she had never become a nicely plump woman.

"Your mother was the kindest woman in the world," my father said the night before her cremation. He was lying in bed, his head propped up by the stack of pillows my mother had used when she read. I told him to eat a little and then rest, but the noodle soup I had made for him remained untouched, and he insisted on watching me pack up my mother's side of the bedroom. Her clothes— many of them from her youth—were to be cremated with her; her collection of novels and ancient poetry I was to put into boxes and move out to the foyer. My father, like uneducated people in his generation, revered anything in print; he told me to keep the books, that I should use them as I continued my education. "She was never happy to be married to an old man, but she kept her promise."

I examined each book, hoping to find the handmade bookmark that I had once discovered. I did not know what promise my father was talking about, but I knew I need not press him for an explanation. In the past two days, he had talked more than he had for years. Stories of my mother's childhood and youth—of being the middle daughter sandwiched between many siblings and feeling neglected by her parents, of her loving books despite her parents' decision to send her to a factory as an apprentice at fifteen, of her favorite three-legged cat named Sansan, of her delight in painting her fingernails with the petals of balsams every spring, red or pink or lavender, depending on which color was blooming in her best friend's garden—all this was related to me. I wondered if my mother had told my father these stories in the early years of their marriage—but she had already been a madwoman then, so how could he have been certain that she was not just making up tales the same way she had made up her love story with a married man?

"She asked me if twenty years was enough," my father said after a moment. "Twenty years was a long time for an older man like me, I told her. So she said, Let's be husband and wife for twenty years. People said I was out of my mind to marry a madwoman, but you see, she was only unhappy. She did not break her promise."

I placed a romance novel on top of a pile quietly. I wondered if my mother had calculated it all out—an older man in love with her was better than an asylum or the reign of her disgraced parents and siblings—but no matter, she had returned his kindness with twenty years of a life she had no desire to live.

"Of course it's not fair for you, Moyan," my father said. "I thought twenty years enough time to bring up a child together. She did not want you at first."

"Why did she agree?"

"A child gives a marriage a future. That was what people told me. I thought when we had you she would forget that foolish deal of twenty years," my father said, his voice so low I could barely hear him. "I am sorry we haven't had much to offer you as parents."

I turned my back to my father, pretending to pick at another stack of books so he would not see my tears. Neither he nor I, in the end, had given her more reason to live than the obligation to fulfill a simple promise, though even in her maddest years, she hadn't given up the pretense that she was my birth mother. I wished Professor Shan had never told me about my adoption.

The next day my father and I saw my mother off at the funeral home. There was no memorial service for her, nor did any of her siblings come and acknowledge her departure. My father insisted on waiting by the furnace alone, so I wandered into one of the meeting halls and sat through a memorial service for a stranger whose children and grandchildren wailed when it was time for the man to go to the furnace.

On the bus ride home, my father carried the wooden box, inside of which was an ivory-colored silk bag that contained what was left of my mother. I had tried to convince him to bury her in the municipal cemetery, but he had refused. He wanted to be buried with her on the same day, he explained to me. Not right next to her, he said, since she had fulfilled her promise and he should fulfill his of leaving her alone—but also not too far from her, he added after a moment. "I'm sorry we have to burden you," my father said when I said nothing about his request. I knew that he had guessed by then that I had found out about my adoption, as one's birth father would not have to apologize for his own last request. "You deserve a better life, but this is all we could do for you."

12.

The pigs would continue lying in the sunshine after meals until they were butchered for the farewell banquet in late July. The new grass at the shooting range would soon be tall enough for small children to play hide-and-seek in, though no children would ever know the place, where bronze bullet shells that would otherwise have made thrilling toys remained undisturbed. At the exhibition drill, on an extremely hot August day, several girls fainted from standing in the sun and listening to the speeches of a general and several senior officers. Lieutenant Wei, along with other junior officers, stood in formation and saluted by the camp entrance until the last lorry carrying boys and girls eager to go home had left for the train station. While the cooking squad cleaned up the mess hall after the banquet, they sipped cheap liquor, and when they became drunk they cried and later fought among themselves. At night Lieutenant Wei walked through the barracks and picked up a few items left behind—a stamp, a ballpoint pen almost out of ink, an army-issue tiepin, golden-colored, with a red star at one end. There were other things for me to remember, details I had not seen with my eyes yet nevertheless had become part of my memory, some gathered from a chat with Nan in college, others imagined.

I did not report back to the army after my mother's cremation. On the last day of my five-day leave I sent a telegram to the camp, addressing no one and giving mental breakdown as the reason for not being able to return. I did not know what would happen to me—if, without the last two months of training, I would still be qualified to go to college in September—and I did not care enough to worry about it. My father had become a shaky old man, and the department store where he had worked for thirty years had to let him go, apologetically granting him half his salary as his pension and an expensive-looking gilded clock as a retirement present. We talked a lot at the beginning, about my mother and sometimes my childhood, but these conversations wore us out, as neither of us was used to talking, and in the end my father replaced my mother in their bedroom, lying in bed all day long; I wandered my days away till sunset as my mother had once done.

A few weeks after I had come home, I was standing by the roadside and watching workers brush the trunks of elm trees with white paint mixed with pesticide when Professor Shan approached me. "I see that you're back," she said. "Come with me."

I had not been to Professor Shan's flat since I had left her, yet from the look of things, time had stopped in her world.

"I heard about your mother's passing," Professor Shan said and signaled me to sit down on her bed. "Is your father doing all right?"

A few days earlier my father had asked me if I thought he had been responsible for my mother's death—would she have had a longer life if he had not married her? he asked me, and I assured him that my mother, despite her unhappiness, had loved him as she never loved anyone else. My father looked at me sadly and did not speak—he must have been thinking of the married man who had never returned my mother's love, so I showed him the bookmark I had saved from her books. What does the poem mean? he asked after reading the lines many times, and I said it was a love song from a younger woman to an older man.

"Love leaves one in debt," Professor Shan said. I nodded, though I wondered whether she meant that my father was forever paying back his debt to my mother because of his love for her, or that being loved and unable to love back had made her indebted to him. "Best if you start free from all that, do you understand?"

I had read enough love stories to be interested in one more, I said, and Professor Shan seemed satisfied by my answer. After that I resumed my daily visit to her flat, and I continued for the next twelve years. At the beginning she read to me, and later, when her eyesight deteriorated, I took over, though she was always the one to tell me which book to read. She never asked me about my life in the army, and she showed little interest in the civilian life I'd led in college, and later as a schoolteacher. When I reached marriage-able age, people began to press me, subtly at first and later less so, saying that a young woman's best years were brief, saying that I was becoming less desirable by the day, like a fresh lychee that had not found a buyer in time. Professor Shan must have suspected all this talk but, as always, she refused to let the mundane into her flat. Instead, we read other people's stories, more real than our own; after all, inadequate makers of our own lives, we were no match for those masters.

My father died less than a year after my mother, and against his wish I buried their urns next to each other. I visit them every year on my birthday, my only trip outside the district where I live and teach. My mother fell in love at an early age, my father late; they both fell for someone who would not return their love, yet in the end their story is the only love story I can claim, and I live as proof of that story, of one man's offering to a woman from his meager existence, and of her returning it with her entire adult life.

I think of visiting Professor Shan's grave in Shanghai, too, but I know I will never do it, as the location is kept from me by her children. In the last days of her life they came back from America to arrange the funeral and the sale of her flat. They were alarmed by my friendship with their mother, and before she was transferred from the geriatric ward to the morgue they told me that I was wrong if I thought they would give me a share of the inheritance.

I laughed and said that had never been my intention, though I could see they did not believe me. Why would they, when life to them was a simple transaction between those who owe and those who own? Before she entered the hospital, Professor Shan had watched me pack up her books. Take them home before my children sell them to the recycling station, she told me, and I packed them all, including the book of D. H. Lawrence's stories that I had once stolen from her. The summer after I left the army, Lieutenant Wei had mailed it to me, along with my half-empty suitcase, with the bar of Lux soap wrapped in my civilian clothes, and a letter expressing her condolences. "I wish we had met under different circumstances," the letter concluded.

I did not write to thank Lieutenant Wei for sending the suitcase, nor did I reply, a few months later, when she sent another letter, saying that she and the other two platoon officers had been officially invited to visit my college, and she would love to see me in my city. After that there was one more letter, and then a wedding invitation, and now, twenty years later, a funeral notice. Professor Shan would have approved of my silence, though I wonder if she was wrong to think that without love one can be free. What was not understood when I was younger is understood now. Lieutenant Wei's persistence in seeking my friendship came from the same desire as Professor Shan's to make me a disciple. Both women had set their hearts on making a new person, though, unlike Professor Shan, Lieutenant Wei was too curious and too respectful to be a successful hijacker of other people's lives. Sometimes I wonder if I would have become her friend had I not met Professor Shan. Perhaps I would have subjected myself to her will as I had Professor Shan's, and I would have become a happier person, falling in love with a suitable man, because that is what Lieutenant Wei would have considered happiness. But what is the point of talking about the past in this haphazard way? Kindness binds one to the past as obstinately as love does, and no matter what you think of Professor Shan or Lieutenant Wei, it is their kindness that makes me indebted to them. For that reason, I know Lieutenant Wei will continue coming to me in my dreams, as Professor Shan's voice still reads to me when I sit in my flat with one of her books in hand.

I now memorize ancient poems from my mother's books. I reread the romantic stories and never tire of them. They are terrible stories, terribly written, yet they are about fate, a kinder fate that unites one with her lover despite hardships and improbability—and they never fail to give me a momentary hope, as they must have given my mother years ago, as if all will be well in the end.

But it is Professor Shan's collection that I truly live with, Dickens and Hardy and Lawrence, who once saw me as a young girl and who will one day see me as an old woman. The people who live out their lives in those books, like their creators, are not my people, and I wonder if it is this irrelevance that makes it easy for me to wander among them, the same way that my not being related to my parents by blood makes it easy for me to claim their love story as mine.

The girls I served with in the army must be mothers and wives by now. I imagine them continuing with their daily lives, unaware of Lieutenant Wei's death: Ping, in a warm cocoon, once provided by her father, now by her husband; Jie, married but perhaps keeping a lover from time to time; and our squad leader, the most militant eighteen-year-old of us all, providing a warm home for her family, for even a militant girl could turn out to be a loving wife and mother. I have never forgotten any person who has come into my life. As I am on my way to work this morning, I see Nan's face on a TV screen in a shop window. I watch her through the glass pane—I cannot hear what the program is saying, but by the way she smiles and talks, you can tell she is an important person. I study her, still petite and beautiful, still able to pass for a young woman in a choir. For a moment my heart mourns for the passing of time as it has never mourned the deaths of my parents, or Professor Shan, or Lieutenant Wei. If I close my eyes I can hear again Nan's beautiful voice, singing "The Last Rose of Summer" at the shooting range, a random act of kindness that will continue living on in the memory of someone who is a stranger to her now.

Steven Millhauser

Phantoms

THE PHENOMENON

The phantoms of our town do not, as some think, appear only in the dark. Often we come upon them in full sunlight, when shadows lie sharp on the lawns and streets. The encounters take place for very short periods, ranging from two or three seconds to perhaps half a minute, though longer episodes are sometimes reported. So many of us have seen them that it's uncommon to meet someone who has not; of this minority, only a small number deny that phantoms exist. Sometimes an encounter occurs more than once in the course of a single day; sometimes six months pass, or a year. The phantoms, which some call Presences, are not easy to distinguish from ordinary citizens: they are not translucent, or smokelike, or hazy, they do not ripple like heat waves, nor are they in any way unusual in figure or dress. Indeed they are so much like us that it sometimes happens we mistake them for someone we know. Such errors are rare, and never last for more than a moment. They themselves appear to be uneasy during an encounter and swiftly withdraw. They always look at us before turning away. They never speak. They are wary, elusive, secretive, haughty, unfriendly, remote.

EXPLANATION #1

One explanation has it that our phantoms are the auras, or visible traces, of earlier inhabitants of our town, which was settled in 1636. Our atmosphere, saturated with the energy of all those who have preceded us, preserves them and permits them, under certain conditions, to become visible to us. This explanation, often fitted out with a pseudoscientific vocabulary, strikes most of us as unconvincing. The phantoms always appear in contemporary dress, they never behave in ways that suggest earlier eras, and there is no evidence whatever to support the claim that the dead leave visible traces in the air.

HISTORY

As children we are told about the phantoms by our fathers and mothers. They in turn have been told by their own fathers and mothers, who can remember being told by their parents—our great-grandparents—when they were children. Thus the phantoms of our town are not new; they don't represent a sudden eruption into our lives, a recent change in our sense of things. We have no formal records that confirm the presence of phantoms throughout the diverse periods of our history, no scientific reports or transcripts of legal proceedings, but some of us are familiar with the second-floor Archive Room of our library, where in nineteenth-century diaries we find occasional references to "the others" or "them," without further details. Church records of the seventeenth century include several mentions of "the devil's children," which some view as evidence for the lineage of our phantoms; others argue that the phrase is so general that it cannot be cited as proof of anything. The official town history, published in 1936 on the three-hundredth anniversary of our incorporation, revised in 1986, and updated in 2006, makes no mention of the phantoms. An editorial note states that "the authors have confined themselves to ascertainable fact."

HOW WE KNOW

We know by a ripple along the skin of our forearms, accompanied by a tension of the inner body. We know because they look at us and withdraw immediately. We know because when we try to follow them, we find that they have vanished. We know because we know.

CASE STUDY #1

Richard Moore rises from beside the bed, where he has just finished the forty-second installment of a never-ending story that he tells each night to his four-year-old daughter, bends over her for a goodnight kiss, and walks quietly from the room. He loves having a daughter; he loves having a wife, a family; though he married late, at thirty-nine, he knows he wasn't ready when he was younger, not in his doped-up twenties, not in his stupid, wasted thirties, when he was still acting like some angry teenager who hated the grown-ups; and now he's grateful for it all, like someone who can hardly believe that he's allowed to live in his own house. He walks along the hall to the den, where his wife is sitting at one end of the couch, reading a book in the light of the table lamp, while the TV is on mute during an ad for vinyl siding. He loves that she won't watch the ads, that she refuses to waste those minutes, that she reads books, that she's sitting there waiting for him, that the light from the TV is flickering on her hand and upper arm. Something has begun to bother him, though he isn't sure what it is, but as he steps into the den he's got it, he's got it: the table in the side yard, the two folding chairs, the sunglasses on the tabletop. He was sitting out there with her after dinner, and he left his sunglasses. "Back in a sec," he says, and turns away, enters the kitchen, opens the door to the small screened porch at the back of the house, and walks from the porch down the steps to the back-yard, a narrow strip between the house and the cedar fence. It's nine-thirty on a summer night. The sky is dark blue, the fence lit by the light from the kitchen window, the grass black here and green over there. He turns the corner of the house and comes to the private place. It's the part of the yard bounded by the fence, the side-yard hedge, and the row of three Scotch pines, where he's set up two folding chairs and a white ironwork table with a glass top. On the table lie the sunglasses. The sight pleases him: the two chairs, turned a little toward each other, the forgotten glasses, the enclosed place set off from the rest of the world. He steps over to the table and picks up the glasses: a good pair, expensive lenses, nothing flashy, stylish in a quiet way. As he lifts them from the table he senses something in the skin of his arms and sees a figure standing beside the third Scotch pine. It's darker here than at the back of the house, and he can't see her all that well: a tall, erect woman, fortyish, long face, dark dress. Her expression, which he can barely make out, seems stern. She looks at him for a moment and turns away—not hastily, as if she were frightened, but deci-sively, like someone who wants to be alone. Behind the Scotch pine she's no longer visible. He hesitates, steps over to the tree, sees nothing. His first impulse is to scream at her, to tell her that he'll kill her if she comes near his daughter. Immediately he forces himself to calm down. Everything will be all right. There's no dan-ger. He's seen them before. Even so, he returns quickly to the house, locks the porch door behind him, locks the kitchen door behind him, fastens the chain, and strides to the den, where on the TV a man in a dinner jacket is staring across the room at a woman with pulled-back hair who is seated at a piano. His wife is watching. As he steps toward her, he notices a pair of sunglasses in his hand.

THE LOOK

Most of us are familiar with the look they cast in our direction before they withdraw. The look has been variously described as proud, hostile, suspicious, mocking, disdainful, uncertain; never is it seen as welcoming. Some witnesses say that the phantoms show slight movements in our direction, before the decisive turning away. Others, disputing such claims, argue that we cannot bear to imagine their rejection of us and misread their movements in a way flattering to our self-esteem.

HIGHLY QUESTIONABLE

Now and then we hear reports of a more questionable kind. The phantoms, we are told, have grayish wings folded along their backs; the phantoms have swirling smoke for eyes; at the ends of their feet, claws curl against the grass. Such descriptions, though rare, are persistent, perhaps inevitable, and impossible to refute. They strike most of us as childish and irresponsible, the results of careless observation, hasty inference, and heightened imagination corrupted by conventional images drawn from movies and television. Whenever we hear such descriptions, we're quick to question them and to make the case for the accumulated evidence of trustworthy witnesses. A paradoxical effect of our vigilance is that the phantoms, rescued from the fantastic, for a moment seem to us normal, commonplace, as familiar as squirrels or dandelions.

CASE STUDY #2

Years ago, as a child of eight or nine, Karen Carsten experienced a single encounter. Her memory of the moment is both vivid and vague: she can't recall how many of them there were, or exactly what they looked like, but she recalls the precise moment in which she came upon them, one summer afternoon, as she stepped around to the back of the garage in search of a soccer ball and saw them sitting quietly in the grass. She still remembers her feeling of wonder as they turned to look at her, before they rose and went away. Now, at age fifty-six, Karen Carsten lives alone with her cat in a house filled with framed photographs of her parents, her nieces, and her late husband, who died in a car accident seventeen years ago. Karen is a high school librarian with many set routines: the TV programs, the weekend housecleaning, the twice-yearly visits in August and December to her sister's family in Youngstown, Ohio, the choir on Sunday, dinner every two weeks at the same restaurant with a friend who never calls to ask how she is. One Saturday afternoon she finishes organizing the linen closet on the second floor and starts up the attic stairs. She plans to sort through boxes of old clothes, some of which she'll give to Goodwill and some of which she'll save for her nieces, who will think of the collared blouses and floral-print dresses as hopelessly old-fashioned but who might come around to appreciating them someday, maybe. As she reaches the top of the stairs she stops so suddenly and completely that she has the sense of her own body as an object standing in her path. Ten feet away, two children are seated on the old couch near the dollhouse. A third child is sitting in the armchair with the loose leg. In the brownish light of the attic, with its one small window, she can see them clearly: two barefoot girls of about ten, in jeans and T-shirts, and a boy, slightly older, maybe twelve, blond-haired, in a dress shirt and khakis, who sits low in the chair with his neck bent up against the back. The three turn to look at her and at once rise and walk into the darker part of the attic, where they are no longer visible. Karen stands motionless at the top of the stairs, her hand clutching the rail. Her lips are dry, and she is filled with an excitement so intense that she thinks she might burst into tears. She does not follow the children into the shadows, partly because she doesn't want to upset them, and partly because she knows they are no longer there. She turns back down the stairs. In the living room she sits in the armchair until nightfall. Joy fills her heart. She can feel it shining from her face. That night she returns to the attic, straightens the pillows on the couch, smooths out the doilies on the chair arms, brings over a small wicker table, sets out three saucers and three teacups. She moves away some bulging boxes that sit beside the couch, carries off an old typewriter, sweeps the floor. Downstairs in the living room she turns on the TV, but she keeps the volume low; she's listening for sounds in the attic, even though she knows that her visitors don't make sounds. She imagines them up there, sitting silently together, enjoying the table, the teacups, the orderly surroundings. Now each day she climbs the stairs to the attic, where she sees the empty couch, the empty chair, the wicker table with the three teacups. Despite the pang of disappointment, she is happy. She is happy because she knows they come to visit her every day, she knows they like to be up there, sitting in the old furniture, around the wicker table; she knows; she knows.

EXPLANATION #2

One explanation is that the phantoms *are not there*, that those of us who see them are experiencing delusions or hallucinations brought about by beliefs instilled in us as young children. A small movement, an unexpected sound, is immediately converted into a visual presence that exists only in the mind of the perceiver. The flaws in this explanation are threefold. First, it assumes that the population of an entire town will interpret ambiguous signs in precisely the same way. Second, it ignores the fact that most of us, as we grow to adulthood, discard the stories and false beliefs of childhood but continue to see the phantoms. Third, it fails to account for innumerable instances in which multiple witnesses have seen the same phantom. Even if we were to agree that these objections are not decisive and that our phantoms are in fact not there, the explanation would tell us only that we are mad, without revealing the meaning of our madness.

OUR CHILDREN

What shall we say to our children? If, like most parents in our town, we decide to tell them at an early age about the phantoms, we worry that we have filled their nights with terror or perhaps have created in them a hope, a longing, for an encounter that might never take place. Those of us who conceal the existence of phantoms are no less worried, for we fear either that our children will be informed unreliably by other children or that they will be dangerously unprepared for an encounter should one occur. Even those of us who have prepared our children are worried about the first encounter, which sometimes disturbs a child in ways that some of us remember only too well. Although we assure our children that there's nothing to fear from the phantoms, who wish only to be left alone, we ourselves are fearful: we wonder whether the phantoms are as harmless as we say they are, we wonder whether they behave differently in the presence of an unaccompanied child, we wonder whether, under certain circumstances, they might become bolder than we know. Some say that a phantom, encountering an adult and a child, will look only at the child, will let its gaze linger in a way that never happens with an adult. When we put our children to sleep, leaning close to them and answering their questions about phantoms in gentle, soothing tones, until their eyes close in peace, we understand that we have been preparing in ourselves an anxiety that will grow stronger and more aggressive as the night advances.

CROSSING OVER

The question of "crossing over" refuses to disappear, despite a history of testimony that many of us feel ought to put it to rest. By "crossing over" is meant, in general, any form of intermingling between us and them; specifically, it refers to supposed instances in which one of them, or one of us, leaves the native community and joins the other. Now, not only is there no evidence of any such regrouping, of any such transference of loyalty, but the overwhelming testimony of witnesses shows that no phantom has ever remained for more than a few moments in the presence of an outsider or given any sign whatever of greeting or encouragement. Claims to the contrary have always been suspect: the insistence of an alcoholic husband that he saw his wife in bed with *one of them,* the assertion of a teenager suspended from high school that a group of phantoms had threatened to harm him if he failed to obey their commands. Apart from statements that purport to be factual, fantasies of crossing over persist in the form of phantom-tales that flourish among our children and are half-believed by naïve adults. It is not difficult to make the case that stories of this kind reveal a secret desire for contact, though no reliable record of contact exists. Those of us who try to maintain a strict objectivity in such matters are forced to admit that a crossing of the line is not impossible, however unlikely, so that even as we challenge dubious claims and smile at fairy tales we find ourselves imagining the sudden encounter at night, the heads turning toward us, the moment of hesitation, the arms rising gravely in welcome.

CASE STUDY #3

James Levin, twenty-six years old, has reached an impasse in his life. After college he took a year off, holding odd jobs and traveling all over the country before returning home to apply to grad school. He completed his coursework in two years, during which he taught one introductory section of American History, and then surprised everyone by taking a leave of absence in order to read for his dissertation (*The Influence of Popular Culture on High Culture in Post–Civil War America, 1865–1900*) and think more carefully about the direction of his life. He lives with his parents in his old room, dense with memories of grade school and high school. He worries that he's losing interest in his dissertation; he feels he should rethink his life, maybe go the med-school route and do something useful in the world instead of wasting his time wallowing in abstract speculations of no value to anyone; he speaks less and less to his girlfriend, a law student at the University of Michigan, nearly a thousand miles away. Where, he wonders, has he taken a wrong turn? What should he do with his life? What is the meaning of it all? These, he believes, are questions eminently suitable for an intelligent adolescent of sixteen, questions that he himself discussed passionately ten years ago with friends who are now married and paying mortgages. Because he's stalled in his life, because he is eaten up with guilt, and because he is unhappy, he has taken to getting up late and going for long walks all over town, first in the afternoon and again at night. One of his daytime walks leads to the picnic grounds of his childhood. Pine trees and scattered tables stand by the stream where he used to sail a little wooden tugboat—he's always bumping into his past like that—and across the stream is where he sees her, one afternoon in late September. She's standing alone, between two oak trees, looking down at the water. The sun shines on the lower part of her body, but her face and neck are in shadow. She becomes aware of him almost immediately, raises her eyes, and withdraws into the shade, where he can no longer see her. He has shattered her solitude. Each instant of the encounter enters him so sharply that his memory of her breaks into three parts, like a medieval triptych in a museum: the moment of awareness, the look, the turning away. In the first panel of the triptych, her shoulders are tense, her whole body unnaturally still, like someone who has heard a sound in the dark. Second panel: her eyes are raised and staring directly at him. It can't have lasted for more than a second. What stays with him is something severe in that look, as if he's disturbed her in a way that requires forgiveness. Third panel: the body is half turned away, not timidly but with a kind of dignity of withdrawal, which seems to rebuke him for an intrusion. James feels a sharp desire to cross the stream and find her, but two thoughts hold him back: his fear that the crossing will be unwelcome to her, and his knowledge that she has disappeared. He returns home but continues to see her standing by the stream. He has the sense that she's becoming more vivid in her absence, as if she's gaining life within him. The unnatural stillness, the dark look, the turning away—he feels he owes her an immense apology. He understands that the desire to apologize is only a mask for his desire to see her again. After two days of futile brooding he returns to the stream, to the exact place where he stood when he saw her the first time; four hours later he returns home, discouraged, restless, and irritable. He understands that something has happened to him, something that is probably harmful. He doesn't care. He returns to the stream day after day, without hope, without pleasure. What's he doing there, in that desolate place? He's twenty-six, but already he's an old man. The leaves have begun to turn; the air is growing cold. One day, on his way back from the stream, James takes a different way home. He passes his old high school, with its double row of tall windows, and comes to the hill where he used to go sledding. He needs to get away from this town, where his childhood and adolescence spring up to meet him at every turn; he ought to go somewhere, do something; his long, purposeless walks seem to him the outward expression of an inner confusion. He climbs the hill, passing through the bare oaks and beeches and the dark firs, and at the top looks down at the stand of pine at the back of Cullen's Auto Body. He walks down the slope, feeling the steering bar in his hands, the red runners biting into the snow, and when he comes to the pines he sees her sitting on the trunk of a fallen tree. She turns her head to look at him, rises, and walks out of sight. This time he doesn't hesitate. He runs into the thicket, beyond which he can see the whitewashed back of the body shop, a brilliant blue front fender lying up against a tire, and, farther away, a pickup truck driving along the street; pale sunlight slants through the pine branches. He searches for her but finds only a tangle of ferns, a beer can, the top of a pint of ice cream. At home he throws himself down on his boyhood bed, where he used to spend long afternoons reading stories about boys who grew up to become famous scientists and explorers. He summons her stare. The sternness devastates him, but draws him, too, since he feels it as a strength he himself lacks. He understands that he's in a bad way; that he's got to stop thinking about her; that he'll never stop thinking about her; that nothing can ever come of it; that his life will be harmed; that harm is attractive to him; that he'll never return to school; that he will disappoint his parents and lose his girlfriend; that none of this matters to him; that what matters is the hope of seeing once more the phantom lady who will look harshly at him and turn away; that he is weak, foolish, frivolous; that such words have no meaning for him; that he has entered a world of dark love, from which there is no way out.

MISSING CHILDREN

Once in a long while, a child goes missing. It happens in other towns, it happens in yours: the missing child who is discovered six hours later lost in the woods, the missing child who never returns, who disappears forever, perhaps in the company of a stranger in a baseball cap who was last seen parked in a van across from the elementary school. In our town there are always those who blame the phantoms. They steal our children, it is said, in order to bring them into the fold; they're always waiting for the right moment, when we have been careless, when our attention has relaxed. Those of us who defend the phantoms point out patiently that they always withdraw from us, that there is no evidence they can make physical contact with the things of our world, that no human child has ever been seen in their company. Such arguments never persuade an accuser. Even when the missing child is discovered in the woods, where he has wandered after a squirrel,

even when the missing child is found buried in the yard of a troubled loner in a town two hundred miles away, the suspicion
remains that the phantoms have had something to do with it. We
who defend our phantoms against false accusations and wild
inventions are forced to admit that we do not know what they
may be thinking, alone among themselves, or in the moment
when they turn to look at us, before moving away.

DISRUPTION

Sometimes a disruption comes: the phantom in the supermarket,
the phantom in the bedroom. Then our sense of the behavior of
phantoms suffers a shock: we cannot understand why creatures
who withdraw from us should appear in places where encounters
are unavoidable. Have we misunderstood something about our
phantoms? It's true enough that when we encounter them in the
aisle of a supermarket or clothing store, when we find them sitting on the edge of our beds or lying against a bed pillow, they
behave as they always do: they look at us and quickly withdraw.
Even so, we feel that they have come too close, that they want
something from us that we cannot understand, and only when
we encounter them in a less-frequented place, at the back of the
shut-down railroad station or on the far side of a field, do we
relax a little.

EXPLANATION #3

One explanation asserts that we and the phantoms were once a
single race, which at some point in the remote history of our town
divided into two societies. According to a psychological offshoot
of this explanation, the phantoms are the unwanted or unac-
knowledged portions of ourselves, which we try to evade but continually encounter; they make us uneasy because we know them;
they are ourselves.

FEAR

Many of us, at one time or another, have felt the fear. For say you are coming home with your wife from an evening with friends. The porch light is on, the living room windows are dimly glowing before the closed blinds. As you walk across the front lawn from the driveway to the porch steps, you become aware of something, over there by the wild cherry tree. Then you half-see one of them, for an instant, withdrawing behind the dark branches, which catch only a little of the light from the porch. That is when the fear comes. You can feel it deep within you, like an infection that's about to spread. You can feel it in your wife's hand tightening on your arm. It's at that moment you turn to her and say, with a shrug of one shoulder and a little laugh that fools no one: "Oh, it's just one of them!"

PHOTOGRAPHIC EVIDENCE

Evidence from digital cameras, camcorders, iPhones, and old-fashioned film cameras divides into two categories: the fraudulent and the dubious. Fraudulent evidence always reveals signs of tampering. Methods of digital-imaging manipulation permit a wide range of effects, from computer-generated figures to digital clones; sometimes a slight blur is sought, to suggest the uncanny. Often the artist goes too far, and creates a hackneyed monster-phantom inspired by third-rate movies; more clever manipulators stay closer to the ordinary, but tend to give themselves away by an exaggeration of some feature, usually the ears or nose. In such matters, the temptation of the grotesque appears to be irresistible. Celluloid fraud assumes well-known forms that reach back to the era of fairy photographs: double exposures, chemical tampering with negatives, the insertion of gauze between the printing paper and the enlarger lens. The category of the dubious is harder to disprove. Here we find vague, shadowy shapes, wavering lines resembling ripples of heated air above a radiator, half-hidden forms concealed by branches or by windows filled with reflections. Most of these images can be explained as natural effects of light that have deceived the credulous person recording them. For those who crave visual proof of phantoms, evidence that a photograph is fraudulent or dubious is never entirely convincing.

CASE STUDY #4

One afternoon in late spring, Evelyn Wells, nine years old, is playing alone in her backyard. It's a sunny day; school is out, dinner's a long way off, and the warm afternoon has the feel of summer. Her best friend is sick with a sore throat and fever, but that's all right: Evvy likes to play alone in her yard, especially on a sunny day like this one, with time stretching out on all sides of her. What she's been practicing lately is roof-ball, a game she learned from a boy down the block. Her yard is bounded by the neighbor's garage and by thick spruces running along the back and side; the lowest spruce branches bend down to the grass and form a kind of wall. The idea is to throw the tennis ball, which is the color of lime Kool-Aid, onto the slanted garage roof and catch it when it comes down. If Evvy throws too hard, the ball will go over the roof and land in the yard next door, possibly in the vegetable garden surrounded by chicken wire. If she doesn't throw hard enough, it will come right back to her, with no speed. The thing to do is make the ball go almost to the top, so that it comes down faster and faster; then she's got to catch it before it hits the ground, though a one-bouncer isn't terrible. Evvy is pretty good at roof-ball—she can make the ball go way up the slope, and she can figure out where she needs to stand as it comes rushing or bouncing down. Her record is eight catches in a row, but now she's caught nine and is hoping for ten. The ball stops near the peak of the roof and begins coming down at a wide angle; she moves more and more to the right as it bounces lightly along and leaps into the air. This time she's made a mistake—the ball goes over her head. It rolls across the lawn toward the back and disappears under the low-hanging spruce branches not far from the garage. Evvy sometimes likes to play under there, where it's cool and dim. She pushes aside a branch and looks for the ball, which she sees beside a root. At the same time she sees two figures, a man and a woman, standing under the tree. They stare down at her, then turn their faces away and step out of sight. Evvy feels a ripple in her arms. Their eyes were like shadows on a lawn. She backs out into the sun. The yard does not comfort her. The blades of grass seem to be holding their breath. The white wooden shingles on the side of the garage are staring at her. Evvy walks across the strange lawn and up the back steps into the kitchen. Inside, it is very still. A faucet handle blazes with light. She hears her mother in the living room. Evvy does not want to speak to her mother. She does not want to speak to anyone. Upstairs, in her room, she draws the blinds and gets into bed. The windows are above the backyard and look down on the rows of spruce trees. At dinner she is silent. "Cat got your tongue?" her father says. His teeth are laughing. Her mother gives her a wrinkled look. At night she lies with her eyes open. She sees the man and woman standing under the tree, staring down at her. They turn their faces away. The next day, Saturday, Evvy refuses to go outside. Her mother brings orange juice, feels her forehead, takes her temperature. Outside, her father is mowing the lawn. That night she doesn't sleep. They are standing under the tree, looking at her with their shadow-eyes. She can't see their faces. She doesn't remember their clothes. On Sunday she stays in her room. Sounds startle her: a clank in the yard, a shout. At night she watches with closed eyes: the ball rolling under the branches, the two figures standing there, looking down at her. On Monday her mother takes her to the doctor. He presses the silver circle against her chest. The next day she returns to school, but after the last bell she comes straight home and goes to her room. Through the slats of the blinds she can see the garage, the roof, the dark green spruce branches bending to the grass. One afternoon Evvy is sitting at the piano in the living room. She's practicing her scales. The bell rings and her mother goes to the door. When Evvy turns to look, she sees a woman and a man. She leaves the piano and goes upstairs to her room. She sits on the throw rug next to her bed and stares at the door. After a while she hears her mother's footsteps on the stairs. Evvy stands up and goes into the closet. She crawls next to a box filled with old dolls and bears and elephants. She can hear her mother's footsteps in the room. Her mother is knocking on the closet door. "Please come out of there, Evvy. I know you're in there." She does not come out.

CAPTORS

Despite widespread disapproval, now and then an attempt is made to capture a phantom. The desire arises most often among groups of idle teenagers, especially during the warm nights of summer, but is also known among adults, usually but not invariably male, who feel menaced by the phantoms or who cannot tolerate the unknown. Traps are set, pits dug, cages built, all to no avail. The nonphysical nature of phantoms does not seem to discourage such efforts, which sometimes display great ingenuity. Walter Hendricks, a mechanical engineer, lived for many years in a neighborhood of split-level ranch houses with backyard swing sets and barbecues; one day he began to transform his yard into a dense thicket of pine trees, in order to invite the visits of phantoms. Each tree was equipped with a mechanism that was able to release from the branches a series of closely woven steel-mesh nets, which dropped swiftly when anything passed below. In another part of town, Charles Reese rented an excavator and dug a basement-size cavity in his yard. He covered the pit, which became known as the Dungeon, with a sliding steel ceiling concealed by a layer of sod. One night, when a phantom appeared on his lawn, Reese pressed a switch that caused the false lawn to slide away; when he climbed down into the Dungeon with a high-beam flashlight, he discovered a frightened chipmunk. Others have used chemical sprays that cause temporary paralysis, empty sheds with sliding doors that automatically shut when a motion sensor is triggered, even a machine that produces flashes of lightning. People who dream of becoming captors fail to understand that the phantoms cannot be caught; to capture them would be to banish them from their own nature, to turn them into us.

EXPLANATION #4

One explanation is that the phantoms have always been here, long before the arrival of the Indians. We ourselves are the intruders. We seized their land, drove them into hiding, and have been careful ever since to maintain our advantage and force them into postures of submission. This explanation accounts for the hostility that many of us detect in the phantoms, as well as the fear they sometimes inspire in us. Its weakness, which some dismiss as negligible, is the absence of any evidence in support of it.

THE PHANTOM LORRAINE

As children we all hear the tale of the Phantom Lorraine, told to us by an aunt, or a babysitter, or someone on the playground, or perhaps by a careless parent desperate for a bedtime story. Lorraine is a phantom child. One day she comes to a tall hedge at the back of a yard where a boy and girl are playing. The children are running through a sprinkler, or throwing a ball, or practicing with a hula hoop. Nearby, their mother is kneeling on a cushion before a row of hollyhock bushes, digging up weeds. The Phantom Lorraine is moved by this picture, in a way she doesn't understand. Day after day she returns to the hedge, to watch the children playing. One day, when the children are alone, she steps shyly out of her hiding place. The children invite her to join them. Even though she is different, even though she can't pick things up or hold them, the children invent running games that all three can play. Now every day the Phantom Lorraine joins them in the backyard, where she is happy. One afternoon the children invite her into their house. She looks with wonder at the sunny kitchen, at the carpeted stairway leading to the second floor, at the children's room with the two windows looking out over the backyard. The mother and father are kind to the Phantom Lorraine. One day they invite her to a sleepover. The little phantom girl spends more and more time with the human family, who love her as their own. At last the parents adopt her. They all live happily ever after.

ANALYSIS

As adults we look more skeptically at this tale, which once gave us so much pleasure. We understand that its purpose is to overcome a child's fear of the phantoms, by showing that what the phantoms really desire is to become one of us. This of course is wildly inaccurate, since the actual phantoms betray no signs of curiosity and rigorously withdraw from contact of any kind. But the tale seems to many of us to hold a deeper meaning. The story, we believe, reveals our own desire: to know the phantoms, to strip them of mystery. Fearful of their difference, unable to bear their otherness, we imagine, in the person of the Phantom Lorraine, their secret sameness. Some go further. The tale of the Phantom Lorraine, they say, is a thinly disguised story about our hatred of the phantoms, our wish to bring about their destruction. By joining a family, the Phantom Lorraine in effect ceases to be a phantom; she casts off her nature and is reborn as a human child. In this way, the story expresses our longing to annihilate the phantoms, to devour them, to turn them into us. Beneath its sentimental exterior, the tale of the Phantom Lorraine is a dream-tale of invasion and murder.

OTHER TOWNS

When we visit other towns, which have no phantoms, often we feel that a burden has lifted. Some of us make plans to move to such a town, a place that reminds us of tall picture books from childhood. There, you can walk at peace along the streets and in the public parks, without having to wonder whether a ripple will course through the skin of your forearms. We think of our children playing happily in green backyards, where sunflowers and honeysuckle bloom against white fences. But soon a restlessness comes. A town without phantoms seems to us a town without history, a town without shadows. The yards are empty, the streets stretch bleakly away. Back in our town, we wait impatiently for the ripple in our arms; we fear that our phantoms may no longer be there. When, sometimes after many weeks, we encounter one of them at last, in a corner of the yard or at the side of the car wash, where a look is flung at us before the phantom turns away, we think: Now things are as they should be, now we can rest awhile. It's a feeling almost like gratitude.

EXPLANATION #5

Some argue that all towns have phantoms, but that only we are able to see them. This way of thinking is especially attractive to those who cannot understand why our town should have phantoms and other towns none; why our town, in short, should be an exception. An objection to this explanation is that it accomplishes nothing but a shift of attention from the town itself to the people of our town: it's our ability to perceive phantoms that is now the riddle, instead of the phantoms themselves. A second objection, which some find decisive, is that the explanation relies entirely on an assumed world of invisible beings, whose existence can be neither proved nor disproved.

CASE STUDY #5

Every afternoon after lunch, before I return to work in the upstairs study, I like to take a stroll along the familiar sidewalks of my neighborhood. Thoughts rise up in me, take odd turns, vanish like bits of smoke. At the same time I'm wide open to striking impressions—that ladder leaning against the side of a house, with its shadow hard and clean against the white shingles, which project a little, so that the shingle-bottoms break the straight shadow-lines into slight zigzags; that brilliant red umbrella lying at an angle in the recycling container on a front porch next to the door; that jogger with shaved head, black nylon shorts, and an orange sweatshirt that reads, in three lines of black capital letters: EAT WELL / KEEP FIT / DIE ANYWAY. A single blade of grass sticks up from a crack in a driveway. I come to a sprawling old house at the corner, not far from the sidewalk. Its dark red paint could use a little touching up. Under the high front porch, on both sides of the steps, are those crisscross lattice panels, painted white. Through the diamond-shaped openings come pricker branches and the tips of ferns. From the sidewalk I can see the handle of an old hand mower, back there among the dark weeds. I can see something else: a slight movement. I step up to the porch, bend to peer through the lattice: I see three of them, seated on the ground. They turn their heads toward me and look away, begin to rise. In an instant they're gone. My arms are rippling as I return to the sidewalk and continue on my way. They interest me, these creatures who are always vanishing. This time I was able to glimpse a man of about fifty and two younger women. One woman wore her hair up; the other had a sprig of small blue wildflowers in her hair. The man had a long straight nose and a long mouth. They rose slowly but without hesitation and stepped back into the dark. Even as a child I accepted phantoms as part of things, like spiders and rainbows. I saw them in the vacant lot on the other side of the backyard hedge, or behind garages and toolsheds. Once I saw one in the kitchen. I observe them carefully whenever I can; I try to see their faces. I want nothing from them. It's a sunny day in early September. As I continue my walk, I look about me with interest. At the side of a driveway, next to a stucco house, the yellow nozzle of a hose rests on top of a dark green garbage can. Farther back, I can see part of a swing set. A cushion is sitting on the grass beside a three-pronged weeder with a red handle.

THE DISBELIEVERS

The disbelievers insist that every encounter is false. When I bend over and peer through the openings in the lattice, I see a slight movement, caused by a chipmunk or mouse in the dark weeds, and instantly my imagination is set in motion: I seem to see a man and two women, a long nose, the rising, the disappearance. The few details are suspiciously precise. How is it that the faces are difficult to remember, while the sprig of wildflowers stands out clearly? Such criticisms, even when delivered with a touch of disdain, never offend me. The reasoning is sound, the intention commendable: to establish the truth, to distinguish the real from the unreal. I try to experience it their way: the movement of a chipmunk behind the sunlit lattice, the dim figures conjured from the dark leaves. It isn't impossible. I exercise my full powers of imagination: I take their side against me. There is nothing there, behind the lattice. It's all an illusion. Excellent! I defeat myself. I abolish myself. I rejoice in such exercise.

YOU

You who have no phantoms in your town, you who mock or scorn our reports: are you not deluding yourselves? For say you are driving out to the mall, some pleasant afternoon. All of a sudden—it's always sudden—you remember your dead father, sitting in the living room in the house of your childhood. He's reading a newspaper in the armchair next to the lamp table. You can see his frown of concentration, the fold of the paper, the moccasin slipper half-hanging from his foot. The steering wheel is warm in the sun. Tomorrow you're going to dinner at a friend's house—you should bring a bottle of wine. You see your friend laughing at the table, his wife lifting something from the stove. The shadows of telephone wires lie in long curves on the street. Your mother lies in the nursing home, her eyes always closed. Her photograph on your bookcase: a young woman smiling under a tree. You are lying in bed with a cold, and she's reading to you from a book you know by heart. Now she herself is a child and you read to her while she lies there. Your sister will be coming up for a visit in two weeks. Your daughter playing in the backyard, your wife at the window. Phantoms of memory, phantoms of desire. You pass through a world so thick with phantoms that there is barely enough room for anything else. The sun shines on a hydrant, casting a long shadow.

EXPLANATION #6

One explanation says that we ourselves are phantoms. Arguments drawn from cognitive science claim that our bodies are nothing but artificial constructs of our brains: we are the dream-creations of electrically charged neurons. The world itself is a great seeming. One virtue of this explanation is that it accounts for the behavior of our phantoms: they turn from us because they cannot bear to witness our self-delusion.

FORGETFULNESS

There are times when we forget our phantoms. On summer afternoons, the telephone wires glow in the sun like fire. Shadows of tree branches lie against our white shingles. Children shout in the street. The air is warm, the grass is green, we will never die. Then an uneasiness comes, in the blue air. Between shouts, we hear a silence. It's as though something is about to happen, which we ought to know, if only we could remember.

HOW THINGS ARE

For most of us, the phantoms are simply there. We don't think about them continually, at times we forget them entirely, but when we encounter them we feel that something momentous has taken place, before we drift back into forgetfulness. Someone once said that our phantoms are like thoughts of death: they are always there, but appear only now and then. It's difficult to know exactly what we feel about our phantoms, but I think it is fair to say that in the moment we see them, before we're seized by a familiar emotion like fear, or anger, or curiosity, we are struck by a sense of strangeness, as if we've suddenly entered a room we have never seen before, a room that nevertheless feels familiar. Then the world shifts back into place and we continue on our way. For though we have our phantoms, our town is like your town: sun shines on the house fronts, we wake in the night with troubled hearts, cars back out of driveways and turn up the street. It's true that a question runs through our town, because of the phantoms, but we don't believe we are the only ones who live with unanswered questions. Most of us would say we're no different from anyone else. When you come to think about us, from time to time, you'll see we really are just like you.

Jim Shepard

Boys Town

Here's the story of *my* life: whatever I did wasn't good enough, anything I figured out I figured out too late, and whenever I tried to help I made things worse. That's what it's been like for me as far back as I can remember. Whenever I was about to get somewhere, something would step in and block me. Whenever I was about to finally have something, something would happen to take it away.

"The story of *your* life is that you're not to blame for anything," my mother always said when I told her that. "Out of everybody on earth, you're the only one who never did anything wrong. Whatever happens, it's always somebody else's fault."

"It *is* always somebody else's fault," I told her.

"Poor you," she always said back. "Screwed by the world."

"Hey, Dr. Jägermeister's calling," I used to tell her. "Bottoms up." And she'd just go back to whatever she was watching.

"So what's the deal with dinner?" sometimes I'd say. "You have a busy day?"

"Go to Pizza Hunt," she'd tell me.

"That's *Hut,* you fucking idiot," I'd tell her back. And then she'd say something else wrong the next time, just to frost my ass.

I was thirty-nine years old and living with my mother. I hadn't had a good year.

"What was your last good year?" my friend Owen asked me. "1992?"

He wasn't doing too well himself, but he managed to come over once or twice a week to eat whatever we had lying around.

I made some comment about whatever it was we were watching and he said, "What do you like? Do you like anything?"

"He likes to complain," my mother told him. "He likes to make trouble."

I liked to complain. I almost choked.

What did I like? I liked my dog. I liked hunting in the woods. I liked target shooting. I liked my kid, when I was first getting to know him. I liked women who weren't all about money or what I planned to do with my future.

"It'd be different with you if you ever got laid," Owen said during a commercial. My mother snorted.

"Hey, you're the one with the hand in your pants," I said.

"Now he's going to tell us about Stacey," my mother told him. But I didn't say a word.

My kid was down there in Stacey's house a thousand miles away. I was supposed to send checks but otherwise not come around more than once or twice a year. I mean, try to cram a whole year's worth of family time into one week. Maybe it'd work for you, but it didn't for me.

Stacey said the kid was asking where his dad was, and that if I wanted to see him I had to send money. It got so I let my mother answer when she called. They'd stay on the phone telling each other stories about me. "You think *that's* bad," my mother would say.

A guy in basic told me that girls who weren't good-looking

were the smart move because they were more grateful and weren't as likely to run off with somebody, and that made sense to me. I met Stacey at Fort Sill and liked her family better than her. I was a 71 Golf, which is like a clerk, hospital stuff, administrative. She was, too. I'd be dropping off discharge batches and she kept her head down when I teased her, but I could see her smile.

We went out for a year and five months and then we got married and had a kid. She was always saying she was going to move out, but she finally did the deed when I pushed her down the stairs. She was all like "You coulda killed me," and I was like "Hey, you shoved *me* first, and there was a railing, and there was carpet." She said, "You don't shove somebody at the top of the stairs," and I said, "Well, what did you do to *me?*" And the cop who showed up was a guy who had had a crush on her in high school and he was all "You can't be with this person. You want to press charges?"

He's standing over her while she's crying at the kitchen table and I'm in the den thinking, Why don't you rub her fucking back. And she was all Miss Generous: "No, just get him out of here. I don't feel safe."

Out here in the fucking sticks, you don't meet anybody. I went to this singles social in the basement rec room of the church. You had to fill out forms so they could match people up. These two women were running the thing. They asked if I could read and write. When they saw my face, they said it was just a question on the form.

But then I always reminded myself I didn't have it so bad. Our next-door neighbor's nineteen-year-old had some kind of thing, muscular dystrophy maybe, and they told her that kids like him only lived to be about twenty-one. When she came over for coffee with my mother, she told us to pray that his heart muscle stopped before his lungs, because that'd be a less horrible way to go.

I had all kinds of jobs. If it was some fucking thing no one else wanted to do, I did it. I worked in a hospital laundry. I washed pots and pans. I separated metals in a scrap yard. I drove a shuttle.

That job had a little pin that came with it that said "Martin, for Comfort Inn." Whenever I said stuff to my mother like I could see why my dad walked out, she'd go, "Where's your pin? Don't lose your pin."

I started thinking I should just go off the grid. You know: if I wasn't using anything or spending anything, I didn't need to make anything. I'd grow my own garden and shit. In the winter there'd still be rabbits and deer. I'd work out. Read a book. Improve my mind, unlike the other fucking imbeciles around here.

"Who says you're not using anything or spending anything?" my mother said when I told her. "*Somebody's* cleaning out the refrigerator every two days."

"That'd be your friend Owen," I said. "Your TV pal."

"*My* friend Owen?" she said. "He doesn't come over to see me."

"Well, I never asked him to come over and see me," I told her.

"So why's he come?" my mother said.

"Because he's a fucking *bum,* like me," I told her. " 'Cause he's got nothing else to do with himself."

"All right, all right," she said. "Don't get excited."

"Don't get excited," I said.

"Don't get excited," she said. "Put that down."

The Comfort Inn was my last job. I took two days off to go to my grandmother's funeral and they never let me forget it. The week I was back, even when I did a good job on something, all I heard was "You never told anybody you weren't coming in, you didn't let us know we were supposed to cover for you, you left us holding the bag." I'm working and the supervisor's just standing there running me down instead of doing his job. I finally told him that kind of horseshit was all well and good but, you know, it was pretty unprofessional.

You get *lonely,* is what it is. A person's not supposed to go through life with absolutely nobody. It's not normal. The longer you go by yourself the weirder you get, and the weirder you get the longer you go by yourself. It's a loop and you gotta do something to get out of it.

There was this girl Janice who I saw a lot at the store. I started talking to her, because it seemed like she was always out, and I was always out. I'd go to the library, or the store, and I'd see her. She seemed like a good person, and when I was with her I found myself thinking maybe I could do this or maybe that. Sit down at a restaurant with someone and eat like a human being. Take her back to my place and maybe watch a movie or something, if my mother would ever leave the house.

Naturally, this Janice had an ex-husband who was a cop. But as far as I could tell she didn't see too much of him.

I didn't need to be near any cops. The last thing I needed was somebody running a check on me.

My mother and Owen didn't know about Janice. They didn't know that I had a plan all worked out, that asshole here hadn't completely given up.

One of the times I saw her in the library, she was taking out like three DVDs about Milo and Otis. I said to her, "So you like dogs, huh?" and she said she did. I asked if she had one and she said yes to that, too. I told her I had one and she asked what kind and I told her. She said when she was leaving that maybe she'd see me walking it and I told her that maybe she would.

I went over there twice with my dog and couldn't get myself to go up to the front door either time. The second time, I was talking to myself and it still didn't work. And while I was standing there my dog took a dump on her sidewalk.

I walked the woods for however many years and know the whole area better than anybody. Down the end of the logging road where people went to park, on the edge of state forest, I hid a bag, a big duffel, that had a sleeping bag and two knives and one of my rifles in it. One of the knives was really more like a machete and ax combined. I had some bug spray in there, too. I thought it would be like a survival bag, if it came to that. I had it all in a big plastic garbage bag to keep it dry. Then somebody stole the whole thing.

I got everything in Wichita Falls at a gun-and-knife show after I got out of the military. I still had the .308 and a .357 Desert Eagle and a lot of ammo, so I started another bag. This one I made sure I hid better.

Fifth grade, we used to play this capture-the-flag game where anybody who got touched had to go stand on the base and there'd be fewer and fewer kids left after one side started winning. Fifth grade for some reason everybody decided it was boys against girls, and they'd pick out who they wanted to get caught by. You had to use two hands to touch and I would always tear free and so I'd be one of the last ones running around. This horrible cold day, the girls were looking at their first win if they could just get me. Four or five of them boxed me in and everybody on both sides was going crazy. This girl named Katie Kiely was right in front of me and all she had to do was step forward. I remember not being able to stop myself from grinning. And her expression changed when she saw my teeth, and she couldn't make that last move. The other girls were shouting at her and then it was like they caught what she had and they couldn't step forward, either. It was like I was a hair in their food. The teacher rang the recess bell and we all just stood there looking at each other. Then she rang it again and we all went inside.

My dad left the year before, or the year before that. I was in either third or fourth grade. Apparently, when he and my mother could still joke around it was always about me coming to a bad end. At least, that's what she said later. Like anybody could tell anything about anybody when they were nine years old. One Christmas, she said that as part of the joke he gave her a VHS of *Boys Town,* the movie where Spencer Tracy's the priest and Mickey Rooney's the tough kid who goes straight because he gets a new baseball glove or smells some home-cooked bread or some fucking thing.

She watched it every year around Christmas. I think it might've been the only thing he gave her that she didn't throw out after he took off. She'd always go, "Your movie's on," after she put it in the machine, but she always ended up watching it by herself.

There was one scene in it I liked, where a kid at one of the big lunch tables at the home tells Mickey Rooney how easygoing the place is, and how if he wants he can go on being Catholic or Protestant or whatever. And Rooney tells him, "Well, I'm nothin'." And the kid says back, "Then you can go right on bein' nothin'. And nobody cares." And one of the other kids showing him around says that on a clear day you can see Omaha from there. And Rooney goes, "Yeah? *Then* what've you got?"

I didn't think I'd seen the movie that often, but I got it in my head, so I must've watched it a lot. There's this other scene where they're about to strap a guy who didn't pan out into the electric chair. And the guy goes to Spencer Tracy, "How much time have I got, Father?" And Tracy goes, "Eternity begins in forty-five minutes, Dan." And the guy asks him, "What happens then?" And Tracy goes, "Oh, a bad minute or two." And the guy's like "Yeah, I know. After that?" And Tracy tells him, "Dan, that's been a mystery for a million years. You can't expect to crack *that* in a few seconds."

There were a lot of things I wanted to do about my appearance, but only so much could get accomplished until I got certain things squared away. I recognized that. I had a lot of stress. That's what nobody understood. I was in the military and after that I was working two jobs and trying to raise a family, and it seemed like even so, living at home and doing nothing, I had more stress than I had back then. Back then I never complained about it, I just did it, but people didn't realize that I was doing whatever the average person did times two. I took whatever shit the average person took times four. And I never said anything. I did my job and worked my eighty-hour weeks and knew as sure as shit that whatever I wanted was going to get taken away from me.

And the kind of thoughts I started to have people had all the time. But it was like everybody said: thinking and doing are two different things.

After my dog took the dump on her sidewalk, I didn't see Janice around for like three weeks. I thought maybe she was avoiding me. Or maybe she'd gone to Florida. Or maybe she was dead. I wrote a note, finally, and stuck it in her screen door: "ARE YOU STILL INTERESTED IN DOG WALKING?" And then when I got home I remembered I hadn't put my number on it. And then I remembered I hadn't put my name on it.

That third week my dog finally flushed a turkey in the state forest and I blew its wing off. I took it home to my mother and she said, "I'm not cleaning that fucking thing." And I said, "I bring you a whole turkey and you act like all I'm doing is making work for you?" And she said, "I'm not gonna start up with you," and went back to her show. So I threw the turkey in our Dumpster. Then when I was walking the woods I thought that was stupid, so I hiked all the way back and pulled it out. I'd give it to some charity or church so some poor kid could have some decent meat. So somebody could get something good out of it.

The guy who sold me my Desert Eagle told me that it was the last of the Israeli ones and that no more were going to be imported. Somebody else told me later that that was bullshit. I got all the extras at the same time and taught myself how to change the barrel length, so the version I had in my new bag had the ten-inch barrel instead of the six. The guy at Gilbert's Gun & Sportsman kept telling me he wanted to see it again. He called it the Hand Cannon. I joined an owners' forum on one of the USA Carry Web sites for a little while to get some tips and just talk to somebody. My user name was MrNoTrouble and somebody trying to be funny asked if that was the name my mother gave me and I said yeah. I met some guys online who seemed okay and some of them said they knew what I was going through. One guy, triplenutz, didn't live too far away and said we should meet up and go hunting together, but we never did. Another guy talked about taking his old toilet out back and letting fly at it with his Eagle from eighty yards. He recommended the experience for all Eagle owners. He said a piece of the flush tank broke the garage window behind him.

I got my dog from the stray facility at Fort Sill when I was leaving. I saw his photo on the Morale, Welfare, and Recreation Web site. The poor little fuck was just sitting there behind the chainlink looking at his paws. The adoption fee was fifty-two dollars, but that came with rabies and distemper-parvo shots, plus deworming and the heartworm test.

I stayed away a couple of days after the turkey incident and when I got back I sat on the porch and cleaned my rifle in the cold. After a while, the porch light went on and finally the door opened and my mother asked me to take her shopping. She had the door open only a little, to keep the heat in. "I need some things," she said after I didn't answer, like she was explaining.

"Why didn't you have Owen take you?" I said. She'd had trouble driving since she hurt her back. It didn't bother her to ride, though.

"He hasn't been around since you left," she said. "So you gonna take me or what?"

We went to the Price Chopper and the state package store. "It's not for me," she said when she told me about the second stop. "I'm getting stocking stuffers for Daryl."

I went up and down the AM dial while she was in there. Every single song I heard was what my father used to call a complete and utter piece of shit. "Don't ask me who Daryl is," I said to her when she finally came out.

"You know who Daryl is," she said. She dumped the bags on the seat between us.

"I thought this wasn't for you," I said, looking at the Jägermeister.

"I was here, I figured I might as well get something for myself," she said.

The other bag was filled with little travel bottles of liquor. "I got an assortment," she said. "He likes those and peppermint patties."

"I think you got that thing they talk about on the news," she said when we were halfway home. "PTSD. Is that what it is? I think you need to talk to somebody."

"PMS," I told her.

"I think you need to talk to somebody," she said.

"I talk to somebody every day," I told her. "Believe me, it's no fucking picnic."

"Owen said you could file a claim," she said. "Everyone gets something from the government except my kid."

"That's because your kid's an imbecile," I told her. "We already know that."

"All I'm saying is I think you need to talk to somebody," she said. "And now I'm gonna drop the subject."

When we got home, the poor fucking dog had wrapped himself around the tree with his chain. I don't know why we left him outside, anyway. "You're not gonna help me carry stuff in?" my mother said when I left her in the car.

She showed up at the door to my room a few hours later, after I was in bed. "There's phone numbers and stuff you can find," she said. "Owen told me."

"So have Owen call them, then," I said.

"Owen doesn't need them," she said.

"You got enough money," I told her. "And I been through worse shit in this house than I been through out of it." And that shut her up for like three days.

. . .

When she was finally ready to talk, I went back to the woods. I took the dog, but of course he ran away. I only found him again when I got back to the house. People like to talk about cancer or strokes, but if I was going to get something I'd want to get cholera. I came across it on the Plagues & Epidemics Web site and somewhere else it said that cholera killed thirty-eight million people in India in less than a hundred years. It even sounds like nothing you want to fuck with: *cholera*.

After basic at Fort Sill, I was in for four and a half active and then four in the reserves. In the reserves I trained to be a 91 Bravo, which was a field medic, but I washed out. When they gave me the news, they said not to worry, they'd still find me something to do. I ended up working out at the Casualty and Mortuary Affairs Operations Center. "What'd you do there?" my mother wanted to know when I got back. "Oh, you know, a little bit of this, little bit of that," I told her. I think she was watching *The Farmer's Daughter*. Even Owen had to laugh.

You want to talk about sad: even after all I been through, one of the saddest things I ever saw was a year after I got home, when my mother pulled over at a stop sign, it must've been ten below, and she's got the window down and she's scooping snow from the side mirror and trying to throw it on her windshield to clean it. We'd gone about three blocks and couldn't see a thing before she finally pulled over. I'm sitting there watching while she leans forward and tosses snow around onto the outside of the glass. Then every so often she hits the wipers.

She did this for like five minutes. We're pulled over next to a Stewart's. They got wiper fluid on sale in the window twenty-five feet away. She doesn't go get some. She doesn't ask me to help. She doesn't even get out of the car to try and do it herself.

. . .

My hair started falling out. I found it on my comb in the mornings. I could see where it was coming from. Not that anybody gives a shit, but you put that together with the teeth and you have quite the package.

I came in from thirty minutes of sliding slush off the porch and there was my kid's voice on the machine. My mother was playing it over again and turned it off when I got inside. She went back to whatever she was doing at the sink.

"Were you gonna tell me he called?" I asked.

"You cleaned up all that ice already?" she asked me back.

"I didn't do the ice. I did the slush," I told her.

"What am I supposed to do about the ice?" she wanted to know. I left her and went into the living room. She said, "There's a message from his mother, too. She says she's gonna get a lawyer to hop your ass unless you start sending some money. And somebody else called," she added once she was back with me in front of the TV.

I went out to the kitchen and played the machine. There was only one message and it was from the kid, saying he wanted to wish me a happy holiday. He said, "There was a thing about your unit in the paper, so I sent it up to you." I could hear a little buzzing, maybe something in our phone, maybe something in his. "Let me know if you get it," he said after a minute, like he was waiting for someone to answer.

I'd been getting a headache that felt like lights going on and off and trying to crack my skull. "Who else called?" I asked. I was still standing at the machine. The water from my boots was black from all the shit in the snow.

"How would I know?" my mother called from the living room. "She didn't leave a name."

"It was a woman?" I asked. "She wanted me? Was her name Janice?"

"I just said she didn't leave a name," she said. When I went back to the living room and stood in front of her, she said, "I can't see," meaning the television. "You got in *here* fast," she added, after I sat on the sofa. "What do you got, a girlfriend?"

I kept thinking this was my one chance, and then about how Janice could've found my number. Maybe she asked someone at the library?

"You're not answering me now?" my mother said.

"I'm trying to *think* here," I told her.

She shut up for a while. Then she finally said, "I don't know why anybody would want to give you the time of day."

I was thinking I should get the dog and go over to Janice's house, but it was sleeting. I figured I'd do it when it got better out. But I couldn't sit still, and my mother finally said, "You're shaking the whole floor," meaning with my leg, so I went up to my room. The dog came up to check on me and took one look and went downstairs again.

Then it got so bad I had to go out anyway, so I hiked down to the creek and checked some of my traps. I was wearing my field jacket with the hood, but I still got soaked. Two of the traps I couldn't find and there was nothing in the third, because I don't even know if I'm setting them right, but a month ago I found one snapped shut with some blood around it in the snow. When I got back, there were police cars all around my house. I hid in the sandpit a few houses down and watched until they went away.

What is *this* what is this what is this? I was thinking. I was surprised how much it freaked me out. I had some tricks I'd come up with over the years to keep from losing it, and I used them all. I waited half an hour after the cop cars left and lay there banging my chin on my gloves. Who else did I know who'd be in a sandpit in the snow outside somebody else's house?

The sleet changed to rain. It was so cold my head was rattling. One of the medics supposedly training me in the reserves used to call me TBI, for Traumatic Brain Injury. The first time he called me that, I told him I hadn't had any brain injuries, and he said, "Well, maybe it happened when you were a baby."

Finally, I stood up and came down the hill and circled my house on the outside. The backyard was like a lake. The light was on in my mother's bedroom and I went up to the window. On the dresser under the lamp there was a pamphlet that said "Your Service Member Is Home!" The TV was going in the living room, but maybe she was in the cellar. I waited until she came up the stairs and then pushed through the back door.

"They're looking for *you*, boy," she said when she saw me. Not "You must be fucking freezing." Not "How about a warm shower?"

"What'd they want?" I asked.

"They said they had a number of things they wanted to talk to you about," she said. "They wanted to look in your room and I said, 'You got a warrant?' I told them you'd be back tonight."

"What'd you say that for?" I asked.

"What was I supposed to tell them?" she said. "That you were out looking for a job?"

I went up to my room to think. There were some issues about prescriptions at the local pharmacy. Some bad checks back in Wichita Falls. There was a girl I'd scared by not letting her past me when we ran into each other in the woods. She'd torn her sleeve when she finally got away. It could've been a lot of things.

"I gotta go," I said when I came back downstairs. "I'm gonna do some camping for a while."

"Camping," she said. "In this." She put her hand out to the window.

"Don't tell them where I went," I said. "Far as you know, I never came home."

"I should be so lucky," she said.

I changed into dry clothes and put on like twelve layers and got together a rain fly and a cooking stove and a tent and a big pack full of cans of food and other shit and got out of there. "You taking your dog?" she called, but I never heard what she said after that.

It took me an hour to get to the end of the logging road, because I was covering my tracks with a pine branch as I went, and then another hour to find the duffel bag in the snow, and from there I followed a creek uphill way into the forest. I found a spot I already knew that had good cover and visibility and got everything set up and then started going through what I had and just what it was I thought I was going to do.

There was a trail fifty yards below that did a hairpin, and snowmobilers used it and cross-country skiers. Farther down was a waterfall and swimming hole and I remembered a notice on the library's Christian Outings bulletin board about a faith hike for teens called the Polar Bear Mixer.

I figured, well, if I'm going to jail I might as well get something to eat first, so I made some stew. And while I was eating I started thinking that once the cops had me one thing would lead to another and I knew what went on in jail, I'd heard stories. So I emptied the duffel in the tent and got all geared up. I had stuff I didn't even know I had. A bipod mount for the rifle and a winter-camo wrap for the stock and barrel and scope. Even winter-camo field bandages. When I was finished, I felt like this way I was at least ready for whatever.

But nobody came down the trail. It got dark. I got some sleep. Nobody came the next day, either. I had little meatballs for breakfast and sat around and waited and finally went out looking for rabbits, but the snow was too deep, so I had to come back.

I'd stepped in the creek and even with three layers of socks my feet were freezing. In the credits part of *Boys Town* right at the beginning there was a kid in an alley warming his hands over a fire in a bucket. I'd forgotten that.

The guy that gets electrocuted is the one who gives Spencer Tracy the idea for the orphans' home in the first place. When they're getting ready to take the guy to the chair, the governor tells him he owes a debt to the state, and the guy goes nuts on them. He asks where the state was when he was a little kid crying himself to sleep in a flophouse with drunks and hoboes. He says if he had one friend when he was twelve he wouldn't be standing here like this. Then he throws everybody but Tracy out of his cell.

I spent the afternoon keeping the stove going and sitting on a tarp and squeezing my head with my hands. The difference between where I was and my mother's house was that where I was I didn't have to listen to TV.

I had everything I needed in front of me and I still couldn't let well enough alone. That night, it sleeted again and the next morning my stove was covered with ice. I washed my face and changed my socks and got my Desert Eagle and hiked back down to the road and through the woods to the culvert that led the back way into town. It was sunny and I was sweating like a pig by the time I climbed out of the culvert at the turnaround at the end of Janice's street, but I didn't want to hang around for too long, so I stood there for a few minutes with my field jacket open, flapping it to dry myself off, and then went up to her house and rang the bell. The Eagle hung in the big inside pocket like a tire iron and I thought, I don't know what you brought *that* for. A guy swung the door open like he'd been waiting for me. He had to be the ex-husband. He looked me up and down and said, "What can I help you with?" But I let it go and just said, "Is Janice here?" And he gave me another look and I remembered how sweaty I was and that I was wearing four shirts under my field jacket. Collars were sticking up all over the place.

He said, "Yeah, she's in the back. What can we help you with?"

I stood there bouncing my leg for a second and reached under my coat like my Eagle might've fallen out. Then Janice came up behind him and I saw her get a good look at me. And I just said, "Nothing. I'll come back," and I left.

"Hey," the guy called from behind me, and I heard Janice

laugh. Halfway down the block, I cut through somebody's yard into the culvert. My heart was going so fast I was sure I was having a heart attack. She was probably still laughing. He was laughing with her. It was a comedy. I crouched at the bottom of the culvert and stepped around like a midget taking a walk. Even my outside shirts were soaked. I can never believe how fast I sweat through my clothes at times like that.

I worked my way up the culvert to Janice's backyard and then ran up to their window but it was too high to see in so I just reached up as far as I could and squeezed off four rounds. From that angle, I probably just hit the ceiling. The Eagle's so loud that at first your ears can't believe it. After the second round, somebody yelled something but I couldn't tell what. After the last one, I was booking back through the yard for the culvert. I could hear somebody whooping from the next house over. They probably thought it was fireworks. And while I was hauling down the culvert to my path through the woods I got to hear sirens from every cop car in upstate New York.

The whole way back through the woods and up into the hills, I thought, *You're* going to be hard to track. I mean, the snow was three feet deep. Even the town cops weren't going to be able to screw this up.

I had to rest on the logging road and again along the creek but finally got back to the tent. I pulled out my sleeping bag and threw my rifle and the Eagle and all the rounds I had on top of it. I could hear guys on the logging road already, the sound carried that far.

People talk about, Oh, this kid's sick and that kid's bipolar and this and that and I always say, Well, does he piss all over himself? And the answer's always no. That's because he *chooses* to go to the bathroom. Because he *knows* better. He *controls* himself. People *control* what they do. Most people don't know what it's like to look down the road and see there's nothing there. You try to tell somebody that, but they just look at you. I don't know why people need to hear the same thing ten thousand times, but they do.

Guys are breaking through the brush down below to my left and right, which tells me they're not only coming but they're coming in numbers. I can start to see them even through the trees.

I haven't cleaned the rifle. Mr. Logistical Planning. Even when I try to make lists for myself I can't follow the lists.

At least I tried, though. I tried harder than most people think. But what I did was, in life you're supposed to leave yourself an out, and I didn't.

I can hear even more sirens, way off in the distance. The cops down below have stopped short of the hairpin. They're keeping their voices low. They might be starting to catch on. I shove my elbows deeper into the snow, wipe my eyes, and put my face back to the scope, sighting back and forth. I don't even know if I'll open fire. I never know what I'm going to do next. They'll probably just come up here and pull me to my feet and push me all the way down the hill. Another scene that always got me in that movie was when the kids were waiting for Spencer Tracy to bring something home for Christmas. Of course, he didn't have any money, so all he can pull out and show them is a package of cornmeal mush. And this one little kid just stares at him. And then the kid finally says, like he wants to kill somebody, "What else you got in that bag?" And when Tracy has to tell him that he doesn't have anything else, the kid goes, "I thought you said that if we were good, somebody would help us."

Mark Slouka

The Hare's Mask

ODD HOW I MISS his voice, and yet it's his silences I remember now: the deliberateness with which he moved, the way he'd listen, that particular smile, as if, having long ago given up expecting anything from the world, he continually found himself mugged by its beauty. Even as a kid I wanted to protect him, and because he saw the danger in this, he did what he could.

By the time I was five I'd figured out—the way kids usually do, by putting pieces together and working them until they fit—that he'd lost his parents and sister during the war. That they'd been there one morning, like keys on a table, then gone. When I asked he said it had been so long ago that it seemed like another life, that many bad things had happened then, that these were different times, and then he messed up my hair and smiled and said, "None of us are going anywhere, trust me." When we went to the doctor he'd make funny faces and joke around while the doctor put a needle in his arm to show me it didn't hurt. And it came to me that everything he did—the way he'd turn the page of a book, or laugh with me at Krazy Kat, or call us all into the kitchen on Saturday evenings to see the trout he'd caught lying on the counter, their sticky skin flecked with bits of fern—was just the same.

He used to tie his own trout flies. I'd come down late at night when we still lived in the old house, sneaking past the yellow bedroom where my sister slept in her crib, stepping over the creaking mines, and he'd be sitting there at the dining-room table with just the one lamp, his hooks and feathers and furs spread out on the wood around him, and when he saw me he'd sit me on his knee, my stockinged feet dangling around his calves, and show me things. "Couldn't sleep?" he'd say. "Look here, I'll show you something important." And he'd catch the bend of a hook in the long-nosed vise and let me pick the color of the thread, and I'd watch him do what he did, his thin, strong fingers winding the waxed strand back from the eye or stripping the webbing off a small feather or clipping a fingernail patch of short, downy fur from the cheek of a hare. He didn't explain and I didn't ask. He'd just work, now and then humming a few notes of whatever he'd been listening to—Debussy or Chopin, Mendelssohn or Satie—and it would appear, step by step, the slim, segmented thorax, the gossamer tail, the tiny, barred wings, and he'd say, "Nice, isn't it?" and then, "Is it done?" and I'd shake my head, because this was how it always went, and he'd say, "Okay, now watch," and his fingers would loop and settle the thread and draw it tight so quickly it seemed like one motion, then clip the loose end close to the eye with the surgical scissors.

"Some things you can finish," he'd say.

I don't know how old I was when I was first drawn to their faces on the mantelpiece—not old. Alone, I'd pull up a chair and stand on it and look at them: my grandfather, tall, slim, stooped, handsome, his hair in full retreat at thirty; my grandmother with her sad black eyes and her uncomfortable smile—almost a wince—

somehow the stronger of the two; my aunt, a child of four, half-turned toward her mother as if about to say something . . . My father stood to the right, an awkward eight-year-old in a high-necked shirt and tie, a ghost from the future. I'd look at this photograph and imagine him taking it down when we weren't around, trying to understand how it was possible that they could be gone all this time and only him left behind. And from there, for some reason, I'd imagine him remembering himself as a boy. He'd be standing in the back of a train at night, the metal of the railing beneath his palms. Behind him, huddled together under the light as if on a cement raft, he'd see his family, falling away so quickly that already he had to strain to make out their features, his father's hat, his mother's hand against the black coat, his sister's face, small as a fingertip . . . And holding on to the whitewashed mantel-piece, struggling to draw breath into my shrinking lungs, I'd quickly put the picture back as though it were something shameful. Who knows what somber ancestor had passed on to me this talent, this precocious ear for loss? For a while, because of it, I misheard almost everything.

It began with the hare's mask. One of the trout flies my father tied—one of my favorites because of its name—was the Gold Ribbed Hare's Ear, which required, for its bristly little body, a tiny thatch of hare's fur, complete with a few long, dark guard hairs for effect. My father would clip the hair from a palm-size piece of fall-colored fur, impossibly soft. For some reason, though I knew fox was fox and deer hair was deer hair, I never read the hare's mask as the face of a hare, never saw how the irregular outline spoke the missing eyes, the nose . . . Whatever it was—some kind of optical illusion, some kind of mental block—I just didn't see it, until I did.

I must have overheard my parents talking one night when they thought I was sleeping and made of it what I could, creeping back up to my room with a new and troubling puzzle piece that I would have to place, and would, in my way. I couldn't have known much.

The full story was this. As a young boy growing up on Táborská Street in Brno, Czechoslovakia, my father would have to go out to the rabbit hutch in the evenings to tend the rabbits and, on Fridays, kill one for dinner. It was a common enough chore in those days, but he hated doing it. He'd grow attached, give them names, agonize endlessly. Often he'd cry, pulling on their ears, unable to choose one or, having chosen, to hit it with the stick. Sometimes he'd throw up. Half the time he'd make a mess of it anyway, hitting them too low or too high so they'd start to kick, and he'd drop them on the floor and have to do it again. Still, this is what boys did then, whether they liked it or not.

In September of 1942, when he was nine, a few months after the partisans assassinated Reichsprotektor Reinhard Heydrich in Prague, my father's family hid a man in the rabbit hutch. My grandfather, who had fought with the Legionnaires in Italy in 1917, built a false wall into the back, making a space two meters long and a half meter wide. There was no light. You couldn't stand up. The man—whose name my father never knew, but who may have been Miloš Werfel, who was captured soon afterward and sent to Terezín, where he was killed the following spring—stayed for nine days.

Both had their burdens. My father, who had to go on making his miserable trips to the hutch to keep from attracting the neighbors' attention, now had to slide a food plate through the gap between the false wall and the floorboards, then take the bucket of waste to the compost pile, dump it, clean it out, return it. By the time he was done taking care of the rabbits, the plate would be empty. Werfel, for his part, lying quietly in the dark, broken out in sores, had to endure my father's Hamlet-like performances. To whack or not to whack. There were bigger things than rabbits.

Nine days. What strange, haunted hours those must have been that they spent in each other's company, neither one able to acknowledge the other (my father was under strict orders, and Werfel—if it *was* Werfel—knew better), yet all the time aware of the other's presence, hearing the slow shift of cloth against wood or air escaping the nose, or even, in Werfel's case, glimpsing some splinter of movement through a crack.

Who knows what Werfel thought? Poet, partisan, journalist, Jew—each an indictment, any two worthy of death—he must have known where things stood. Not just with himself, but with the boy who brought him food and took the bucket with his waste. Partisans weren't supposed to have children—this was just one of those things. As for my father, he didn't think about Werfel much. He didn't think how strange it was that a grown man, his suit carefully folded in a rucksack, should be lying in his underwear behind a board in the rabbit hutch. He didn't think about what this meant, or what it could mean. He thought about Jenda and Eliška.

Jenda and Eliška were rabbits, and they were a problem. That September, for whatever reason, my father's Uncle Lada hadn't been able to bring the family any new rabbits, and the hutch was almost empty. Jenda and Eliška were the last. My father, who had been protecting the two of them for months by taking others in their place, thought about little else. With that unerring masochism common to all imaginative children, he'd made them his own. They smelled like fur and alfalfa. They trusted him. Whenever he came in, they'd hop over to him and stand up like rabbits in a fairy tale, hooking their little thick-clawed feet on the wire. They couldn't live without each other. It was impossible. What he had yet to learn was that the impossible is everywhere; that it hems us in at every turn, trigger set, ready to turn when touched.

And so it was. Locked in by habit, my father had to go to the hutch to keep Mrs. Čermáková from asking after his health because the other evening she'd just happened to notice my grandfather going instead, had to go because habit was safety, invisibility, because it held things together, or seemed to; because even in this time of routine outrages against every code and norm—*particularly* in this time—the norm demanded its due. And so off he went, after the inevitable scene, the whispering, the tears, shuffling down the dirt path under the orchard, emerging ten minutes later holding the rabbit in his arms instead of by its feet, disconsolate, weeping, schooled in self-hatred . . . but invisible. The neighbors were used to his antics.

It wasn't enough, something had been tripped; the impossible opened like a bloom. Two days after my father, his eyes blurring and stinging, brought the stick down on the rabbit's back, the hutch felt different; Werfel was gone. Five days later, just before nine o'clock on the morning of October 16, 1942, my father's parents and sister were taken away. He never saw them again. He himself, helping out in a neighbor's garden at the time, escaped. It shouldn't have been possible.

Sixteen years later my father had immigrated to New York, married a woman he met at a dance hall who didn't dance, and moved into an apartment on 63rd Road in Queens, a block down from the Waldbaum's. Four years after that, having traded proximity to Waldbaum's for an old house in rural Putnam County, he'd acquired a son, a daughter, and the unlikely hobby of trout fishing. And in 1968, that daughter came to the table, poured some milk on her Cap'n Crunch, and announced that she wanted a rabbit for her sixth birthday.

I'd begun to understand some things by then—I was almost nine. I knew, though he'd never show it, how hard this business with the rabbit would be for him, how much it would remind him of. Though I couldn't say anything in front of him, I did what I could behind the scenes. I offered my sister my gerbils, sang the virtues of guinea pigs, even offered to do her chores. When she dug in, predictably—soon enough it was a rabbit or death—I called her stupid, and when she started to cry, then hit me in the face with a plastic doll, I tried to use that to get the rabbit revoked. It didn't work. She'd been a good girl, my mother said, incredibly. We lived in the country. I had gerbils. It wasn't unreasonable.

That weekend we drove to the pet store in Danbury (I could come too if I behaved myself, my mother said), and after a last attempt to distract us from our mission by showing my sister the hamsters running on their wheels or pawing madly at the glass, I watched as my father leaned over the pen, lifting out one rabbit after the other, getting pine shavings on his lap while she petted their twitching backs or pulled their stupid ears . . . I wanted to hit her. When I took my father's hand at one point he looked down at me and said, "You okay?" and I said, "Sure." My sister picked out an ugly gray one with long ears, and as we were leaving the store I stuck out my foot and she hit herself on one of the metal shelves and my father grabbed me and said, "What's the matter with you, what's gotten into you these days?" and I started to cry.

It got worse. I wouldn't help set up its cage. I wouldn't feed it. I refused to call it by its name. I started calling it Blank for some reason. When my sister asked me something about it, I'd say, "Who? You mean Blank?" and when she started to cry I'd feel bad but I couldn't stop and part of me felt better. When it kept my sister up at night with its thumping and rustling and my parents moved its cage to the living room, I started walking around the other way, through the kitchen. I'd pretend to myself that I couldn't look at it, that something bad would happen if I did, and even watching TV I'd put my hand up as if scratching my forehead, or thinking, so that my eye couldn't slip. Sometimes I'd catch my father looking at me, and once he asked me if I'd like a rabbit of my own. When I said no, he pretended to be surprised.

It was sometime that fall that I had a bad dream and came down the stairs to find him sitting at the table under the lamp, tying his trout flies. He looked up at me over the silly half glasses that went over his regular glasses that helped him to see. "Well, hello," he said. "Haven't done this in a while."

"I couldn't sleep," I said.

"Bad dream?"

"No," I said. I could hear the rabbit in the dark behind us, thumping around in his cage.

"He can't sleep either," my father said.

"What's that one called?" I said, pointing to the fly he had in the vise.

My dad was looking at me. "This one?" he said. And he told me, then showed me how it was made, clipping four or five blue-gray spears for the tail, then selecting a single strand from a peacock feather for the body. I watched him secure it with a few loops of thread, then start to wind it toward the eye of the hook, the short dark hairs sparking green with every turn through the light . . . And that's when I saw it, not just the thick, familiar chestnut fur of the cheeks and head and neck, but now, for the first time, the missing nose and ears, the symmetrical cavities of the eyes, even the name itself, reaching back to deepest childhood through the medium of my father's voice saying, "Pass me the hare's mask," "Let's take a little bit off the hare's mask."

It was the next day that I took the hare's mask and hid it in my room. When he asked me if I'd seen it I lied, and when he came back upstairs after going through everything in the dining room (as though that piece of fur could have jumped from the table and hidden itself behind his books), I swore I didn't have it and even let myself get indignant over the fact that he wouldn't believe me. Eventually, he left. "For Christ's sake," I heard him saying to my mother downstairs, "it didn't just disappear," and then, "That's not the point and you know it."

I slept with it under my pillow. I'd keep it in my pocket and run my thumb over the thin edge of the eye socket and the soft bristly parts where my father had clipped it short. When no one was home I'd hold it up to the rabbit cage and, appalled at myself, thrilled and shaky, yell "Look, look, this was you" to the rabbit who would sometimes hop over and try to nibble at it through the wires. I pushed my nose into it, breathing in that indescribable deep fur smell.

And that's how he found me, holding the hare's mask against my face, crying so hard I didn't hear him come into the room, two days before my ninth birthday. Because he'd understood about dates, and how things that aren't connected can seem to be, and that he'd been nine years old when it happened. And he held me for a long time, petting my hair in that slightly awkward, fatherly way, saying, "It's okay, everything's going to be okay, everything's just fine."

It was some years later that I asked him and he told me how it went that night. How he'd opened the dirt-scraping door to the hutch and entered that too-familiar smell of alfalfa and steel and shit already sick with the knowledge that he couldn't do what he absolutely had to do. How he lit the lamp and watched them hop over to him. How he stood there by the crate, sobbing, pulling first on Jenda's ears, then Eliška's, picking up one, then the other, pushing his nose into their fur, telling them how much he loved them . . . unaware of the time passing, unaware of anything, really—this is how miserable he was—until suddenly a man's voice speaks from behind the wall and says, "You're a good boy. Let me choose." My father laughed—a strange laugh: "And I remember standing there with my hands in the wire and feeling this stillness come over me, and him saying, 'Jenda. Take Jenda, he's the weaker of the two. It's not wrong. Do it quickly.' "

Lauren Groff

Eyewall

IT BEGAN WITH the chickens. They were Rhode Island Reds and I'd raised them from chicks. Though I called until my voice gave out, they'd huddled in the darkness under the house, a dim mass faintly pulsing. Fine, you ungrateful turds! I'd yelled before abandoning them to the storm. I stood in the kitchen at the one window I'd left unboarded and watched the hurricane's bruise spreading in the west. I felt the chickens' fear rising through the floorboards to pass through me like prayers.

We waited. The weatherman on the television mimicked the swirl of the hurricane with his body like a valiant but inept modern dancer. All the other creatures of the earth flattened themselves, dug in. I stood in my window watching, a captain at the wheel, as the first gust filled the oaks on the far side of the lake and raced across the water. It shivered my lawn, my garden, sent the unplucked zucchini swinging like church bells. And then the wind smacked the house with an open hand. Bring it on, I shouted. Or, just maybe, this is yet another thing in my absurd life that I whispered.

. . .

At first, though, little happened. The lake goosebumped; I might have been looking at the sensitive flesh of an enormous lizard. The swing in the oak made larger arcs over the water. The palmettos nodded, accepting the dance.

The wine I had been drinking was very good. I opened another bottle. It had been left in a special cooler in the butler's pantry that had been designed to replicate precisely the earthy damp of the *caves* under Bourgogne. One bottle cost a year of retirement, or an hour squinting down the barrel of a hurricane.

My neighbor's Jeep kicked up hillocks of pale dust on the road. He saw me in the window and skidded to a halt. He rolled down the window, shouting, his face squared into his neck, the warm hue of a brick. But the wind now was so loud that his voice was lost, and I felt a surge of affection for him as he leaned out the window, gesticulating. We'd had a moment a few years back at a Conservation Trust benefit just after my husband left, our fortyish bodies both stuffed into finery. There was the taste of whiskey and the weirdness of his mustache against my teeth. Now I toasted him with my glass, and he shouted so hard he turned purple, and his hunting dog stuck her head from the back window and began to howl. I raised two fingers and calmly gave him a pope's blessing. He bulged, affronted, and rolled up the window. He made a gesture as if wadding up a hunk of paper and tossing it behind his shoulder and then he pulled away to join the last stragglers pushing north as fast as their engines could strain. The great hand of the storm would wipe them off the road like words from a chalkboard. I'd hear of the way my neighbor's Jeep, going a hundred miles per hour, lovingly kissed the concrete riser of an overpass. His dog would land clear over the six lanes in the southbound culvert and dig herself down. When the night passed and the day dawned calm, she'd pull herself to the road and find herself the sole miraculous survivor of a mile-long flesh and metal sandwich.

. . .

I began to sing to myself, songs from childhood, songs with lyrics I didn't understand then and still don't, folk songs and commercial jingles and the Hungarian lullaby my father sang during my many sleepless nights when I was small. I was a high-strung, beetle-browed girl, and the songs only made me want to stay awake longer, to outlast him until he fell asleep crookedly against my headboard and I could watch the way his dreams moved beneath his handsome face. Enervated and watchful in school the next day, I'd be unable to follow the teacher's voice, the ropes of her sentences as she led us through history or English or math, and would fill my notebooks with drawings—a hundred different houses, floors and windows and doors. All day I'd furiously scribble. If I only drew the right place to hold me, I could escape from the killing hours of school and draw myself all the way safely home.

The house sucked in a shuddery breath, and the plywood groaned as the windows drew inward. Darkness fell over the world outside. Rain unleashed itself. It was neither freight train nor jet engine nor cataract crashing around me, but, rather, everything. The roof roared with water, the window blurred. When the storm cleared, I saw a branch the size of a locomotive cracking off the heritage oak by the lake and falling languorously down, the wet moss floating outstretched like useless dark wings.

I felt, rather than saw, the power go out. Time erased itself from the appliances and the lights winked shut. The house went sinister behind me, oppressive with its dark humidity. When I turned, I saw my husband in the far doorway.

You're drinking my wine, he said. I could hear him perfectly, despite the storm. He was a stumpy man, thirty years older than me. I could smell the mint sprigs he chewed and the skin ointment for his psoriasis.

I didn't think you'd mind, I said. You don't need it anymore.

He put both hands over his chest and smiled. A week after he left me, his heart broke itself apart. He was in bed with his mistress. She was so preposterously young that I assumed they conversed in baby talk. He hadn't wanted children until he ended up fucking one. I was glad that she was the one who'd had to be stuck under his moist and cooling body, the one to shout his name and have it go unanswered.

He came closer and stood next to me in the window. I went very still, as I always did near him. We watched the world on its bender outside. My beautiful tomatoes had flattened and the metal cages minced away across the lawn, as if ghosts were wearing them as hoopskirts.

You're still here, of course, he said. Even though they told you to get out days ago.

This house is old, I said. It has lived through other storms.

You never listen to anyone, he said.

Have some wine, I said. Stand with me. Watch the show. But for God's sake, shut it.

He looked at me deeply. He had huge brown eyes that were young no matter how alligatored his skin got. His eyes were what had made me fall for him. He was a very good poet. The night I met him I sat, spellbound, at a reading my friend had dragged me to, his words softening the ground of me so that when he looked up, those brown eyes could tunnel all the way through.

He drank a swig of wine and moaned in appreciation. At its peak, he said. Perfection. Drink it now.

I plan to, I said.

He began to go vague on me. I knew his poems were no good when they began to go vague. How's my reputation? he said, the fingers of his hands melding into mittens. I was his literary executor; he hadn't had time to change that one last thing.

I'm letting it languish, I said.

Ah, he said. *La belle dame sans merci.*

I don't speak Italian, I said.

French, he said.

Oh, dear, I said. My ignorance must have been so maddening.

Honey, he said, you don't know the half of it.

Well, I said. I *do* know my half.

I didn't say, I had never said: Lord, how I longed for a version of you I could hold, entire, in my arms.

He winked at me, and the mint smell intensified, and there was a pressure on my mouth, then a lessening. And then it was only the storm and the house and me.

The darkness redoubled, the sound intensified. There were pulsing navy veins within the clouds; I remembered a hunting trip with my husband once, the buck's organs gutted onto the ground. The camphor and magnolia and crepe myrtles pressed their crowns to the earth, backbending, acrobats. My teak picnic table galumphed itself toward the road, chasing after the chairs that had already fled away.

My best laying hen was scraped from under the house and slid in a horrifying diagonal across the window. For a moment, we were eye to lizardy eye. I took a breath. The glass fogged, and when it cleared, my hen had blown away. Then the top layer of the lake seemed to rise in one great sheet and crush itself against the house. When the wind swept the water into the road, my garden became a pit in which a gar twisted and a baby alligator dug furiously into the mud. From behind the flattened blueberries, a nightmare creature of mud stood and leaned against the wind. It showed itself to be a man only moments before the wind picked him up and slammed him into the door. I didn't think before I ran and heaved it open so that the man tumbled in. I was blown off my feet, and had to clutch the doorknob to keep from flying. The wind seized a flowerpot and smashed it through the microwave. The man crawled and helped me push the door until at last it closed and the storm was banished, howling to find itself outside again.

The man was mudstruck, naked, laughing. A gold curl emerged from the filth of his head, and I wiped his face with the hem of my dress until I saw that he was my college boyfriend. I sat down on the floor beside him, scrabbling the dirt from him with my fingernails until I could make him out in his entirety.

Oh! he shouted when he could speak. He'd always been a jovial boy, garrulous and loving. He clutched my face between his hands and said, You're old! You're old! You should wear the bottoms of your trousers rolled.

I don't wear trousers, I said, and snatched my head away. There was still water in the pipes, and I washed him until he was clean. He fashioned a loincloth out of a kitchen towel. He kept his head turned from me, staring at me from the corners of his eyes until I took his chin in my fingers and turned it. There it was, the wet rose blossoming above his ear. He took a long swallow of wine and I watched a red ligament move over the bone.

So you really did it, I said.

A friend of a friend of a friend had told me something: Calgary, the worst motel he could find, the family's antique dueling pistol. But I didn't trust either the friend or the friend of the friend, certainly not the friend to the third power, and this act seemed so out of character for such a vivid soul that I decided it couldn't possibly have been true.

It's so strange, I said. You were always the happiest person I knew. You were so happy I had to break up with you.

He cocked his head and pulled me into his lap. Happy, eh? he said.

I rested against his thin young chest. I thought of how I had been so tired after two years of him, how I couldn't bear the three a.m. phone calls when he *had* to read me a passage from Benjamin, the Saturdays when I had to search for him in bars or find him in strangers' living rooms, how, if I had to make one more goddamn egg sandwich to fill his mouth and quiet him and make him fall asleep at dawn, I would shatter into fragments myself.

Our last month was in Spain. I had sold one of my ovaries to get us there, and lost him in Barcelona. For an hour I wept at the center of a knot of concerned Spaniards, until he came loping down the street toward me, some stranger's stolen Afghan hound tugging at the leash in his hand. A peculiar light had been kindled in his eye; it blazed before him, a herald announcing his peculiar vibrancy. I looked up at him in the dim of the house, the hole in the side of his head.

He smiled, expectant, brushing my knuckles with his lips. I said, Oh.

Bygones, he said. He downed half of the bottle of wine as if it were a plastic cup of beer. A swarm of palmetto bugs burst up through the air-conditioning vent and paraded politely by in single file. I could feel the thinness of the dishcloth between his skin and my legs, the way this beautiful boy had always stirred me.

My God, I loved you, I said. I had played it close to my chest then; I had thought not telling him was the source of my power over him.

Also bygones, he said. Now tell me what you're doing here.

The rowboat skipped over the lake, waggling its oars like swimmers' arms. It launched itself into the trunks of the oaks and pinned itself there. I saw the glass of the window beating, darkness so deep in it that I could see myself, gray at the temples, lined from nostril to lip. The house felt cavernous around me. I had thought it would be full by now: of husband, of small voices, at the very least of chickens.

Do you remember our children? I asked.

He beamed. Clothilde, he said. Rupert. Haricot and Abricot, the twins. Dodie. Australopithecus. And Dirk. All prodigies, with your brains and my looks.

You forgot Cleanth, I said.

My favorite! he said. How could I have forgotten? Maker of crossword puzzles, National Spelling Bee champion. Good old Cleanth.

He lifted the back of my hand to his lips and kissed it. It's too bad, he murmured.

Before I could ask what was too bad, the window imploded, showering us with glass. The wind reached in and sucked him out. I clutched at the countertops and saw my beautiful boy swan-dive into the three-foot-deep pond that had been my yard. He turned on his back and did a few strokes. Then he imitated one of my dead chickens floating about in the water, her two wings cocked skyward in imprecation. Like synchronized swimmers, they swirled about each other, arms to the sky, and then, in a gulp, both sank.

I tucked two bottles and a corkscrew into my sleeves and pulled myself to the doorway against the tug of the wind. I could barely walk when I was through. The house heaved around me and the wind followed, overturning clocks and chairs, paging through the sheet music on the piano before snatching it up and carrying it away. It riffled through my books one by one as if searching for marginalia, then toppled the bookshelves. The water pushed upward from under the house, through the floor cracks, through the vents, turning my rugs into marshes. Rats scampered up the stairs to my bedroom. I trudged over the mess and crawled up, step by step, on my hands and knees. A terrapin passed me, then a raccoon with a baby clutched to its back, gazing at me with wide robbers' eyes. Peekaboo, I said, and it hid its face in its mother's ruff. In the light of a battery-powered alarm clock, I saw rats, a snake, a possum, a heap of bugs scattered across the room, as if gathered for a slumber party, all those gleaming eyes in the dark. The bathroom was the sole windowless place at the heart of the house, and when I was inside, I locked them all out.

I sat in the bathtub, loving its cool embrace of my body. I have always felt a sisterhood with bathtubs; without someone else within us, we are smooth white cups of nothing. It was thick black in the bathroom, sealed tight. The house twisted and shook; above, the roof peeled itself slowly apart. The wind played the chimney until the whole place wheezed like a bagpipe. I savored each sip of wine and wondered what the end would be: the roof gone and the storm galloping in; the house tilting on its risers and rolling me out; a water moccasin crawling up the pipes and finding a warm place to nest between my legs.

Above the scream of the storm, there came the hiss and sputter of a wet match. Then a weak flame licked brightly near the toilet and went out. There rose in its place the sweet smell of pipe smoke.

Jesus Christ, I said.

No. Your father, he said in his soft accent. He had a smile in his voice when he said, Watch your language, my love.

I felt him near, sitting at the edge of the bathtub as if it were the side of a bed. I felt his hand brushing the wet hair out of my mouth. I lifted my own hand and caught his, feeling the sop of his flesh against the fragile bone. I was glad it was dark. He'd been eaten from the inside by cancer. My mother, after too many gin and tonics, always turned cruel. She had once described my father's end to me. The last few days, she'd said, he was a sack of swollen flesh.

I hadn't been there. I didn't even know he was sick. I'd been sent to Girl Scout camp. While he slowly died, I learned how to tie knots. While he hallucinated about his village, the cherry trees, the bull in the field that bellowed at night for sex, I kissed a girl named Julia Pfeffernuss. I believed for years afterward that tongues should taste like the clovers we'd sucked for the honey at their roots. When my father was forgetting his English and shouting for his mother in Hungarian, I stole a sailboat and went alone to the quiet heart of the reservoir. Before the dam had been built, there had been a village there. I took down the sails and dropped the anchor and dove. I opened my eyes to find myself outside a young girl's room, her brushes and combs still laid out on her vanity, me in the algaed mirror, framed by the window. I saw a catfish lying on a platter in the dining room as if serving himself up; he looked at me and shook his head and sagely swam away. I saw sheets forgotten on the line, waving upward toward the sun. I came out of the lake and climbed into the boat and tacked for camp, and didn't tell a soul what I had seen, never, not once, not even my husband, who would have made it his own.

I might have told my friends, I think. I don't think I'd meant to keep the miracle to myself. But the camp's director had been waiting for me on the dock, a hungry pity pressing her lips thin, the red hood of her sweatshirt waggling in the air behind her. It stirred still, in my memory, still, a big and ugly tongue.

When we first saw this house on its sixty acres, I didn't fall for the heart-pine floors or the attic fan that kept the house cool all summer without air-conditioning or the magnolias blooming their goblets of white light. I fell for the long swing in the heritage oak over the lake, which had thrilled some child, which was waiting for another. My husband looked at the study, mahogany-paneled, and said under his breath, Yes. I stood in the kitchen and looked at the swing, at the way the sun hit the wood so gently, the promise it held, and thought, Yes. Every day for ten years, watching the swing move expectantly in the light wind of morning, thinking, Yes, the word quietly piercing the diaphragm, that same Yes until the day my husband left, and even after he left, and then even after he died; even then, still hoping.

For a very long time, we sat there like that: my dad's hand in mine, in the roaring black. I waited for him to speak, but he had always been a man who knew how to groom the silence between people. He smoked, I drank, and the world tired itself out with its tantrum.

I lost awareness of my body. There was only the smoothness of the porcelain beneath me, the warmth of my father's hand. Time passed, endless, a breath.

Slowly, the wind softened. Sobbed. Stopped. The house trembled and moaned itself back to pitch. A trickle of dawn painted a gray strip under the door. My body returned to itself. I could only hear my heartbeat and rain off the roof when I said, Remember when you used to call your family in Hungary?

You were always so furious, he said. You would scream at me when I tried to talk. Your mother had to take you out to get ice cream every time I wanted to call.

I couldn't eat it. I just watched it melt, I said.

I know, he said.

I still can't eat it, I said. I hated that, suddenly, you opened your mouth and became another person

We waited. The air felt poached, both sticky and wet. I said, I never thought I could be so alone.

We're all alone, he said.

You had me, I said.

True, he said. He squeezed the back of my neck, kneaded the knots out.

I listened to the shifting of the world outside. This is either the eye or we've made it through, I said.

Well, he said. There will always be another storm, you know.

I stood, woozy, the bottles clanking off my body back into the bathtub. I know, I said.

You'll be A-OK, he said.

That's no wisdom coming from you, I said. Everything's all right for the dead.

When I opened the door to the bedroom, the room was blazing with light. The plywood over the windows had caught the wind like sails and carried the frames from the house. There were rectangular holes in the wall. The creatures had left the room. The storm had stripped the sheets like a good guest, and they had all blown away, save one, which hung pale and perfect over the mirror, saving me from the sight of myself.

The damage was done: three-hundred-year-old trees smashed, towns flattened as if a fist had come from the sun and twisted. My life was scattered into three counties. Someone found a novel with my bookplate in it sunning itself on top of a car in Georgia. Everywhere I looked, the dead. A neighbor child, come through the storm, had wandered outside while the rest of the family was salvaging what remained, and fallen into the pool and drowned. The high school basketball team, ignoring all warnings, crossed a bridge and was swallowed up by the Gulf. Old friends were carried away on the floods; others, seeing the little that remained, let their hearts break. The storm had stolen the rest of the wine and the butler's pantry, too. My chickens had drowned, blown apart, their feathers freckling the ground. For weeks, the stench of their rot would fill my dreams. Over the next month, mold would eat its way up the plaster and leave gorgeous abstract murals of sage and burnt sienna behind. But the frame had held, the doors had held. The house, in the end, had held.

On my way downstairs, I passed a congregation of exhausted armadillos on the landing. Birds had filled the Florida room, cardinals and whip-poor-wills and owls. Gently the insects fled from my step. I sloshed over the rugs that bled their vegetable dyes onto the floorboards. My brain was too small for my skull and banged from side to side as I walked. Moving in the humidity was like forcing my way through wet silk. Still, I opened the door to look at the devastation outside.

And there I stopped, breathless. I laughed. Isn't this the fucking kicker, I said aloud. Or perhaps I didn't.

Houses contain us; who can say what we contain? Out where the steps had been, balanced beside the drop-off: one egg, whole and mute, holding all the light of dawn in its skin.

Keith Ridgway

Rothko Eggs

S HE LIKED ART. She liked paintings and video art and photography. She liked to read about artists and she liked to hear
them talk. She had been to all the big London art museums
already, and she had been to some small ones too, and some galleries. She wanted to be an artist, she thought. She liked how the
world looked and felt one way when you looked at it or breathed
or walked about, and looked another way completely when you
looked at art, even though you recognized that the art was about
the world, or had something to do with the world—the world you
looked at or breathed or walked about in. She didn't mean realism. She didn't like realism very much, really, because usually
there was no room in it. She would look at it, and everything was
already there. But she liked abstract art because it was empty.
Sometimes it was only empty a tiny amount, and it was easy for
her to see what the artist was trying to say or make her feel, and
sometimes that was okay, but she usually liked the art that had lots
of empty in it, where it was really hard to work out what the artist
wanted, or whether the artist wanted anything at all, or was just,
you know, trying to look like he had amazing ideas. But really

good artists had lots of empty in their paintings or whatever they did. They left everything out, or most things, anyway, but suggested something, so that she could take her own things into the painting (or the installation or the video or whatever), and the best art of all was when she didn't really know what she was taking in with her, but it felt right, and when she looked at that art and took herself into it she felt amazing.

She wanted to be able to do that. Make that.

Photography was a bit different. She hadn't worked out why yet.

Her Dad was having a text fit. She put her phone on silent and stuck it in a drawer.

She was trying to finish her history essay but Beth kept on popping up on MSN asking her stupid questions. She didn't answer her for a while and then set her status to *away* and tried to think about why Churchill lost the election after the war.

There were some artists that she couldn't really understand. She could see that they had left her lots of space, but she didn't know what to fill it with. Sometimes, if they were not very well known or respected artists she decided that they just weren't very good— that they were faking it and they didn't know what they were doing really. But if they were famous and supposed to be amazing, then they just made her feel stupid. It was easier the farther back in history you went, because art became more realist and you could just like something or not like it. More or less. Though sometimes when you didn't like something and then read about it, or read about the artist, you could start to see things you didn't notice before, or you could feel things differently, and start to like it. Unless you went back to when everything was sort of cartoonish, like Fra Angelico, and then she didn't really understand what was going on there either, because it just looked so sloppy and bad. But apparently it was amazing.

On her laptop the wallpaper was a self-portrait by Frida Kahlo.

She liked it. She thought it was sort of funny, because it looked so serious. She liked this woman. She had seen a film about her. That wasn't why she liked her though. She liked the way she made people fit her world, and be a bit ugly, but still made them beautiful. And funny. There were not enough women artists in history. She paid them extra attention when she came across them. She wondered if that was fair, and then wondered why she wondered that. It was not a competition. She was not a judge. So she decided she could pay them more attention if she wanted.

On her wall she had some small postcards lined up in a grid. There were quite a few now. It was useless to look at any one of them really, because the prints were so small, and you could get only the vaguest sort of idea of what they were really like. She had seen some of them for real. But there were thirty-eight now, in seven rows of five, and one row of three at the top. Two more and then she'd start another grid. Her Dad had sent most of them. Or just given them to her. But there were ones from her Gran as well, and from friends, and her mother had picked up a few when she'd gone to the National Gallery in Edinburgh on her weekend away. She suspected her mother had just gone into the shop.

The grid was really neatly spaced and aligned. She didn't like that now. She wished it was more disorganized. She'd made it look like a chart. But she'd decided to leave it as it was and make the next one messy in contrast. She thought that would be interesting. It had started by accident, when she just stuck her first postcard, of the Thames, by Turner, on the wall above her desk. It was only when she'd added the third that she lined them up properly. And then she told people she liked art postcards. So more came. She'd only been doing it about a year. She wondered how long it would take to fill all the empty space on the walls.

She had a Francis Bacon exhibition poster that her Dad had bought for her. She had a really nice print of a young Rembrandt self-portrait where he looked mad and sort of handsome. She also had a poster of van Gogh's *Starry Night*, which she hated, but which she had to leave there, at least for now, because her mother had bought it for her. She didn't *hate* it. But it was so clichéd that she couldn't help deciding not to like it. Her favourite print was the one over her bed. It was *Judith Slaying Holofernes* by Artemisia Gentileschi. Her mother didn't like it at all. She said it would give her nightmares. All that blood. But it didn't. It was very violent, but it was like that wasn't the point. The point was something else. It was the way Judith gritted her teeth. It was good.

Her mother was calling her. She shouted back. She opened the drawer and looked at her phone. Okay. No new texts from her Dad. She read the last one. He was panicking about the summer holidays. It wasn't even Easter yet. If they talked to each other and left her out of it everything would be sorted in about ten seconds. She hated clichés. Except maybe it would be a cliché if they got on really well and were all mature all the time and made sure she never felt like a football or whatever, and were super civilized and cool. That would be another cliché. At least it would be a more pleasant cliché. Maybe it wouldn't. Maybe it wouldn't because it would feel forced and unnatural, whereas at least this was them being honest.

—Is he annoying you?

—What?

—Your father?

—No. Why?

—You're sighing at your phone. You always sigh at your phone when he's texting you.

—I don't. It's not him. It's Michele.

—Why are you sighing at Michele?

—Oh, she thinks she's pregnant. Again.

Her mother stared at her for a second. And relaxed.

—Jesus, Cath, don't do that. It's not funny. I am . . . God almighty. Just don't.

Cath smiled. Her mother stood in the doorway.

—Washing.

—No, I put it all in the basket.

—What's that then?

There was a pair of socks on the bed.

—They're clean. They're today's.

—All right. Come down for a cuppa.

—I will in a minute. I'm doing an essay.

—Well I'm putting the kettle on. Come down and have a cuppa with me. I'm bored. Do you want to go to the shops?

—No. I'll be down in a minute.

She waited until she was alone again and then replied to her father. *Yes. No. I did. There is. It will be all right. Shut up.* She knew that if something terrible happened to her, her parents would have to meet in casualty or the morgue or something and they would break down and cry and hug each other and all the dumb fighting would be forgotten and they would love each other again, because she was dead or a vegetable and that was all they had. And then she imagined herself thinking that if she really loved them she'd kill herself and she laughed. Then she thought that if something terrible happened they would blame each other and spend the rest of their lives tied together by hatred and her death.

Everything was a cliché.

Sometimes when she was out with her Dad and they were talking with other people, he would refer to her Mum as "*my ex-wife.*" One day she asked him if he ever referred to her as his ex-daughter. They had a row. But since then he referred to her Mum as *Catherine's mother.* Which made it sound like her fault.

Churchill lost the postwar election because people were tired. When you have a fire in your house you want the fire brigade to come. When the fire is out you want them to leave. She wrote this in her essay and was really pleased with it. She thought it was a brilliant analogy. But when she got it back she'd been given 65% and there were no comments at all, and the bit where she said that wasn't even ticked or marked. She didn't know why she bothered.

. . .

He waited for her sometimes in a coffee shop near her school. She'd get a text at exactly 3:30 saying "fancy a quick coffee"? even though she never actually had a coffee, she had one of their herbal teas, or sometimes a smoothie. Sometimes she couldn't meet him because she had something on, or was going somewhere with Beth or Michele. Sometimes she pretended she had something on. Well, just once or twice. Usually it was fun to see him. He was usually in a good mood. He'd tell her funny things about work. About people at work or people he'd met. Sometimes he'd get a call and have to leave in a hurry. She liked that. He'd say *What* into his phone and then listen and grunt or say *yes* or *no,* and then he'd sigh and say *all right ten minutes,* and he'd stand up and kiss her on the forehead and whisper that he loved her and he'd be gone.

The coffee shop was at a crossroads. She had to walk past it on the way home. Down the road from the school. Then the zebra crossing. One time she was walking past it and she glanced in and her Dad was sitting there. He hadn't seen her. He was reading a newspaper. She just looked at him. She was with a couple of people. Stuart and Byron and Felice, or someone. So she couldn't really just stop. But she lingered. And looked at him. He was reading. Every so often he'd look up. But he was looking out toward the crossing. He'd missed her. He looked worried. He looked sad and worried and tired. He looked the way he always looked whenever she caught sight of him before he saw her. Then when he saw her he'd light up, or, well, not light up, but his face changed. He would smile. And yeah, he'd brighten up a little. And she liked that. But his face when she wasn't in front of him worried her. He sat slumped. He looked old. Older. Did he fake it when he saw her? Or did seeing her just make him happier than he really was? She didn't like either idea. She caught up with the others. Later she got the text that he must have sent at 3:30. It had been lost somewhere. She replied immediately and he texted back saying it didn't matter, it was no big deal, he'd just been passing. Love.

She and Stuart had sort-of-sex in his bedroom one Saturday afternoon. Everyone thought he was gay, and he never really cared one way or the other about that and never denied it or got angry or anything, so she had thought he was gay, too. And he liked books and art, so . . . and he wore a scarf in a sort of gay way, and he was good friends with Byron, who was actually gay. But it turned out he wasn't gay. Or wasn't very gay, anyway. He was a really good kisser. Kissing him was . . . really good. She talked to Beth about it, and she wanted to describe what the kissing was like; and she wanted to tell her that kissing Stuart was *like being inside a Jackson Pollock painting.* She really wanted to say that. She was determined to say that. But when it came to it she just said that it was *really good* and *bare sexy.* It made her think that maybe Beth and her weren't as close as she had thought. Because why else would she not say what she wanted to say? It was just stupid.

Stuart had talked to her about art. She knew more than he did. He had seemed interested in listening to her. He sent her an e-mail saying he'd looked up Francis Bacon online and thought he was mad and brilliant. But she thought he was faking it a bit. And it was the first she'd heard from him since the sort-of-sex, and he didn't mention that at all, or her really either, or mention anything about meeting up again outside school or whatever. He had film posters on his wall. *Watchmen* and *Superbad,* and an old *Finding Nemo* one that she thought was cute but which made him blush when she mentioned it.

When he took off his jeans she saw a big scar on his leg. Just above his knee, on the back of his leg. She wanted to know what it was, but she didn't ask.

She read about horrible things on the news. She read about fathers who killed their kids because they hated their ex-wives. They

332 / KEITH RIDGWAY

strangled them or poisoned them or drove them off a cliff. She
read that stuff all the time. Just when she had forgotten about one
case, a new one would turn up. Or she'd hear them on the TV or
the radio. Her mother always went dead quiet when stuff like that
came on. And sometimes she'd mutter something. Something like
the poor things, or *what a bastard.* And Cath would think about
her father. About him slouched over his coffee without her. She
could scare herself for a short while thinking like that. But not for
very long. Her father was very gentle. Very kind. He had never
smacked her, even when she was little and screamed all the time.
Her mother had smacked her. He'd never even shouted at her. Or
not that she could remember. Or not in a way that made her
remember. He was always gentle. He would say nothing, just
open his arms, and she would lie against him and he would wrap
her up and she would stay like that for ages. That was when she
was little. They hadn't done that in a long time. But she would do
that again without even thinking.

She wanted to ask him whether he had ever had a case like that.
A father who kills his kids. Or anything like that. But he never
told her any of the bad stuff. She knew he had to investigate all
sort of things—murders and everything. She'd seen him on the
news once. The London news. Detective Inspector Mark Rivers.
It was weird, seeing his name like that. And him asking for witnesses after a boy was stabbed somewhere. He'd been really good.
He talked about the boy like he'd known him, about his family
and stuff. It was all good—the way people are after they're dead. It
had made her nearly cry, because she was proud of him she supposed. But he only ever told her about the funny stuff.

—No, Dad, that's Pollock.
   —Watch your language.
   She laughed.
   —Pollock. Jackson Pollock. He does the ones with the paint all
over the place all scrambled and splattered and stuff.

—Do you like them?

—Yeah.

—Not so much though?

—Well, I like them. They're fun. I'd like to see them for real, because the paint is meant to be really thick and that would be amazing to see them up close. But they're like . . .

—A mess.

—No. They're like the idea of having an idea, instead of having an idea.

She laughed at herself. Her Dad made an *ooh* noise. They turned a corner.

—Is that art teacher of yours any good?

—Yes she's okay.

—Are you smarter than her?

She laughed, thinking *yes!*

—No.

—Have you told her you want to go to art college?

—I don't know if I want to go to art college.

—Oh. I thought you did.

—Well I want to do art, but I don't know if I want to go to an art college or do art history. First.

—First?

—Maybe.

—Well. No hurry.

He pulled in to the curb in front of the house. She leaned across and kissed him. She knew he wanted a hug. But it was awkward, hugging in the car, and she didn't like it.

—Will you call me during the week?

—Yes.

—How's your mother?

He always left it to the last minute. So that she could only say:

—She's fine.

—Okay. I love you.

—I love you too.

—Speak soon.

He waited for her to get to the door. As if something might happen to her between the car and the front door. Then when she put her key in the lock he drove off, as if nothing could happen to her then until the next time.

She liked Tracey Emin, even though everyone else she knew didn't like her, and some people seemed to hate her. She liked her voice best of all, and she loved to hear her talk. She saw her once, walking through the Smithfield Market looking really hungover. She'd wanted to talk to her, but she'd been too shy, and her friend Michele didn't know who she was and there was no one else to be excited with. She didn't like Damien Hirst at all. She thought he was an idiot. And his work was ugly and full of boyish things, like he was a permanently horny boy trying to get some, and everyone was just embarrassed to have him around. She thought Sarah Lucas was like that too. But she didn't say it. She just said that Lucas didn't really move her. It was a way she had of dismissing something without sounding judgmental. She had learned it from a documentary about Francis Bacon. She couldn't remember now whether it was Bacon who said it about some other artist, with a smirk on his face, or whether it was someone else who'd said it about Bacon. She liked Jake and Dinos Chapman. She liked the way that they could make her feel a bit sick, but that she kept on peering at their models and their pictures anyway because all the detail had something in it that was important but it kept on shifting somewhere else, like when you have a floater in your eye. She liked Grayson Perry. She liked his voice too, and she liked hearing him talk about art, and she had some podcasts of a radio show he'd done. But she didn't really know his art. She liked the way he shocked his mother whenever he turned up on the telly in one of his mad frocks. She'd been to the Turner Prize exhibition for the last three years. She had liked Zarina Bhimji most in 2007. In 2008 her favorite was either the photographer or Goshka Macuga's wooden things like people trees. In 2009 she hadn't really liked any of them. They didn't move her.

On the Tuesday after the Saturday when they'd had sort-of-sex and Stuart had sent her an e-mail about Bacon, and a couple of texts about nothing, he came up to her in a corridor in school and, blushing very red, asked her did she want to go for a coffee after school, just the two of them. She didn't know why he was blushing. Well, she did, and she thought it was funny, but it made her blush as well. The two of them just standing there going red. She rushed out a *Yeah, okay, see you after* as casually as she could and walked off. It was completely stupid. They'd had about six million conversations in the school corridors before.

One time in the café two men came in and sort of stood there looking at her Dad. He stared back at them.

—What.

It was the same voice he used on the phone.

—Sorry to interrupt, sir.

The one talking was a really good-looking black man with dark-framed glasses and hair shaved close to his head. He was wearing a dark gray suit, with a black V-neck jumper under the jacket and his tie done up. He looked really interesting. The other one was a white guy with a funny face. Like he was peeking through a keyhole. Or maybe it was normal. He had a stupid smile and was carrying a big envelope and he was looking at her. He was wearing a neat suit too, but he looked more like he was going for a job interview. They didn't look like police.

—What.

—Need you to have a look at a couple of things. Somewhat urgent.

He pushed his glasses up his nose and looked at Cath and nodded.

—I'm very sorry to bother you.

She smiled and felt herself blush.

Her Dad went outside with them. She looked through the window. The three of them hunched over the envelope, and stuff was pulled out of it, and her Dad peered at it. She thought maybe it was photographs. She couldn't see. Her Dad made a call on his phone. The black guy made one on his. The white guy came back in and bought himself a bottle of water.

—Sorry about this, he said.

—That's okay.

—He'll be back in a minute.

He seemed nice. She wanted to ask him stuff. About her Dad. What's he like to work with? Is he tough? Does he beat people up? Is he a racist? Does he curse all the time? Is he good at being a detective? Is he clever? Is he sexist? Does he have a girlfriend? Do you do cases where fathers kill their kids? What does he think about them? But she couldn't form any sort of question at all before he had gone back outside. The two of them walked to a car and drove away and her father came back in and patted her shoulder and apologized.

—That's the first time I've ever met anyone you work with.

—No, it's not. Is it?

—Yeah. You're very rude to them.

He laughed.

—I am not.

—You didn't say anything to them. Just *what*. You should have asked them to sit down.

—They should have called me.

—They seemed really nice. You should have introduced me.

He smiled at her as he sipped his coffee.

—They are not nice. Really. And anyway, one of them is married and the other is gay and they're both old enough to be your father. And if your mother and I agree on anything then we agree that you should never, ever, ever get involved with a policeman.

. . .

They went up toward Muswell Hill to a place Stuart knew where there'd be no one from the school. He bought her a strawberry tea, and got himself a cappuccino. He talked about music and kept on wiping his lips. He was into all these bands that she had never heard of. She thought he was trying to match her art talk. Trying to balance it. That was okay. He said he'd send her a playlist and they talked for a while about the best ways of sharing files, and about the computers they had and about stuff on Facebook, and she was sure they'd had all these conversations a dozen times before. It was like he'd forgotten that he'd known her for about two years. On and off.

They walked down the hill and he held her hand for a while. When they got to a bus stop that was good for her, he kissed her again, and it was great. He leaned against her and she could feel his body warm against her and she liked it and she thought about his scar. When the bus came he smiled at her like he was shy again, and she liked that, too, and he said, "*See ya, gorgeous*" in a stupid voice and they both laughed, and they were laughing at themselves, at how stupid they were being and that it was all right to be stupid, it was fun. On the bus she dozed and held her phone in her hand and leaned her head against the window.

She didn't know what to do about Rothko. She didn't understand Rothko. Everything about Rothko made her want to like him. All the things people who liked him said and wrote made her want to like him. They talked about warmth and love and comfort and feelings like religious feelings. She wondered about herself, about what was wrong with her that she couldn't feel those things. Or not feel them when she looked at Rothko. She had been, twice, to the Rothko Room in the Tate. And her Dad had taken her to the big exhibition of lots of his stuff. But she didn't get it. Soft-focus blocks of dusty color. One of them made her think of sunsets on summer holidays in Cornwall, so she liked that one, a bit. But Rothko. He did not move her.

Whenever her father took her to one of the Tates, or to the National Gallery or something, she could sense his boredom make his back straight, and his eyes water. She would forget he was there sometimes and then turn to find him looking at his phone, or looking at a woman, or yawning. She'd laugh at him and they'd go for a coffee and he'd get her something in the shop. Some postcards usually, or a book. She didn't like him spending much. She didn't know why. He wasn't hard up.

Her mother was jealous of these trips. She didn't want to be, and she battled with herself to cover it up, but Cath could feel it, in the kitchen. It was like she was plugged into something.

She started going to museums and galleries with Stuart. They went to the Whitechapel Gallery together—the first time she'd been there. They had to stand on the Tube and he held her hand. She liked when they had to let go for some reason and then she'd wait to see how long it took him to reach out for her again. Sometimes it wasn't quick enough and she grabbed his hand, and she liked that she felt able to do that, and liked that it made him smile. She liked the fact that they were turning into a really annoying couple who held hands all the time and that their other friends, if they knew, would dedicate their lives to taking the piss.

They went to the National Gallery and spent a couple of hours wandering around. Stuart wasn't scared of stuff that other boys were scared of. He stood in front of a picture of a naked man and said out loud to her that it was beautiful. He looked at another picture and wanted her to tell him whether it was supposed to suggest a vagina. She blushed and he didn't. When she used a word he didn't understand, he told her he didn't understand it and asked her what it meant. She had to admit once that she didn't really know what *crescendo* meant. He laughed at her and put his arm around her shoulder and gave her a little kiss on her cheek.

She had told her mother that she and Stuart were sort-of-seeing each other now. Her mother took a couple of minutes to work out which of her friends she meant. Then she told her that he was welcome to come over to the house whenever Cath wanted. That made her laugh. Not whenever Stuart wanted, but whenever Cath wanted. She liked that. She wondered if he'd be allowed to stay the night. Maybe. In the spare room. She wondered if he'd even want to. She wanted him to. Sometime. For some reason. She wanted to see him first thing in the morning. She imagined bringing him a cup of tea in bed. She imagined him lying asleep in the spare bed in the spare room. She imagined it for ages.

Her Dad was obsessing now about the crossing outside the café, near the school.

—Some kid is going to get run over there one of these days.

—Why?

—Cos you lot never look. You just walk across. And cars come up that road too fast. There should be traffic lights there. Not just a crossing.

She looked. Most of the younger kids were gone by now. There were a few people she recognized outside the shop on the other side. She'd never seen anyone even come close to getting run over.

—You should be careful.

She laughed.

—Don't laugh. I worry about things like that. They may seem stupid to you but there you have it. I can't help it, I'm your father.

He was in a mood.

—You need to be careful. The number of teenagers killed on the road in London is horrific. You know? Never mind knife crime and drugs and all the stuff you get warned about all the time. Well, do mind them, but you know about that stuff. It's the traffic you might just forget about. Forget to look out for. You're to be careful about that.

A group of uniforms passed the window. She looked up and saw Byron, who gave her a wave. And Stuart's head appeared from behind him, smiling at her. Her Dad looked.

—Your friends?

They walked on. Stuart looked back, still smiling. She found herself smiling and blushing.

—How's the flat, she asked, to cover it.

—Do you have a boyfriend?

—Oh Dad.

He was smiling at her. She was so obvious. She was a cliché. Her cheeks burned.

—Which one? The black boy?

He was turned around in his chair now, looking after them. Stuart noticed and looked away, and then they disappeared.

—The one who looked back?

—They're just friends.

—So why are you blushing like a berry?

She laughed.

—Like a berry?

—Like a strawberry.

—People don't blush like berries.

—Which one was he then? What's his name?

So she told him a bit about Stuart. But nothing like as much as she'd told her mother. He smiled at her and nodded but she could tell he was sad. Because she was growing up and all that clichéd crap.

She imagined walking from school one day and hearing a bang and a scream, and another scream, and seeing something happening at the crossing. She imagined running up, and as she got closer her friends trying to hold her back. She imagined seeing Stuart lying on the ground, pale, a trickle of blood coming out of his mouth. She imagined kneeling beside him and holding his head, and looking into his eyes and him looking at her with the most intense eyes that she had ever seen, and dying. She imagined a girl screaming and sobbing, and Byron crying and holding her hand,

and she imagined her Dad arriving with the two men from the coffee shop, and her Dad helping her up and moving her away, and the good-looking black man and the other one trying to restart Stuart's heart, and the black guy looking up at her Dad and her and shaking his head, and Stuart being beautiful.

Then she imagined that she was the one hit by a car, and Stuart holding her, tears running down his face. She preferred the idea of him dying. She laughed and wondered whether she could tell him about all this and knew that of course she couldn't.

She told Byron that she'd met a gay cop.

—Cop's a cop, he sneered. Then he remembered her Dad was a cop, and smiled and touched her arm.

Byron told her that Stuart was really happy about, you know. Them. The two of them. Byron said it was a really good thing. He said they were two of his most favorite people, and he was made up to see them together. He said Stuart deserved some happiness. She laughed and asked him what he meant.

—Oh you know.

—More than me?

—No. Just.

—What?

—Oh nothing.

Stuart's parents were still together, but his father was always away and his mother worked in the city and Stuart had the house to himself most of the time and she would go there and they would end up kissing, of course, and they would do various things, but they still hadn't had actual-sex. She wondered whether he was really only interested in sex. And was really clever. And by not ever pressing her into stuff, he made her want stuff that she might not want if he suggested it out loud. Maybe he was devious like that and everything, all his niceness and his calm and the way he looked out for her, they were all a disguise for the fact that he was just a horny boy like other horny boys and that he was following some sort of Plan and every night he called his friends to bring them up to date about the progress of The Plan.

And even though he never blatantly pushed her into doing anything, he had a way of making her do stuff anyway, by getting the two of them arranged in such and such a way and leaving the opportunity open for her to do it if she wanted to, but not to do it if she didn't want to. Which was how she ended up giving her first ever blowjob for example. In her life. Which was something that even a year ago she thought she would never do. But now she'd done it. And she had liked it. And it had been completely different from what she had expected, and it had not been gross or embarrassing or weird tasting or any of the things she had thought it was going to be, and she was doing it even before she'd decided to do it, she was just suddenly doing it, because of the devious way Stuart had arranged their bodies on his bed, with both of them still mostly dressed and the CD by Micachu playing that he'd got for her and that she really liked. Stuart had to stop her almost as soon as she started. He gasped and wriggled and pushed her head away from him and came all over his T-shirt like he'd been shot, and she couldn't help laughing, and then worried almost immediately that he would think she was some sort of *expert*. But all he could say was *wow*, and he laughed too, and they both giggled for a while and he kissed her, and then he took off his T-shirt and mopped up and they hugged and kissed under the covers and laughed at each other and chatted for ages.

He said that no one had ever done that before.

He said that Byron had offered, but that was all.

He said that he and Byron had kissed once, and he had liked it, but he had stopped because he didn't want to do anything else and Byron did, and Byron had sulked for a while, but they were okay again now.

He said Byron was his best friend. Him and Byron talked about everything.

He said she was a better kisser than Byron.

He said he loved her skin and he loved her breasts and her neck. He said he wanted to hold her every time he saw her in school. He said he'd wanted to kiss her from the first time he met her. He said that he had never done anything because she'd seemed uninterested in him, in that way.

He said he really wanted to have full sex with her, but there was no hurry.

He said he wasn't a virgin. But he'd only had sex once before and it had been a real mess, a disaster, and he wouldn't tell her who it was, and she didn't know her anyway, and they had both been drunk and it was all a sort of horrible blur of a bad memory.

She told him that she was a virgin. He asked about other boys and she told him about some of them. He stroked her hair and smiled at her and they wrapped their legs around each other under the duvet.

She liked him so much that she couldn't do any work.

Her Dad came to the house on a Tuesday. "To speak to your Mum," he said, which made her immediately suspicious. Something was up. Something had happened. They talked in the kitchen, and she couldn't hear a thing. It was good, she supposed, that they weren't shouting at each other. But it was creepy too. There wasn't a sound. She tried to work out what it was. He had seen her with Stuart and didn't approve. He was worried that she wasn't doing as well as she had been, at school. Maybe it wasn't about her. He had lost his job. He couldn't afford to pay maintenance anymore. He was leaving London. He had prostate cancer. She sat on the stairs and thought about Stuart having cancer.

He wouldn't tell her what it was about. He seemed impatient. He wanted to be gone.

—See you Saturday?

—Yeah.

—It's not about us. Ask your mother what it's about. She can tell you if she wants. Up to her.

So she had to nag. Her mother was sitting in the kitchen looking at the wall. She had put out mugs but she hadn't filled them. She didn't want to talk about it. Cath whined at her. *What? What's going on?*

—Someone died.

All Cath's breathless wondering stopped. And then restarted, and she tripped on relief and shock and a new fear.

—Who? What happened?

—Misha. You don't know her. She used to . . . I was at uni with her.

—What happened?

—I don't want to, Cath.

And her mother started crying.

She didn't know what to do. She gave her a sort of hug. She got her a box of tissues. She made a pot of tea. She sat at the table and listened to the story. She caught herself wondering if it was made up. Invented by her mother and father together to warn her of how badly wrong everything could go. Because it was *that* story. About the pretty, clever girl who everyone knows is going to turn out to be a genius but she starts to drink, and then she meets the wrong boy, and then she drinks too much, and then she starts taking other stuff, and before anyone knows what's happened she's living in a junkie squat somewhere in King's Cross and she's got a string of arrests and all her old friends and her traumatized parents are really just waiting for the police to show up at the door to say she's dead. Then she goes away and disappears. She goes to Spain. Years pass. She comes home and she's okay. She's sober and she's done some courses, and everyone thinks that she's better, she's through it. She's not the same, but at least she's not a mess anymore, and even if she is a bit fragile, a bit pathetic, she can hold down a sort of office admin job and she can pay a rent and it's okay. But she's never what she was. And she's never what she might have been. And they notice that she's probably still drinking. Secretly. And eventually, after everyone stops thinking about her and she has become just a sad friend who doesn't have much of a life and who they never see unless they have to, then she hangs herself in her kitchen.

Her mother choked and spluttered on all her guilt and her grief, and she banged the table and cried so loud that Cath was terrified and called her father, but she couldn't reach him, and left an angry message accusing him of being a *heartless bastard.* And her mother might have overheard, because she hugged Cath then and told her *sorry sorry sorry,* she was just *so sad. So sad.* And she went to bed, and Cath could hear her still, wailing, as if she'd lost everything and had nothing left, not even Cath. And then Cath was crying.

She called Stuart. He wanted to come over but she wouldn't let him. She tried to be cold about her mother. She tried to tell him that she was being stupid, but he didn't fall for it, and soon she was crying, and he told her he was coming over, and she told him not to, *thank you,* but she'd prefer if he didn't, because it was her mother, her mother's privacy, and he said okay.

Her Dad called. He didn't give out to her about being called a heartless bastard, but he didn't apologize either. *She's bound to be upset,* he said. *She'll be okay.* She accused him of not caring. That it was easy for him, it wasn't his friend who had died. And then he was quiet for a minute and told her that actually it was his friend. That he'd known Misha as long as he'd known her mother. That they'd dated a couple of times. And that he'd seen more of her in the last couple of years than anyone else had. Cath apologized, and for no reason that she could understand other than having a dig, her father told her that he loved her.

Then there was someone at the door. It was her mother's friend Heather, and then everything was okay. Heather gave her a hug, and went up to her mother. Then their other friends Scan and Lillian arrived. And then everyone was in her mother's bedroom, and coming and going with cups of tea and she even heard laughter.

She called Stuart again. To say sorry. To tell him that everything was okay now. They talked for an hour, each of them lying on their beds. She wrapped his voice around her and made him promise that he wouldn't let her become a junkie. He laughed. *Okay,* he said. *I promise.* He thought it was a joke. But she knew they would remember it always, that it was a promise to look after her, and that it was made now and could not be retracted, and that even if they did not stay together there were things between them that would never be between her and anyone else. And that wasn't being stupid or romantic or saying that it was *special* or anything. It was just the truth.

She slept late, was late for school. Her mother stayed in bed. Beth nagged at her. Stuart kept an eye on her. Byron asked her if she was okay, and gave her a hug. She was fine. She was tired. She couldn't remember most of the things she'd talked to Stuart about. She wondered what he'd said to the others. Whether she came across as needy, weepy, clingy. Those things. She ignored him.

She was still annoyed at her Dad.

He closed down when he needed to be open. That was what she thought. When there was something wrong he became efficient, busy. He dealt with it. Like a policeman. Like you'd want from a policeman. He would arrive and sort it out. Then he'd leave. And it was sorted. It was fixed. It was a closed case and he was closed and everything was shut off and quiet and finished and he forgot about it.

But when there was nothing wrong he was funny and kind and patient and open.

She thought it through again. She wasn't sure what she was complaining about.

It was too hot. They took the Tube down through London, holding hands and allowing themselves to be pressed against each other. She had a sheen of sweat on her forehead. Stuart was wearing a T-shirt and kept on lifting and flapping the front over his stomach.

They hadn't been anywhere together for a while. She'd been spending time with her mother, who was still wobbly. She'd sob in front of the television. She'd sit at the kitchen table just staring into space. Cath didn't know why. Well, she knew why, but she didn't understand why the grief was so intense. There was something she didn't know about, she was sure of it. Something more to the story. This Misha. How it was that she had never been heard of before, and now she was all over Cath's life, even though she was dead. Nothing, then dead, then everything.

Her father came around a few times. More than he ever had before. They would sit in the kitchen chatting quietly. She sometimes sat with them for a while. But it was too weird. They just talked to her, about her, while she was there. So she would go and watch television, or go to her bedroom, and she would hear them murmur together, for a long time. Once, after she had gone to bed and fallen asleep, the front door woke her. It was her father leaving. She heard his car start up. She looked at her clock. It was 4:30 in the morning.

She didn't know what it was.

She tried to ask her father. He would not help. All he said was that they'd been good friends once, her mother and this Misha. That was it. She wondered whether they'd been lovers or something. She couldn't imagine it. She wondered whether the three of them had been mixed up in some sort of love triangle thing.

Her father didn't want to talk about it.

It was cruel. It was unfair. She was the one who had to live with her mother. And for a week now she'd been weird and silent and weepy. The day of the funeral Cath had come home to find her mother in bed still wearing her black dress. She'd had to call Heather again. What was wrong with these people? It was like they forgot she existed. As soon as their own stuff hit them, they forgot about her. She had to fend for herself, knowing nothing.

She'd told her father that she couldn't see him that day. That she was seeing Stuart.

They arrived at Waterloo and walked along the river, strolling, holding hands. He looked so good. Byron had said to her a few days before that Stuart was always good-looking, but now that he was going out with her he was beautiful. He'd said it really nicely, quietly, with a big smile. Then he'd made her promise not to tell Stuart he'd said it, or he'd kill her.

The Tate was quiet. There were still tourists and some big groups of kids, but it was nice, it was okay, it was easier to stand and look at things than it usually was. They went searching for the Rothko Room. She had told Stuart about Rothko, a little. About how he did not move her. And he had wanted to see. He said he knew a song about Rothko, by an American singer that he liked. She rolled her eyes. The only things he knew about were things he'd heard in songs. He laughed at her.

They looked at the paintings. The room was almost empty. Large flat blocks of color frayed at the edges, set against the dark. It was gloomy in there. Why was it so gloomy? It was cool, at least. Cath sat on a bench and tried again with Rothko. Stuart stood at first. Then he sat beside her for a while. They didn't say anything. She wanted to let him decide for himself. He stood up again and walked around the room. Then he stopped in front of one of them and his head dropped onto his chest. Then she saw him wipe his eyes and look up again. She thought he was bored. He didn't get it either. She stood and went to him and took his hand, meaning to lead him out of the room so they could look at some other stuff or get a coffee. He turned to her. He was crying. Not sobbing. But there were a couple of tears running down the side of his nose, and his eyes were red. She stared at him.

He wanted to stay in the room. He moved around. She watched him. He breathed deeply. He stood still. Really still. He sat on the seats a couple of times and just looked. She wondered if he was taking the piss. She went and sat beside him.

—What do you think?

—They're beautiful. I don't understand how they work. But they're just beautiful.

He wanted to stay there for ages. He looked at the Rothkos, and she looked at him.

In the café afterward she complained about her parents. She told him that there was something they weren't telling her about this dead woman Misha. She told him it wasn't fair. That they just weren't thinking about her. He nodded.

—Maybe they can't, he said.

—They could try.

—Maybe you had to be there. Some things you can't share, you know?

He got a second coffee. He wanted to talk about the Rothko Room. He seemed a bit embarrassed now, that he'd been so moved by it. He smiled and shook his head.

—They're so great though. I could look at those things all day.

She told him about her Dad and the eggs.

—I made my Dad scrambled eggs one morning, yeah? When I was staying at his place for a weekend. He sleeps late, you know. And I made him breakfast when he got up, you know—good little girl. And it was like, scrambled eggs on toast, and some bacon and a tomato. Stuff like that. And a pot of tea. Glass of orange juice. All posh. And he really liked it, and then he was trying to show off that he knew about art—he's always doing this—and he said, *Rothko eggs*. Points at the scrambled eggs. *Rothko eggs*. I didn't know what he was on about. *They look like a Rothko painting*, he said, all pleased with himself. And then I realized that he'd gotten Rothko mixed up with Pollock!

She laughed.

Stuart smiled.

—So now he still calls scrambled eggs *Rothko eggs*. I never corrected him. He hasn't realized yet. So he's always asking for *Rothko eggs*. I bet he does it at work and everything. Trying to show off how cultured he is. Down the police station, you know? Pretending he knows his art. *Had some great Rothko eggs this morning.* And no one has a clue what he's on about. It's so funny.

And she laughed, to show how funny it was.

Stuart smiled at her. He looked at her and smiled and said nothing, and he rubbed his eyes.

Later that day she asked him about the scar.

—What happened?

—What?

—There. How did you get it?

—Shark bite.

—Really though.

He said nothing for a minute. Then he lay on his back and looked at the ceiling.

—A few years ago. I was swimming in a river. Sort of a river thing, near where we were staying on holiday in France. Me and a friend went swimming. He was a local guy. And we got snagged on some stuff under the water. There was some old farm machinery or something dumped in there. And we were kind of diving down and exploring it. It wasn't very deep but we were trying to . . . I don't know . . . pretending it was a shipwreck or something. He pushed a bit of it, I think. Or pulled it. Or maybe he didn't. But it shifted. We got . . .

He stopped.

—What?

—Some part of it caught my leg when I was freeing myself. Some sharp edge. And cut it.

—Shit. Did it hurt?

—Yeah. Well. Yeah, after a bit. I didn't notice at first.

—Cos you have arteries and stuff in there. You could bleed to death.

—Yeah.

He said nothing. She looked at him.

He was quiet. He had drifted off somewhere. She traced shapes and words and pictures on his chest with her fingers. The sun lit the curtains and the music made her drowsy. She was lulled by his heartbeat into feeling nothing more than a vague wonder that nothing in her life had really started yet.

She went home. She thought about their day. Something had gone wrong but she didn't know what.

Anthony Doerr

The Deep

Tom is born in 1914 in Detroit, a quarter mile from International Salt. His father is offstage, unaccounted for. His mother operates a six-room, underinsulated boardinghouse populated with locked doors, behind which drowse the grim possessions of itinerant salt workers: coats the color of mice, tattered mucking boots, aquatints of undressed women, their breasts faded orange. Every six months a miner is fired or drafted or dies and is replaced by another, so that very early in his life Tom comes to see how the world continually drains itself of young men, leaving behind only objects—empty tobacco pouches, bladeless jackknives, salt-caked trousers—mute, incapable of memory.

Tom is four when he starts fainting. He'll be rounding a corner, breathing hard, and the lights will go out. Mother will carry him indoors, set him on the armchair, and send someone for the doctor.

Atrial septal defect. Hole in the heart. The doctor says blood sloshes from the left side to the right side. His heart will have to do three times the work. Life span of sixteen. Eighteen if he's lucky. Best if he doesn't get excited.

Mother trains her voice into a whisper. *Here you go, there you are, sweet little Tomcat.* She smothers the windows with curtains. She moves Tom's cot into an upstairs closet—no bright lights, no loud noises. Mornings she serves him a glass of buttermilk, then points him to the brooms or steel wool. *Go slow,* she'll say. He scrubs the coal stove, sweeps the marble stoop. Every so often he peers up from his work and watches the face of the oldest boarder, Mr. Weems, as he troops downstairs, a fifty-year-old man hooded against the cold, off to descend in an elevator a thousand feet underground. Tom imagines his descent, sporadic and dim lights passing and receding, cables rattling, a half dozen other miners squeezed into the cage beside him, each thinking his own thoughts, sinking down into that city beneath the city, where mules stand waiting and oil lamps burn in the walls and glittering rooms of salt recede into vast arcades beyond the farthest reaches of the light.

Sixteen, thinks Tom. *Eighteen if I'm lucky.*

School is a three-room shed aswarm with the offspring of salt workers, coal workers, ironworkers. Irish kids, Polish kids, Armenian kids. *Don't run, don't fight,* whispers Mother. *No games.* For Tom the schoolyard seems a thousand acres of sizzling pandemonium. His first day, he lasts an hour. Mother finds him beneath a tablecloth with his fist in his mouth. *Shhh,* she says, and crawls under there with him and wraps her arms around his like ropes.

He seesaws in and out of the early grades. By the time he's ten, he's in remedial everything. *I'm trying,* he mumbles, but letters spin off pages and hang themselves in the branches outside. *Dunce,* the other boys declare, and to Tom that seems about right.

Tom sweeps, scrubs, scours the stoop with pumice one square inch at a time. *Slow as molasses in January,* says Mr. Weems, but he winks at Tom when he says it.

Every day, all day, the salt finds its way in. It encrusts washbasins, settles on the rims of baseboards. It spills out of the boarders, too: from ears, boots, handkerchiefs. Furrows of glitter gather in the bedsheets; a daily lesson in insidiousness.

Start at the center, then scrub out to the edges. Linens on Thursdays. Toilets on Fridays.

He's twelve when Ms. Fredericks asks the children to give reports. Ruby Hornaday goes sixth. Ruby has flames for hair, Christmas for a birthday, and a drunk for a daddy. She's one of two girls to make it to fourth grade.

She reads from notes in controlled terror. *If you think the lake is big you should see the sea. It's three-quarters of Earth. And that's just the surface.* Someone throws a pencil. The creases in Ruby's forehead deepen. *Land animals live on ground or in trees rats and worms and gulls and such. But sea animals they live everywhere they live in the waves and they live in mid water and they live in canyons six and a half miles down.*

She passes around a thick, red book. Inside are blocks of text and full-color photographic plates that make Tom's heart boom in his ears. A blizzard of green fish. A kingdom of purple corals. Five orange starfish cemented to a rock.

Ruby says, *Detroit used to have palm trees and corals and seashells. Detroit used to be a sea three miles deep.*

Ms. Fredericks says, *Ruby, where did you get that book?* but by then Tom is hardly breathing. See-through flowers with poison tentacles and fields of clams and pink monsters with kingdoms of whirling needles on their backs. He tries to say, *Are these real?* but quicksilver bubbles rise from his mouth and float up to the ceiling. When he goes over, the desk goes over with him.

The doctor says it's best if Tom stays out of school. *Keep indoors,* the doctor says. *If you get excited, think of something blue.* Mother lets him come downstairs for meals and chores only. Otherwise he's to stay in his closet. *We have to be more careful, Tomcat,* she whispers, and sets her palm on his forehead.

Tom spends long hours on the floor beside his cot, assembling and reassembling the same jigsaw puzzle: a Swiss village. Five hundred pieces, nine of them missing. Sometimes Mr. Weems sits and reads to Tom from adventure novels. They're blasting a new vein down in the mines and little cascades of plaster sift from the ceiling. In the lulls between Mr. Weems's words, Tom can feel explosions reverberate up through a thousand feet of rock and shake the fragile pump in his chest.

He misses school. He misses the sky. He misses everything. When Mr. Weems is in the mine and Mother is downstairs, Tom often slips to the end of the hall and lifts aside the curtains and presses his forehead to the glass. Children run the snowy lanes and lights glow in the foundry windows and train cars trundle beneath elevated conduits. First-shift miners emerge from the mouth of the hauling elevator in groups of six and bring out cigarette cases from their overalls and strike matches and spill like little salt-dusted insects out into the night, while the darker figures of the second-shift miners stamp their feet in the cold, waiting outside the cages for their turn in the pit.

In dreams he sees waving sea fans and milling schools of grouper and underwater shafts of light. He sees Ruby Hornaday push open the door of his closet. She's wearing a copper diving helmet; she leans over his cot and puts the window of her helmet an inch from his face.

He wakes with a shock and heat pooled in his groin. He thinks, *Blue, blue, blue.*

One drizzly Saturday when Tom is thirteen, the bell rings. He's scrubbing behind the stove, Mother is changing linens upstairs, and Mr. Weems is in the armchair reading the newspaper. When Tom opens the door, Ruby Hornaday is standing on the stoop in the rain.

Hello. Tom blinks a dozen times. Raindrops set a thousand intersecting circles upon the puddles in the road. Ruby holds up a jar: six black tadpoles squirm in an inch of water.

Seemed like you were interested in water creatures.

Tom tries to answer, but the whole sky is rushing through the open door into his mouth.

You're not going to faint again, are you?

Mr. Weems stumps into the foyer. *Jesus, boy, she's damp as a church, you got to invite a lady in.*

Ruby stands on the tiles and drips. Mr. Weems grins. Tom mumbles, *My heart.*

Ruby holds up the jar. *Keep 'em if you want. They'll be frogs before long.* Drops shine in her eyelashes. Rain glues her shirt to her clavicles. *Well, that's something,* says Mr. Weems. He nudges Tom in the back. *Ain't it, Tom?*

Tom is opening his mouth. He's saying, *Maybe I could*—when Mother comes down the stairs in her big, black shoes. *Trouble,* hisses Mr. Weems. Heat crashes over Tom like a wave.

Mother dumps the tadpoles in a ditch. Her face says she's composing herself but her eyes say she's going to wipe all this away. Mr. Weems leans over the dominoes and whispers, *Mother's as hard as a cobblestone, but we'll crack her, Tom, you wait.*

Tom whispers, *Ruby Hornaday,* into the space above his cot. *Ruby Hornaday. Ruby Hornaday.* A strange and uncontainable joy inflates dangerously in his chest.

Mr. Weems has long conversations with Mother in the kitchen. Tom overhears scraps: *Boy needs to move his legs. Boy should get some air.*

Mother's voice is a whip. *He's sick.*

He's alive! What're you saving him for? How much time he got left?

Mother consents to let Tom retrieve coal from the depot and tinned goods from the commissary. Tuesdays he'll be allowed to walk to the butcher's in Dearborn. *Careful, Tomcat, don't hurry.*

Tom moves through the colony that first Tuesday with something close to rapture in his veins. Down the long gravel lanes, past pit cottages and surface mountains of blue and white salt, the warehouses like dark cathedrals, the hauling machines like demonic armatures. All around him the monumental industry of Detroit pounds and clangs. The boy tells himself he is a treasure hunter, a hero from one of Mr. Weems's adventure stories, a knight on important errands, a spy behind enemy lines. He keeps his hands in his pockets and his head down and his gait slow, but his soul charges ahead, sparking through the gloom.

In May of that year, 1929, fourteen-year-old Tom is walking along the lane thinking spring happens beneath the snow, beyond the walls—spring happens in the dark while you dream—when Ruby Hornaday steps out of the weeds. She has a shriveled rubber hose coiled over her shoulder and a swim mask in one hand and a tire pump in the other. *Need your help.* Tom's pulse soars.

I got to go to the butcher's.

Your choice. Ruby turns to go. But really there's no choice at all.

She leads him west, away from the mine, through mounds of rusting machines. They hop a fence, cross a field gone to seed, and walk a quarter mile through pitch pines to a marsh where cattle egrets stand in the cattails like white flowers.

In my mouth, she says, and starts picking up rocks. *Out my nose. You pump, Tom. You understand?* In the green water two feet down Tom can make out the dim shapes of fish gliding through weedy enclaves.

Ruby pitches the far end of the hose into the water. With waxed cord she binds the other end to the pump. Then she fills her pockets with rocks. She wades out, looks back, says, *You pump,* and puts the hose into her mouth. The swim mask goes over her eyes; her face goes into the water.

The marsh closes over Ruby's back, and the hose trends away from the bank. Tom begins to pump. The sky slides along overhead. Loops of garden hose float under the light out there, shifting now and then. Occasional bubbles rise, moving gradually farther out.

One minute, two minutes. Tom pumps. His heart does its fragile work. He should not be here. He should not be here while this skinny, spellbinding girl drowns herself in a marsh. If that's what she's doing. One of Mr. Weems's similes comes back to him from some dingy corner of memory: *You're trembling like a needle to the pole.*

After four or five minutes underwater, Ruby comes up. A neon mat of algae clings to her hair, and her bare feet are great boots of mud. She pushes through the cattails. Strings of saliva hang off her chin. Her lips are blue. Tom feels dizzy. The sky turns to liquid.

Incredible, pants Ruby. *Fucking incredible.* She holds up her wet, rock-filled trousers with both hands, and looks at Tom through the wavy lens of her swim mask. His blood storms through its lightless tunnels.

He has to trot to make the butcher's by noon. It is the first time Tom can remember permitting himself to run, and his legs feel like glass and his breath like quicksand. At the end of the lane, a hundred yards from home, he stops and pants with the basket of meat in his arms and spits a pat of blood into the dandelions. Sweat soaks his shirt. Dragonflies dart and hover. Swallows inscribe letters across the sky. The lane seems to ripple and fold and straighten itself out again.

Just a hundred yards more. He forces his heart to settle. *Everything,* Tom thinks, *follows a path worn by those who have gone before: egrets, clouds, tadpoles. Everything.*

The following Tuesday Ruby meets him at the end of the lane. And the Tuesday after that. They hop the fence, cross the field; she leads him places he's never dreamed existed. Places where the structures of the saltworks become white mirages on the horizon. Places where sunlight washes through groves of maples and makes the ground quiver with leaf-shadow. They peer into a foundry where shirtless men in masks pour molten iron from one vat into another; they climb a tailings pile where a lone sapling grows like a single hand thrust up from the underworld. Tom knows he's risking everything, but how can he stop? How can he say no? To say no to Ruby Hornaday would be to say no to the world.

Some Tuesdays Ruby brings along her red book, with its images of corals and jellies and underwater men breathing from hoses. She tells him that when she grows up she'll go to parties where hostesses row guests offshore and everyone puts on special helmets and goes for strolls along the sea bottom. She tells him she'll be a diver who sinks herself a half mile into the sea in a steel ball with one window. In the basement of the ocean she'll find a world of lights: schools of fish glittering green, whole galaxies wheeling through the black.

In the ocean, says Ruby, *the rocks are alive and half the plants are animals.*

They hold hands; they chew Indian gum. She stuffs his mind full of kelp forests and seascapes and dolphins. *When I grow up,* thinks Tom. *When I grow up . . .*

Four more times Ruby walks around beneath the surface of a River Rouge marsh while Tom stands on the bank working the pump. Four more times he watches her rise back out like a fever. *Amphibian.* She laughs. *It means two lives.*

Then Tom runs to the butcher's and runs home, and his heart races, and spots spread like inkblots in front of his eyes. *Blue, blue blue.* But how does he know the blue he sees is the right color? Sometimes in the afternoons, when he stands up from his chores, his vision slides away in violet streaks and is a long while returning. Other colors spiral through his mind's eye, too: the glowing white of the salt tunnels, the red of Ruby's book, the orange of her hair—he imagines her all grown up, standing on the bow of a ship, and feels a core of lemon yellow light flaring brighter and brighter within him. It spills from the slats between his ribs, from between his teeth, from the pupils of his eyes. He thinks: *It is so much! So much!*

. . .

So now you're fifteen. And the doctor says sixteen?

Eighteen if I'm lucky.

Ruby turns her book over and over in her hands. *What's it like? To know you won't get all the years you should?*

I don't feel so shortchanged when I'm with you, he says, but his voice breaks at *short-* and the sentence falls apart.

They kiss only that one time. It is clumsy. He shuts his eyes and leans in, but something shifts and Ruby is not where he expects her to be. Their teeth clash. When he opens his eyes, she is looking off to her left, smiling slightly, smelling of mud, and the thousand tiny blonde hairs on her upper lip catch the light.

The second-to-last time Tom and Ruby are together, on the last Tuesday of October, 1929, everything is strange. The hose leaks, Ruby is upset, a curtain has fallen somehow between them.

Go back, Ruby says. *It's probably noon already. You'll be late.* But she sounds as if she's talking to him through a tunnel. Freckles flow and bloom across her face. The light goes out of the marsh.

On the long path through the pitch pines it begins to rain. Tom makes it to the butcher's and back home with the basket and the ground veal, yet when he opens the door to Mother's parlor the curtains seem to blow inward. The chairs seem to leave their places and come scraping toward him.

The daylight thins to a pair of beams, waving back and forth. Mr. Weems passes in front of his eyes, but Tom hears no footsteps, no voices: only an internal rushing and the wet metronome of his exhalations. Suddenly he's staring through a thick, foggy window into a world of immense pressure. Mother's face disappears and reappears. Her lips say, *Haven't I given enough? Lord God, haven't I tried?* Then she's gone.

In something deeper than a dream Tom walks the salt roads a thousand feet beneath the house. At first it's all darkness, but after what might be a minute or a day or a year, he sees little flashes of green light out there in distant galleries, hundreds of feet away. Each flash initiates a chain reaction of further flashes beyond it, so that if he turns in a slow circle he can perceive great flowing signals of light in all directions, tunnels of green arcing out into the blackness—each flash glowing for only a moment before fading, but in that moment repeating everything that came before, everything that will come next. Like days, like hours, like heartbeats.

He wakes to a deflated world. The newspapers are full of suicides; the price of gas has tripled. The miners whisper that the saltworks is in trouble. The Ford plant is shedding men; the foundry shuts down.

Quart milk bottles sell for a dollar apiece. There's no butter, hardly any meat. Most nights Mother serves only cabbage and soda bread. Salt.

No more trips to the butcher or the depot or the commissary. No more outside. He waits for Ruby to come to the door.

By November, Mother's boarders are vanishing. Mr. Beeson goes first, then Mr. Fackler. Still, Ruby doesn't come. Her face doesn't appear among the faces Tom watches from the upstairs window. Each morning he clambers out of his closet and carries his traitorous heart down to the kitchen like an egg. Images of Ruby climb the undersides of his eyelids, and he rubs them away.

No addresses, mumbles Mr. Weems. *The world is swallowing people like candy, boy. No one is leaving addresses.*

Mr. Hanson goes next, then Mr. Heathcock. By April the saltworks is operating only two days a week, and Mr. Weems, Mother, and Tom are alone at supper.

Sixteen. Eighteen if he's lucky. Tom moves his few things into one of the empty boarders' rooms on the first floor, and Mother doesn't say a word. He thinks of Ruby Hornaday: her pale blue eyes, her loose flames of hair. *Is she out there in the city, somewhere, right now? Or is she three thousand miles away?* Then he puts his questions aside.

Mother catches a fever in 1931. It eats her from the inside. She still puts on her high-waisted dresses, ties on her apron. She still cooks every meal and presses Mr. Weems's suit every Sunday. But within a month she has become somebody else, an empty demon in Mother's clothes—perfectly upright at the table, eyes smoldering, nothing on her plate.

She has a way of putting her hand on Tom's forehead while he works. Tom will be hauling coal or mending a pipe or sweeping the parlor, the sun glowing behind the curtains, and Mother will appear from nowhere and put her icy palm over his eyebrows, and he'll close his eyes and feel his heart tear just a little more.

Amphibian. It means two lives.

Mr. Weems is let go. He puts on his suit, packs up his dominoes, and leaves an address downtown.

I thought no one was leaving addresses.

You're true as a map, Tom. True as the magnet to the iron. And tears spill from the old miner's eyes.

One blue, icy morning not long after that, for the first time in Tom's memory, Mother is not at the stove when he enters the kitchen. He finds her upstairs sitting on her bed, fully dressed in her coat and shoes and with her rosary clutched to her chest. The room is spotless, the house wadded with silence.

Now remember, payments are due on the fifteenth. Her voice is ash. *The flashing on the roof needs replacing. There's ninety-one dollars in the dresser.*

Mother, Tom says.

Shhh, Tomcat, she hisses. *Don't get yourself worked up.*

Tom manages two more payments. Then the saltworks closes and the bank comes for the house. He walks in a daze through blowing sleet to the end of the lane and turns right and staggers over the dry weeds awhile till he finds the old path and walks beneath the creaking pitch pines to Ruby's marsh. Ice has interlocked in the shallows, but the water in the center is dark as molten pewter.

He stands there a long time. Into the gathering darkness he says, *I'm still here, but where are you?* His blood sloshes to and fro, and snow gathers in his eyelashes, and three ducks come spiraling out of the night and land silently on the water.

The next morning he walks past the padlocked gate of International Salt with fourteen dollars in his pocket. He rides the trackless trolley downtown for a nickel and gets off on Washington Boulevard. Between the buildings the sun comes up the color of steel, and Tom raises his face to it but feels no warmth at all. He passes catatonic drunks squatting on upturned crates, motionless as statues, and storefront after storefront of empty windows. In a diner a goitrous waitress brings him a cup of coffee with little shining disks of fat floating on top.

The streets are filled with faces, dull and wan, lean and hungry; none belongs to Ruby. He drinks a second cup of coffee and eats a plate of eggs and toast, and then another. A woman emerges from a doorway and flings a pan out onto the sidewalk, and the wash water flashes in the light a moment before falling. In an alley a mule lies on its side, asleep or dead. Eventually the waitress says, *You moving in?* and Tom goes out. He walks slowly toward the address he's copied and recopied onto a sheet of Mother's writing paper. Frozen furrows of plowed snow are shored up against the buildings, and the little golden windows high above seem miles away.

It's a boardinghouse. Mr. Weems is at a lopsided table playing dominoes by himself. He looks up, says, *Holy shit sure as gravity,* and spills his tea.

By a miracle Mr. Weems has a grandniece who manages the owl shift in the maternity ward at City General. Maternity is on the fourth floor. In the elevator Tom cannot tell if he is ascending or descending. The niece looks him up and down and checks his eyes and chest for fever and hires him on the spot. *World goes to Hades, but babies still get born,* she says, and issues him white coveralls.

Rainy nights are the busiest. Full moons and holidays are tied for second. God forbid a rainy holiday with a full moon. Ten hours a night, six nights a week, Tom roves the halls with carts of laundry, taking soiled blankets down to the cellar, bringing clean blankets up. He brings up meals, brings down trays.

Doctors walk the rows of beds injecting expectant mothers with morphine and something called scopolamine that makes them forget. Sometimes there are screams. Sometimes Tom's heart pounds for no reason he can identify. In the delivery rooms there's always new blood on the tiles to replace the old blood Tom has just mopped away.

The halls are bright at every hour, but out the windows the darkness presses very close, and in the leanest hours of those nights Tom gets a sensation like the hospital is deep underwater, the floor rocking gently, the lights of neighboring buildings like glimmering schools of fish, the pressure of the sea all around.

He turns eighteen, nineteen. All the listless figures he sees: children humped around the hospital entrance, their eyes vacant with hunger; farmers pouring into the parks; families sleeping without cover—people for whom nothing left on earth could be surprising. There are so many of them, as if somewhere out in the countryside great factories pump out thousands of new men every minute, as if the ones shuffling down the sidewalks are but fractions of the immense multitudes behind them.

And yet is there not goodness, too? Are people not helping one another in these ruined places? Tom splits his wages with Mr. Weems. He brings home discarded newspapers and wrestles his way through the words on the funny pages. He turns twenty, and Mr. Weems bakes a mushy pound cake full of eggshells and sets twenty matches in it, and Tom blows them all out.

He faints at work: once in the elevator, twice in the big, pulsing laundry room in the basement. Mostly he's able to hide it. But one night he faints in the hall outside the waiting room, and a nurse named Fran hauls him into a closet. *Can't let them see you like that,* she says, and he washes back into himself.

Fran's face is brown, lived-in. She sits him on a chair in the corner and wipes his forehead. The air is warm, steamy; it smells like soap. For a moment he feels like throwing his arms around her neck and telling her everything.

The closet is more than a closet. On one wall is a two-basin sink; heat lamps are bolted to the undersides of the cabinets. Set in the opposite wall are two little doors.

Tom returns to the chair in the corner of this room whenever he starts to feel dizzy. Three, four, occasionally ten times a night, he watches a nurse carry an utterly newborn baby through the little door on the left and deposit it on the counter in front of Fran.

She plucks off little knit caps and unwraps blankets. Their bodies are scarlet or imperial purple; they have tiny, bright red fingers, no eyebrows, no kneecaps, no expression except a constant, bewildered wince. Her voice is a whisper: *Why here you are, there you go, okay now, baby, just lift you here.* Their wrists are the circumference of Tom's pinkie.

Fran takes a new washcloth from a stack, dips it in warm water, and wipes every inch of the creature—ears, scrotum, armpits, eyelids—washing away bits of placenta, dried blood, all the milky fluids that accompanied it into this world. Meanwhile the child stares up at her with blank, memorizing eyes, peering into the newness of all things. Knowing what? Only light and dark, only mother, only fluid.

Fran dries the baby and splays her fingers beneath its head and tugs its hat back on. She whispers, *Here you are, see what a good girl you are, down you go,* and with one free hand lays out two new, crisp blankets, and binds the baby—wrap, wrap, turn—and sets her in a rolling bassinet for Tom to wheel into the nursery, where she'll wait with the others beneath the lights like loaves of bread.

In a magazine Tom finds a color photograph of a three-hundred-year-old skeleton of a bowhead whale, stranded on a coastal plain in some place called Finland and covered with moss. He tears it out, studies it in the lamplight. *See,* he murmurs to Mr. Weems, *how the flowers closest to it are brightest? See how the closest leaves are the darkest green?*

Tom is twenty-one and fainting three times a week when he sees, among the drugged, dazed mothers in their rows of beds, the unmistakable face of Ruby Hornaday. Flaming orange hair, freckles sprayed across her cheeks, hands folded in her lap, and a thin gold wedding ring on her finger. The material of the ward ripples. Tom leans on the handle of his cart to keep from falling.

Blue, he thinks. *Blue, blue, blue.*

He retreats to the chair in the corner of the washing room and tries to suppress his heart. *Any minute,* he thinks, *her baby could come through the door.*

Two hours later, he pushes his cart into the postdelivery room, and Ruby is gone. Tom's shift ends; he rides the elevator down. Outside, an icy January rain settles lightly on the city. The streetlights glow yellow. The early morning avenues are empty except for the occasional automobile, passing with a damp sigh. Tom steadies a hand against the bricks and closes his eyes.

A police officer helps him home. Tom lies on his stomach in his rented bed all that day and recopies the letter until little suns burst behind his eyes. *Deer Ruby, I saw you in the hospital and I saw your baby to. His eyes are viry prety. Fran sez later they will probly get blue. Mother is gone and I am lonely as the arctic see.*

That night at the hospital Fran finds the address. Tom includes the photo of the whale skeleton from the magazine and sticks on an extra stamp for luck. He thinks: *See how the flowers closest to it are brightest. See how the closest leaves are the darkest green.*

He sleeps, pays his rent, walks the thirty-one blocks to work, and checks the mail each day. And each day winter pales and spring strengthens and Tom loses a little bit of hope.

One morning over breakfast, Mr. Weems looks to him with concern and says, *You ain't even here, Tom. You got one foot across the river. You got to pull back to our side.*

But three weeks later, it comes. *Dear Tom, I liked hearing from you. It hasn't been ten years but it feels like a thousand. I'm married, you probably guessed that. The baby is Arthur. Maybe his eyes will turn blue. They just might.*

A bald president is on the stamp. The paper smells like paper, nothing more. Tom runs a finger beneath every word, sounding it out. Making sure he hasn't missed anything.

I know your married and I dont want anything but happyness for you but maybe I can see you one time? We could meet at the acquareyem. If you dont rite back thats okay I no why.

Two more weeks. *Dear Tom, I don't want anything but happiness for you, too. How about next Tuesday? I'll bring the baby, okay?*

The next Tuesday, the first one in May, Tom leaves the hospital after his shift. His vision wavers at the edges, and he hears Mother's voice: *Be careful, Tomcat. It's not worth the risk.* He walks slowly to the end of the block and catches the first trolley to Belle Isle, where he steps off into a golden dawn.

There are few cars about, all parked, one a Ford with a huge present wrapped in yellow ribbon on the backseat. An old man with a crumpled face rakes the gravel paths. The sunlight hits the dew and sets the lawns aflame.

The face of the aquarium is Gothic and wrapped in vines. Tom finds a bench outside and waits for his pulse to steady. The reticulated glass roofs of the flower conservatory reflect a passing cloud. Eventually a man in overalls opens the gate, and Tom buys two tickets, then thinks about the baby and buys a third. He returns to the bench with the three tickets in his trembling fingers.

By eleven the sky is filled with a platinum haze and the island is busy. Men on bicycles crackle along the paths. A girl flies a yellow kite.

Tom?

Ruby Hornaday materializes before him—shoulders erect, hair newly short, pushing a chrome-and-canvas baby buggy. He stands quickly, and the park bleeds away and then restores itself.

Sorry I'm late, she says.

She's dignified, slim. Two quick strokes for eyebrows, the same narrow nose. No makeup. No jewelry. Those pale blue eyes and that hair.

She cocks her head slightly. *Look at you. All grown up.*

I have tickets, he says.

How's Mr. Weems?

Oh, he's made of salt, he'll live forever.

They start down the path between the rows of benches and the shining trees. Occasionally she takes his arm to steady him, though her touch only disorients him more.

I thought maybe you were far away, he says. *I thought maybe you went to sea.*

Ruby doesn't say anything. She parks the buggy and lifts the baby to her chest—he's wrapped in a blue afghan—and then they're through the turnstile.

The aquarium is dim and damp and lined on both sides with glass-fronted tanks. Ferns hang from the ceiling, and little boys lean across the brass railings and press their noses to the glass. *I think he likes it,* Ruby says. *Don't you, baby?* The boy's eyes are wide open. Fish swim slow ellipses through the water.

They see translucent squid with corkscrew tails, sparkling pink octopi like floating lanterns, cowfish in blue and violet and gold. Iridescent green tiles gleam on the domed ceiling and throw wavering patterns of light across the floor.

In a circular pool at the very center of the building, dark shapes race back and forth in coordination. *Jacks,* Ruby murmurs. *Aren't they?*

Tom blinks.

You're pale, she says.

Tom shakes his head.

She helps him back out into the daylight, beneath the sky and the trees. The baby lies in the buggy sucking his lips, and Ruby guides Tom to a bench.

Cars and trucks and even a limousine pass slowly along the white bridge, high over the river. The city glitters in the distance.

Thank you, says Tom.

For what?

For this.

How old are you now, Tom?

Twenty-one. Same as you. A breeze stirs the trees, and the leaves vibrate with light. Everything is radiant.

World goes to Hades, but babies still get born, whispers Tom.

Ruby peers into the buggy and adjusts something, and for a moment the back of her neck shows between her hair and collar. The sight of those two knobs of vertebrae, sheathed in her delicate skin, fills Tom with a longing that cracks the lawns open. For a moment it seems Ruby is being slowly dragged away from him, as if he were a swimmer caught in a rip, and with every stroke the back of her neck recedes farther into the distance. Then she sits back, and the park heels over, and he can feel the bench become solid beneath him once more.

I used to think, Tom says, *that I had to be careful with how much I lived. As if life was a pocketful of coins. You only got so much and you didn't want to spend it all in one place.*

Ruby looks at him. Her eyelashes whisk up and down.

But now I know life is the one thing in the world that never runs out. I might run out of mine, and you might run out of yours, but the world will never run out of life. And we're all very lucky to be part of something like that.

She holds his gaze. *Some deserve more luck than they've gotten.*

Tom shakes his head. He closes his eyes. *I've been lucky, too. I've been absolutely lucky.*

The baby begins to fuss, a whine building to a cry, and Ruby says, *Hungry.*

A trapdoor opens in the gravel between Tom's feet, black as a keyhole, and he glances down.

You'll be okay?

I'll be okay.

Good-bye, Tom. She touches his forearm once, and then she goes, pushing the buggy through the crowds. He watches her disappear in pieces, first her legs, then her hips, then her shoulders, and finally the back of her bright head.

And then Tom sits, hands in his lap, alive for one more day.

Salvatore Scibona

The Woman Who Lived
in the House

HE LEARNED OF Sergei's arrest and imprisonment when a
waiter switched the television to CNN. Ásmundur and his
wife watched the screen with horror in the Amsterdam café where
they habitually took their Sunday coffee and pastries, reading two
papers, his in English, hers in Dutch. The Soviets—rather the
Russians, rather Putin—would seize all the money too, wouldn't
they? asked Ásmundur's wife hopelessly.

Ásmundur's whole head boiled with blood. He mistook the
bowl of sugar cubes for an ashtray and stabbed his cigarette in it.
He said, "Perhaps." They both knew he meant, *Yes, everything.*

Sergei's development of a Siberian natural gas field was such a
sure thing, his kleptocratic credentials so spotless, that they had
tied to him millions of their own guilders and even taken a second
mortgage on their house to make the minimum investment.

"This is what we *get.* This is what we *get*," she cried on the walk
home—otherwise their week's most tender hour, when she would
hook her arm in his and wrap her small hands in the tail of his
scarf. Whatever the weather she felt a chill outdoors.

Then a cyclist neglecting his bell careened into her on a foot-bridge, and Ásmundur made the mistake of asking after the health of the drug-addled young man, who'd just bloodied his head on the stone bridge rail. That she had only stumbled a little made no difference. Ásmundur should first have thought of her. And so the deep screw in the joint between them came out another turn.

She had warned him off Sergei—his occasional squash partner, a Russian with the face of Saddam Hussein and fingers as soft as soup dumplings. Once, the man had come to Twelfth Night sup-per while Ásmundur's sister, Íris, was visiting from Iceland with her infant daughter, Frigg. When the girl awoke howling during dessert, Sergei fetched her and dipped her pacifier in his rum pud-ding. She went to sleep again on his belly while he petted her like a cat. Nevertheless Ásmundur's wife had been right about that man, and now she compulsively said so.

Later on, Ásmundur saw that God had sent them the cyclist to foretell that, after twenty years of giving them the stamina and will that makes young Eros turn into the companionship of mar-ried love, he would now send bicycle accidents; a toilet seat that cracked under her behind at a friend's dinner party; brackish water that pooled from untraceable faults in their basement just as they had to sell their house for debts; spoiled milk in fresh cartons; and contempt for all the differences between their characters that, before, they had turned into more and more baroque demonstra-tions that their love gained strength with exercise.

Ásmundur Gudmundsson had been born a hayseed and made himself a modern man. Twenty years of typing at a computer key-board while pressing a telephone receiver or a mobile to his right ear with his shoulder had permanently twisted his neck. Through-out his career his clever intestines convulsed in sympathy with otherwise undetectable shifts in the mood of the currency markets in distant capitals. When he had begun to lose his hair he won-dered which of his daring investments had caused it, and only concluded long after his ruin that he might just have been taking part in the common life of his species, as when a maturing frog loses its tail.

He had married a woman he admired. She taught him the knack of talking with strangers, simply asking them questions about themselves. She worked for an NGO devoted to transparency in government but had usually held her tongue about his own dealings. Her slender neck bore a crown, like a seeding dandelion, of hair that had gone to shining white in her twenties.

He had wanted two children, and she wanted none, and they made none. It was only once they went bankrupt that he saw his recitations that he was "okay" with having no children as the reading of a hostage from a script before a video camera, while his captor pointed a Kalashnikov at the place where the hostage's spine met his skull.

After the Sergei affair, Ásmundur revealed a distemper, a callowness he'd never shown from his Lutheran boyhood to his early middle age. He made lewd jokes at her friends' expense while drinking with them. Then he began to take long drives in the countryside with a red-headed Danish university student, whose silly fixation on such a lopsided figure as him briefly inspired the delusion that he had been meant for rakishness. The girl's muddy English, learned from text messaging, bewitched him. He did not understand a word of it, and for three months it seemed to hold out all the wrecked promise of continental Europe.

His wife confirmed her terrified intuition by smelling his pants. She demanded divorce immediately. Her father, a Dutch magistrate, began its execution with dispatch and feeling for both sides. He was a man, too, after all, as he told Ásmundur in an e-mail; and he himself had let his weakness play games. Only his own wife's loyalty to the Church and her fear of hell had saved them.

But Ásmundur's wife's resolve to be free, she said, and then— she knew exactly the words that could dismember him forever— to "love somebody who really understands me," at last tore out the screw. It didn't matter that he would have done anything to drill it back in at a different place. She did not take his calls.

At his father-in-law's billiard club, Ásmundur scratched the cue ball with force; and the old man, fit as a pony, contracted his great red brow and said, "You should strike it more gently. Maybe that stick is bowed."

"Alexis, please," Ásmundur snapped, but immediately he repented his tone. He looked up. In the rafters, a fat spider awaited a fly. He said, "Alexis, I have to, I have to do something *rash* or I'll never get out of this."

"I thought your fling was rash," the old man enunciated. "I thought you rather needed to do something careful for a change— I'm sorry. I withdraw that. You have an idea?" He ran the table except for the eight ball, an easy shot he seemed to botch from pity.

Ásmundur declared, but with a hint of inquiry, the hope of approval, "I'm thinking I will go home."

"Hogwash," spat the old man. "Who do you think you are, Thomas Jefferson? He went broke on *his* farm."

"I'm broke *now*," Ásmundur retorted.

As a young man, Ásmundur had studied economics in the hope of little more than a one-bedroom flat in Germany or the Low Countries, where he might keep the vow he'd sworn that he would not die incarcerated on the smallholding in Iceland where his mother and grandparents had raised him.

And yet at fifty, a year after the divorce was final; long after he had told Hulda, the student, to leave him alone, that he had never cared for her; his reputation among his colleagues intact but his capital destroyed—he found himself in a London airport listening to his native language spoken by a ticketing agent of Icelandair while his own ears swelled with the new promise, maybe the last promise, that, notwithstanding the experience of revenant fools everywhere, he might find a warmer future in his cold past. He knew how to get by on a farm.

. . .

In the terminal, he threw his tabloid in the trash and moved down the nave of the radiant concourse. His physical possessions included a boarding ticket, the clothes he was wearing, a credit card, a passport, and nothing else, but they seemed too much. He had stopped in Barcelona, Frankfurt, and London, closing his affairs. He owned nothing of value but his teenage savings and a little of his mother's old bonds, in the Landsbanki in Reykjavík, denominated in a currency he had not spent in twenty years. Whenever his family had wanted to see him, he always insisted they come to Holland, and he paid their fares.

A voice from everywhere like the call to prayer invited the crowd in Icelandic and English to begin boarding zone three. He took the air in, feeling the chill as far down as his stomach. As he inhaled, the place entered him; as he exhaled, he left some of himself behind.

He fed his ticket to a laser scanner and embarked through the long umbilical of the Jetway. He drank a vodka on board. He sat still, feet flat, attending to the air that entered and departed his lungs in a stream of present moments, each of them the very center of time.

The manufacturer had disguised the fuselage as a narrow living room fitted out for a civil wedding.

He had rarely referred to his wife by name. To her father, he called her "she" or "your girl"; to others, "my wife" or, satirizing himself, "the woman who lives with me in the house." He liked the name and saved it like a child with Easter chocolate for private moments when the lights burned brightly in his mind.

"Am I your only one?" she used to ask him.

"Yes," he replied—but all that was past.

Now he was only a thing that breathed.

. . .

The home in the southlands had not changed from the last time he had visited, during his university days. It half-rose from the basalt rubble at the cliff's sloping base, like a seal poking its head from under a wave. His grandfather had ordered the corrugated-iron house from a Norwegian catalog before the Great War, and the pieces came delivered in a crate with unintelligible instructions. Of the house's eight sides, only the southern face was not partly buried in earth. The red roof shone in the endless summer days and for a month or two in winter lay buried in snow. Íris, six years his junior, used it as a vacation house, riding the bus to a stop three kilometers up the road. She met him at the farm today, running to the car he had rented at the airport in Reykjavík, and welcomed her brother's crinkled face, his crooked head, the inborn grimace that she understood was his way of grinning. She kissed him through the window on top of his flimsy hair.

The sea began two kilometers away, visible across the lava-pebble beach where no vegetation grew. In the rear of the home field, a hot spring suitable for six persons steamed year-round with a sulfurous odor as homeful to him as haddock-head soup. Their mother and grandparents were long dead. Their cousins had taken jobs in Denmark, Canada, Shanghai, and Houston. Íris was delighted to let him stay there now. She clerked at an electronics store in the capital and had always clung to Ásmundur, her only sibling, when she visited in Amsterdam; even holding his hand in bars as a lover does. In recent years she had come with the little daughter, whose other parent she had never met again after a night of hash and dancing four years ago.

Before Ásmundur could open the door, his niece figured out the latch, climbed his leg, ensconced herself in his lap, seized the wheel, and demanded to drive the car.

He bought as many sheep as his feeble mother had had left when she died—fourteen ewes and three rams. He would never stop hating sheep. He fed them chewing tobacco to stave off worms. Given luck, he might pull a peasant profit from the fleece and mutton in two years.

A project gripped him right away that he knew would keep his hands moving: the repair of the derelict glasshouse, between the dwelling and the spring, that his grandfather had surrounded with blueberries. Steam pipes from the volcanic drama under the earth heated the glasshouse, and Ásmundur bought a new steam generator for electricity that represented his only vain purchase. He wanted to subsist on his own power. The steam was free. The steam rose like rage everywhere whether you liked it or not. When he switched on the machine, the turbid glass became an enormous crystal that burned all night with the sodium lamps he'd bought for a song from a neighbor who was getting out of the tulip business.

His wife's father wrote a letter, dictated to his secretary and FedExed to the door of the farmhouse.

> My only hopes for you, dear Ásmundi, are that you will compose a scheme of daily work, socialize a little, drink only a little, pay close attention to the fats in your blood, forget your sins, keep your feet dry, keep the holidays with your sister and Frigg, always iron your shirts, keep oil in the crankcase of your car, and do not skimp on a mechanic when your ingenuity fails you. I remain
> Your father-out-of-law,
> Alexis

He slept in his grandfather's room, where a hot tap emptied into a basin and a shaving brush still sat in a cup before a little mirror. The furnishings were handmade though they didn't look so. The old man had built the bed from birch scraps and the few iron stays left over once he'd figured out, more or less, how to piece the house together. Barley straw filled the mattress, which reeked of mildew, but after a week's airing on the line outside, the mattress suited Ásmundur well enough. He oiled the barrel of the ancient shotgun that hung over the mirror and bought fresh shells and tested them by firing at gulls on the beach. Most comforting: the new sheets and pillowcases of Egyptian cotton that his sister brought from the city as a housewarming present. The stucco walls of the interior bore the trowel strokes of the dead man— who had taught young Ásmundur to shear a ewe, to sever its child's throat, to wash the child's intestines and stuff them with its ground-up shoulder, and to smoke its head over charcoal.

Yet all that winter, he woke in the bed from dreams in which he spoke and walked with none of the house's former inhabitants, but instead with the woman who had attended the second half of his life. The two of them vacationed on Saturn. In a café that boasted an excellent view of the planet's rings, she looked away from the window and said, "You never understood me; I never understood you."

He needed so little that he let the bonds languish in the bank at their geriatric interest rates. He did buy a rusted car, used parts, gasoline, silage, oatmeal, some whiskey. He might have used a little more money, but when was that ever not the case? Money was water filling a balloon at a faucet; the balloon was only ever *almost* full as it swelled, and swelled, until it burst. Up to now, he had expended his adulthood changing money from guilders to pounds to rubles, later to euros. Money existed only in order that you should exchange it. Even male friends could be exchanged. His gym and investment partners did not accumulate but rotated.

The woman on Saturn, however—the woman who used to share his drink, in their shiny kitchen in Amsterdam, so they wouldn't have to wash a second glass—she was not, as they say, fungible. She cost exactly nothing. You found her yourself, or you didn't. She was the only one of her.

He moved the mattress to his granny's room and slept somewhat sounder, a little warmer there. It had a separate radiator that burbled with a noise like a lamb coughing up its blood.

The spring after Ásmundur had settled into the farm, he resolved to sow one of the pastures with barley for feed. The gunked carburetor in his mother's Ford tractor needed replacing, and he drove to the gas station that doubled as a junk parts store. Into this place he was followed by a yearling spitz dog. And when he walked out, the dog came along, at a distance of ten meters, respectful but determined.

A week later, once the dog's adoption of Ásmundur and the farm had become an established fact, he needed something to call her. He named her Hulda, the joke being that the bitch would never leave him alone. He had tried to make a clean break from Hulda—the red-headed Dane—but months afterward she would surprise him by leaping into the restaurant in Amsterdam where he and Alexis were divvying up the scraps of Ásmundur's assets among his creditors, or by telephoning at his rented flat on Christmas morning. Once, when Frigg was visiting in Holland, she answered the phone in Icelandic and called out, "Uncle, it's the bad elf again!" as her mother basted the goose. Ásmundur was malt and the girl Hulda was juice, and together they had made the kind of drink that only tastes good on a holiday.

If his impulse with that name was to cure himself by ridiculing himself, he failed. However, once he admitted the futility of letting his remorse have his ear whenever it asked, the dog began to get mixed up in the very feelings he had come home to Iceland with the goal of never feeling again.

"Come here, Hulda, my sweet," he cooed, as the dog presented its woolly neck to his fingernails.

In Ásmundur's youth, no one would have called this animal a breed; it was simply the sort of dog that came from Iceland. She was curious, frolicsome, industrious, unafraid. She groomed meticulously her blonde coat, rummaging it with her snub muzzle. Her tail curled over her back like a scorpion's. She spoke only one word, *Hello!* Her ears never lay down. Her lips were black.

Her tongue was all of Hulda's animal perfection condensed into a single organ. Still and imperceptible like a private mind when she slept, wagging like a tail when she played at chasing her master through the barley, showing only the tongue's tip when she looked cock-headed into a mink's den in a marsh, arched like a spoon when she drank from a puddle; instrument of kisses, tidier of her privates, dislodger of fleas. To think, Ásmundur had one of these himself, a tongue, of which he rarely took notice except when it smarted on a cocoa mug.

Ásmundur Gudmundsson was a modern man, yes; but despite their common language of looks and yips, Hulda was a creature of deep antiquity. She knew the memory of her kind far better than she knew her own life. It costs a dog months of grief to learn a skill as simple as playing dead, while its clairvoyant gift for tracking livestock lost in a crag excels any similar talent human beings have ever acquired. We are born crippled and stupid, with a vast cavern of mind to fill with memories, conclusions, judgments: a warehouse where we build the store of implements with which we nightly torture ourselves in our dreams. But a dog is born already knowing nearly everything it will ever know.

Thus when a collarless dog lopes down a mountain of mossy lava into an Icelandic town and follows a man into a junk store, then runs untiringly the twenty paved highway kilometers after his car until later in the dark afternoon she sits at his stockade gate sweeping her tail with such force as to wobble her paws in the mud—then the man will feel something quite different from the thrill of a woman choosing him. A woman's choice, however fraught with feelings, is still a judgment of his prospects, his personality, his fitness, and all the things in which a man's ego rejoices. A dog does not *choose*. A dog *recognizes*. In this way, Hulda saw in Ásmundur Gudmundsson the soul of the human being to which the prehistoric process that had fashioned her own soul had arranged that she would attach.

It was one thing to make love with a woman; to sign a contract at church; to grow rich; to fear death; to be forgiven for sin; to eat fresh chops by the fire; even at night in bed to be scratched by a wife on the flank of the thigh at the place where the hip bone protrudes, and to have one's own withers petted by her through the wool of one's jacket while walking over a canal after breakfast. All these things, according to Ásmundur Gudmundsson, were very fine. But surely it was another thing to be followed home by a dog who takes you at one whiff to be a part of herself.

Hulda ate salmon, the guts of the ptarmigans he shot in the mountains, barley mash, even cucumbers, and always licked her bowl clean. So when she lost her appetite, suddenly, the fall after her investiture at the farm, Ásmundur noticed right away. She made a squealing noise addressed to no one. She seemed always underfoot and woke him one morning in his granny's bed by licking his toes. Her stomach hardened like the cooked yolk of an egg. Her flushed teats protruded. Within the month, her abdomen waggled under her while she walked. Ásmundur could no longer deny it. She was pregnant.

And so young!

His jealousy flared like an ulcer and impeded his breath. Who was this cad to whom she had submitted, and where did she find the time? She never strayed farther than a shout, and she believed that every word he spoke meant *come*.

One day, in a flash of wishful insight, Ásmundur thought he discovered her violator on the way to Selfoss. A black Labrador mixed with something weaselish and longer-haired was harassing one of his ewes by the road. The ewe took cover among his silage bales, and the dog gave up and loped along the shoulder and stopped to lift a leg on a guidepost. Ásmundur eased toward the far lane to avoid the creature; then, in a florescence of wrath, swerved back to crush it under the tires of his Opel car, so small it might have overturned if he had acted in time. His adversary only bounded away in the grass of the plain.

At length, at home, Hulda began to tremble and vomit. She had never been a neurotic dog before, but now paced around the stockade where his horse ate its hay. Ásmundur packed a wine crate with lyme-grass straw, fluffing it and smoothing it out like a nervous boy with his hair before a dance. Hulda hobbled into it. She scratched her nipples on the unplaned edge of the box and yelped, and bedded down.

She panted in spasms.

And when he brushed with his fingers the fur at her ribs, the contents of her mind opened themselves to him, as when a human toddler simply hugs his mother's knee and the mother's whole being vibrates with comprehension.

Hulda needed air, and it was everywhere around her, and yet she lacked the force to draw it fully into her lungs. She stood up in the straw, turned herself in circles, scratched at the floor of the box, unsure for what she was digging, where any hole she might dig here would have led, what she would bury in it. He watched as spasms rippled her midriff. She squatted as though in hope of relieving a strain in her bowels, and yet not in her bowels. But everything was wrong. She was surely starving, yet at the offer of her master's lamb-bone supper she recoiled. She lay down on her side, rheum streaming from her nose. Her face asked, What on earth is happening to me?

Ásmundur wondered if anything could be more piteous than a proud animal showing you the whites of its eyes.

The bitch's privy parts went convex, as though trying to grow a second neck and head from behind. She stretched her legs rigidly. Her hot breath stank. Her tail broomed the straw. A bubble appeared on her vulva, yellowish and dripping pale fluid. The bubble grew. Its surface was hard and slick. With a heave, she emitted it, an ovoid mass with no discernible parts.

She snapped herself double, lapping feverishly between her legs. She nipped with her teeth and licked passionately at an end of the thing, which revealed itself to be a face with ears, and a tongue poking out. She licked the thing's ventral side, all in a mania as though of appetite, and gnawed at the cord with her molars until it frayed and broke. The thing made a mew and bumbled in the straw, found its mother's hind leg, crawled up it—all the while impeded by Hulda's mad lapping—and miraculously found a teat, affixed itself, and nursed.

Ásmundur looked on with wonderment and disgust at the spectacle of new life.

The bitch expelled three more sleek globs before she had finished, each in turn transforming, under the force of her tongue, into pups: all of them yellower even than she, with fawn-colored splotches across the snouts. Thus Ásmundur reconsidered his black adversary, though he had no regret left to spend on the dog he had nearly run down on the road.

The blood and mucus from Hulda's innards and the amniotic bath that still covered her haunches and much of the pups—all this Hulda began to clear with strokes of her stretching tongue. She birthed the final two placentas. She lapped them out and fed on them in slurps as though swallowing oysters, and went back to licking at the pups, which were truly animals now, with tails and legs and greed for milk.

She sneezed with fatigue.

Her master ran inside the parlor to fetch a blanket onto which to move the new family once the mess was cleared.

Where was the sire of the pups in all this? Or in the birthing and rearing of nearly all the animals dearest to us? Tomcats, studhorses, rams, his own father and Frigg's, bulls, boars, and billies—none of them lost a bead of sweat for their young. The fatherly sentiments of human beings must come, when they do, from the extra hands farming used to require before machines. Men are only good, Ásmundur said to himself, insofar as we are womanly.

When he returned, Hulda had tidied the box. Two of the pups seemed to have lost their teats and gotten buried in the loose straw. He picked through it but didn't find them.

Hulda went on bathing the two children at her breast. Her cavernous eyes caught her master, as though distracted by love. She licked and looked up.

"My good sweet," he said. He unfolded the blanket on the floor and scratched her snout.

Hulda licked again, and looked up at Ásmundur, licked again—then she lifted the smaller of the pups with her long tongue, and, in a flick of her jaw, swallowed the panting babe.

Ásmundur Gudmundsson was paralyzed.

The dog bathed the other pup at her breast, which went on working her flesh with its forepaws. Then she repeated the whole business, eating the pup quite delicately, retracting the flesh of her muzzle from the teeth as though to avoid smearing lipstick on a fork.

He lifted her from the box and dumped it out, raking the wet straw for life, and found nothing. Meantime Hulda fell asleep on the blanket, her stomach growling with strange effort.

Ásmundur went outside and vomited in the mud.

By the following year, while he was consumed with the autumn hay harvesting and Íris and Frigg were visiting to celebrate Frigg's fifth birthday, Hulda was giving birth again. In a half-hidden pile of slag under the porch, she whelped a litter of three and had swallowed two before Frigg took matters into her own hands and plucked the last one from Hulda's gooey mouth.

Frigg handed the thing to her mother, who washed it in the kitchen sink and dried it. Then Frigg held it in a dishrag inside her coat, petting it with the end of her pigtail and singing it the lullaby about the outlaw woman who threw her baby down a waterfall.

The three of them deliberated a means of breaking Hulda of her passion for her own meat and bones. "They're wet, like food," Frigg said with authority. And her uncle agreed that if they only gave Hulda a dry pup she might, having no precedent in her own life, refer to the buried memory of all lady mammals and suckle it.

Frigg named the surviving puppy Vigdís, although she called the pup from the beginning by its full Icelandic name, Vigdís Huldasdóttir. And Ásmundur followed her lead, hoping to append some of his feelings for the bitch to its offspring.

Hulda let it nurse for a week, then ran off to tell the sheep what to do. She followed Ásmundur into the shower stall until he had to nudge her out with his foot and bar the door.

Íris's yearly municipal stipend for day care ran out, and Frigg stayed with her uncle at the farm, feeding the pup with ewe's milk from an eyedropper. She kept the infant in a fanny pack she wore frontward, so that wherever the girl hopped along the pup looked out from her pouch.

Meantime, the girl co-opted her uncle's ardor for repairing the glasshouse and kept him at it every morning. The finished lights dangled ten feet overhead on pulleys strung with rope he could raise or lower as the season dictated. For the time being, he had wrapped the ceiling with plastic to keep drips out of his wires. But the walls' cracked glass panes and sashes needed laborious patching.

He could not simply go to the capital and buy new panes. None would fit. His grandfather had spent years rummaging flea markets where people were getting rid of old windows, which he assembled into long walls and a ceiling, fitting the glass in wood sashes.

Every tenth pane or so had broken, and Ásmundur passed his evenings shaping new ones from scrap glass with a steel cutter he had dug up at the junk store and bought for the promise of a joint of spring lamb.

Why the girl had such patience for tedium with her uncle he could never comprehend. She had satellite television at home, but so did he. In the dark mornings, she waited for him at the breakfast table and said, "Good morning, Uncle. What do we do today? Caulk?"

It was nearly Christmas again, and time under the warm lamps kept him sane as the darkness pervaded every other hour at that time of year. He turned the thermostat up to twenty-five Celsius and they worked in T-shirts. Hulda followed always, looking querulously at the girl and her sagging pouch.

Today the man and the girl worked on sashes. Frigg walked along the scaffold with a candle, tracing them. Where the flame flickered, Ásmundur pumped the caulking gun and laid a bead of silicone where the air was drafting. Then Frigg dipped her finger in a glass of water and smoothed the patch.

Frigg had great hopes for banana trees, which she had learned in day care were grown elsewhere in Iceland in such houses. We could "make a killing," she said, using the English phrase she had picked up long ago from his wife.

The pup squeaked in its pouch, which she carried even to the bedroom, where her mother had slept as a girl. Frigg was good about changing the straw in the pouch but she did smell perpetually of urine. If Hulda lurked nearby, Frigg zipped the pouch entirely, leaving only a hole she had cut with a scissors for air.

"Frigg, you really must let Vigdís Huldasdóttir out to play," he said.

"But the other one," she said, pointing her foot at the dog that lay dozing two meters beneath where her master stood.

"Let's just try for a little while and see."

Frigg replied, "No."

"Frigg, you *must*. How would you like to spend your days and nights in a bag?"

"Just okay," she said. "I would like it just okay."

In fact, she might. Like her mother, she always sought to share a blanket on the couch, touching toes.

"I told you let her *down*," he said. "For one hour. Then you see how she likes it."

He had let his temper out. Frigg gave a start, squeezed her mouth, and her eyes welled.

"Don't cry at me, now," he said. With all the strength in his ghoulish face, he tried to make his muscles do what other people's did when they smiled.

Frigg rattled down the scaffold steps. Her nerve, rather than her obedience, impressed him. She sat on the bottom step and whipped the puppy out and set it on the floor. The light dazzled the animal, and it sat awhile on her foot winking, before it sniffed at the pipes and jumped back when its nose tapped the hot metal.

At the moment Ásmundur relit the candle, Frigg let out a cracking scream.

Hulda had woken up, snapped at the puppy's hind, and bitten off its tail. In a second snatch, she now had the head of Vigdís Huldasdóttir down her throat; and Frigg was furiously beating the bitch about the ears and baying.

Ásmundur leapt from the scaffold—he later learned that he sprained his ankle—and with the toe of his overshoe punted Hulda's breast. The bitch screeched and coughed the wet puppy onto the floor.

The girl clutched Vigdís Huldasdóttir to her shirt while blood dappled it.

Hulda sprang back from the corner where she had landed and embraced Ásmundur's waist in her forelegs. She barked: *Hello!* And her tongue shot out, and she did her best to wash the tacky silicone from his fingers.

Almost everything he told Íris on the phone the next morning was true. The girl was unharmed. The pup had no tail anymore. He had dabbed iodine on the stub and taped it. He gave the pup back to Frigg, who went to bed with it that night. While she slept, Ásmundur had indeed driven off with the bitch in the car— Hulda always jubilated to taste the breeze through the passenger window.

But he had not in fact driven east through the pasture and shot her and buried her in the snow. He had driven two hours west to the capital, weeping wickedly, and found the park in Reykjavík where he had seen other dogs congregate, eating garbage and mice. The city would probably catch and euthanize her. It was treason all over again, of the worst kind, against someone—no, she was a *thing*, an *it*, he kept saying aloud—whose love for him no trespass of his would ever challenge.

In the park, he reached over her and popped the passenger door. Snow fell. The green aurora moved like a theater curtain in a breeze. She would not get out—*it* would not get out. He went around the side of the car, the frigid wind petrifying his snot and biting his ears, and found a lava rock and threw it into the trees. She was not normally the fetching sort. She was the sort that sought out and gathered. He made to run in his galoshes across the snow at high speed. She tore after him, as always desperate to get ahead, bounding in the snow gleefully at the game. Then he ran back to the car and raced away, closing the passenger door at a stop sign.

He made a maze of turns through the classier parts of the city, with wide boulevards where it was possible to speed and turn suddenly. But in the mirror he did not see her trailing. And at the main highway he slammed the accelerator, rocketing at twice the legal speed through the endless night.

Íris took time off from work for the holidays and came to stay at the farm for a week.

"Children forget everything," she said with insouciance, as though either she or her brother had mislaid a single harsh word from their mother and could not recall in detail the shape of the stick their grandfather had used to thrash them.

Frigg did seem okay though, and let Vigdís Huldasdóttir play outside the pouch, but only in the glasshouse with its lights burning so she could trace the puppy's every step.

Íris roasted a goose Ásmundur had shot. He read through two weeks of the London *Times* that she had brought him from Reykjavík. Frigg sat close beside him at the kitchen table, paging through seed catalogs from Germany in search of exotic fruits and inquiring after their suitability for the climate of the glasshouse.

"Whatever you like, my dear," Ásmundur murmured. "But avocado can take many years." Other farmers nearby had done well lately selling roses and tomatoes in the city. *Well* meant earning in a season what he had used to blow on a night out in Moscow, with the woman who had lived with him in the house, in the old days.

It was the greatest happiness left to him to eat goose with his sister and the girl on New Year's Eve, picking pellets from the meat. And to keep the old family custom of a nap afterward on the sheepskin couches still firm with horsehair stuffing. And then to wake up in the evening and to run outside to the hot spring, barefoot in their robes.

All three climbed naked into the well of the spring. The steam that always enshrouded it swelled in its obscurity throughout the winter like an enormous fun house. The silica in the water had accreted over the years into pearly walls in the pool basin. Their grandparents had maintained that the water there cured ailments from eczema to pimples to the curses of witches that lived under rocks. His sister's red breasts drooped now as his mother's had, the areolas still wide from Frigg's nursing. The adults drank beer, and Frigg malt with juice. When the water got too warm, they scooped some snow into it.

Every so often on the distant highway cars passed. Frigg counted them. She had persuaded them to allow the puppy to swim in the spring; they agreed only on the condition that she be vigilant lest it defecate in the water. "Eleven!" Frigg said at a car from the west.

Íris had stretched an extension cord from the glasshouse generator and plugged a boom box into it that played at terrible volume the thudding club music Ásmundur could tolerate only if he was drinking.

The music blared so loudly that at first when Frigg claimed she heard something cracking the snow outside the great cloud of steam, they didn't believe her.

"Shush, it's only a Christmas elf," her mother said.

But then he heard it too. Steps. Assertive then tentative, as though nosing about.

And Frigg, with a mother's weird sensual acuity, screamed, "Hulda! Hulda! Hulda!"

Ásmundur sprang from the pool, naked, and ran limping around the far edge of the cloud to the farmhouse.

The shotgun shells were in a teacup at the bottom of the linen chest. He loaded the gun at a sprint. He threw his foot in a galosh and slipped to the floor, his coccyx smacking the tile. He pulled on the boot and ran into the warm cloud.

At the spring, Frigg cried in furious whispers, "It will eat her! It will eat her!" clutching the squirming pup and pointing into the steam in the direction of the glasshouse.

Ásmundur stayed at the spring long enough to perceive his sister grip the girl and mutter with flagging confidence, "Hulda is back in the rocks, dear, where she came from." And then he turned back toward the glasshouse.

He emerged from the bright fog into brighter light still, where the glasshouse lights blazed over the spinach they had planted the week before. And the light blinded him. He really could not see anything. His eyes were in pain. His foreskin froze excruciatingly in a blistering gust. But his need now to kill the animal approaching around the other side of the glasshouse overpowered him. He heard *it* coming, crack by crack in the snow. The wind stung his lungs, and the veins in his thighs stuck out blue and monstrous.

He wanted to breathe, though the air was ice itself, and he breathed, and aimed his heart at the animal approaching the corner of the crystal box, the butt of the gun jammed to his shoulder. Blinking his one open eye to keep its surface from freezing.

His treasonous thumping throat called out, "Come here, my sweet."

And the animal rounded the corner, its shape somehow elongated by the sodium lamps. Trusting his voice, it approached him. Too tall. Far too tall, as fear is. His exposed pupil shrank. The thing kept coming.

It was a woman.

It was a woman with hardly any neck at all and a hat tied around the white mass of her hair. She stood on two human legs, in a blue parka, shivering.

It was a woman.

It was you.

Alice Munro

Corrie

"IT ISN'T A good thing to have the money concentrated all in the one family, the way you do in a place like this," Mr. Carlton said. "I mean, for a girl like my daughter Corrie here. For example, I mean, like her. It isn't good. Nobody on the same level."

Corrie was right across the table, looking their guest in the eye. She seemed to think this was funny.

"Who's she going to marry?" her father continued. "She's twenty-five."

Corrie raised her eyebrows, made a face.

"You missed a year," she said. "Twenty-six."

"Go ahead," her father said. "Laugh all you like."

She laughed out loud, and, indeed, what else could she do? the guest thought. His name was Howard Ritchie, and he was only a few years older than she was, but already equipped with a wife and a young family, as her father had immediately found out.

Her expressions changed very quickly. She had bright-white teeth and short, curly, nearly black hair. High cheekbones that caught the light. Not a soft woman. Not much meat on the bone, which was the sort of thing her father might find to say next.

Howard Ritchie thought of her as the type of girl who spent a lot of time playing golf and tennis. In spite of her quick tongue, he expected her to have a conventional mind.

He was an architect, just getting started on a career. Mr. Carlton insisted on referring to him as a church architect, because he was at present restoring the tower of the town's Anglican church. A tower that had been on the verge of toppling until Mr. Carlton came to its rescue. Mr. Carlton was not an Anglican—he had pointed that out several times. His church was the Methodist, and he was Methodist to the core, which was why he kept no liquor in the house. But a fine church like the Anglican ought not to be let to go to wrack and ruin. No hope looking to the Anglicans to do anything—they were a poor class of Irish Protestants, who would have taken the tower down and put up something that was a blemish on the town. They didn't have the shekels, of course, and they wouldn't understand the need for an architect, rather than a carpenter. A church architect.

The dining room was hideous, at least in Howard's opinion. This was the mid-fifties, but everything looked as if it had been in place before the turn of the century. The food was barely all right. The man at the head of the table never stopped talking. You'd think the girl would be exhausted by it, but she seemed mostly to be on the verge of laughing. Before she was done with her dessert, she lit a cigarette. She offered Howard one, saying, quite audibly, "Don't mind Daddy." He accepted, but didn't think the better of her.

Spoiled rich miss. Unmannerly.

Out of the blue, she asked him what he thought of the Saskatchewan Premier, Tommy Douglas.

He said that his wife supported him. Actually, his wife didn't think Douglas was far left enough, but he wasn't going to get into that.

"Daddy loves him. Daddy's a Communist."

This brought a snort from Mr. Carlton that didn't squelch her.

"Well, you laugh at his jokes," she told her father.

Shortly after that, she took Howard out to look at the grounds. The house was directly across the street from the factory, which made men's boots and work shoes. Behind the house, however, were wide lawns and the river that curled halfway around the town. There was a worn path down to its bank. She led the way, and he was able to see what he hadn't been sure of before. She was lame in one leg.

"Isn't it a steep climb back up?" he asked.

"I'm not an invalid."

"I see you've got a rowboat," he said, meaning that as a partway apology.

"I'd take you out in it but not right now. Now we've got to watch the sunset." She pointed out an old kitchen chair that she said was for watching the sunset, and demanded that he sit there. She herself sat on the grass. He was about to ask if she would be able to get up all right, but thought better of it.

"I had polio," she said. "That's all it is. My mother had it, too, and she died."

"That's too bad."

"I suppose so. I can't remember her. I'm going to Egypt next week. I was very keen on going, but now I don't seem to care so much. Do you think it'd be fun?"

"I have to earn a living."

He was amazed at what he'd said, and, of course, it set her off giggling.

"I was speaking in general terms," she said grandly, when the giggling finished.

"Me, too."

Some creepy fortune hunter was bound to snap her up, some Egyptian or whatever. She seemed both bold and childish. At first, a man might be intrigued by her, but then her forwardness, her self-satisfaction, if that was what it was, would become tiresome.

Of course, there was money, and to some men that never became tiresome.

"You mustn't ever mention my leg in front of Daddy or he will go apoplectic," she said. "Once he fired not just a kid who teased me but his entire family. I mean, even cousins."

From Egypt there arrived peculiar postcards, sent to his firm, not his house. Well, of course, how could she have known his home address?

Not a single pyramid on them. No Sphinx.

Instead, one showed the Rock of Gibraltar with a note that called it a pyramid in collapse. Another showed some flat, dark brown fields, God knows where, and said, "Sea of Melancholia." There was another message in fine print: "Magnifying glass obtainable send money." Fortunately, nobody in the office got hold of these.

He did not intend to reply, but he did: "Magnifying glass faulty please refund money."

He drove to her town for an unnecessary inspection of the church steeple, knowing that she had to be back from the Pyramids but not knowing whether she would be at home or off on some other jaunt.

She was home, and would be for some time. Her father had suffered a stroke.

There was not really much for her to do. A nurse came in every other day. And a girl named Sadie Wolfe was in charge of the fires, which were always lit when Howard arrived. Of course, she did other chores as well. Corrie herself couldn't quite manage to get a good fire going or put a meal together; she couldn't type, couldn't drive a car, not even with a built-up shoe to help her. Howard took over when he came. He looked after the fires and saw to various things around the house and was even taken to visit Corrie's father, if the old man was able.

He hadn't been sure how he would react to the foot, in bed. But in some way it seemed more appealing, more unique, than the rest of her.

She had told him that she was not a virgin. But that turned out to be a complicated half-truth, owing to the interference of a piano teacher, when she was fifteen. She had gone along with what the piano teacher wanted because she felt sorry for people who wanted things so badly.

"Don't take that as an insult," she said, explaining that she had not continued to feel sorry for people in that way.

"I should hope not," he said.

Then he had things to tell her about himself. The fact that he had produced a condom did not mean that he was a regular seducer. In fact, she was only the second person he had gone to bed with, the first being his wife. He had been brought up in a fiercely religious household and still believed in God, to some extent. He kept that a secret from his wife, who would have made a joke of it, being very left-wing.

Corrie said she was glad that what they were doing—what they had just done—appeared not to bother him, in spite of his belief. She said that she herself had never had any time for God, because her father was enough to cope with.

It wasn't difficult for them. Howard's job often required him to travel for a daytime inspection or to see a client. The drive from Kitchener didn't take long. And Corrie was alone in the house now. Her father had died, and the girl who used to work for her had gone off to find a city job. Corrie had approved of this, even giving her money for typing lessons, so that she could better herself.

"You're too smart to mess around doing housework," she had said. "Let me know how you get along."

Whether Sadie Wolfe spent the money on typing lessons or on something else was not known, but she did continue to do housework. This was discovered on an occasion when Howard and his wife were invited to dinner, with others, at the home of some rather important people in Kitchener. There was Sadie waiting on table, coming face-to-face with the man she had seen in Corrie's house. The man she had seen with his arm around Corrie when she came in to take the plates away or fix the fire. An unknown woman with him, who, the conversation soon made plain, was his wife. It was also made plain that his wife had not come recently into the picture. Her time had overlapped with Corrie's.

Howard did not tell Corrie about the dinner right away, because he hoped it would become unimportant. The host and hostess of the evening were nothing like close friends of his, or of his wife. Certainly not of his wife, who made fun of them on political grounds afterward. It had been a social business event. And the household wasn't likely the sort in which the maids gossiped with the mistress.

Indeed, it wasn't. Sadie said that she had not gossiped about it at all. She said this in a letter. It was not her mistress whom she had a notion of speaking to, if she had to. It was his own wife. Would his wife be interested in getting this information? was the way she put it. The letter was sent to his office address, which she had been clever enough to find out. But she was also acquainted with his home address. She had been spying. She mentioned that and also referred to his wife's coat with the silver-fox collar. This coat bothered his wife, and she often felt obliged to tell people that she had inherited, not bought, it. That was the truth. Still, she liked to wear it on certain occasions, like that dinner party, to hold her own, it seemed, even with people whom she had no use for.

"I would hate to have to break the heart of such a nice lady with a big silver-fox collar on her coat," Sadie had written.

"How would Sadie know a silver-fox collar from a hole in the ground?" Corrie said, when he felt that he had to break the news to her. "Are you sure that's what she said?"

"I'm sure."

He had burned the letter at once, had felt contaminated by it.

"She's learned things, then," Corrie said. "I always thought she was sly. I guess killing her is not an option?"

He didn't even smile, so she said very soberly, "I'm just kidding."

It was April, but still cold enough that you would like to have a fire lit. She had planned to ask him to do it, all through supper, but his strange, somber attitude had prevented her.

He told her that his wife hadn't wanted to go to that dinner. "It's all just pure rotten luck."

"You should have taken her advice," she said.

"It's the worst," he said. "It's the worst that could happen."

They were both staring into the black grate. He had touched her only once, to say hello.

"Well, no," Corrie said. "Not the worst. No."

"No?"

"No," she said. "We could give her the money. It's not a lot, really."

"I don't have—"

"Not you. I could."

"Oh, no."

"Yes."

She made herself speak lightly, but she had gone deathly cold. For what if he said no? No, I can't let you. No, it's a sign. It's a sign that we have to stop. She was sure that there'd been something like that in his voice, and in his face. All that old sin stuff. Evil.

"It's nothing to me," she said. "And, even if you could get hold of it easily, you couldn't do it. You'd feel you were taking it away from your family—how could you?"

Family. She should never have said that. Never have said that word.

But his face actually cleared. He said no, no, but there was doubt in his voice. And then she knew that it would be all right.

After a while, he was able to speak practically and he remembered another thing from the letter. It had to be in bills, he said. She had no use for checks.

He spoke without looking up, as if about a business deal. Bills were best for Corrie, too. They would not implicate her.

"Fine," she said. "It's not an outrageous sum, anyway."

"But she is not to know that we see it that way."

A postal box was to be taken, in Sadie's name. The bills in an envelope addressed to her, left there twice a year. The dates to be set by her. Never a day late. Or, as she had said, she might start to worry.

He still did not touch Corrie, except for a grateful, almost formal good-bye. This subject must be altogether separate from what is between us, was what he seemed to be saying. We'll start fresh. We will be able again to feel that we're not hurting anybody. Not doing any wrong. That was how he would put it in his unspoken language. In her own language she made one half-joke that did not go over.

"Already we've contributed to Sadie's education—she wasn't this smart before."

"We don't want her getting any smarter. Asking for more."

"We'll cross that bridge when we come to it. Anyway, we could threaten to go to the police. Even now."

"But that would be the end of you and me," he said. He had already said good-bye and turned his head away. They were on the windy porch.

He said, "I could not stand for there to be an end of you and me."

"I'm glad to hear that," Corrie said.

The time came quickly when they did not even speak of it. She handed over the bills, already in their envelope. At first he made a small grunt of disgust, but later that turned into a sigh of acquiescence, as if he had been reminded of a chore.

"How the time goes around."

"Doesn't it just?"

"Sadie's ill-gotten gains," Corrie might say, and though he didn't care for the expression at first, he got used to saying it himself. In the beginning, she would ask if he'd ever seen Sadie again, if there had been any further dinner parties.

"They weren't that kind of friends," he reminded her. He hardly ever saw them, didn't know if Sadie was still working for them or not.

Corrie hadn't seen her, either. Her people lived out in the country, and if Sadie came to see them they weren't likely to shop in this town, which had rapidly gone downhill. There was nothing now on the main street but a convenience store, where people went to buy Lotto tickets and whatever groceries they had run out of, and a furniture store, where the same tables and sofas sat forever in the windows, and the doors seemed never to be open—and maybe wouldn't be, until the owner died in Florida.

After Corrie's father died, the shoe factory had been taken over by a large firm that had promised—so she believed—to keep it running. Within a year, however, the building was empty, such equipment as was wanted moved to another town, nothing left, except a few outmoded tools that had once had to do with making boots and shoes. Corrie got it into her head to establish a quaint little museum to display these things. She herself would set it up and give tours describing how things used to be done. It was surprising how knowledgeable she became, helped by some photographs that her father had had taken to illustrate a talk that perhaps he himself had given—it was badly typed—to the Women's Institute when they were studying local industries. Already by the end of the summer Corrie had shown a few visitors around. She was sure that things would pick up the next year, after she had put a sign up on the highway and written a piece for a tourist brochure.

In the early spring, she looked out of her window one morning and saw some strangers starting to tear the building down. It turned out that the contract she'd thought she had to use the building so long as a certain amount of the rent was paid did not allow her to display or appropriate any objects found within the building, no matter how long they had been considered worthless. There was no question of these ancient bits of hardware belonging to her, and, in fact, she was fortunate not to be hauled up in court now that the company—which had once seemed so obliging— had found out what she was up to.

If Howard had not taken his family to Europe the previous summer, when she embarked on this project, he could have looked at the agreement for her and she would have been saved a lot of trouble.

Never mind, she said when she had calmed down, and soon she found a new interest.

It began with her deciding that she was sick of her big and empty house—she wanted to get out, and she set her sights on the public library down the street.

It was a handsome, manageable red brick building and, being a Carnegie Library, was not easy to get rid of, even though few people used it anymore—not nearly enough to justify a librarian's wages.

Corrie went down there twice a week and unlocked the doors and sat behind the librarian's desk. She dusted the shelves if she felt like it, and phoned up the people who were shown by the records to have had books out for years. Sometimes the people she reached claimed that they had never heard of the book—it had been checked out by some aunt or grandmother who used to read and was now dead. She spoke then of library property, and sometimes the book actually showed up in the returns bin.

The only thing not agreeable about sitting in the library was the noise. It was made by Jimmy Cousins, who cut the grass around the library building, starting again practically as soon as he'd finished because he had nothing else to do. So she hired him to do the lawns at her house—something she'd been doing herself for the exercise, but her figure didn't really need it and it took forever with her lameness.

Howard was somewhat dismayed by the change in her life. He came more seldom now, but was able to stay longer. He was living in Toronto, though working for the same firm. His children were teenagers or else in college. The girls were doing very well, the boys not quite so well as he might have wished, but that was the way of boys. His wife was working full-time and sometimes more than full-time in the office of a provincial politician. Her pay was next to nothing, but she was happy. Happier than he'd ever known her.

The past spring he had taken her to Spain, as a birthday surprise. Corrie hadn't heard from him for some time then. It would have been lacking in taste for him to write to her from the birthday-present holiday. He would never do a thing like that, and she would not have liked him to do it, either.

"You'd think my place were a shrine, the way you carry on," Corrie said after he got back, and he said, "Exactly right." He loved everything about the big rooms now, with their ornate ceilings and dark, gloomy paneling. There was a grand absurdity to them. But he was able to see that it was different for her, that she needed to get out once in a while. They began to take little trips, then somewhat longer trips, staying overnight in motels—though never more than one night—and eating at moderately fancy restaurants.

They never ran into anyone they knew. Once upon a time they would have done so—they were sure of it. Now things were different, though they didn't know why. Was it because they weren't in such danger, even if it did happen? The fact being that the people they might have met, and never did, would not have suspected them of being the sinful pair they still were. He could have introduced her as a cousin without making any impression—a lame relation he had thought to drop in on. He did have relatives whom his wife never wanted to bother with. And who would have gone after a middle-aged mistress with a dragging foot? Nobody would have stored that information up to spill at a dangerous moment. *We met Howard up at Bruce Beach with his sister, was it? He was looking good. His cousin, maybe. A limp?* It wouldn't have seemed worth the trouble.

They still made love, of course. Sometimes with caution, avoiding a sore shoulder, a touchy knee. They had always been conventional in that way, and remained so, congratulating themselves on not needing any fancy stimulation. That was for married people.

Sometimes Corrie would fill up with tears, hiding her face against him.

"It's just that we're so lucky," she said.

She never asked him whether he was happy, but he indicated in a roundabout way that he was. He said that he had developed more conservative, or maybe just less hopeful, ideas in his work. (She kept to herself the thought that he had always been rather conservative.) He was taking piano lessons, to the surprise of his wife and family. It was good to have that kind of interest of your own, in a marriage.

"I'm sure," Corrie said.

"I didn't mean—"

"I know."

One day—it was in September—Jimmy Cousins came into the library to tell her that he wouldn't be able to cut her grass that day. He had to go to the cemetery and dig a grave. It was for someone who used to live around here, he said.

Corrie, with her finger in *The Great Gatsby,* asked for the person's name. She said that it was interesting how many people showed up here—or their bodies did—with this last request and bother for their relatives. They might have lived their entire lives in cities nearby or distant, and seemed quite satisfied in those places, but had no wish to stay there when they were dead. Old people got such ideas.

Jimmy said that it wasn't such an old person. The name was Wolfe. The first name slipped his mind.

"Not Sadie? Not Sadie Wolfe?"

He believed it was.

And her name proved to be right there, in the library edition of the local paper, which Corrie never read. Sadie had died in Kitchener, at the age of forty-six. She was to be buried from the Church of the Lord's Anointed, the ceremony at two o'clock.

Well.

This was one of the two days a week that the library was supposed to be open. Corrie couldn't go.

The Church of the Lord's Anointed was a new one in town. Nothing flourished here but what her father had called "freak religions." She could see the building from one of the library windows.

She was at the window before two o'clock, watching a respectably sized group of people go in.

Hats didn't seem to be required nowadays, on women or men.

How would she tell him? A letter to the office, it would have to be. She could phone there, but then his response would have to be so guarded, so matter-of-fact, that half the wonder of their release would be lost.

She went back to *Gatsby*, but she was just reading words, not taking in the meaning—she was too restless. She locked the library and walked around town.

People were always saying that this town was like a funeral, but in fact when there was a real funeral it put on its best show of liveliness. She was reminded of that when she saw, from a block away, the funeral-goers coming out of the church doors, stopping to chat and ease themselves out of solemnity. And then, to her surprise, many of them went around the church to a side door, where they reentered.

Of course. She had forgotten. After the ceremony, after the closed coffin had been put in its place in the hearse, everybody except those close enough to follow the dead and see her put into the ground would head for the after-the-service refreshments. These would be waiting in another part of the church, where there was a Sunday-school room and a hospitable kitchen.

She didn't see any reason that she shouldn't join them.

But at the last moment she would have walked past.

Too late. A woman called to her in a challenging—or, at least, confidently unfunereal—voice from the door where the other people had gone in.

This woman said to her, close up, "We missed you at the service."

Corrie had no notion who the woman was. She said that she was sorry not to have attended but she'd had to keep the library open.

"Well, of course," the woman said, but had already turned to consult with somebody carrying a pie.

"Is there room in the fridge for this?"

"I don't know, honey, you'll just have to look and see."

Corrie had thought from the greeting person's flowered dress that the women inside would all be wearing something similar. Sunday best if not mourning best. But maybe her ideas of Sunday best were out-of-date. Some of the women here were just wearing slacks, as she herself was.

Another woman brought her a slice of spice cake on a plastic plate.

"You must be hungry," she said. "Everybody else is."

A woman who used to be Corrie's hairdresser said, "I told everybody you would probably drop in. I told them you couldn't till you'd closed up the library. I said it was too bad you had to miss the service. I said so."

"It was a lovely service," another woman said. "You'll want tea once you're done with that cake."

And so on. She couldn't think of anybody's name. The United church and the Presbyterian church were just hanging on; the Anglican church had closed ages ago. Was this where everybody had gone?

There was only one other woman at the reception who was getting as much attention as Corrie, and who was dressed as Corrie would have expected a funeral-going woman to be. A lovely lilac-gray dress and a subdued gray summer hat.

The woman was being brought over to meet her. A string of modest genuine pearls around her neck.

"Oh, yes." She spoke in a soft voice, as pleased as the occasion would allow. "You must be Corrie. The Corrie I've heard so much about. Though we never met, I felt I knew you. But you must be wondering who I am." She said a name that meant nothing to Corrie. Then shook her head and gave a small, regretful laugh.

"Sadie worked for us ever since she came to Kitchener," she said. "The children adored her. Then the grandchildren. They truly adored her. My goodness. On her day off I was just the most unsatisfactory substitute for Sadie. We all adored her, actually."

She said this in a way that was bemused, yet delighted. The way women like that could be, showing such charming self-disparagement. She would have spotted Corrie as the only person in the room who could speak her language and not take her words at face value.

Corrie said, "I didn't know she was sick."

"She went that fast," the woman with the teapot said, offering more to the lady with the pearls and being refused.

"It takes them her age faster than it does the real old ones," the tea lady said. "How long was she in the hospital?" she asked in a slightly menacing way of the pearls.

"I'm trying to think. Ten days?"

"Shorter time than that, what I heard. And shorter still when they got around to letting her people know at home."

"She kept it all very much to herself." This from the employer, who spoke quietly but held her ground. "She was absolutely not a person to make a fuss."

"No, she wasn't," Corrie said.

At that moment, a stout, smiling young woman came up and introduced herself as the minister.

"We're speaking of Sadie?" she asked. She shook her head in wonder. "Sadie was blessed. Sadie was a rare person."

All agreed. Corrie included.

"I suspect Milady the Minister," Corrie wrote to Howard, in the long letter she was composing in her head on the way home.

Later in the evening she sat down and started that letter, though she would not be able to send it yet—Howard was spending a couple of weeks at the Muskoka cottage with his family. Everybody slightly disgruntled, as he had described it in advance—his wife without her politics, him without his piano—but unwilling to forgo the ritual.

"Of course, it's absurd to think that Sadie's ill-gotten gains would build a church," she wrote. "But I'd bet she built the steeple. It's a silly-looking steeple, anyway. I never thought before what a giveaway those upside-down ice-cream-cone steeples are. The loss of faith is right there, isn't it? They don't know it, but they're declaring it."

She crumpled the letter up and started again, in a more jubilant manner.

"The days of the Blackmail are over. The sound of the cuckoo is heard in the land."

She had never realized how much it weighed on her, she wrote, but now she could see it. Not the money—as he well knew, she didn't care about the money, and, anyway, it had become a smaller amount in real terms as the years passed, though Sadie had never seemed to realize that. It was the queasy feeling, the never-quite-safeness of it, the burden on their long love, that had made her unhappy. She'd had that feeling every time she passed a postbox.

She wondered if by any chance he would hear the news before her letter could get it to him. Not possible. He hadn't reached the stage of checking obituaries yet.

It was in February and again in August of every year that she put the special bills in the envelope and he slipped the envelope into his pocket. Later, he would probably check the bills and type Sadie's name on the envelope before delivering it to her box.

The question was, had he looked in the box to see if this summer's money had been picked up? Sadie had been alive when Corrie made the transfer but surely not able to get to the mailbox. Surely not able.

It was shortly before Howard left for the cottage that Corrie had last seen him and that the transfer of the envelope had taken place. She tried to figure out exactly when it was, whether he would have had time to check the box again after delivering the money or whether he would have gone straight to the cottage. Sometimes while at the cottage in the past he'd found time to write Corrie a letter. But not this time.

She goes to bed with the letter to him still unfinished.

And wakes up early, when the sky is brightening, though the sun is not yet up.

There's always one morning when you realize that the birds have all gone.

She knows something. She has found it in her sleep.

There is no news to give him. No news, because there never was any.

No news about Sadie, because Sadie doesn't matter and she never did. No post office box, because the money goes straight into an account or maybe just into a wallet. General expenses. Or a modest nest egg. A trip to Spain. Who cares? People with families, summer cottages, children to educate, bills to pay—they don't have to think about how to spend such an amount of money. It can't even be called a windfall. No need to explain it.

She gets up and quickly dresses and walks through every room in the house, introducing the walls and the furniture to this new idea. A cavity everywhere, most notably in her chest. She makes coffee and doesn't drink it. She ends up in her bedroom once more, and finds that the introduction to the current reality has to be done all over again.

But then there is a surprise. She is capable, still, of shaping up another possibility.

If he doesn't know that Sadie is dead he will just expect things to go on as usual. And how would he know, unless he is told? And who would he be told by, unless by Corrie herself?

She could say a thing that would destroy them, but she does not have to.

What a time it has taken her, to figure this out.

She could say right now, what does it matter? Whatever goes on will go on. Someday, she supposes, there will have to be an end to it. But in the meantime, if what they had—what they have—demands payment, she is the one who can afford to pay.

When she goes down to the kitchen again she goes as if gingerly, making everything fit into a proper place.

She has calmed down mightily. All right.

But in the middle of her toast and jam she thinks, No.

Fly away, why don't you, right now? Fly away.

What rot.

Yes. Do it.

Reading *The PEN/O. Henry Prize Stories 2012*
The Jurors on Their Favorites

Every year our jurors read the twenty PEN/O. Henry Prize Stories *in a blind manuscript in which each story appears in the same type and format with no attribution of the magazine that published it or the author. The jurors don't consult the series editor or one another, and they write their essays without knowledge of the author's name (though occasionally the name of the author is inserted into the essay later for the sake of clarity).* —LF

Mary Gaitskill on "Kindness" by Yiyun Li

This is a terrible story. It is an ordinary story. It is terrible, how ordinary it is. In it, a woman tells a girl named Moyan that her parents adopted her in order to make their artificial marriage appear real and then reads to her with a melodic voice never present in her speaking voice. Moyan learns that her mother is a "mental case" who ran through the streets crying for a married man. Her father offered to marry her mother, and her mother's parents agreed because otherwise they'd have to send their mental-case daughter to an asylum. The woman reads to Moyan: *There was a woman who was beautiful, who started with all the advantages, yet she had no luck. She married for love, and the love turned to dust.* Moyan joins the army and there meets a painlessly beautiful girl who sings in a voice made beautiful by pain. Her lieutenant is kind to her, which revolts her; her lieutenant makes her cry by forcing her to sing in a tuneless voice in front of everyone. She sings "It Is a Shame to Be a Lonely Person." She cries. A sow is stretched across a road, suckling. Children cry for candy from the "Auntie Soldiers." There is a baby in a basket handed up to an old man at the train station. Moyan waves to the stranger who drove her there and goes home. Her mother is dead. Her father says she was the "kindest woman in the world" because she kept her promise. Moyan cannot visit the grave of the woman who read to her because the woman's estranged children won't let her know where it is. She gets a wedding invitation from the lieutenant. She reads her mother's romantic novels. They give her hope that it will all be well in the end. She is invited to the lieutenant's funeral. She doesn't go. Because she lives her life in the same neighborhood she has many acquaintances and so does not feel alone in her aging.

Kindness seems to me a story of terrible loneliness made bearable because the woman suffering it is exquisitely sensitive to the most subtle acts of kindness, which are acceptable to her only when they come from strangers. It seems a story of a starving soul who every now and then senses a feast in the occasional scrap, which keeps her barely alive. It seems a story in which love hides in tiny places, in the memory of sunlight on the floor of a long-dead person's apartment, in the voice of someone reading to you about imaginary people, or in the heart of someone you have never really cared much about.

But that is interpretation, and interpretation of any kind seems nearly disrespectful to this work, this narrator. Moyan's voice is void of superfluous emotion; she says what happened, and while she might speculate in a small way about why or what someone felt, her speculation is unfailingly modest; it is perhaps this modesty that gives her story its quiet, desolate beauty. There is no transcendence here, no heroism, no self-deprecating humor; that is to say, there are no contemporary literary conventions. In this story there is human feeling, which turns and changes as life turns and changes, and for Moyan—as for most people—that must be enough. Her inability to take more than the bare minimum of what life offers to her becomes, in this story, a kind of dignity that lives and dies alone, unrecognized. I felt touched and grateful to read of it.

Mary Gaitskill is the author of the novels *Two Girls, Fat and Thin* and *Veronica,* as well as the story collections *Bad Behavior, Because They Wanted To,* and *Don't Cry.* Her stories and essays have appeared in *The New Yorker, Harper's, Granta, The Best American Short Stories,* and *The O. Henry Prize Stories.* Last year she was a Cullman fellow at the New York Public Library, where she was researching a novel.

Daniyal Mueenuddin on "Kindness" by Yiyun Li

Kindness. Even the title is deceptive, warm and uncomplicated as the story certainly is not. Yiyun Li plays a subtle game with her readers, concealing hard conflict in the shadows of what appears to be the quietest, the mildest of stories. The narrator Moyan, in her cat-footed voice, begins by telling us that her life has been without notable event, subdued and blameless. She has traveled very little, has neither family nor friends, never married, teaches math but doesn't particularly care for the job, has no hobbies. And yet, from this plain material, Li has created a story as dramatic and complex and penetrating as anything I've read in a good long time.

The story is idiosyncratic in other ways. Is it a short story at all, or is it that contentious thing, a novella, which operates under a different code? Certainly it is longer than any of the other pieces in this collection and strains the limit of what will likely be read in one sitting—my definition of a short story. Given extra space, Li has not merely added detail, she has also freed herself from the characteristic arrow trajectory of a short story. Pilots describe helicopters, which are aerodynamically unstable, as a collection of parts flying in tight formation; the same can be said of *Kindness,* which has several different points of narrative weight, the emphasis distributed.

What holds the story together, in fact, is not the cumulative development of the narrative, but rather, the voice. The story circles around the elements of Moyan's life, reinforcing and deepening our knowledge of her, by making us privy to her thoughts and reflections, dropping in and out of the stories within the story. The narrator's subtlety, which is a form of good manners, of hygiene, draws us increasingly into sympathy with her; Moyan is a *knowing* narrator—we take her at her word. Here she is, speaking of her single romantic adventure, which marked her entire life yet barely rose to the level of a relationship, with only a single moment of near avowal, in the shade of a wisteria:

> There had not been a boyfriend and perhaps there never would be one—the man who had not wiped away my tears under the wisteria trellis had later done so, repeatedly, when my memories were revised into dreams, and he who had chosen not to claim the love had left no space for others to claim it: In high school there had been a boy or two, like there is a boy or two for most girls during those years, but I had returned their letters in new envelopes, never adding a line, thinking that would be enough to end what should not have been started.

There is neither self-pity in this nor a plea for our pity, and even this resignation, which can so often be merely a cover for timidity, leaves the impression of being sincere, deliberate.

Moyan's quiet intelligence, her resignation, and her stoicism serve as a foil for the drama of the story. Her beautiful, intellectual mother is bedridden, unbalanced years ago by her unrequited love for a married man; her uneducated father drifts through life, deeply in love with this woman who agreed to marry and live with him, but only on the most limited terms; Moyan discovers by accident that she is adopted; she falls in love with a pauper, a derelict, who later becomes a great flautist; her mother commits suicide. This is a heavy load for a story to carry, is almost baroque, and yet the reader accepts it without demur, because the tone and the matter of the story so blend with and so balance each other.

There is another quieter drama running through the story, a backbone on which the rest of the narrative is hung. The story jumps back and forth in time, but if it were straightened out and laid flat, we would see that a series of characters approach Moyan, wanting intimacy from her, and that each in turn is rejected in favor of the isolation—or the independence—that she feels is her inevitable portion. Professor Shan, Lieutenant Wei, Nini's father, even the Jeep driver who takes her to the train station after she is informed of her mother's death, all seek to overcome her resistance to their touch, the touch of their minds more than their hands. Moyan allows the approach—without that there would be no story—but fleetingly, while drawing away. We acquiesce in this, find it sufficient that these relationships are unresolved, that these characters loom up to Moyan—and then back away, the moment passing unconsummated. Moyan's distinct sensibility binds the story together, her unexpected lonely affirmative power.

Daniyal Mueenuddin's debut collection of short stories, *In Other Rooms, Other Wonders,* was the winner of the Story Prize, the Rosenthal Family Foundation Award from the American Academy of Arts and Letters, and the 2010 Commonwealth Writers' Prize (Best First Book, Europe and South Asia). It was also a finalist for the National Book Award, the Pulitzer Prize, the Los Angeles Times Book Prize, and a number of other awards. His work has appeared in *The New Yorker, Granta, Zoetrope, The PEN/O. Henry Prize Stories,* and elsewhere. Mueenuddin lives in Pakistan's southern Punjab.

Ron Rash on "Corrie" by Alice Munro

When I agreed to be a juror for this year's *PEN/O. Henry Prize Stories,* I suspected choosing a single short story out of many excellent ones would be a daunting task, and so it has proven to be. A first reading narrowed my list to ten, a second to five, and a third to three: Anthony Doerr's "The Deep," Miroslav Penkov's "East of the West," and Alice Munro's "Corrie." As is always the case with the best short stories, each rereading only enhanced my appreciation of all three and made me more reluctant to choose one. I placed them on a couch in my living room, perhaps in hopes that two of them, like impatient suitors, would weary of my indecision and simply vanish. None left voluntarily, so after a few days I reread each a final time and made my decision.

I have always believed that short stories are closer to poems than to novels, and no story in this volume is more poetic than Anthony Doerr's "The Deep." The level of the language is astonishing, both in its vividness and its cadences. The story is worth reading for the elegance of the language alone. Yet "The Deep" completely satisfies as a story. Not only are the characters fully realized but so are the time and the place. Doerr has the ability to render Depression-era Detroit as a vibrant presence, yet his research, which must have been considerable, is invisible within the story.

Miroslav Penkov's "East of the West" has many instances of memorable language, too, but what made this story most unforgettable is the scene in which Vera and Nose clutch the steeple of the drowned church. Serving as a visual refrain, this image resonates on many levels. Though the steeple and the clinging couple defy any pat interpretation, they clearly embody a whole culture's tragedy.

Alice Munro's "Corrie," however, is the story I chose as my favorite. As with "The Deep," Munro's narrative is constructed with the precision of a formal poem. Each time I read "Corrie," I became more aware of how integral each detail is to the whole. As in Flannery O'Connor's best work, everything in "Corrie," from paragraph breaks to commas, has been set down in its essential place. Account, accounting, and accountability. Money and religion are center stage at the story's beginning, and they return at its conclusion when the revelation about the blackmail money occurs inside a church. (Another of the story's many nuances is that the decrepit, nearly abandoned church at the story's beginning, which we see only from the outside, is replaced by a bustling newer one at the end.) Corrie has always held a belief that there would be a reckoning, a payment due, for the affair. The crucial question is to whom. The answer may surprise the reader as much as Corrie, but the story's architecture, beginning with the opening line, makes the denouement almost inevitable.

And yet—and this may be Munro's greatest gift as a writer—the story feels as if it is telling itself, operating at its own internal pace. Years and decades pass, and many other important events, inevitably, occur in the lovers' lives, but the reader is not made aware of them because they are not important to the story. And I do mean *to the story*. Part of this organic effect is created by a seeming disinterestedness. The story doesn't appear to care much if we find Corrie a sympathetic or unsympathetic character. Aspects that normally would elicit sympathy—Corrie's polio, her mother's early death—are muted, as are the less appealing aspects of her idle life of privilege. We do care though, because, like Corrie, we all must find ways to account for our actions as well as for the actions of others. We must, as Munro puts it at the story's end, find a way of "making everything fit into a proper place."

"The role of the artist is to deepen the mystery," Muriel Spark once said, echoing a quote of Francis Bacon's. I kept thinking of that quote as I read and reread "Corrie," for Munro's story takes us deep into the mystery of how we make accommodations in our lives. Do we really know if we act out of selfishness or selflessness, this remarkable story asks us. Do we even know which is which?

. . .

Ron Rash was born in 1953 and grew up in Boiling Springs, North Carolina. He is the author of four novels, *One Foot in Eden, Saints at the River, The World Made Straight,* and *Serena;* three collections of poems; and three collections of stories, among them *Burning Bright,* winner of the 2010 Frank O'Connor International Short Story Award. Twice a finalist for the PEN/Faulkner Award, he is a previous recipient of the PEN/O. Henry Prize as well as National Endowment for the Arts grants in poetry and fiction. He teaches at Western Carolina University and lives in Clemson, South Carolina.

Writing *The PEN/O. Henry Prize Stories 2012*

The Writers on Their Work

John Berger, "A Brush"
I hope the story is most itself when read out loud. The hair of "the reader" still a little damp from the water of the swimming pool.

John Berger was born in London in 1926. He is well known for his novels and stories as well as for his works of nonfiction, including several volumes of art criticism. His first novel, *A Painter of Our Time*, was published in 1958, and since then his books have included the novel *G.*, which won the Man Booker Prize in 1972. His latest book is *Bento's Sketchbook*. In 1962 he left Britain permanently, and he lives in a small village in the French Alps.

Wendell Berry, "Nothing Living Lives Alone"
"Nothing Living Lives Alone," published with much kindness and editorial indulgence by *The Threepenny Review*, seems to me to impose some strain on the term *story*. It belongs to a stretch of new work attempting to deal directly and explicitly with what I see as the paramount change in my time and place: Until the end of World War II, the life of the rural landscapes of my home country was predominately creaturely. The countryside then was mainly, as we would now say, solar-powered. The farms worked mainly by sunlight converted to usable energy by plants and the

bodies of animals and people. After 1945, by the industrialization of farming, and of everything else, life here has become increasingly mechanical. Machines of various kinds now dominate work and economy, and also the thoughts and aspirations of the people. I would like, so far as I am able, to understand what is implied by this.

Wendell Berry was born in Newcastle, Kentucky, in 1934. He is an essayist, poet, and fiction writer, and has received fellowships from the Guggenheim, Lannan, and Rockefeller foundations and the National Endowment for the Arts, and also the T. S. Eliot Award, the Aiken Taylor Award, and the John Hay Award of the Orion Society. Forthcoming books include a volume of collected poems as well as a collection of twenty new stories, *A Place in Time*. Berry lives with his family on a farm in his native Henry County, Kentucky.

Anthony Doerr, "The Deep"

For pretty much all of human history, we've assumed the deep oceans were devoid of life. Plato concluded the sea bottom was "corroded by the brine, and there is no vegetation worth mentioning, and scarcely any degree of perfect formation, but only caverns and sand and measureless mud."

For millennia, no one bothered to disagree. Who would? Deep water is cold, food-poor, and utterly dark. And the pressure increases as we descend: Two and a half miles down, the pressure exerted on a square inch (picture your big toe) is 5,880 pounds (picture a Ford F-150 on your big toe). Oceanographers are fond of putting Styrofoam coffee cups in socks and attaching them to deepwater instruments. Sink a cup to 10,000 feet, and it will come back to the surface the size of a thimble.

What could possibly live under those circumstances?

Plenty, it turns out. "Untold billions of organisms," as one oceanographer puts it, and we have barely begun to understand what's down there. There are coral reefs a quarter mile from the surface. There are vast feeding communities swirling above underwater mountaintops. The diversity of animal life on the deep seafloor alone, estimates one marine biologist, "may exceed that of the Amazon rain forest and the Great Barrier Reef combined."

So I started to write a story about how much was down there. That was four years ago. I dreamed up two oceanographers, one glamorous and redheaded, one slow and methodical and married. Early versions of the story included melodrama and sweaty submarine scenes and sentences like, "The storm comes in Indonesia."

It was heavy on atmosphere and light on humanity. I abandoned it for several months to write other stuff. Then in an airport one day I watched multiple faces on CNN say, "This is the worst recession since the Great Depression." It made me want to try to understand: Are our lives *really* like the lives of Americans in the Great Depression?

Eventually I decided to braid the two interests: the deep sea and the Great Depression. In some tenuous and inarticulable way they seemed linked to me. It took me another year to find the right pressure for the story, the F-150 on the big toe—Tom's heart condition. Once I had those three concerns in place, I started making more headway.

The story owes a debt to my friend Cort Conley, who gave me Annie Dillard's *For the Time Being,* which includes glimpses of a nurse washing newborn babies, as well as a very old pamphlet called *A Book of Striking Similes,* from which I wrenched much of Mr. Weems's dialogue.

Anthony Doerr was born in Cleveland, Ohio. He's the author of four books: *Memory Wall, The Shell Collector, About Grace,* and *Four Seasons in Rome.* His writing has won the Story Prize, two

Pushcart Prizes, the Rome Prize, the New York Public Library's Young Lions Fiction Award, the Barnes & Noble Discover Prize, a Guggenheim fellowship, and three previous O. Henry prizes. He also writes a column about science books for *The Boston Globe*. "The Deep" won the 2011 Sunday Times EFG Private Bank Short Story Award in the U.K. He lives in Boise, Idaho.

Dagoberto Gilb, "Uncle Rock"

My fiction always comes from an experience—personal or observed—that gets loaded onto and chipped away at and artistically distorted by the various obsessions I have. For example, it's been pointed out even by nontherapists that I appear to have a bit of a *mami* issue. For a dude, that should be embarrassing. But what if, whenever you were broke, you knew you had a treasure chest of gold coins? So okay, the fact is that when I was around the age of Uncle Rock's Erick, I was with my own single mom and her date, who'd paid for the baseball game we went to at Dodger Stadium, getting autographs from a busload of the famous New York Yankees. When I got a note not unlike the one Erick did, it was one of those pieces of paper that becomes light and moans hymnal, until moments later when I was pissed. I shouldn't cash in that gold coin? Add the fact that I made Erick verging on mute, as Mexican Americans are both not heard and trained to feel, and the story's on. I loved those years when Fernando Valenzuela was the biggest star in baseball—what pride there was in Los Angeles then! And that's what I wanted the story to be.

Dagoberto Gilb was born and raised in Los Angeles, and then lived in El Paso. He is the author of seven previous books, most recently *Before the End, After the Beginning,* as well as *The Flowers, Gritos, Woodcuts of Women, The Last Known Residence of Mickey Acuña,* and *The Magic of Blood.* His fiction and nonfiction have appeared in *The New Yorker, Harper's, The Threepenny Review, Callaloo,* and many others. His work won the PEN/Hemingway

Award and has been a finalist for the PEN/Faulkner Award and National Book Critics Circle Award. He lives in Austin, Texas.

Karl Taro Greenfeld, "Mickey Mouse"

In the fall of 2009 I was editing the English translation of my mother's paired novellas *Wasabi for Breakfast*. My mother, Foumiko Kometani, is a well-known author in Japan, and the translator had done a fine job, but the book still needed some work. I was struggling to uncover in the novellas a voice that seemed organic and to sound like my mother. It was trying work, and I never quite got the book to where I would have liked.

One character in my mother's book is a graphic artist who goes back to a reunion of her old art school in Kyoto. The details about the art scene in postwar Japan got me thinking about what it must have been like during the war. Nazi Germany's suppression of artists and condemnation of so-called degenerate art has been well-covered. But I hadn't read much about the same period in Imperial Japan, which was every bit as fanatic as Nazi Germany. That was a period I wanted to write about. If I recall, I set out to write a story that was more about the corruption of the artist in those circumstances than the story I actually ended up writing.

I think the germ of it came from reading about artists in post-war Japan in my mother's novellas.

Karl Taro Greenfeld was born in Kobe, Japan, in 1964. He is the author of six books, including the novel *Triburbia,* the story collection *Now Trends,* and the memoir *Boy Alone,* a Washington Post Best Book of 2009, about his autistic brother, Noah. His fiction has appeared in *The Best American Short Stories, The Paris Review, One Story, Commentary,* and *The Missouri Review,* among other journals. His nonfiction has appeared in *The Best American Nonrequired Reading, The Best American Travel Writing, The Best American Sports Writing,* and *The Best Creative Nonfiction.* He lives in Los Angeles, California.

Lauren Groff, "Eyewall"

Stories come to me differently, depending on their need. Sometimes a story or fragment that I read long ago will collide with a story or fragment I have just read; sometimes a character will just step in front of me; sometimes there's an image that is so compelling that it gathers disparate parts of the story to it like an industrial-strength junkyard magneto. This particular story announced itself in terms of structure. I was baking in my little unair-conditioned writing studio behind my house in Florida, looking at a storm cloud roaring near and feeling unbearably fragile and exposed. It wasn't a hurricane, but I thought it might have been—there are always hurricanes lurking like assassins here—and when the word *hurricane* came into my head, the structure did, too. I saw a despairing character who was at the center of some harsh circular winds that were, in turn, whipping enormously urgent leitmotifs around and around her at blinding speed. Everyone knows what the eye of a storm is; an eyewall is where the eye meets the storm again, the circle of terrifying black clouds where the weather is at its worst.

Lauren Groff was born in Cooperstown, New York, in 1978. She is the author of the novel *The Monsters of Templeton* and the story collection *Delicate Edible Birds.* Her fiction has appeared in *The New Yorker, The Atlantic Monthly,* and *Ploughshares,* among other publications, and has been anthologized in the Pushcart Prize anthology and two editions of *The Best American Short Stories.* Her second novel is *Arcadia.* She lives in Gainesville, Florida.

Yiyun Li, "Kindness"

"Kindness" was inspired by William Trevor's novella *Nights at the Alexandra,* which is narrated by an older Irish man in a provincial town who has never married; "Kindness" is narrated by a middle-aged woman in Beijing who has chosen not only to stay single but also not to love anyone. *Nights at the Alexandra* is one of my favorite books by Trevor, so I wrote "Kindness" as a homage to the book. I opened the novella with three sentences that echoed the opening sentences of *Nights at the Alexandra,* and while writing it, I imagined my narrator speaking to the narrator in Trevor's novella—both characters lead a stoically solitary life, yet both are capable, and are proofs, of love and affection and loyalty. Their conversation would not have happened in reality, but I hope that by speaking to one person in her mind, my narrator, in the end, speaks to many.

Yiyun Li is a native of Beijing and a graduate of the Iowa Writers' Workshop. She is the recipient of a 2010 MacArthur Foundation fellowship, as well as the Frank O'Connor International Short Story Award, the PEN/Hemingway Foundation Award, the Whiting Writers' Award, and the Guardian First Book Award. In 2007, *Granta* named her one of the best American novelists under thirty-five; in 2010, she was named as one of the top twenty fiction writers under forty by *The New Yorker.* She is the author of *A Thousand Years of Good Prayers, The Vagrants,* and *Gold Boy, Emerald Girl.* Her work has appeared in *The New Yorker, A Public Space, The Best American Short Stories,* and *The O. Henry Prize Stories,* among others. She teaches writing at the University of California, Davis, and lives in Oakland, California.

Hisham Matar, "Naima"
"Naima" is a story about a family secret. Nuri, the boy protagonist of the story, is, in some subtle and poignant ways, detecting the echoes of a distant secret, a secret he was born into. Sometimes it is hard not to conclude that families are not only given to secrets but rely on them. The story picks a strand from my new novel, *Anatomy of a Disappearance;* it compresses and alters that strand slightly. I think it was Borges who once said that certain stories have more than one possibility. I enjoyed seeing how the light changes on the same characters.

. . .

Hisham Matar was born in New York City to Libyan parents and spent his childhood first in Tripoli and then in Cairo. His first novel, *In the Country of Men,* was short-listed for the Man Booker Prize, the Guardian First Book Award, and the National Book Critics Circle Award. It won six international literary awards, including the Commonwealth Writers' Prize (Best First Book, Europe and South Asia), the Royal Society of Literature Ondaatje Prize, and the inaugural Arab American Book Award. It has been translated into twenty-six languages. *Anatomy of a Disappearance,* his second novel, was published in 2011. Matar lives in London, Cairo, and New York, where he is a visiting associate professor at Barnard College.

Alice Mattison, "The Vandercook"

I'm not interested in writing about flawless people, and the people in "The Vandercook," indeed, are all flawed. But in most of my stories and novels, the characters find in themselves some strength, however minimal or partial, that makes it possible to keep from doing the worst they are capable of. The people in "The Vandercook" can't solve their problem, and I knew that about them as I wrote: it was this thought that I began with. Still, I wish they could.

Alice Mattison grew up in Brooklyn. Her new novel, *When We Argued All Night,* will be published in 2012, and she is the author of five previous novels, four collections of stories, and a book of poems. Her work has appeared in many magazines, including *The New Yorker, Ploughshares, The Threepenny Review,* and *Ecotone.* She teaches fiction in the Bennington Writing Seminars and lives in New Haven, Connecticut, where she is a longtime volunteer in a soup kitchen.

Steven Millhauser, "Phantoms"

"Phantoms" began as an idea that at first excited me but gradually interested me less and less: the story of a young man and a phantom. I abandoned it—still only an idea—and began dreaming my way into a story that had nothing to do with phantoms. At some point, as if it had been taking shape secretly, without my knowledge, a new version of the phantom story sprang into my mind, and this is the one that demanded to be written down.

Steven Millhauser was born in Brooklyn and grew up in Connecticut. His books include *The Knife Thrower; Martin Dressler; Edwin Mullhouse: The Life and Death of an American Writer, 1943–1954, by Jeffrey Cartwright;* and *Dangerous Laughter.* His work has appeared in *Harper's, Tin House, The New Yorker,* and *McSweeney's Quarterly Concern.* His most recent book is *We Others: New and Collected Stories.* He lives in Saratoga Springs, New York.

Alice Munro, "Corrie"

I don't remember whether I knew a Corrie, but I did know lonely, idle, small-town rich girls—just the outside of their lives. I was not at all interested in them, being of Sadie's class myself. Then a cousin told me how she, working as a maid, saw a guest, plus his wife, dining in her employer's house, and what a shock it was, because she had known him as the long-time gentleman caller of an unmarried, well-to-do woman in our town. This story came to me years after it happened, but it stuck. I put the foot on her quite naturally, no symbolic crap, then was embarrassed a bit but left it. Same in a way with Gatsby. Will anyone get that now?

I must say I like these characters. Him, too. It would be too boring to make him an utter stinker.

. . .

Alice Munro grew up in Wingham, Ontario, and attended the University of Western Ontario. She has published twelve collections of stories—*Dance of the Happy Shades; Something I've Been Meaning to Tell You; The Beggar Maid; The Moons of Jupiter; The Progress of Love; Friend of My Youth; Open Secrets; The Love of a Good Woman; Hateship, Friendship, Courtship, Loveship, Marriage; Runaway; The View from Castle Rock;* and *Too Much Happiness*—as well as a novel, *Lives of Girls and Women,* and a *Selected Stories.* During her distinguished career, she has been the recipient of many awards and prizes, including three of Canada's Governor General's Literary Awards and two of its Giller Prizes, the Rea Award for the Short Story, the Lannan Literary Award, England's W. H. Smith Book Award, the United States' National Book Critics Circle Award, and the Man Booker International Prize. Her stories have appeared in *The New Yorker, The Atlantic Monthly, The Paris Review,* and other publications, and her collections have been translated into thirteen languages. She lives in Clinton, Ontario, near Lake Huron.

Ann Packer, "Things Said or Done"

In "Things Said or Done" I did something I'd never done before: revisited characters from a previous work. Sasha and Dan and the rest of the Horowitz family started life in a novella, *Walk for Mankind,* which is about a teenage boy named Richard Appleby into whose life thirteen-year-old Sasha and her family intrude. I knew "Walk for Mankind" was going to be the opening piece in a collection of short fiction (ultimately published under the title *Swim Back to Me*), and even before I'd finished it I decided that the final story in the book would catch up with the same characters several decades later. I began the story by imagining the adult Sasha fielding health complaints from the elderly Dan, but in the first couple of drafts Dan was actually ill, and I had Sasha flying from Seattle (where she lived with a spouse who would not survive the writing process) to Boston (where he lived, also with a spouse who would not survive the writing process) so she could support him through some medical treatment. The only thing working at that point was the way they related to each other, and in a slash-and-burn revision I converted Dan's complaining to hypochondria, extracted the spouses, resettled Sasha in western Massachusetts and Dan in Hartford, imagined Sasha's brother and mother back into being, and transferred the action to a family wedding in California. After that, the story started to make sense, and I could devote myself to refining the characters' interactions and deciding where I wanted to leave them. I had originally thought that Richard Appleby would reappear, too, but once I had the shape of the piece I found there wasn't a place for him, which I think ended up benefitting both the story and the book.

Ann Packer was born in Stanford, California, in 1959. She is the author of the novels *The Dive from Clausen's Pier* and *Songs Without Words* and two books of short fiction, *Mendocino and Other Stories* and *Swim Back to Me*. Her stories have appeared in *The New Yorker, Zoetrope, Ploughshares,* and *Narrative Magazine,* among other publications. *The Dive from Clausen's Pier* received a Great Lakes Book Award, an American Library Association award, and the Kate Chopin Literary Award. A past recipient of support from the Michener Copernicus Society and the National Endowment for the Arts, she lives in San Carlos, California.

Miroslav Penkov, "East of the West"

I wanted to write a story about those Bulgarians who, at the will of the Great Powers, were severed from our country, and who inevitably will lose, if they haven't already, their sense of being Bulgarian. At the same time, I wanted to write a story about myself, abroad and alone, with a huge body of water between me and the people I love.

This is the only story I've ever written in which I've posed myself a question and tried to answer it. I believe that at the end of the story Nose is liberated—from his family, nationality, country—that he is ready to begin a new life, in freedom. A kind of freedom that he has earned through loss. I want to be like Nose, and yet I'm terrified of such a possibility. I lack the strength to lose, let go, and carry on—and in the comfort of my cowardice all I could do was imagine—a river where there is none, a drowned church, two lovers who would never reunite. And even if I myself lack the courage to break the chains, a part of me now roams the dirt roads of Bulgaria, already free.

My deepest gratitude to Mr. Andrew Blechman and *Orion* for publishing the story. Thank you, dear reader, for reading.

Miroslav Penkov was born in 1982 in Bulgaria. He holds an MFA in Creative Writing from the University of Arkansas. His stories have won *The Southern Review*'s Eudora Welty Prize and have appeared in *A Public Space, One Story, Orion,* and *The Best American Short Stories 2008.* Author of the story collection *East of the West,* he teaches creative writing at the University of North Texas, where he is editor of the *American Literary Review.* He lives in Denton, Texas.

Keith Ridgway, "Rothko Eggs"

I used to sit and write in a coffee shop around the corner from where I lived in Finsbury Park, North London. And in the late afternoon I would see the kids coming out of school, and sometimes some would come into the coffee shop and I would eavesdrop on their conversations. And I was struck several times how, against expectations, these kids were gentle and funny and seemed to treat their friends with genuine kindness. And I used to see one girl who would sometimes meet a man who was obviously her father. And he always looked miserable before she arrived, and would light up when he saw her. There was something quite lovely but also fragile about all of that. So I stole it.

· · ·

Keith Ridgway was born in 1965 in Dublin and brought up there. He lived in London for ten years. His first novel, *The Long Falling*, received the Prix Femina Étranger in 2001 and was made into a film directed by Martin Provost. Ridgway was awarded the Rooney Prize for his short-story collection *Standard Time*. He is also the author of the novels *The Parts* and *Animals*. His newest book is *Hawthorn & Child*. He lives in Edinburgh.

Sam Ruddick, "Leak"

The first draft of "Leak" was a solemn and dull affair. I showed it to Frederick Barthelme and he said, "This is a story that would benefit from being hit by a fiery rock from outer space." It would be tedious to explain all the differences between the original version and the one you see here, but I would be remiss if I didn't mention that he gave me a few ideas, and it led to a breakthrough in the way I think about writing. I used to be overly concerned with plausibility: The actions of my characters had to make sense. People don't work that way. I don't know why I thought fictional characters would. Ridding myself of the notion has made the work much more interesting.

Sam Ruddick was born in 1971, in Chicago Heights, Illinois. His work has appeared in *Glimmer Train*, *The Threepenny Review*, and *Prairie Fire*. He is a graduate of the Center for Writers at the University of Southern Mississippi and currently teaches at the University of Massachusetts, Lowell. He received the Henfield Prize for Fiction in 2007. He lives in Boston, Massachusetts.

Salvatore Scibona, "The Woman Who Lived in the House"

I had forgotten my computer at home in the States and wrote the story longhand at the Hotel Bergs in Riga, Latvia: in the ample bathtub, or on the balcony, or pacing the city through crowds of courteously misbehaving Swiss soccer hooligans. For a month I knew perfect urban solitude, punctuated by drink and dinner dates with absorbing raconteurs and speech makers and twenty-something dredging magnates worried about the Latvian real estate market, suspicious of Russia, enormously proud of their national language, gracious, and warm. Then I would go home to the hotel and take the sleek elevator up to the farm in the private Iceland inside my room.

Salvatore Scibona was born in Cleveland, Ohio, in 1975. His first book, *The End,* was a finalist for the 2008 National Book Award and winner of the Young Lions Fiction Award. It is published or forthcoming in six languages. His work has appeared in *The Pushcart Book of Short Stories, Best New American Voices, A Public Space, The Threepenny Review, The New Yorker, The New York Times, San Francisco Chronicle, D di La Repubblica,* and *Il Sole 24 Ore.* He has received a Fulbright fellowship, Pushcart Prize, Whiting Writers' Award, and Guggenheim fellowship. In 2010, *The New Yorker* named him to its "20 Under 40" list of writers to watch. He administers the writing fellowship at the Fine Arts Work Center in Provincetown, Massachusetts, and lives in Provincetown.

Jim Shepard, "Boys Town"

Lately it's started to seem to me that here in America our fetishization of self-reliance has taken a wrong turn and has helped enable us to jettison compassion as a national value while still maintaining a vision of ourselves as essentially well-meaning. It hasn't taken a whole lot of common sense, given the evidence of the last few years, to puzzle out the heartlessness of unregulated capitalism, and yet our political class has embraced even more fervently the notion of every man for himself, even given the ever-growing numbers such a philosophy leaves behind.

I grew up around some of those people left behind, and I'm interested in the way somebody in that position whipsaws between blaming himself for having been unable to keep up and understanding that he never had a chance in the first place. Either way you start to get enraged at your own ineffectuality, and you start to consider acting on that rage and making a mark *one* way or the other.

And of course, when we're *talking* about the shit end of the stick, we're also talking about those people who fight our wars now that we've abolished the semidemocracy of the draft.

I've known my share of guys who sound like my narrator in "Boys Town," but the story got its start when I came across a short piece by Calvin Trillin about Scott Johnson, an ex-serviceman convicted of the murder of three teenagers on the Wisconsin-Michigan border in 2008. That led me to the transcript of the police interview with Johnson once he was in custody, where I came across this moment in which he was trying to explain to his interrogators why he felt like he never got through to people: "I don't know why people need to hear the same thing ten thousand times, but it seems like they want to hear anything but the truth." And something just went off in me. I thought: *That* guy. I know *that* guy. And the story was off and running.

Jim Shepard was born in Bridgeport, Connecticut, and is the author of six novels, including most recently *Project X,* and four story collections, including the latest, *You Think That's Bad.* His third collection, *Like You'd Understand, Anyway,* was a finalist for the National Book Award and won the Story Prize. *Project X* won the 2005 Library of Congress/Massachusetts Book Award for Fiction, as well as the Alex Award from the American Library Association. His short fiction has appeared in, among other magazines, *Harper's, McSweeney's, The Paris Review, The Atlantic Monthly, Esquire, DoubleTake, The New Yorker, Granta, Zoetrope,* and *Playboy,* and he was a columnist on film for the magazine *The Believer.* Four of his stories have been chosen for *The Best American Short Stories* and one for a Pushcart Prize. He's won an artist fellowship from the Massachusetts Cultural Council and a Guggenheim fellowship. He teaches at Williams College and lives in Williamstown, Massachusetts.

Mark Slouka, "The Hare's Mask"

At the heart of "The Hare's Mask" are two historical facts: My father's family sheltered a Jewish refugee in a rabbit hutch during the war, and as a boy my father had to kill rabbits for dinner. After that the imagination gets its foot in the door, and the story begins to shape itself to other needs. I'm the trout fisherman, not my father. Though there's a picture of my father's family on our mantelpiece, his actual parents and sister survived the war by some years. I never had a sister *or* a rabbit, while my son, now grown, had both.

Who knows where our stories begin, really? I suppose, looking at the picture on the mantel, recalling the anecdotes my father told, listening to our daughter's rabbit thumping around in the dark, I sensed a story about history's losses, time's compensations, and a child's ability to misread the world. To get at it, I had to mix three generations. It was easy; in my heart, they had blurred already.

Mark Slouka was born in New York City in 1958. His books, which have been translated into eighteen languages, include the story collection *Lost Lake;* the novels *God's Fool* and *The Visible World;* and two works of nonfiction, *War of the Worlds,* a cultural critique of technological society, and, most recently, *Essays from the Nick of Time,* winner of the PEN/Diamonstein-Spielvogel Award for the Art of the Essay. He is a contributing editor at *Harper's,* and his stories and essays have appeared in *Harper's, Granta, Agni, Orion,* and *The Paris Review,* among other publications, as well as in *The Best American Essays, The Best American Short Stories,* and *The PEN/O. Henry Prize Stories.* He lives in Canton, New York.

Christine Sneed, "The First Wife"

Movies are important to so many people, and some of us, whether we admit to it or not, have personal and often irrational attachments to movie stars and to other celebrities whom we've fallen a little in love with because we admire the way they sing or look or act. The famous also have attributes or opportunities that most of us don't have but wish we did—whether it be extreme wealth or beauty or the most attractive lovers on the planet.

Adding fuel to this bonfire is the rise of reality TV, which allows some participants, whether or not they have talent, to become famous overnight. One result of this phenomenon is that more people than ever before hope to become famous but don't really have any idea what it's like to be a celebrity. I have a few friends who work in Hollywood, and what I've learned from them is something that we've been told before, but it rarely ever seems to stick: All that glitters isn't gold.

Despite the somber tone of "The First Wife," this short story was a lot of fun to write. I liked the formal challenge of writing a story that began at its chronological end and progressed backward. As I wrote it, I was thinking of a particular famous couple and the first wife who was left behind (and against her will was featured on tabloids the world over, often with an unflattering expression on her face). I felt compassion for this woman and for my title character, but not pity, because she's smart and knows that she took an enormous risk by marrying a movie star, even if she is also somewhat famous. Like so many of us, she loves fairy tales and wanted to believe in them, too.

Christine Sneed was born in 1971 in Berlin, Wisconsin. Her story collection, *Portraits of a Few of the People I've Made Cry*, won the 2009 Grace Paley Prize in Short Fiction and was a finalist for the 2010 Los Angeles Times Book Prize, first fiction category, and long-listed for the 2011 Frank O'Connor International Short

Story Award. *Portraits* also received *Ploughshares*'s 2011 John C. Zacharis First Book Award. Her stories have appeared in *The Best American Short Stories 2008, The Southern Review, New England Review, Pleiades, TriQuarterly Online, The Massachusetts Review, Ploughshares,* and a number of other journals. Her novel, *Little Known Facts,* is forthcoming. She teaches at DePaul University and Northwestern University and lives in Evanston, Illinois.

Kevin Wilson, "A Birth in the Woods"

In the years before my wife and I decided to have a baby, I tortured myself by writing story after story about monstrous babies that ruined the lives of their parents. I could not stop doing it. This was one such story. Now that I have a beautiful son, Griff, who is pure light, I wonder what dark part of my brain contained these narratives, and I hope that it is closed to me for the near future.

Kevin Wilson was born in Nashville, Tennessee. He is the author of a story collection, *Tunneling to the Center of the Earth,* which won the Shirley Jackson Award, and a novel, *The Family Fang.* He is an assistant professor of English at the University of the South and lives in Sewanee, Tennessee.

Recommended Stories 2012

The task of picking the twenty PEN/O. Henry Prize Stories each year is most difficult at the end when more than twenty admirable and interesting stories remain. Here are our Recommended Stories, listed, along with the place of publication, in the hope that readers will seek them out and enjoy them. Please go to our website, www.penohenryprizestories.com, for excerpts from each year's recommended stories and information about the writers.

Jamil Ahmad, "The Sins of the Mother," *Granta*
Mary-Beth Hughes, "The Widow of Combarelles," *A Public Space*
James Terry, "Road to Nowhere," *The Iowa Review*
Alix Ohlin, "The Cruise," *World Literature Today*
Mary Swan, "Washington's Teeth," *Zoetrope*

Publications Submitted

Stories published in American and Canadian magazines are eligible for consideration for inclusion in *The PEN/O. Henry Prize Stories*. Stories must be written originally in the English language. No translations are considered. Sections of novels are not considered. Editors are asked not to nominate individual stories, and stories may not be submitted by agents or writers.

Beginning with *The PEN/O. Henry Prize Stories 2013*, editors may submit online fiction for consideration, but such submissions must be sent in hard copy to the address below. The publication's contact information and the date of the story's publication must accompany the submissions.

Because of production deadlines for the 2013 collection, it is essential that stories reach the series editor by May 1, 2012. If a finished magazine is unavailable before the deadline, magazine editors are welcome to submit scheduled stories in proof or manuscript. Publications received after May 1, 2012, will automatically be considered for *The PEN/O. Henry Prize Stories 2014*.

Please see our website, www.penohenryprizestories.com, for more information about submission to *The PEN/O. Henry Prize Stories*.

The address for submission is:
Laura Furman, Series Editor, The PEN/O. Henry Prize Stories
The University of Texas at Austin
English Department, B5000
1 University Station
Austin, TX 78712

The information listed below was up-to-date when *The PEN/O. Henry Prize Stories 2012* went to press. Inclusion in this listing does not constitute endorsement or recommendation by *The PEN/O. Henry Prize Stories* or Anchor Books.

African American Review
Saint Louis University
Adorjan Hall 317
3800 Lindell Boulevard
St. Louis, MO 63108
Nathan Grant, editor
aar.slu.edu
quarterly

Agni Magazine
Boston University
236 Bay State Road
Boston, MA 02215
Sven Birkerts, editor
agni@bu.edu
agnimagazine.org
biannual

Alaska Quarterly Review
University of Alaska Anchorage
3211 Providence Drive
Anchorage, AK 99508

Ronald Spatz, editor
www.uaa.alaska.edu/aqr
biannual

Alimentum
PO Box 776
New York, NY 10163
Paulette Licitra and Peter Selgin,
    editors
editor@alimentumjournal.com
alimentumjournal.com
biannual

Alligator Juniper
Prescott College
220 Grove Avenue
Prescott, AZ 86301
Abby Durden, managing editor
aj@prescott.edu
prescott.edu/alligator_juniper
annual

American Literary Review
PO Box 311307
University of North Texas
Denton, TX 76203-1307
Miroslav Penkov, editor
engl.unt.edu/alr
biannual

The American Scholar
1606 New Hampshire Avenue
  NW
Washington, DC 20009
Robert Wilson, editor
scholar@pbk.org
theamericanscholar.org
quarterly

American Short Fiction
PO Box 301209
Austin, TX 78703
Jill Meyers, editor
americanshortfiction.org
quarterly

The Antioch Review
PO Box 148
Yellow Springs, Ohio
  45387-0148
Robert S. Fogarty, editor
antiochreview.org
quarterly

Apalachee Review
PO Box 10469
Tallahassee, FL 32302
Michael Trammell, editor
apalacheereview.org
biannual

**Arkansas Review: A Journal of
  Delta Studies**
PO Box 1890
Arkansas State University
State University, AR 72467
Janelle Collins, editor
arkansasreview@astate.edu
altweb.astate.edu/arkreview
triannual

Ascent
Concordia College
Department of English
901 South Eighth Street
Moorhead, MN 56562
W. Scott Olsen, editor
ascent@cord.edu
readthebestwriting.com
triannual

**The Asian American Literary
  Review**
c/o Gerald Maa
6243 Adobe Circle
Irvine, CA 92617
Lawrence-Minh Bùi Davis and
  Gerald Maa, editors in chief

editors@aalrmag.org
aalrmag.org
biannual

The Atlantic Monthly
600 New Hampshire Avenue NW
Washington, DC 20037
C. Michael Curtis, senior fiction editor
theatlantic.com
monthly

Avery Anthology
Stephanie Fiorelli, Adam Koehler, Nicolette Kittinger, editors
submissions@averyanthology.org
averyanthology.org
biannual

Baltimore Review
PO Box 36418
Towson, MD 21286
Barbara Westwood Diehl, senior editor
baltimorereview.org
annual

The Bark
2810 Eighth Street
Berkeley, CA 94710
Claudia Kawczynska, editor in chief
editor@thebark.com
thebark.com
bimonthly

Belles Lettres: A Literary Review
Washington University in St. Louis
The Center for the Humanities
Campus Box 1071
One Brookings Drive
St. Louis, MO 63130
Gerald Early, editor
cenhum.artsci.wustl.edu/publications/belle_lettres
biannual

Bellevue Literary Review
Department of Medicine
NYU Langone Medical Center
550 First Avenue OBV-A612
New York, NY 10016
Ronna Wineberg, JD, senior fiction editor
blreview.org
biannual

Black Clock
California Institute of the Arts
24700 McBean Parkway
Valencia, CA 91355
Steve Erickson, editor
info@blackclock.org
blackclock.org
biannual

Black Warrior Review
PO Box 862936
Tuscaloosa, AL 35486
Danilo John Thomas, fiction
    editor
http://bwrsubmissions.ua.edu
bwr.ua.edu
biannual

BOMB
New Art Publications
80 Hanson Place
Suite 703
Brooklyn, NY 11217
Betsy Sussler, editor in chief
generalinquiries@bombsite.com
bombsite.com
quarterly

Boulevard Magazine
6614 Clayton Road
Box 325
Richmond Heights, MO 63117
Richard Burgin, editor
boulevardmagazine.org
triannual

**Brain, Child: The Magazine for
    Thinking Mothers**
PO Box 714
Lexington, VA 24450
Stephanie Wilkinson and Jennifer
    Niesslein, editors
editor@brainchildmag.com

brainchildmag.com
quarterly

The Briar Cliff Review
3303 Rebecca Street
PO Box 2100
Sioux City, IA 51104-2100
Tricia Currans-Sheehan, editor
currans@briarcliff.edu
briarcliff.edu/bcreview
annual

Brick
Box 609, Station P
Toronto, ON M5S 2Y4
Canada
Nadia Szilvassy, managing editor
info@brickmag.com
brickmag.com
biannual

Callaloo
English Department
Texas A&M University
4212 TAMU
College Station, TX 77843-4212
Charles Henry Rowell, editor
callaloo@tamu.edu
callaloo.tamu.edu
quarterly

Calyx: A Journal of Art and Literature by Women
PO Box B
Corvallis, OR 97339
Rebecca Olson, senior editor
editor@calyxpress.org
calyxpress.org
biannual

Camera Obscura
c/o Sfumato Press
PO Box 2356
Addison, TX 75001
M. E. Parker, editor in chief
editor@obscurajournal.com
obscurajournal.com
biannual

The Carolina Quarterly
CB# 3520 Greenlaw Hall
University of North Carolina
Chapel Hill, NC 27599-3520
Phil Sandick and Lindsay Starck, fiction editors
thecarolinaquarterly.com
triannual

Chicago Review
5801 South Kenwood Avenue
Chicago, IL 60637
Joel Calahan and Michael Hansen
chicago-review@uchicago.edu
humanities.uchicago.edu/orgs/review
quarterly

Cimarron Review
205 Morrill Hall
Oklahoma State University
Stillwater, OK 74078-4069
Toni Graham, editor
cimarronreview@okstate.edu
cimarronreview.okstate.edu
quarterly

The Cincinnati Review
PO Box 210069
Cincinnati, OH 45221-0069
Michael Griffith, fiction editor
editors@cincinnatireview.com
cincinnatireview.com
biannual

Coal City Review
c/o Brian Daldorph
English Department
University of Kansas
Lawrence, KS 66045
Brian Daldorph, editor
coalcityreview.com
annual

Cold Mountain Review
Department of English
ASU Box 32052

Boone, NC 28608-2052
Leigh Ann Henion, editor in
chief
coldmountain@appstate.edu
coldmountain.appstate.edu
biannual

Colorado Review
9105 Campus Delivery
Department of English
Colorado State University
Fort Collins, CO 80523-9105
Stephanie G'Schwind, editor
creview@colostate.edu
coloradoreview.colostate.edu
triannual

Concho River Review
Angelo State University
ASU Station #10894
San Angelo, TX 76909–0894
Mary Ellen Hartje, editor
www.angelo.edu/dept/english
_modern_languages/concho
_river_review.html
biannual

Confrontation Magazine
English Department
C. W. Post of Long Island
University
Brookville, NY 11548
Jonna Semeiks, editor in chief
confrontationmag@gmail.com

confrontationmagazine.org
biannual

Conjunctions
21 East 10th Street, 3E
New York, NY 10003
Bradford Morrow, editor
conjunctions.com
biannual

Crab Orchard Review
Southern Illinois University
Carbondale
Faner Hall 2380—Mail Code
4503
1000 Faner Drive
Carbondale, IL 62901
Allison Joseph, editor
craborchardreview.siuc.edu
biannual

Crazyhorse
Department of English
College of Charleston
66 George Street
Charleston, SC 29424
Garrett Doherty, managing editor
crazyhorse@cofc.edu
crazyhorse.cofc.edu
biannual

Cream City Review
Department of English
University of Wisconsin-
Milwaukee

PO Box 413
Milwaukee, WI 53201
Ann Steward McBee, editor in
    chief
creamcityreview.org
biannual

Daedalus
American Academy of Arts and
    Sciences
Norton's Woods
136 Irving Street
Cambridge, MA 02138
Phyllis S. Bendell, managing
    editor
daedalus@amacad.org
mitpressjournals.org/page/
    editorial/daed
quarterly (publication by
    invitation only)

Dappled Things
Katy Carl, editor in chief
dappledthings.editor@gmail.com
dappledthings.org
quarterly

Denver Quarterly
University of Denver
Department of English
2000 East Asbury
Denver, CO 80208
Bin Ramke, editor

denverquarterly.com
quarterly

descant
Department of English
Texas Christian University
TCU Box 297270
Fort Worth, TX 76129
Dave Kuhne and Lynn Risser,
    editors
descant@tcu.edu
descant.tcu.edu
annual

Dogwood
Department of English
Fairfield University
1073 North Benson Road
Fairfield, CT 06824-5195
Kim Bridgford and Pete Duval,
    editors
faculty.fairfield.edu/dogwood
annual

Downstate Story
1825 Maple Ridge
Peoria, IL 61614
Elaine Hopkins, editor
ehopkins7@prodigy.net
wiu.edu/users/mfgeh/dss/
    index.html

Ecotone
Department of Creative Writing
University of North Carolina
  Wilmington
601 South College Road
Wilmington, NC 28403-5938
Ben George, editor
info@ecotonejournal.com
ecotonejournal.com
biannual

Electric Literature
325 Gold Street, Suite 303
Brooklyn, NY 11201
Andy Hunter, editor in chief
editors@electricliterature.com
electricliterature.com
quarterly

Ep;phany: A Literary Journal
Willard Cook, editor in chief
epiphany.magazine@gmail.com
epiphanyzine.com
biannual

Epoch
Cornell University
251 Goldwin Smith Hall
Ithaca, NY 14853-3201
Michael Koch, editor
www.arts.cornell.edu/english/
  publications/epoch
triannual

Event
Douglas College
PO Box 2503
New Westminster, BC V3L 5B2
Canada
Elizabeth Bachinsky, editor
event@douglas.bc.ca
event.douglas.bc.ca
triannual

Exile
134 Eastbourne Avenue
Toronto, ON M5P 2G6
Canada
Barry Callaghan, editor in chief
exilequarterly.com
quarterly

Explosion-Proof
Alex Ludlum, editor in chief
contact@explosion-proof.net
explosionproof.wordpress.com
quarterly

Fantasy & Science Fiction
PO Box 3447
Hoboken, NJ 07030
Gordon Van Gelder, editor
fsfmag@fandsf.com
fandsf.com
bimonthly

The Farallon Review
1017 L Street
Number 348
Sacramento, CA 95814
Tim Foley, editor
editor@farallonreview.com
farallonreview.com
annual

Fence
Science Library 320
University at Albany
1400 Washington Avenue
Albany, NY 12222
Lynne Tillman, fiction editor
fence@albany.edu
fenceportal.org
biannual

Fiction
Department of English
The City College of New York
138th Street and Convent Avenue
New York, NY 10031
Mark Jay Mirsky, editor in chief
fictionmagazine@yahoo.com
fictioninc.com
biannual

The Fiddlehead
Campus House
11 Garland Court
PO Box 4400
University of New Brunswick

Fredericton, NB E3B 5A3
Canada
Ross Leckie, editor
fiddlehd@unb.ca
thefiddlehead.ca
quarterly

Fifth Wednesday Journal
PO Box 4033
Lisle, IL 60532-9033
Vern Miller, editor
editors@fifthwednesdayjournal.org
fifthwednesdayjournal.org
biannual

The First Line
PO Box 250382
Plano, TX 75025-0382
David LaBounty, editor
info@thefirstline.com
thefirstline.com
quarterly

Five Points
Georgia State University
PO Box 3999
Atlanta, GA 30302-3999
David Bottoms and Megan
    Sexton, editors
fivepoints@gsu.edu
fivepoints.gsu.edu
triannual

Fjords
2932 B Langhorne Road
Lynchburg, VA 24501
John Gosslee, editor
editors@fjordsreview.com
fjordsreview.com
biannual

The Florida Review
Department of English
University of Central Florida
PO Box 161346
Orlando, FL 32816-1346
Jocelyn Bartkevicius, editor
flreview@mail.ucf.edu
floridareview.cah.ucf.edu
biannual

Fourteen Hills
Creative Writing Department
San Francisco State University
1600 Holloway Avenue
San Francisco, CA 94132
Stephanie Doeing, fiction editor
14hills.net
biannual

Gargoyle
3819 North 13th Street
Arlington, VA 22201
Lucinda Ebersole and Richard
    Peabody, editors
gargoyle@gargoylemagazine.com

gargoylemagazine.com
annual

The Georgia Review
320 South Jackson Street
The University of Georgia
Athens, GA 30602-9009
Stephen Corey, editor
thegeorgiareview.com
quarterly

The Gettysburg Review
Gettysburg College
Gettysburg, PA 17325-1491
Peter Stitt, editor
www.gettysburgreview.com
quarterly

Glimmer Train
1211 NW Glisan Street,
    Suite 207
Portland, OR 97209-3054
Susan Burmeister-Brown and
    Linda B. Swanson-Davies,
    editors
editors@glimmertrain.org
glimmertrain.org
quarterly

Grain Magazine
PO Box 67
Saskatoon, Saskatchewan S7K 3K1
Canada

Rilla Friesen, editor
grainmag@sasktel.net
grainmagazine.ca
quarterly

Granta
12 Addison Avenue
London W11 4QR
United Kingdom
John Freeman, editor
editorial@granta.com
granta.com
quarterly

The Greensboro Review
MFA Writing Program
3302 HHRA Building
University of North Carolina at
    Greensboro
Greensboro, NC 27402-6170
Jim Clark, editor
greensbororeview.org
biannual

Grey Sparrow Journal
812 Hilltop Road
Mendota Heights, MN 55118
Diane Smith, editor
greysparrowpress.net
quarterly

Gulf Coast
Department of English
University of Houston

Houston, TX 77204-3013
Nick Flynn, faculty editor
editors@gulfcoastmag.org
gulfcoastmag.org
biannual

Harper's Magazine
666 Broadway, 11th Floor
New York, NY 10012
harpers.org
monthly

Harvard Review
Lamont Library
Harvard University
Cambridge, MA 02138
Christina Thompson, editor
info@harvardreview.org
hcl.harvard.edu/harvardreview
biannual

Hayden's Ferry Review
Arizona State University
Box 875002
Tempe, AZ 85287-5002
Beth Staples, managing
    editor
HFR@asu.edu
haydensferryreview.org
biannual

Hobart
Aaron Burch, editor
aaron@hobartpulp.com

hobartpulp.com
biannual

The Hudson Review
684 Park Avenue
New York, NY 10021
Paula Deitz, editor
hudsonreview.com
quarterly

The Idaho Review
Department of English
Boise State University
1910 University Drive
Boise, ID 83725-1525
Mitch Wieland, editor in chief
mwieland@boisestate.edu
idahoreview.org
annual

Image
3307 Third Avenue West
Seattle, WA 98119
Mary Kenagy Mitchell, managing
   editor
image@imagejournal.org
imagejournal.org
quarterly

Indiana Review
Indiana University
Ballantine Hall 465
1020 East Kirkwood Avenue
Bloomington, IN 47405-7103

Alessandra Simmons, editor
inreview@indiana.edu
indianareview.org
biannual

The Iowa Review
The University of Iowa
308 EPB
Iowa City, IA 52242-1408
Russell Scott Valentino, editor
iowa-review@uiowa.edu
iowareview.org
triannual

Iron Horse Literary Review
Texas Tech University
Department of English
Box 43091
Lubbock, TX 79409-3091
Leslie Jill Patterson, editor
mail@ironhorsereview.com
ironhorsereview.com
published six times a year

Jabberwock Review
Department of English
Mississippi State University
Drawer E
Mississippi State, MS 39762
Michael P. Kardos, editor
jabberwockreview@english
   .msstate.edu
jabberwock.org.msstate.edu
semiannual

The Journal
The Ohio State University
Department of English
164 West 17th Avenue
Columbus, OH 43210
Kathy Fagan and Michelle
    Herman, editors
thejournalmag@gmail.com
thejournalmag.org
biannual

Juked
110 Westridge Drive
Tallahassee, FL 32304
J. W. Wang, editor
info@juked.com
juked.com
annual

The Kenyon Review
Kenyon College
Finn House
102 West Wiggin Street
Gambier, OH 43022
Geeta Kothari, fiction editor
kenyonreview@kenyon.edu
kenyonreview.org
quarterly

**Lady Churchill's Rosebud
    Wristlet**
150 Pleasant Street, #306
Easthampton, MA 01027

Kelly Link and Gavin Grant,
    editors
info@smallbeerpress.com
smallbeerpress.com/lcrw
biannual

The Lindenwood Review
400 North Kingshighway
St. Charles, MO 63301
Beth Mead, editor
thelindenwoodreview@
    lindenwood.edu
lindenwood.edu/
    lindenwoodreview
annual

Literary Imagination
Peter Campion, editor
litimag.oxfordjournals.org
triannual

The Literary Review
285 Madison Avenue
Madison, NJ 07940
Minna Proctor, editor
editorial@theliteraryreview.org
theliteraryreview.org
quarterly

The Long Story
18 Eaton Street
Lawrence, MA 01843
R. P. Burnham, editor

rpburnham@mac.com
homepage.mac.com/rpburnham/
   longstory.html
annual

Louisiana Literature
Southeastern Louisiana University
SLU Box 10792
Hammond, LA 70402
Jack Bedell, editor
lalit@selu.edu
louisianaliterature.org
biannual

The Louisville Review
Spalding University
851 South Fourth Street
Louisville, KY 40203
Sena Jeter Naslund, editor
louisvillereview@spalding.edu
louisvillereview.org
biannual

Low Rent Magazine
Robert Liddell, fiction editor
fiction@lowrentmagazine.com
lowrentmagazine.com
six issues annually

The Malahat Review
University of Victoria
PO Box 1700
Station CSC
Victoria, British Columbia
   V8W 2Y2

Canada
John Barton, editor
malahat@uvic.ca
malahatreview.ca
quarterly

Manoa
University of Hawai'i
English Department
1733 Donaghho Road
Honolulu, HI 96822
Frank Stewart, editor
mjournal-1@lists.hawaii.edu
manoajournal.hawaii.edu
biannual

**McSweeney's Quarterly
   Concern**
849 Valencia Street
San Francisco, CA 94110
Dave Eggers, editor
printsubmissions@mcsweeneys
   .net
mcsweeneys.net
quarterly

Meridian
University of Virginia
PO Box 400145
Charlottesville, VA 22904-4145
Juliana Daugherty, editor in chief
meridianuva@gmail.com
readmeridian.org
biannual

Michigan Quarterly Review
University of Michigan
0576 Rackham Building
915 East Washington Street
Ann Arbor, MI 48109-1070
Jonathan Freedman, editor
mqr@umich.edu
michiganquarterlyreview.com
quarterly

The Minnesota Review
Virginia Tech
ASPECT, 202 Major Williams
   Hay (01 92)
Blacksburg, VA 24061
Janell Watson, editor
editors@theminnesotareview.org
theminnesotareview.org
biannual

MiPOesias
Didi Menendez, founding editor
mipoesias.com

Mission at Tenth
c/o California Institute of Integral
   Studies
1453 Mission Street
San Francisco, CA 94103
Randall Babtkis, editor
missionattenth.com
annual

Mississippi Review
The University of Southern
   Mississippi
118 College Drive
Box 5144
Hattiesburg, MS 39406-0001
Julia Johnson, editor
elizabeth@mississippireview.com
usm.edu/mississippi-review
biannual

The Missouri Review
357 McReynolds Hall
University of Missouri
Columbia, MO 65211
Speer Morgan, editor
question@moreview.com
missourireview.com
quarterly

n+1
68 Jay Street, #405
Brooklyn, NY 11201
Keith Gessen and Mark Greif,
   editors
editors@nplusonemag.com
nplusonemag.com
triannual

Narrative Magazine
Carol Edgarian and Tom Jenks,
   editors
info@narrativemagazine.com

narrativemagazine.com
annual

New England Review
Middlebury College
Middlebury, VT 05753
Stephen Donadio, editor
nereview@middlebury.edu
nereview.com
quarterly

New Letters
University of Missouri-Kansas
    City
University House
5101 Rockhill Road
Kansas City, MO 64110-2499
Robert Stewart, editor
newletters@umkc.edu
newletters.org
quarterly

New Ohio Review
English Department
360 Ellis Hall
Ohio University
Athens, OH 45701
Jill Allyn Rosser, editor
noreditors@ohio.edu
ohiou.edu/nor
biannual

New Orleans Review
Box 195
Loyola University
New Orleans, LA 70118
Christopher Chambers, editor
noreview@loyno.edu
neworleansreview.org
biannual

The New Yorker
4 Times Square
New York, NY 10036
Deborah Treisman, fiction editor
fiction@newyorker.com
newyorker.com
weekly

Nimrod International Journal
University of Tulsa
800 South Tucker Drive
Tulsa, OK 74104-3189
Francine Ringold, editor in chief
nimrod@utulsa.edu
www.utulsa.edu/nimrod
biannual

Ninth Letter
University of Illinois, Urbana-
    Champaign
Department of English
608 South Wright Street
Urbana, IL 61801
Jodee Stanley, editor
info@ninthletter.com

ninthletter.com
biannual

Noon
1324 Lexington Avenue
PMB 298
New York, NY 10128
Diane Williams, editor
noonannual.com
annual

North Carolina Literary Review
Department of English
East Carolina University
Mailstop 555 English
Greenville, NC 27858-4353
Margaret Bauer, editor
bauerm@ecu.edu
ecu.edu/nclr
annual

North Dakota Quarterly
Merrifield Hall Room 110
276 Centennial Drive Stop 7209
Grand Forks, ND 58202-7209
Robert W. Lewis, editor
und.ndq@email.und.edu
arts-sciences.und.edu/north
   -dakota-quarterly
quarterly

Northern New England Review
Humanities Department
Franklin Pierce University

40 University Drive
Rindge, NH 03461
Edie Clark, managing editor
nner@franklinpierce.edu
biannual

Northwest Review
5243 University of Oregon
Eugene, OR 97403-5243
nweditor@uoregon.edu
nwr.uoregon.edu
biannual

Notre Dame Review
840 Flanner Hall
University of Notre Dame
Notre Dame, IN 46556
William O'Rourke, fiction editor
english.ndreview.1@nd.edu
ndreview.nd.edu
biannual

One Story
232 Third Street, #E106
Brooklyn, NY 11215
Hannah Tinti, editor
one-story.com
published about every three weeks

Orion
187 Main Street
Great Barrington, MA 01230
H. Emerson Blake, editor in
   chief

orionmagazine.org
bimonthly

Overtime
PO Box 250382
Plano, TX 75025-0382
David LaBounty, editor
info@workerswritejournal.com
workerswritejournal.com/
    overtime.htm
six times annually

The Oxford American
201 Donaghey Avenue
Main 107
Conway, AR 72035
Marc Smirnoff, editor
editors@oxfordamerican.org
oxfordamericanmag.com
quarterly

Pakn Treger
The Yiddish Book Center
Harry and Jeanette Weinberg
    Building
1021 West Street
Amherst, MA 01002
Nancy Sherman, editor
pt@bikher.org
yiddishbookcenter.org/
    pakn-treger
triannual

The Paris Review
62 White Street
New York, NY 10013
Fiction Editor
theparisreview.org
quarterly

Pearl
3030 East Second Street
Long Beach, CA 90803
Joan Jobe Smith, founding editor
pearlmag@aol.com
pearlmag.com
biannual

PEN America
c/o PEN American Center
588 Broadway, Suite 303
New York, NY 10012
M. Mark, editor
journal@pen.org
pen.org/journal
biannual

The Pinch
Department of English
The University of Memphis
Memphis, TN 38152-6176
Kristen Iversen, editor
thepinchjournal.com
biannual

Pleiades
Department of English, Martin
  336
University of Central Missouri
Warrensburg, MO 64093
Phong Nguyen and Matthew
  Eck, editors
pleiades@ucmo.edu
ucmo.edu/pleiades
biannual

Ploughshares
Emerson College
120 Boylston Street
Boston, MA 02116-4624
Ladette Randolph, editor in
  chief
pshares@emerson.edu
pshares.org
triannual

PMS poemmemoirstory
HB 217
1530 Third Avenue South
Birmingham, AL 35294-1260
Kerry Madden, editor in chief
poememoirstory@gmail.com
pms-journal.org
annual

Post Road
Chris Boucher, managing editor
fiction@postroadmag.com
postroad@bc.edu

postroadmag.com
biannual

Pot Luck Magazine
280 William Lain Road
Westtown, NY 10998
Amanda Stiebel, editor
potluckmagazine@gmail.com
sites.google.com/site/
  potluckmagazine
quarterly

Potomac Review
Montgomery College
51 Mannakee Street, MT/212
Rockville, MD 20850
Zachary Benavidez, editor
zachary.benavidez@montgomery
  college.edu
montgomerycollege.edu/
  potomacreview
biannual

Prairie Fire
423-100 Arthur Street
Winnipeg, Manitoba R3B 1H3
Canada
Andris Taskans, editor
prfire@mts.net
prairiefire.ca
quarterly

Prairie Schooner
123 Andrews Hall
University of Nebraska
Lincoln, NE 68588-0334
Kwame Dawes, editor in chief
prairieschooner@unl.edu
prairieschooner.unl.edu
quarterly

Prism International
University of British Columbia
Buchanan E-462
1866 Main Mall
Vancouver, BC V6T 1Z1
Canada
Cara Woodruff, fiction editor
prismmagazine.ca
quarterly

A Public Space
323 Dean Street
Brooklyn, NY 11217
Brigid Hughes, editor
general@apublicspace.org
apublicspace.org
quarterly

Puerto del Sol
New Mexico State University
Department of English
PO Box 30001, MSC 3E
Las Cruces, NM 88003

Carmen Giménez Smith, editor
in chief
contact@puertodelsol.org
puertodelsol.org
biannual

Raritan: A Quarterly Review
Rutgers University
31 Mine Street
New Brunswick, NJ 08903
Jackson Lears, editor in chief
raritanquarterly.rutgers.edu
quarterly

Redivider
Emerson College
120 Boylston Street
Boston, MA 02116
David Snyder, editor in chief
redividerjournal.org
biannual

Red Rock Review
College of Southern Nevada
English Department, J2A
3200 East Cheyenne Avenue
North Las Vegas, NV 89030
Richard Logsdon, senior editor
redrockreview@csn.edu
sites.csn.edu/english/
   redrockreview/index.htm
biannual

Relief: A Christian Literary Expression
60 West Terra Cotta
Suite B, Unit 156
Crystal Lake, IL 60014-3548
Brad Fruhauff, editor in chief
reliefjournal.com
biannual

River Styx
3547 Olive Street, Suite 107
St. Louis, MO 63103
Richard Newman, editor
bigriver@riverstyx.org
riverstyx.org
triannual

Roanoke Review
Roanoke College
Salem, VA 24153
review@roanoke.edu
roanokereview.wordpress.com
annual

Rosebud
N3310 Asje Road
Cambridge, WI 53523
Roderick Clark, managing editor
rsbd.net
triannual

Ruminate
140 North Roosevelt Avenue
Fort Collins, CO 80521

Brianna Van Dyke, editor in chief
editor@ruminatemagazine.org
ruminatemagazine.org
quarterly

Salamander
English Department
Suffolk University
41 Temple Street
Boston, MA 02114
Jennifer Barber, editor
salamandermag.org
biannual

Salmagundi
Skidmore College
815 North Broadway
Saratoga Springs, NY 12866
Robert Boyers, editor in chief
salmagun@skidmore.edu
cms.skidmore.edu/salmagundi
quarterly

Santa Monica Review
Santa Monica College
1900 Pico Boulevard
Santa Monica, CA 90405
Andrew Tonkovich, editor
www.smc.edu/sm_review
biannual

Saranac Review
CVH, Department of English
SUNY Plattsburgh

101 Broad Street
Plattsburgh, NY 12901
Matt Bondurant, fiction editor
saranacreview@plattsburgh.edu
research.plattsburgh.edu/
  saranacreview
annual

Seven Days
PO Box 1164
Burlington, VT 05402-1164
Pamela Polston and Paula Routly,
  editors
7dvt.com
weekly

Sewanee Review
University of the South
735 University Avenue
Sewanee, TN 37383-1000
George Core, editor
sewanee.edu/sewanee_review
quarterly

Shenandoah
Washington and Lee University
Lexington, VA 24450-2116
R. T. Smith, editor
shenandoah@wlu.edu
shenandoah.wlu.edu
biannual

Slake: Los Angeles
PO Box 385
2658 Griffith Park Boulevard
Los Angeles, CA 90039
Joe Donnelly and Laurie Ochoa,
  editors
slake@slake.la
slake.la
quarterly

Slice
editors@slicemagazine.org
slicemagazine.org
biannual

Sonora Review
English Department
University of Arizona
Tucson, AZ 85721
Lisa Levine, fiction editor
sonora@email.arizona.edu
sonorareview.com
biannual

The South Carolina Review
Center for Electronic and Digital
  Publishing
Clemson University
Strode Tower Room 611
Box 340522
Clemson, SC 29634-0522
Wayne Chapman, editor
cwayne@clemson.edu

clemson.edu/cedp/cudp/scr/
current.htm
biannual

South Dakota Review

Department of English
University of South Dakota
414 East Clark Street
Vermillion, SD 57069
Brian Bedard and Lee Ann
Roripaugh, editors
sdreview@usd.edu
usd.edu/sdreview
quarterly

Southern Humanities Review

9088 Haley Center
Auburn University
Auburn, AL 36849-5202
Dan R. Latimer and Chantel
Acevedo, editors
auburn.edu/shr
quarterly

Southern Indiana Review

Orr Center, #2009
University of Southern Indiana
8600 University Boulevard
Evansville, IN 47712
Ron Mitchell, editor
usi.edu/sir
biannual

The Southern Review

3990 West Lakeshore Drive
Baton Rouge, LA 70808
Cara Blue Adams, fiction editor
southernreview@lsu.edu
lsu.edu/thesouthernreview
quarterly

Southwest Review

Southern Methodist University
PO Box 750374
Dallas, TX 75275-0374
Willard Spiegelman, editor in chief
swr@smu.edu
smu.edu/southwestreview
quarterly

Spot Literary Magazine

Spot Write Literary Corporation
4729 East Sunrise Drive
Box 254
Tucson, AZ 85718-4535
Susan Hansell, editor
susan.hansell@gmail.com
spotlitmagazine.net
biannual

St. Anthony Messenger

28 West Liberty Street
Cincinnati, OH 45202-6498
Pat McCloskey, OFM, editor
mageditors@americancatholic.org
americancatholic.org
monthly

Subtropics
Department of English
University of Florida
PO Box 112075
4008 Turlington Hall ·
Gainesville, FL 32611-2075
David Leavitt, editor
subtropics@english.ufl.edu
www.english.ufl.edu/subtropics
triannual

Sycamore Review
Purdue University
Department of English
500 Oval Drive
West Lafayette, IN 47907
Jessica Jacobs, editor
sycamore@purdue.edu
sycamorereview.com
biannual

Third Coast
Western Michigan University
Department of English
1903 West Michigan Avenue
Kalamazoo, MI 49008-5331
Emily J. Stinson, editor
editors@thirdcoastmagazine.com
thirdcoastmagazine.com
biannual

The Threepenny Review
PO Box 9131
Berkeley, CA 94709

Wendy Lesser, editor
wlesser@threepennyreview.com
threepennyreview.com
quarterly

Timber Creek Review
8969 UNCG Station
Greensboro, NC 27413
John M. Freiermuth, editor
quarterly

Tin House
2617 NW Thurman Street
Portland, OR 97210
Win McCormack, editor in chief
tinhouse.com
quarterly

Trachodon
PO Box 1468
Saint Helens, OR 97051
John Carr Walker, editor
editor@trachodon.org
trachodon.org
biannual

TriQuarterly
Northwestern University
339 East Chicago Avenue
Chicago, IL 60611-3008
Susan Firestone Hahn, editor
triquarterlyonline@northwestern
   .edu
triquarterly.org
triannual

upstreet
PO Box 105
Richmond, MA 01254-0105
Vivian Dorsel, editor
editor@upstreet-mag.org
upstreet-mag.org
annual

The Virginia Quarterly Review
One West Range
PO Box 400223
Charlottesville, VA 22904
Ted Genoways, editor
vqr@vqronline.org
vqronline.org
quarterly

Weber—The Contemporary West
Weber State University
1405 University Circle
Ogden, UT 84408-1405
Michael Wutz, editor
weberjournal@weber.edu
weber.edu/weberjournal
biannual

West Marin Review
c/o Tomales Bay Library
    Association
PO Box 984
Point Reyes Station, CA 94956
info@westmarinreview.org

westmarinreview.org
annual

Western Humanities Review
University of Utah
English Department
255 South Central Campus
    Drive, LNCO 3500
Salt Lake City, UT 84112-0494
Barry Weller, editor
wh@mail.hum.utah.edu
hum.utah.edu/whr
triannual

Whistling Shade
PO Box 7084
Saint Paul, MN 55107
Anthony Telschow, executive
    editor
editor@whistlingshade.com
whistlingshade.com
biannual

Willow Springs
501 North Riverpoint Boulevard,
    Suite 425
Spokane, WA 99202
Samuel Ligon, editor
willowspringsewu@gmail.com
willowsprings.ewu.edu
biannual

Witness Magazine
Black Mountain Institute
University of Nevada, Las Vegas
Box 455085
Las Vegas, NV 89154-5085
Amber Withycombe, editor
witness@unlv.edu
witness.blackmountaininstitute
.org
annual

WLA: War, Literature & the Arts
Department of English and Fine Arts
2354 Fairchild Drive
Suite 6D-149
United States Air Force Academy
Colorado Springs, CO
80840-6242
Colonel Kathleen Harrington,
managing editor
editor@wlajournal.com
wlajournal.com
annual

The Worcester Review
One Ekman Street
Worcester, MA 01607
Rodger Martin, managing editor
wreview.homestead.com
annual

Workers Write!
PO Box 250382
Plano, TX 75025–0382
David LaBounty, editor
info@workerswritejournal.com
workerswritejournal.com
annual

Yale Review
Yale University
PO Box 208243
New Haven, CT 06520-8243
J. D. McClatchy, editor
yalereview@aol.com
yale.edu/yalereview
quarterly

Zoetrope: All-Story
916 Kearny Street
San Francisco, CA 94133
Michael Ray, editor
info@all-story.com
all-story.com
quarterly

Zone 3
Austin Peay State University
Box 4565
Clarksville, TN 37044
Susan Wallace, managing editor
apsu.edu/zone3
biannual

Permissions

Associate Member Registration

NAME: _____

ADDRESS: _____

CITY/STATE/ZIP: _____

TELEPHONE: _____

E-MAIL ADDRESS: _____

I AM A(N): ❑ WRITER ❑ ACADEMIC ❑ BOOKSELLER ❑ EDITOR
❑ JOURNALIST ❑ LIBRARIAN ❑ PUBLISHER ❑ TRANSLATOR ❑ OTHER_____

❑ I AM INTERESTED IN VOLUNTEER OPPORTUNITIES WITH PEN.

❑ I ENCLOSE $40, MY ANNUAL ASSOCIATE MEMBERSHIP DUES.
　　　-- OR --
❑ I ENCLOSE $20, MY ANNUAL STUDENT ASSOCIATE MEMBERSHIP DUES.

❑ I ALSO ENCLOSE A TAX-DEDUCTIBLE CONTRIBUTION IN ADDITION TO MY DUES TO PROVIDE MUCH-NEEDED SUPPORT FOR THE *READERS AND WRITERS* PROGRAM AT PEN, WHICH ENCOURAGES LITERARY CULTURE THROUGH OUTREACH PROGRAMS AND LITERARY EVENTS, INCLUDING AUTHOR PANELS, WRITING AND READING WORKSHOPS FOR HIGH SCHOOL STUDENTS, AND THE WRITING INSTITUTE, WHICH INVITES TEENS TO INTERACT DIRECTLY WITH PROFESSIONAL WRITERS IN A SERIES OF WORKSHOPS. FOR MORE INFO, VISIT: WWW.PEN.ORG/READERSANDWRITERS.

❑ $50 ❑ $100 ❑ $500 ❑ $1,000 PRESIDENT'S CIRCLE
❑ OTHER $_____

TOTAL: $_____

(ALL CONTRIBUTIONS ABOVE THE BASIC DUES OF $40/$20 ARE TAX DEDUCTIBLE TO THE FULLEST EXTENT ALLOWED BY THE LAW.)

PLEASE MAKE YOUR CHECK PAYABLE TO **PEN AMERICAN CENTER.**

MAIL FORM AND CHECK TO:
PEN AMERICAN CENTER, MEMBERSHIP DEPARTMENT
588 BROADWAY, 303, NEW YORK, NY 10012.

TO PAY BY CREDIT CARD PLEASE VISIT **www.pen.org/join.**

PEN IS THE FIRST ORGANIZATION OF ANY KIND I HAVE EVER JOINED.
LET'S HOPE I DON'T REGRET IT!
—HENRY MILLER, 1957

JOIN PEN!

ASSOCIATE MEMBERSHIP IN PEN AMERICAN CENTER IS OPEN TO EVERYONE WHO SUPPORTS PEN'S MISSION. MEMBERS PLAY A VITAL ROLE IN SUPPORTING AND FURTHERING PEN'S EFFORTS ON BEHALF OF WRITERS AND READERS BOTH AT HOME AND ABROAD. BENEFITS INCLUDE:

► A SUBSCRIPTION TO *PEN AMERICA*, OUR AWARD-WINNING SEMI-ANNUAL JOURNAL

► DISCOUNTED ACCESS TO THE ONLINE DATABASE *GRANTS AND AWARDS AVAILABLE TO AMERICAN WRITERS*, THE MOST COMPREHENSIVE DIRECTORY OF ITS KIND

► SELECT INVITATIONS TO MEMBER-ONLY RECEPTIONS

► DISCOUNTS TO PUBLIC PROGRAMS, INCLUDING PEN WORLD VOICES: THE NEW YORK FESTIVAL OF INTERNATIONAL LITERATURE

► FREE WEB PAGE AND BLOG ON PEN.ORG

ANNUAL DUES ARE $40 ($20 FOR STUDENTS). TO JOIN, FILL OUT THE REGISTRATION FORM ON THE OPPOSITE PAGE, AND MAIL THE FORM AND PAYMENT TO:

PEN AMERICAN CENTER
MEMBERSHIP DEPT.
588 BROADWAY, 303
NEW YORK, NY 10012

YOU CAN ALSO JOIN ONLINE:
WWW.PEN.ORG/JOIN